Swallowing the Sun

शंकेरव
—✕—

मंचांचं कारें भूर्जपत्र घरुनं असनाचकीं धरयतां
स्वर्गाचं नवकेरव कुंकुमारसें नीं मंदधर्दचां छिरीं;
रात्रां शांत गभीर अनुभूतिधैन्या आगांठ पुष्टतरें
केंजाकेरव छिंडी विकांपित करे नीं नारदसुंदरी;
इथांना निःसरिणी पुनःपुनःरूपीं सारांत वेलिग्रहीं
मुदाकेरव सुरभ्य सेंअनी छिंटीं मंचांगीं मारुकुळ्ळ
वेळांचं स्वर्रें क्षाप्र घरुनां त्या मंदमंदांतनैं
अठिकेरव वनस्थळांई छिंहिंनीं कांहिंतरां आंगुहैं.
हे बारें मधुकेरव घडतनां जन्नीं नाचीळीं तेथें बनां
गावां गीत शांत नयांस, मनाचीं त्यांचां कडे धरांवेी
केंजागुप्त परीं डोरा कमक्ष तैं हेवूंन मास्यां उरी
स्वसांच्यां कर्णां छिंटी छिंशिंतरां हीं मेणेलाचवेंटी.
सारें ते मझ शंकरव मुंझ्यं गातनां निःशब्दूर्भ्यां
कोलनां,
तीघा अक्षय शंक केरव प्रर्ष अभां मां
मंन पराचंणीं.
— बाकीबव.

Swallowing the Sun

a novel

LAKSHMI MURDESHWAR PURI

ALEPH

ALEPH BOOK COMPANY
An independent publishing firm
promoted by *Rupa Publications India*

First published in India in 2024
by Aleph Book Company
7/16 Ansari Road, Daryaganj
New Delhi 110 002

Copyright © Lakshmi Murdeshwar Puri 2024

The author has asserted her moral rights.

All rights reserved.

This is a work of fiction. Names, characters,
places, and incidents are either the product of
the author's imagination or are used fictitiously
and any resemblance to any actual persons,
living or dead, events or locales is entirely
coincidental.

No part of this publication may be reproduced,
transmitted, or stored in a retrieval system, in
any form or by any means, without permission
in writing from Aleph Book Company.

ISBN: 978-81-19635-86-3

1 3 5 7 9 10 8 6 4 2

Printed in India.

This book is sold subject to the condition that it
shall not, by way of trade or otherwise, be lent,
resold, hired out, or otherwise circulated without
the publisher's prior consent in any form of
binding or cover other than that in which it is
published.

To my mother, Malati Desai, and father, B. G. Murdeshwar, who inspired me to believe that only if you dare can miracles happen.

मुंगी उडाली आकाशी।
तिने गिळिले सुर्यासी
थॉर नवलव झाला ।
बाँझ पुत्र प्रसवला ।
विंचु पाताळासी जाय ।
शेष माथा वंदी पाय ॥
माशी व्याली घार झाली ।
देखोनी मुक्ताई हासली ॥

The ant flies into the sky,
She swallows the sun.
Another miracle!
A barren woman begets a son.
A scorpion burrows down to the nether realms
And Shesha, the snake king, bows his head at its feet.
A fly gives birth to a hawk
Muktabai sees all!
Muktabai laughs!

—Abhang of Muktabai

CONTENTS

Author's Note	xi
1. The Big Fight	1
2. Destiny's Children	7
3. The Mango Season	13
4. A Marriage Made in Heaven	19
5. Divine Madness	26
6. Krishna's Tulsi	33
7. Lifting the Wedding Veil	39
8. A Passage to Heaven	46
9. The Castaways	52
10. Destination Ashram	59
11. Thriving with Slow Poison	66
12. The Reunion	74
13. Prophecies	81
14. The Séance	88
15. Krishna Leela and Shitala Mata	95
16. Whatever Will Be Will Be	103
17. Pleasure Ladies and Fireflies	110
18. Agnikankan—the Branded Oath	117
19. Mud in the Lotus Pond	123
20. Stardust	130
21. Baba's Righteous Empire	137
22. Dangerous Encounters	146
23. Becoming Elphinstonians	151
24. Getting Acquainted	158
25. The Celestial Singer	166
26. Sunflower Faces the Sun	173
27. The Exalted Bombay Company	180
28. The Star of My Motherland	188
29. Metamorphosis	195

30.	Smoke and Mirrors	201
31.	Heir to the Estate	208
32.	The Wilful Snake Goddess	213
33.	Two Suitors	218
34.	Gurudakshina	224
35.	A Play Within the Play	231
36.	Enslaved by Power	238
37.	The Proposals	245
38.	Final Lap to the Finish Line	252
39.	Becoming Artemis	259
40.	The Road to Purna Swarajya	266
41.	Reading the Lines of the Palm	273
42.	The Tryst	280
43.	Exchange of Sacrifices	288
44.	The Birch Bark Offering	295
45.	Love, Letters, Life Apart	302
46.	A Flick of the Puppeteer's Hand	310
47.	To Delay Is to Deny	317
48.	A Pond Eager to Meet the Ocean	324
49.	A Long-distance Marriage	331
50.	The Benares Conspiracy	338
51.	Farewell, My Domain	346
52.	Guru's River of Achievement	353
53.	The Trial	360
54.	Venus Glows Against the Setting Sun	367
55.	The Rejection	375
56.	Among the Cloud Messengers	382
57.	Martyrdom	389
58.	The Separation	396
59.	The Ring of Recognition	402
60.	Swallowing the Sun	408

AUTHOR'S NOTE

The abhang (devotional verse written in praise of Vithoba, a form of Lord Vishnu) of Muktabai, the thirteenth century poet–saint from Maharashtra from which the title of the book, *Swallowing the Sun*, has been derived has possessed me forever. I have used the complete abhang translated by me, as the epigraph for the novel.

Although my novel covers only the first five decades of the twentieth century, the reader today will recognize Malati and other stellar men and women characters who populate in all of us. For, the theme of daring to attain the unattainable, whether miracles happen or not, must resonate universally and across time.

My parents, Malati Desai and Balkrishna Ganesh Murdeshwar, lived by this mantra. Their extraordinary life, love, and times, and stories gave birth to this coming-of-age saga. My lawyer father was a gentle, subtle storyteller, sprinkling his anecdotes with the darshana or the essence of philosophy, the anhad naad or celestial music of Marathi and English poetry and songs, and Sanskrit kavya. The 148 love letters he wrote to Malati a century ago, stirred me to share the mystique of that thing called love, of romance and disillusionment and the intoxicating aromas of a bouquet of small gestures as much as of grand ones these letters reveal.

Malati was the commanding storyteller—always vivid, often fantastical, whimsically dipping her characters into vats of Greek and Hindu mythology, and pulling them out as completely new avatars, proving how 'real' and present myth can be. She amazed us with poignant renditions of her own life, with her photographic memory and her gift for seeing the future! She exuded feisty woman power, tinged with regret that, after taking flight and soaring, she failed to swallow the sun.

My parents inspired me to explore the concept of Ardhanarishwar—that there is in all of us a nari and a purusha and that a man can be as vulnerable as a woman can be strong. That in a man–woman relationship there is a constant intermeshing of domination and surrender, love and sacrifice, self-realization and affirmation by the other! That we in life as in love keep drawing boundaries—the Lakshman Rekhas—only to dissolve them, sometimes with guilt and other times with abandon.

As a student of history, I have tried to evoke the tumultuous social and political movements in British-ruled India that my parents were part of, to capture the sparkle of cultural and literary renaissance and its idioms. My characters relive the discourses, contests, and awkward resolutions they engaged in. Though they were not Gandhiji, Baba Ambedkar, or Veer Savarkar nor Sarojini Naidu and Annie Besant, they were integral to the Indian freedom movement, to the birth of a new India that is Bharat—an ongoing project.

I began to work on the novel when I finally took retirement from the UN to return to India after eighteen years abroad and a lifetime in diplomacy. It was Hardeep Singh Puri, my life partner and soulmate, who stood by me through the ups and downs of self-congratulation and self-doubt of a first-time novelist, insisting that I never give up till I reach my destination.

This novel is in many ways a sisterly labour of love. Without my sister Indira Bhargava's steadfast help—jogging my memory, deciphering love letters, reading and discussing the manuscript—originally 270,000 words—I could not have done it. Her husband Arun was a much-valued commentator throughout.

Himayani—my elder daughter, whose audacious journey of striving and achievement deserves a separate novel—found the time to read and provide ideas. My younger daughter, Tilottama, my sons-in-law Hari and Daniel, and my grandchildren—Amaya, Jai, and Leela, my niece Manasi, along with our larger family and friends, have been a wellspring of my inspiration too.

I am thankful to Sandhya Pandey, a skilled and empathetic editor with a Maharashtrian sensibility, who saw me through the distilling of the manuscript.

I was fortunate that Namita Gokhale, a pre-eminent literary figure of our times, mentored me. She was the first to spot the 'makings of an excellent novel, a major book and an epic saga', all of which kept my morale up till I reached David Davidar and he 'discovered' me.

To David Davidar, my gratitude for championing and believing in the novel, for giving me direction and affirmation, and editing and publishing *Swallowing the Sun* with brilliance and care. My gratitude and thanks to Aienla Ozukum for shepherding the novel through the various stages of the publishing process, and Bena Sareen for making the cover speak eloquently for the novel!

1
THE BIG FIGHT

The excitement flew around in shards and rattled within Malati. Her head had become a two-sided drum. Bhika, her burly classmate, had ballooned into a demon drummer, tapping gently on her head with his claws—*tut tut tut*, then fiercely pounding on it with sticks to rouse it into a *dham dhama dham* beat of the festive Dhol Tasha. A prelude to their wrestling match.

She could hardly concentrate as she sat cross-legged on a reed mat with her sister Kamala on one side of the classroom, separated from the boys. She furiously wrote Bhika's name on her slate and erased it again and again. She was smarting from the insults hurled by the village headman's son earlier that day when she had crossed over to the 'boys' side' of the classroom.

'How dare you cross the boundaries—the Lakshman Rekha! Who are you—two puny, skirt-wearing girls in a school of sixty strong loincloth-wearing warriors—to have the temerity to do something like that? Stay within your limits. Submit to our overlordship or else...' Bhika had warned at the top of his voice that was beginning to comically croak and squeak by turns with the onset of puberty.

Malati laughed mockingly.

'Or else what? Kamala and I see no boundaries. We are more than equal to your sixty so-called veers combined in brains. We can beat you Bhika in anything!' Malati had retorted angrily, no longer able to bear the daily onslaughts on their 'privileged girldom'.

'Arechya! Then you must be able to wrestle with us and beat us, eh?' Bhika had taunted.

'Don't forget I am a Kshatriya warrior! No matter that I am a girl. Sure, I will wrestle with you. Now!' Malati had raised her clenched fists. Bhika and his veers had guffawed out loud.

'Done. And if I defeat you, you retreat into your kitchens as Gangubais, where you belong,' Bhika had said, winking at his mates.

Kamala whispered in Malati's ear, trying to dissuade her. But she could not back down now. The whole class was electrified by the prospect of what was about to happen. Pingle sir, their teacher, came in just then, and Kamala was relieved. Malati was not. She signalled surreptitiously to Bhika to set up the contest after class. Malati declared to Kamala in a loud enough voice to startle Pingle sir, 'Now even the English sahebs who rule us cannot save Bhika.'

The bell rang at last and everyone shot out of the door like arrows released from Lord Rama's bow, scattering in all directions. Cries of 'Jai Hanuman' rent the air. Bhika and his gang ran to a deserted side of the school and beckoned to the girls to follow. Kamala looked out for Khandoba, their father's farm manager who escorted them to and from the school, hoping he could stop Malati's mad venture without her losing honour. But he was late arriving that day.

Bhika's gang formed a circle. Kamala was frightened, but tried not to show it to keep Malati's morale up. Malati prayed hard and tried to recall moves the wrestlers made in the occasional wrestling matches she and Kamala had been taken to by Khandoba. Bhika and Malati faced off in the centre. His friend, Pandu, blew a whistle as Bhika took up his position, hit his chunky thighs with his hands, making an intimidating sound—*thad thad thad.* Bending forward with fists poised in readiness, he donned a wrestler's killer look and swagger.

Malati copied his pose but refrained from slapping her thighs. What if it produced a pathetic *tut tut tut,* muffled by the swirl of her skirt. She stared back at him, trying not to look small and girlish. The gang laughed at her and mocked, 'Bagha, bagha, look a dwarf of a girl is spoiling for a fight with us giants.'

Malati tried to block out the din. Tried to concentrate on a vulnerable part of Bhika's body that she could attack. Pandu blew the whistle again. Before she could move her fist, Bhika's iron arm flew into her face and she fell down on her back with a cry of 'Ayeega'.

Bhika stood above her and leered down.

'Have you had enough already with this first blow itself?' he asked.

Malati was trying not to cry. 'I will fight you, you dog,' she managed to hiss.

Malati glanced at Kamala. She did not look afraid for her brave sister. So, Malati scrambled up, swaying from side to side. Everyone jeered. Suddenly, Malati remembered Baba's story about Ravana, the ten-headed demon king, who was invincible except around his navel. And Lord Rama, tipped off by Ravana's brother, Vibhishan, killed him by shooting an arrow into his navel. To Malati, Bhika was that demon. And she herself was the righteous, victory-deserving Lord Rama.

Just as everyone thought Malati was about to faint, she turned, ran at her tormentor, and swung her fist hard into his navel and below it repeatedly. He shrieked with pain. His hands moved wildly, trying to pummel her. She dodged, running in circles around him. Suddenly, he collapsed on the ground and shouted to his gang to get her. Malati raised her hand in victory. It was her turn to look down on him. But before she could really savour the moment, his shocked friends pounced on her and Kamala and started beating them.

'Bas kara!' Khandoba's loud voice stopped the boys short. They ran away, leaving Bhika writhing in pain on the ground. Kamala and Malati got up, dusted off their skirts. Blood dripped from Malati's nose and there were bruises all over her body from the pounding she had got. Kamala was hurt on her face and had a bleeding arm.

Khandoba was alarmed. 'What happened?' he demanded.

A half-defiant, half-tearful Malati explained why she had to fight and pleaded with him not to tell Baba.

Khandoba went up to Bhika, who was still prone on the ground, pulled him upright and asked, 'Kai re! Why are you fighting with girls? They are younger and smaller than you! And only ten–eleven years old. That is cowardly!'

'I did not. Malati challenged me. We boys let her be a girl, but she wants to be like us,' Bhika replied, not looking Khandoba in the eye.

'I do not want to be like him,' Malati said vehemently, tears streaming down her cheeks. 'He and his gang keep bullying us. Today, he challenged me to a fight and said that otherwise we girls will lose our right to be in school with boys.'

She was ashamed of her tears. Baba always said that if they wanted to be like boys, and do the things that boys did, they couldn't cry like girls.

Khandoba bent close to Bhika, and said menacingly: 'Look here, Bhika. It is not for you to decide if the girls have a right to attend this school. It's for them, their father, and their principal, Sadashiv Pandit. Don't you dare bully or provoke them. I will teach them how to defeat you in a wrestling match, and next time, I will personally also teach you and your gang a lesson. And if you tell your father or Sadashiv Pandit about it, you will not only be in trouble because it was you who hit a girl, but you will also be shamed because you did lose to a girl.'

Realizing his predicament Bhika agreed not to tell anyone provided the girls did not.

'I will not. I promise too. But don't challenge me again. Next time I will come prepared. Already I demolished you like Rama did Ravana,' Malati said through her cracked, bruised lips.

As he turned to leave, Bhika suddenly shouted, 'But remember, you can't be Lord Rama—you are only a girl!'

Khandoba took the girls to the well in the school and unseen by anyone they washed off all the dirt and blood. On the way home, they discussed what story to tell Baba.

Khandoba was torn between his duty as a loyal servant of Baba and his role as the girls' protector-confidant.

Malati came up with a solution that was a mix of the milk of truth and the water of untruth.

'The danger is that our discerning Baba claims to have neer-ksheer vivek, the wisdom of separating the milk from the water. So, we should tell Baba the truth,' Kamala said firmly.

Khandoba agreed. They reached home later than usual. Their worried mother was standing at the door. As soon as Ayee saw them, she rushed to embrace them and looked accusingly at Khandoba.

Baba was home early and called out from the sitting room, 'Aalya ka?'

Malati ran to him and stood before him like an accused before a king in his court. Head down, not daring to cry. Baba saw her injuries and softened. He pulled Malati towards him and examined her.

'Arre, arre, my little soldier! You seem to have battle wounds all over your face, head, and body,' he said.

Kamala also joined Malati quietly.

Khandoba stood at the door, his head bowed. Malati recounted what had happened.

'What? Are you crazy? Bhika is so much bigger than you and stronger,' Baba said and then looking at Kamala added, 'you too are hurt. I thought you were the sober one, Papi, who would stop this hothead from doing such rash things.'

'Baba, these boys have been mocking us as if we are inferior to them. We could not let them get away without a fight. My regret is that I did not join the wrestling match and let my younger sister fight alone. I have proved that I am the frail one after all,' Kamala admitted, tearing up.

'No, you are not,' Baba assured. 'And Malati, I am proud of you, that you fought for your honour like a true Maratha—with courage and clever tactics.'

Malati put her arms around Baba. Giggling uncontrollably! Forgetting her pain.

'Should I now learn to wrestle from Khandoba Kaka and fight Bhika?' she asked.

'Now, now, don't get carried away,' Ayee, who had been listening quietly, interjected. 'You were lucky this time. Next time you could be badly hurt if they decide to attack you by surprise. Wrestling is not for girls,' she said firmly, attending to their wounds.

'I agree with your mother. You have to use your brains and find the right yukti, tactics, to fight this unequal battle. Maybe carry a weapon—a sling and pellet to defend yourself. I know you are good at taking aim, trained well by Khandoba in the mango gardens,' Baba said.

Malati and Kamala beamed. The thought of carrying a sling to school in their satchels was exciting.

'Well, I must persuade Bhausaheb, the sarpanch, to allow other girls from the village to go to school,' Baba announced.

Malati told Baba how the boys said that their destiny was to just be 'Gangubai wives', make babies, bake bhakris, and be ruled by boys and men. Baba looked at them intently.

'Next time he says that, tell him you are going to be the rulers not the ruled,' he said, and he laughed out loud.

Malati and Kamala would never ever forget the sound of that laughter.

'Aga bai, what are you teaching our daughters? Just because we don't yet have a son, you cannot turn them into boys!' said Ayee.

Baba laughed again and said, 'Yes, I can!'

The next day, Baba and Malati went to Bhausaheb's house to ask him to convene a meeting of the village council. Bhika came running, probably worried that Malati was 'breaking his clay pot' as he said to her later. Obviously, he had told his father nothing.

'Ya, ya, Madhav Rao. Is everything all right? Why this urgent request for a meeting?' Bhausaheb asked officiously.

'Bhausaheb. It is 1918 after all and Maharishi Karve, the great social reformer, has already set up the first woman's mahavidyalaya—the highest temple of learning—two years ago. Times have changed. So, I want to propose that all our daughters get to attend the Vidya Mandir School and eventually go to the mahavidyalaya,' Baba said.

'Are you not content with committing blasphemy by sending your daughters to school with the boys? Now you want our daughters to be defiled too?' Bhausaheb asked angrily.

'Bhausaheb, you are the Brahmin, I am only a Kshatriya who protects all, and a Vaidya, who heals people of all castes. I believe you are a worshipper of Goddess Saraswati, are you not?' Baba said, too humbly for Malati's liking.

'Yes, I am, of course—all Brahmins worship and are blessed by Goddess Saraswati,' he replied, all puffed up, his arms interlocked across his hairy, bare chest, with his sacred thread slung prominently across it.

'Can you say, then, that only men and boys can worship her and get her holy benediction of vidya, of learning, and not girls, who, if educated, can grow up to be Saraswatis roaming the earth?'

Bhausaheb was melting.

'Bhausaheb, if you, as a learned Brahmin and respected community leader, make an appeal, others of all castes will also follow your exalted example,' Baba pressed on.

'Well, if this caste mishmash makes boys and girls see each other as potential husbands and wives, I will never be able to support, let alone advocate all this. This is a back-door way to break Manu's injunctions against both lower castes and young girls being elevated to equality with upper castes, boys, and men,' Bhausaheb said firmly.

'But we are allowing boys from all castes to sit in the same class, why not girls?' Baba argued, patiently.

Bhausaheb finally relented and agreed to convene the village council. Baba and the girls went canvassing door to door. The village council met on a hot afternoon the next day under the shade of an ancient banyan tree, its gnarled roots climbing back onto the trunks and branches and reaching down like pillars to the earth. Much like the old ideas of women and girls being the fifth caste!

2
DESTINY'S CHILDREN

The council members sat self-importantly on the brick platform to listen to the case that Baba was going to make. Sadashiv Pandit, the school principal, was present. The villagers packed the ground in front. There were more women than usual, and, of course, girls and boys, all agog, sweaty as much from the anticipation of the drama as from the heat of the sun-soaked air. Bhausaheb asked Baba to begin.

'Dear councillors, brothers, and sisters! If we believe that Saraswati, a woman whom we worship as a goddess, is the repository of knowledge, then every girl has a right to be the recipient of her benediction. In addition, we must heed the teachings of our own great heroes—Maharishi Karve and Mahatma Phule. May I propose that the Ratnagiri Vidya Mandir be allowed to admit any girl who wants to attend and that the village council extend the permission given to my daughters to attend the school to all others?'

Sadashiv Pandit supported Baba. 'Madhav Rao's proposal merits your consideration. After the councillors have spoken, may I ask what our mothers and wives sitting here think?' Bhausaheb said.

The angel of Baba's hopes rose every time a councillor stood up to speak and got thrashed to the ground with their objections to the proposal. Then many of the mothers of the girls, surprisingly, raised their hands to speak. Malati was giddy with excitement. This could be a miracle moment—Chamatkaar! Chamatkaar! Chamatkaar! She intoned! The women, of course, will speak out for girls, she was sure.

But alas, no. They were given the rare chance to speak, and one by one, the women shyly and almost inaudibly said, 'Amahala he nako! We don't want that. We are content with things as they are. That is our fate, our duty.'

A crestfallen Baba turned in desperation to the oldest matriarch of the village—Chandrabai. 'At least you, who are as wise as Rajmata Jijabai, Shivaji Maharaj's mother, must want better for your granddaughters and can speak your mind without fear or favour, unlike their diffident mothers,' he said.

Chandrabai got up shakily from her muda with the help of her stick—one as bent as her back—and walked unsteadily towards the centre of the assembly. Malati had never before heard a voice tremble like the banyan leaves in the wind, and yet ring out so authoritatively. The villagers listened with rapt attention. The daggers of her two front teeth flashed in the dark hollow of her otherwise toothless mouth. Her tongue deftly slipped in and out. Her jaws moved from side to side and Malati was reminded of their cow Vaidehi, forever chewing cud.

'Madhav Rao, this has been ordained for us women since times immemorial. Who are you, Lord Sri Krishna of Bhagavad Gita come to uplift us? You cannot change the laws of our Hindu dharma like this. Even the Gora sahebs could not do that. We are better off in the comfort of our homes being wives and mothers. We are the medium of vanshvriddhi, ensuring the continuity of the Indian race—a role only women are privileged to perform. We leave the heroism of purushartha—study and work outside the home and breadwinning—to the boys and men of our family. I advise you also to follow this dharma with your own daughters. And beget sons, if you want your progeny to do heroic deeds,' she taunted.

Baba, leading the battle for girls going to school, was fighting so far with yukti. When he saw that he had lost that battle, there was no holding him back.

'It is not the spears of betrayal by the men and fathers—which I can bear—it is the mace of perversity and surrender of the women present, who did not stand up for their own kind that has clobbered me into defeat: Maa Saheb, you let down all our daughters by upholding and perpetuating this injustice. You are certainly no Jijabai, alas!'

Chandrabai gave him a sheepish look—the only consolation for Malati. Bhausaheb smiled and twirled his already upturned moustache in triumph. Bhika wagged his thumb derisively at Malati. Baba immediately left the meeting with the girls, angry and hurt.

After this shocking defeat for Baba there was a continuous churning in everyone's mind. Ayee, strangely, seemed convinced that her younger daughters must continue to look beyond the threshold and courtyard of the home. She acknowledged that the fate of wives and mothers is not easy, nor do all women get a husband like hers—a green coconut, hard outside, soft and pulpy inside—a rarity.

Ayee was nevertheless shaken by the panchayat showdown and

wondered aloud, whether in a world where girls were pursuing their age-old destinies, their two daughters would remain unmarried.

'Chhe, Chhe, Chhe! I am not following the path of adharma in educating them nor taking them away from their natural flowering into wives and mothers. But they must go through the stage of celibate scholarship that our ancient lawmakers prescribed, not only for men, as Maharshi Karve pointed out. They will get married at the right time to better grooms. I was possessed by this good spirit of educating our girls—it's too late for Surekha, our eldest daughter, to gain for it. So, you can fulfil all your motherly desires and rituals of marriage you so love with Surekha,' Baba assured her.

Ayee now had the licence to dream separate dreams—one for Surekha and another for Kamala and Malati.

Malati, Kamala, and Surekha shared a room. At night, Surekha would fall asleep the moment her head touched the pillow. However, Malati and Kamala would often lie awake, watching and listening to Ayee–Baba talk to each other in whispers through a crack in the door. They saw Baba being kind and gentle to Ayee and embracing her, though he was aloof when he was with them.

He would tell Ayee over and over again that she was a jewel who came into his rough hands by sheer good luck. Coming from a bigger and richer farming family in nearby Sindhudurga and with her rare beauty, she could have been a queen, he said. Not toil day and night for him in a common farmer's hut, giving birth to and caring for his children.

Ayee replied shyly, 'You see me as your queen, but you are more than a king to me. Unlike other Maratha men in Ratnagiri, you do not go out to the adda to drink nor go to other women. You never raise your hand or touch me except in love. I know I am blessed, but I am afraid this may not last. Our neighbours cast their evil eye on us all the time. When all our male children died at childbirth, but three girls survived, my worst fears were stoked,' she would say.

Every time she became heavy with a baby, he told her that he was not happy and proud like other men.

'I can't stay away from you and feel guilty to see my seed asserting its vigour and growing inside your womb. I am afraid to lose you, frail that you are. Your childbirths put me through more agony than you yourself go through, Pratibhaga,' he would say tenderly.

'You are a man. It is your right. This is my privileged destiny as your wife. Don't worry, I may look delicate, but remember, women are stronger than men. See how our daughters thrive, but our sons are stillborn or die soon after birth,' Ayee said.

Kamala and Malati only half understood their talk. Their parents' love filled them with happiness, but also anxiety about losing Ayee. They were pleased to see an otherwise gruff Baba becoming almost a poet every night, saying to Ayee, 'My love for you is so imperishable that it must come from the infinite, celestial sea that the Konkan is bound by.'

The girls loved Ayee dearly. Her face was beautiful and luminous with whirls of curly black hair framing her chiselled features. She had cat-like eyes. The sweetness and lilt in her voice invoked Goddess Saraswati herself. As she worked, she sang folk songs and angayees—lullabies she had heard not so long ago as a little girl herself.

She was always giving the girls boons like Goddess Annapurna—mouth-watering morsels of food fed with her own hands. She stitched colourful clothes for them, turning them into butterflies. Most of all, she doted on them and did not see them as mere daughters, as so many reminded her.

She worked all the time—for Baba, for the girls, and for those around her in the village. Ayee had cast Surekha, the eldest sister, in her own image and was clearly preparing her, a fifteen-year-old, to be an ideal wife and mother.

'See child, you will be an ardhangini—half the body and soul of your husband, like Goddess Parvati was of Lord Shiva. So, you have to be prepared to do anything for him. He will be your swami!'

'Ho, ho, I know,' Surekha said reluctantly, much like a distracted young boy would to the relentless chanting of mantras in his ears by a Brahmin priest at his sacred thread ceremony.

When she tired of housework, Surekha hid in the garden to rest and fed her beloved sparrows cooked rice. She was delighted when her sisters joined her there and asked them about their games with the village boys and their school.

Her eyes lit up when they told her about what they were learning—the numbers game, history and tales about the Gora sahebs, their rule, their inventions, and their language. The fun they had playing with village boys.

Sometimes, she looked sad at what she was missing. To make her feel better, the girls complained about the miles they had to walk to go to school, the crusty teachers who caned them, or the awful Bhika who teased them for being misfits, and how they were often at the receiving end of rough handling by their village playmates.

Before long, Ayee sought her out from her hiding place.

'Have I not told you not to run away from housework like this,' she scolded.

Surekha blew her cheeks out in mock anger and turned her face away. Ayee held her by her chin and pivoted her back to face her. With a twinkle in her eyes, Surekha offered a justification.

'But you yourself said that I should be Annapurna—who feeds and nurtures others. See I am feeding these helpless little sparrows. I promise you, someday I will feed my helpless husband too when he comes to my doorstep. Don't pester me now,' she said.

'Ayya! When will this child learn to be a woman,' Ayee exclaimed in exasperation.

'Never,' Surekha said and embraced Ayee. 'I want to be always with you and Baba. God knows what a husband will be like.'

Kamala and Malati sometimes felt deprived when they were not given fancy clothes or jewellery meant to kindle vanity. But they were thankful to be spared the drudgery of housework and baby rearing—those trades of the fifth caste which were looked down upon by men as mere duty! And they loved and admired Baba, for daring to set them free; and Ayee, for not stopping him, even though like the ladies in the village assembly, it went against all she knew as stree dharma.

Other eleven–twelve-year-old girls in the neighbourhood were already getting married. Malati and Kamala were scared of marriage, having seen how men ill-treated their wives. Their stomachs turned when their mother went from one miscarriage to another.

They had seen Ayee in the semi-darkness of the oil lamp at night or early morning, dragging herself from her bed to the washroom, leaving a trail of blood. The 'Red River', unknowingly they called it at first, thinking it was a woman's badge of honour as Ayee portrayed. They wondered why Ayee had to swab the floor with cow dung paste to cover the stain. Why did she suffer pain but had to stifle her screams? They sometimes had caught her crying silently, after yet another ritual emptying of her womb and the interment of another dead, lizard-like foetus. And they worried that Surekha was headed to the same place.

'I don't want to be a woman. If we do tapasya—undergo austerity and do penance—will we be given the boon to be a man, Papi?' Malati asked, despairingly one day after Ayee had suffered yet another miscarriage.

'Not in this life. Remember that most boons for a change from who you are now, work out in the next life,' Kamala replied authoritatively, dashing Malati's hopes.

3
THE MANGO SEASON

Koo kuch Koo! Koo kuch Koo! Koo.... Before the cock could crow for the third time, Malati and Kamala woke up with a pleasant start, uncoiled themselves, and flung aside their sheets. They completed their morning rituals in a whirl—only a few lotas of water splashed as an excuse for a bath, their tumblers of milk half gulped, and even their favourite millet, jaggery, and ghee pie was left gnawed, squirrel-like, on leaf bowls. With their well-oiled braids tightly tied behind their heads in wilfully swinging loops, they scurried out of their home, their legs insisting on running, not walking.

They saluted the effulgent Lord Surya, riding his one-wheel chariot with seven golden horses, to herald the commencement of their day as their Baba had told them to. Their glittery brown eyes squinted, as his sharp rays gave blessings. They smiled at each other in joyful anticipation of doing something 'adventurous' during vacation time. Yes! Today they were going to pick mangoes in Baba's orchards.

Their little saris tucked between their legs, they nimbly climbed up and down the trees, leaping from branch to branch like the monkey god Hanuman. Now they hid behind the poppling mesh of dark green leaves under the trees' round canopy. Now the wiggle jiggle sway of branches they traversed gave a clue to their whereabouts. Now they emerged to seek out the pendulous ripe mangoes stretching their arms far and wide to pluck the choicest ones. Now they squealed with glee, 'Arre mala milal', the moment they captured an exceptionally fragrant and luscious specimen.

Baba's orchards were his pride and the Hapus mangoes, with their heavenly fragrance, his specialty. Even Englishmen sent for his mangoes from afar, such was their fame. The mango trees were now heavy with fruit—oval shaped with a lopsided curvy dent, plump yet firm, green turning to saffron, oozing juice. Ready for plucking.

Greedy birds swarmed around, piercing the thick, smooth skin, digging into the warm flesh, drinking the sweet nectar. Zealous orchard keepers thrashed about rhythmically with long sticks—*khut-khut-khut*—daring the airborne thieves to evade their vigil.

The avarice of the crazed birds for the fruit however, was beyond the energy and ingenuity of the human defenders. Swooshing sticks brought but a short respite. Cries of '*hu-tu-tu*' elicited a reluctant tactical withdrawal. The moment the weary guards put away their weapons to eat their meals, smoke a bidi, or take a well-deserved nap in the humid heat, the birds resumed their orgy.

In Baba's orchard, there was a rather more determined warrior fighting the relentless parrots, crows, and mynahs—Khandoba. Swarthy, muscular, bare chested, he was a formidable rival to the winged armies.

His brahmastra—the ultimate weapon—was his sling. Hard, round, clay pellets shot out from it with a rapidity and accuracy that drove away even the most daring birds. He often drew blood. On some days, wounded or dead birds carpeted the field, making the girls squirm.

Baba appreciated Khandoba's devotion to saving his mangoes. His only complaint was that Khandoba was like Duryodhana, the spiteful heir of the Kauravas who was so driven by his desire to destroy his enemies, that he was willing to hurt his own cause. Khandoba's clay bullets made Baba's fruits instant martyrs, thumping to the ground—sometimes half-eaten, unripe, or bruised.

The girls got to work with Khandoba. Their labour was just Baba's way of allowing them to enjoy the open air as boys did elsewhere. Their daily haul was a token. However, it made them feel important to be outside with the men, not with the women inside the house. Baba's friends rebuked him to no avail. He only told the girls to be careful and stay close to Khandoba, who never let them out of his sight.

The best moments were when Papi and Malati brought a part of their haul home, triumphantly presented them to Ayee, and got to eat some themselves.

Eating a mango was a ritual that had no equal. They chose a mango each and removed its stalk. They squeezed it gently from all sides until its flesh became soft and pulpy, taking care that its mouth did not burst open. They let the first greenish white juice drip away to avoid the itching and throat pain, this little poison inflicted on impatient mango-eaters. And then came the moment of supreme ecstasy as they sucked out the sugary, thick pulp with a slurping sound, cheeks and lips moving in and out in tandem, till the mango was hollowed out, the seed and wrinkled skin left forlorn.

The girls also competed with each other in planting mango seeds in their kitchen garden and waited eagerly for the two-leafed seedlings to shoot out of the ground, growing into their Bal Kalpavrikshas—wish-fulfilling heavenly trees.

Ayee was the custodian of the precious fruit and conjurer of mango delicacies—the viscous amras drink or spicy raw mango lonche. She was so busy all the time that she barely had time to sit and talk to the girls except at mealtimes. Her affectionate glances, her knowing smiles when she guessed they had been up to their usual monkey tricks signalled that she was with them and around them, all the time.

Ayee had never gone to school, but she outwitted the girls easily when they tried to flaunt their newly acquired knowledge before her and correctly answered the riddles they posed. So, they asked her to teach them some riddles, eager to show them off to their friends.

'The moon and the sun are neighbours, but they never meet in the universe. What are they in our midst?' Ayee asked.

'They are sawats—rival first and second wives of a man,' Malati replied, thinking of their neighbour who had two wives living in separate houses with a wall between. Ayee laughed.

'Well, but sawats can't help but meet and fight, even if they are instructed not to. The answer, dear girls, stares you in the face! Literally. Is it not impossible for the two eyes in your face to ever meet!' she said triumphantly.

'Unless someone is squint-eyed,' Malati retorted, laughing.

'A winnowing fan full of grain held up high, you can't count, I can't count. What is that?' she asked.

'The upturned fan is the sky and the grains are the countless stars in the firmament,' Kamala said.

> Aha! You guessed this one right,
> Always my shining lamplight,
> It's to no one's great surprise,
> You are Shahani—Papi the Wise!

Malati darted an envious glance at Kamala, stomped her feet and putting her hand on her hips, demanded petulantly to be asked another riddle to win a title too. 'Oh, you have already won a title,' said Ayee and proceeded with the title-giving ceremony in ryhme.

> Malati Yukti—the clever Improviser,
> You go beyond the question for the answer,
> When asked about the Sun and Moon not meeting
> You reply with 'squinty eyes' and 'sawats not greeting'!

'Ayee, how do you know so much and rhyme so effortlessly when you barely went to school nor read many books?' Malati asked amazed.

> Not everything can be learnt from books,
> Don't always go by someone's looks,
> If you keep open your eyes and ears,
> And your mind ever hungry, for years,
> You can learn in an unorthodox way
> From anyone, anywhere, and thereby hold sway.

'Ho Ayee! Pandit Sadashiv told us how the Vedas were transmitted by word of mouth and memory, from generation to generation for centuries in India! That is why rhyme comes so easily to us.'

It was because of impromptu sessions like this that the girls felt that their Ayee was as wise and 'learned' as she was kind and beautiful!

Even when she scolded them occasionally, they didn't hold it against her. Ayee's 'not to go' lines crisscrossed so many of their play theatres that they had to constantly do exactly what she forbade them to do. And were inventive in making excuses.

'Don't go out in the sun or you will get sun burnt and dark-skinned,' Ayee urged.

'But Ayee, we have to help Baba in the mango orchards, like your sons would,' Malati would reply and run out to accompany Khandoba to the orchards.

'Don't wander in the forests alone, who knows which beast will prey on you,' she warned.

'But, Ayee, we don't go to the darkest forest trails the terrifying wild creatures inhabit. We go to the brightest spots where our favourite birds sing and where we can feed and play with the gentle deer and their fawns. And I know you like the wild berries we pick for you from trees aflame with the ber, don't you?' said Papi and extracted a licence to explore the forests unhindered.

'Papi, Malati, don't scream or pretend to be a snake charmer when you come across snake gods. Just walk away quietly,' Ayee counselled.

'We know we are no snake charmers to sway and play the been pipe to hypnotize the snakes. But how can we stop ourselves from screaming when we unexpectedly come upon snakes that accost you in Konkan, shaking their menacing hoods and staring at us with their lidless eyes? Run we will, and ask Khandoba to kill them,' Malati replied.

'Don't you play with the rowdy boys in the neighborhood, only with girls,' scolded Ayee.

'But, Ayee, the girls don't play the games we like. The boys are fun to play with,' Kamala explained.

'Swear on God, you won't tease and chase stray dogs. They could bite you and make you go mad,' Ayee insisted.

'Ho Ayee. We won't chase them, but when they chase us, we run. That's why we can beat the boys in races now!' Malati the racer replied with relish!

'Don't go alone to open the door when mendicants or minstrels come knocking. They could kidnap you,' she warned.

'How can our friends, the monkey man, the acrobat, and the minstrel, whose performances we delight in, be kidnappers? They come to our door and leave with our offerings of food and money. Ayee, you yourself like to make offerings to Shiva's Bull—the decorated Nandi Bail with bells around his neck and you ask for forecasts about our future, don't you?' Papi made clever counterpoints.

'Don't you dare show yourself to childless women or they will cast an evil eye on you,' Ayee cautioned.

'But, Ayee, what's so special about us that they should cast an evil eye. We are just girls, not boys,' Papi retorted.

Ayee would have added 'don't be seen or talk to inauspicious widows', but she stopped herself, because her friend and household help, Ambutai, had recently been widowed.

Ambutai had just given birth to a baby—Bala. Ayee too was heavy with a baby. Not all of Ayee's babies survived. They were plucked away by Yamadeva. Much like baby mangoes falling from the tree before they ripened. Of Ayee's many pregnancies, only Kamala, Malati, and their elder sister Surekha survived. Ayee was being extra careful because this last time, she wanted to try and give Baba a son and heir. The village ladies had pronounced that her high and pointed baby bump foretold her wish coming true. Was she not craving sour and spicy pickles more than ever?

Baba himself seemed very concerned about her well-being. He often said to her, 'You are not like other Maratha women—sturdy and well built, to endure so many pregnancies. You have to become strong and eat well.'

'Agabai,' Ambutai would exclaim, and join Baba in urging Ayee to pump up her strength by eating more. 'If you continue to look like a fragile mango flower, you will be blown away by a strong gust of wind that Maruti, the wind god, so often sends our way in the Konkan.'

Ayee would smile wanly and protest, 'The girls' father (she never took Baba's name) and you feed me as if I am a wrestler. I am strong. Don't worry, I have not been blown away by any wind and mango flowers don't get dissipated in vain, either. They give abundant fruit!'

Kamala and Malati wanted Ayee to be like the mango tree—solid and eternal—not like mango flowers that became fruits and themselves disappeared.

4

A MARRIAGE MADE IN HEAVEN

Surekha was one of the most eligible of Ratnagiri's maidens—fine-boned and light-skinned like Ayee, and tall and strong like Baba. Marriage proposals from local families just did not find favour with Baba. Baba felt she deserved to be a queen. Already people said she was getting too old and may have to marry an older man, when she had only been fifteen short years on earth.

Ayee was anxious about the delay in Surekha's marriage, but Baba told her, 'I have to set right the injustice of your marriage to Madhav Rao's humble farmer family, when you deserved to be married into comfort, if not riches.'

Ayee expectedly protested, 'Find the best boy for my phulrani—who will care for her and be good to her like you are to me. Riches, without her being valued, will be meaningless,' she said.

The girls hoped that Surekha would get the best of both Baba and Ayee's wishes—a rich husband, but also a king of hearts like Baba.

One day, a wily Brahmin matchmaker, Pandit Prakash, came down from the Maratha kingdom of Vaishali in the north to Baba's house. He announced his arrival as much with his loud greeting of 'Narayan! Narayan! Aho koni aahe kaay?' as with his big belly protruding sharply like a vertically hanging Konkan turtle. It greeted them before the rest of his body arrived on the scene on his stout, white dhoti-clad legs. His neatly pleated white and gold angavastram adorned his bare chest on one side and unruly clumps of black hair spread like grass on the other. He wore a necklace of brown, puckered, five-faced rudraksh beads and sleek gold ones to announce that he was no ascetic but a man of God, whose calling it was to make marriages on earth as ordained in heaven

He sat cross-legged on a wooden seat on the floor. Over ladoos and taak yoghurt drink, Pandit Prakash lost no time in telling them that he had brought a proposal of marriage for Surekha that would elicit their eternal gratitude to him. Vilas Rao, the finance minister in the Vaishali Maharaja's court, wanted her hand in marriage. He was from a noble Maratha family, had large tracts of land, spread over several villages and lived in a palatial wada—in Vaishali city.

Maharaja! Minister! Nobleman! Wada! Baba was intrigued. Kamala and Malati were excited and started teasing Surekha. She was shy and uncertain listening to the conversations from behind the door and could not believe the fairy tale that fate seemed to be spinning.

Pandit Prakash's proposal pleased Baba but he was not so naive as to surrender to belief in a seeming miracle. He interrogated the matchmaker as if he were selling faulty goods.

'Tell me, Pandit, why does an aristocrat from a Maratha Sardar family want to marry the daughter of a mere farmer? True, we are of pure Maratha blood and my Surekha is a rare jewel who must be transferred to a discerning owner who cherishes her, but there must be other reasons.'

Pandit Prakash equivocated with the tuft of hair atop his shaven head bobbing up and down like a rabbit's tail for a while before admitting that Vilas Rao was only two–three years younger than Baba, that he had a wife and a daughter nearly Surekha's age. They lived separately, but on the same estate. 'On the suggestion of my relative Bhausaheb here, I proposed Surekha to Vilas Rao. She is sturdy and beautiful and of good stock, will have no airs and be a good, obedient, second wife. Just what he needs!' he explained.

Baba was not satisfied. 'Why does he want to marry again? Does he also have all the other vices of wine and women that noblemen have? What if he tires of Surekha, too, and gets another wife; or the first wife seeks revenge and harms Surekha? Why should I send Surekha so far away—almost a week's travel and I will not be able to keep an eye on her well-being from here.'

Pandit Prakash assured Baba that he could ask these questions of Vilas Rao directly. The mighty Vilas Rao came down all the way from Vaishali to meet and ask for Surekha's hand: Baba was forced to reassess him. He was slim and looked younger than his professed age. He was fair-skinned, like the Gora sahebs, with sharp features and piercing grey eyes.

'Madhav Rao, Pandit Prakash highly recommended your daughter. He told me about your misgivings. I am not a serial wife changer. My first wife Savitri, who has lost her mind, comes from an aristocratic family and I have borne with her for long without looking at another woman. I am marrying again to beget a son, fill the void of a mistress of my house, my ardhangini, my equal half in performing religious rituals and state ceremonies. I have a daughter, Sarala, very wise for her age, but who is almost motherless because of my wife's madness. They live in a different house. They will be no trouble to anyone. I want to assure you that I will make concessions for Surekha being a child-woman, protect her from her sawat and my daughter, Sarala, will be her companion. She will not lack for anything,' Vilas Rao assured Baba.

Baba was silent. The confluence of corrugated lines forming on his forehead led all to think that he was not convinced.

'Madhav Rao, there will be no expense for you, no dowry. In fact, I will gift you with villages as bride price—rich agricultural land in the Maratha areas of the central province. If your family were to move there, you would be near Surekha,' Vilas Rao offered.

Baba looked up and hastened to say, 'That is not a consideration, Vilas Rao. I may not be rich, but I am capable of looking after my family. I do not need your largesse. I am still not sure how Surekha can be the right match for you and you for her!'

'Well, I have had their horoscopes studied by the local astrologer, Kashi Bhau, and they are compatible. Even the stars are conspiring to persuade you to give her hand in marriage to Vilas Rao,' Pandit Prakash said, triumphantly playing his final card.

Baba then did something out of character with his patriarchal privilege. He told Ayee, who was standing hesitantly at the door of the room, to call in Surekha. She entered looking beautiful in a new sari and suitably shy like a Lajoli touch-me-not plant, head covered with her sari padar, her shoulders held straight, her long elegant hands locked self-protectively around her waist.

'Come, come, dear. I want you to meet Vilas Rao who proposes to marry you. I don't want to make the decision on your behalf. I want you to ask him whatever you wish to know. After that tell me freely if you want to be his second wife,' Baba said reassuringly.

Ayee looked at him, stunned.

Surekha was all flustered. She fidgeted with the edge of her sari, twisting and untwisting it repeatedly. She kept staring at the ground, not daring to look up at the man who wanted to be her lord and master—someone she would have to revere as Ayee had taught her. Surekha had never met a man from outside Konkan; that too, an aristocrat and a minister. She was tongue-tied, but gathered courage when Baba insisted.

'Do you have mango gardens in Vaishali? I like to talk to and feed birds. My sisters will not be with me. Are there any girls who can be my friends? Any temples I can visit?' Surekha asked shyly, haltingly, still looking down.

Vilas Rao laughed, eased up, letting go of his stiffness, humoured her and said, 'Yes, I have mango trees in my garden, also exotic lychee and fig trees. We have many birds you can feed. They will swarm around you and hoot, caw, and shriek until you cry for mercy. Even the guards will have to come to your rescue. There are koels and mynahs, too, that will sing your praise like bards to a queen in a royal court. You will have many companions in court ladies and housemaids to take care of you, to regale you with stories including about our crazy ancestors. You can dance the phugadi with your friends. You can visit Vaishali's famous temples in my carriage and pay obeisance at our family goddess temple on the hill near my wada.'

Emboldened by his indulgently replying to her in such detail, she asked, 'I am only a simple girl from Konkan. Will rajwadi people there not look down on me? Will not your first wife hate me and plot against me? You are much older than me—will you be kind to me or be rough with me and beat me?'

Vilas Rao now got the opportunity to allay all her fears.

He said, 'Listen, Surekha. When I bring you to my home as my main wife, everybody will be at your feet. You will learn rajwadi ways. My first wife does not live with me and will not disturb us. Yes, I am older than you are, but I bring position, money, and all the luxuries for you to enjoy. I am not a violent Kshatriya. I only use my gun for hunting animals. Not to hurt my wife. So, I ask you, do you agree to be my wife? Tell your father what your answer is. And don't be afraid to speak your mind now, so that you don't regret later.'

She smiled! She was obviously impressed by how stately he looked in his gold-bordered shirt and pants and rich plumed turban. They would make a handsome, godly, Ram–Sita pair, she thought. The prospect of not having to do housework like Ayee and have dais to do her bidding, to live in a wada in comfort—who would not want that!

No one was surprised when she spoke in a hushed voice, 'Yes. I consider myself lucky to be chosen by you, even as a second wife.'

Therefore, despite Baba's and Ayee's reservations, Surekha's choice became her destiny.

By the time everyone was ready to leave for Vaishali for the wedding, Ayee was too close to delivering her baby so was unable to travel. Her friend and helper, Ambutai, stayed to take care of Ayee.

Surekha, Kamala, and Malati travelled with Baba from Vaishali by road and train—their first journey outside Ratnagiri. The kingdom of Vaishali opened to them quite another, distant world. Vaishali was not blessed with the luxuriant foliage of Konkan or the sea. The tree-lined avenues, grassy open fields, henna bush hedges enclosing well-tended gardens full of trees, flowers and fruits, evoked a lush dream of their own. The distance from the sea was cunningly wished away by the molten, full-bodied Karuna River, with girdles of iron bridges adorning her waist, as she snaked and thrust her way through the city's dusty earth and caringly parcelled it into bustling neighbourhoods, slaking the thirst of all its inhabitants.

Vaishali's rugged fort, cut out of the hills cupping it, stood tall and uncompromising—a stern reminder of the many onslaughts by covetous enemies. Of the gallant battles fought by the defenders, of the many lost and of surrender to the British. The Maharaja now paid tribute to them. They then came upon the Maharaja's palace of white marble and red sandstone, with its crenulated arches and domes, its mirrored pavilions and latticed balconies. It rose like a gem-studded crown on the forehead of the beautiful city. The few huts like in Konkan seemed to be discreetly tucked away, like an embarrassing tear in a beggar woman's sari.

Baba became poetic—a facet of him the girls had not seen so far, except in his declarations of love to Ayee, when no one was supposed to be watching or listening!

'Bagha, bagha,' he said, pointing to the landmarks around them.

'A city of illusions! Doesn't it remind you of the palace and city of the Pandavas that the illusionist, Mayadanava, and the heavenly architect, Vishwakarma built?'

Malati and Kamala were overawed.

'The houses are of brick and stone, meant to last forever. Everything here has a feel of solidity, of a will to endure beyond the monsoon storm,' said Surekha half approvingly.

'True, girls, to us folks from the Konkan, with our fragile homes and lives at the whimsical command of the rain and the sea, such solidity arouses disbelief and amazement,' said Baba. 'And Surekha you are going to live in this city of illusions. Such a place actually exists, outside of books and our nocturnal fantasies,' he added enthusiastically, turning to her.

'Baba, you all will go back and I will have to stay and sort out the illusions from the reality. Figure out which mirrored floor is actually a pool of treacherous water I could step on and drown. Which rippled pool is hard ground I could fall on and break my limbs? Which opaque walls I could walk through and which sheer curtains I could hit my head against. Will Mayadanava, be there to guide me?' Surekha asked.

'Baal, you will get help from our gods and goddesses and make your choices accordingly! Just as you made the choice to marry Vilas Rao.'

They missed Ayee so much at Vaishali. She would have enjoyed the pomp and splendour of the wedding ceremonies, the girls reckoned. The hosts made them feel as if it was Vilas Rao's first marriage, with all the eagerness to please the bride's family and to show off the bridegroom's status, wealth, and sophisticated taste.

Rows of auspicious arches bedecked with flowers covered the entire hill leading up to the Goddess temple. At night, it was lit up with giant torches, their hungry flames licking the skies. Oil lamps, garlands, and intricate rangoli patterns traced with coloured powders on the stone floors decorated the wada. Even Diwali seemed a dark twin! So overflowing was the estate with Vilas Rao's relatives and servants that its largeness, and the absence of their own relatives, was lost on them. They were left gaping at everything with astonishment.

Surekha, as the bride, was not the only one to get all the attention. Kamala and Malati received freshly stitched silk and gold-bordered skirt and blouse sets from Vilas Rao. They never wanted to get out of them, so soft was their touch. The gold borders glistened, and they felt like goddesses in a temple—all dressed up for worshippers. 'Kamala, the dainty' as Malati teased her, did not even want to move around with the fine clothes on. She just sat in one place, close to the bride, where everyone could see her in all her reflected splendour.

'I am not a monkey like you. What if my silk dress gets caught in a thorn bush or becomes dirty trailing the ground?' she said to Malati.

Nothing could stop Malati from running around in excitement, absorbing and enjoying the new sights, smells, and tastes of the wedding household in Vaishali, never mind the fine clothes.

5

DIVINE MADNESS

Maharaj, the chef, allowed Malati privileged entry into the kitchen. When Malati rolled her eyes in delight just watching him wield his magic ladle, he was flattered. But he insisted that her long, curly hair be tightly braided, so that not a wiry wisp floated around in the curries and lentils. She watched him preside over an army of helpers. The hapless onion peelers and choppers incessantly wiped tears that rolled down their cheeks. The masala grinders coaxed out smooth pastes with the circular movement of heavy stone in the corresponding recesses of the ragdas. Dry grinding was being done with heavy wooden pestles beating down on sturdy stone containers. Mounds of vegetables were being cut, heaps of potatoes peeled, and peas being shelled.

There was a bewildering variety of meats being prepared. At first, Malati was revolted by the heartless skinning of birds, rabbits, and deer, and the bloody chopping up of the meats. But Maharaj said that real Kshatriya girls did not cringe at the sight of bloodletting. These were the just fruits of the shikar from the nearby forests and were Vilas Rao's own hunting trophies for his wedding feast.

Malati's Maratha spirit came to the fore once she learnt to savour and discern the texture and flavour of the different meats—the delicate quail, chewy goat, succulent venison, dense and dry rabbit, and even the tender peacock meat that the Maharaj worked his wizardry on.

And oh the curries! That was where Maharaj really shone. He was the royal conjurer, splashing spoonfuls of ghee, mustard, sesame or peanut oil, adding just the right amounts of sour yoghurt, tomatoes, lemon juice, or tamarind. Picking a medley of dry and wet, whole or ground spices Malati did not even know existed and 'awakening their essences' as he called it to create his gourmet dishes.

'You must have been a Brahmin in your past life, Papi,' Malati said to Kamala with a superior air. 'Otherwise, how could you resist these delectable meats?'

'Well, the chef seems to have cast a spell on you and you on him with your ringlet framed round face and the greed in your eyes!' Kamala laughed.

'Well, you know I am now an expert at recognizing the different royal foods and spices, especially the dark, explosive spice of the Marathas—Pathar Phool. Its strong fragrance lingers in the mouth and on our hands long after we have eaten our meals. I have even tested and confirmed a junior cook's claim that even our stools carry the fragrance of the spice,' Malati replied.

Kamala screwed up her nose in disgust. 'Shi shi, a girl should not talk about such indelicate things.'

'But I am Malati, not just a girl,' Malati said, laughed and ran away, hunting for another nibble.

Vilas Rao treated Baba with great respect. But the girls didn't like what other people were saying.

'The son-in-law is behaving like an aristocratic benefactor. You notice that Madhav Rao—the commoner and farmer to boot—has not been invited to the royal palace to pay obeisance to the king, nor to the royal hunt, or to share a royal feast,' Badi Dai, the senior maid assigned to Surekha said to Chhoti Dai, the junior one. Thankfully, they did not say it within Baba's earshot.

Vilas Rao's widowed sister, Meenabai, however made sure she mocked him to Vilas Rao when Baba was standing close by. 'You should have asked me to select a girl for you from a good, blue-blooded family. You need not have brought this peasant girl from Ratnagiri. How will you present her to the ladies of the court? Now her father is going to be a leech and a parasite along with his other two daughters.'

Baba did not react. In Ratnagiri, he was a fiery lion, self-respecting farmer, and authoritative vaidya, brooking no ill-intentioned, vicious diatribe from anyone. But here, in Vaishali, he had to act like the tame father of the bride.

Thankfully, Vilas Rao, stung by his sister's malicious talk, rose magnificently to Baba's defence. 'I should not have invited you bitter, ungrateful widow. I deserve a new start after my travails with Savitri's madness for fifteen years. You could not find anybody like Surekha for me. So beautiful, yet modest and innocent. She will learn to mingle with royalty and will bear me handsome sons who will carry my family line forward. Moreover, we have earned the Sardar blood by our own efforts. Madhav Rao has pure Maratha blood, is a proud and self-respecting man. True, he is a farmer. Nothing wrong with that. But he is also a respected vaidya. He did not come to me to offer his daughter. I went to him. He is not going to be a burden on me. He has his own life to lead. You and your family have been leeches. I have allowed you to suck my blood for too long. It will be best if you all leave for Bhopal forthwith.'

Vilas Rao called his clerk to arrange for Meenabai and her family to leave instantly.

Baba tried to intercede and said, 'Vilas Rao, let it be. She did not offend me with her talk. She is your sister after all, and I want her to bless my daughter, not put a widow's curse on her.'

Vilas Rao, who everyone called Malak—the overlord—brushed Baba aside. 'Madhav Rao, she has already cursed Surekha and me, as she cursed my first marriage. I will not brook her insulting you or Surekha and stirring poison into this auspicious moment.'

Baba was deeply touched and doffed his turban to Malak.

'You know, when you came down to Ratnagiri to ask for Surekha's hand, I had all kinds of doubts. But I also had an intuition that you are a man of character and you have proved me right today. I am proud that you chose Surekha and she chose you,' he said.

Malak was not an emotional man, it seemed. Nor could he take an elder brotherly compliment from his father-in-law.

'Bara bara, bus kara, Madhav Rao,' he said, smiling. 'Don't put me on a pedestal. I am like any other. But one good man deserves another.'

Meenabai left in a huff. From the safety of her carriage, frog-like, she stuck her head out, her bulging eyes rolled, her nostrils flared, and she croaked forth a curse on Malak.

Baba was upset.

'Don't worry. The power to curse only belongs to sages. Moreover, my marriage to Surekha is made on earth, but blessed by the heavens. Let us now get the wedding going!' Malak brushed his concerns away.

'An unseen enemy has the power of a ghost,' Badi Dai told the girls when Malati and Kamala asked about Maa Saheb, Surekha's sawat, and daughter Sarala not being visible. 'Go and see what they are up to. Their caretaker, Bhasker, is an evil man, adept at hatching conspiracies. He came with her as a pathrakha—one who watches her back. But he is always setting her up against Malak to show that he is needed. Be careful and don't fall into their trap. Maa Saheb has the gift of divine madness. She becomes the medium to transmit both good and bad spirits,' she said, much to the girls' alarm.

So, one afternoon, Kamala and Malati went to the Chhota Ghar—a bungalow where Maa Saheb and Sarala lived under Bhasker Kaka's watch. They did not dare to go in through the front door, but decided to peek through the large windows at the back of the bungalow. They could hear faint voices, but couldn't see anything. Kamala lifted Malati on to some bricks to get a better view. Malati rose precariously, the pile wobbled, and she fell with a thud and an involuntary cry of 'Ayeega!' Kamala shooed Malati into silence, but it was too late.

The stern housekeeper, Bhasker, came running to the back of the house, peered at them through thick glasses, and said menacingly, 'Arechya! So, you are the new mistress's sisters. Come in through the front door. You are not thieves. Let Maa Saheb meet you since the sawat herself has not come to greet her and seek her blessings.'

Kamala and Malati had no option but to do as he bade and enter from the front door. The big living room had a damp, musty smell, the windows closed and curtains drawn to shut out the world and ensnare the visitors into a witch's lair it seemed. They were in Maa Saheb's presence and panicked. What if she became possessed by a bad spirit on seeing them and cursed them? They did not dare even to look up at her until Bhasker introduced them to her. They then saw the thin, richly dressed woman reclining on a velvet couch and smiling at them.

'She is not possessed by bad spirits. She smiled at us,' whispered Kamala.

'Pai lago, Maa Saheb,' they said in unison and bowed to touch her feet—a customary way of greeting elders in Vaishali.

'So, your sister sent you to see what her sawat is like, how wasted she is, whether she is mad or not?' Her voice was raspy and tired rather than threatening.

Kamala did not dare to reply. But the ever-blunt Malati managed to say, 'No, our Surekhatai does not even know we are here. We just wanted to meet you because we have heard so much about you from the ladies of the Bada Ghar.'

Visibly embarrassed by Malati's outspokenness, Kamala quickly added, 'And we, of course, wanted to make friends with Sarala.'

'What do they say about me?' asked Maa Saheb, fiercely pulling Malati closer.

Her long, blue veined fingers dug into Malati's arms. She noticed a deep sadness on Maa Saheb's face, the magnetism of her burning black eyes and felt her breath, hot and rancid upon her and she turned away in a spasm of disgust only to turn right back. Malati was momentarily mesmerized by this woman of divine madness and did not listen to Kamala's urgent whispered warning.

'Many people say that you get possessed by good or bad spirits, you get fits, then you can be angry and dangerous and that you may curse anyone in your sight. You may sometimes also give boons, they say,' she blurted out.

Maa Saheb let go of Malati's arm, laughed, and got up from the couch. She was a tall, slim woman. Must have been beautiful once, Malati thought admiringly—not as beautiful as their sister Surekha, but in her own regal way. Her green sari was bridal and she was wearing jewellery that could be the envy of queens.

'Yes, I do get fits. The Mother Goddess of the Hill Temple enters my body and captures my mind and soul. Then I see what others cannot. Sometimes, it is good and I convey blessings. Sometimes, what is going to happen is bad; it's not only Mata's will or my curse. It is the misfortune of the person I behold and concentrate on and their karmas from past life catching up,' Maa Saheb said with a faraway look.

Malati was fascinated and oddly drawn to this rival of their sister, who would probably like to see darkness in Surekha's future. And do everything to make Surekha's life in Vaishali hell.

'Really? Then what do you see in our future now that we are in your presence?' she asked her, with great bravado.

Maa Saheb looked at the girls for a moment as if directing shafts of light at them. She then closed her eyes—for what seemed like an eternity.

The girls waited in silence, looking down, too afraid to look at her. What if she read in their eyes bad karma from a past life and predicted a dark future for them, maybe even curse them? Malati even started thinking of all the bad karma she may have earned in this life, with her naughtiness and tricks!

'I cannot see anything in your near future that is usual for girls,'

Maa Saheb said, at last. 'I see no marriage, no husband, no grihasthi. You are going to lose someone very precious soon, but will also get someone new in your life. You are going to be separated from your family.'

Malati started reasoning out what she had predicted to allay their anxiety.

'Well, we are losing Surekhatai and separating from her and getting Malak as a new member of our family. And yes, we will continue to study and we don't want marriage and husbands for a long time, perhaps never. Yes, all that you say fits into what's happening.'

Maa Saheb smiled and said, 'Well, if that makes you happy, so be it. But remember, what I see is not visible to you mortals here and now. It's shrouded in the fogs of the future.'

She talked as if she were not a mortal herself, but a supernatural being!

Kamala was uneasy.

'What do you see in Surekhatai's future, Maa Saheb?' she asked.

'Now you ask! I have not seen your sister, so if she visits me the Mother Goddess of the Hill Temple will tell me. Mata already warned me that there will be another kind of antarpat—curtain of separation—that will fall between Malak and me forever. Our souls, which had become one, must now be pulled apart,' she said with a sigh of resignation.

'And what do you see for Sarala then?' Malati asked unthinkingly, and then bit her tongue.

'Well, I try not to call upon the Mother Goddess to show me her future, but I know better times are coming for her. She will prevail,' Maa Saheb asserted.

Even as she made these optimistic predictions about Sarala's future, her face clouded over as if trying to push aside troubling visions and she got up saying, 'Bhasker, show them out. I am tired now.'

A slim, tall girl, who looked like one whom God has sculpted and painted with care to perfection, a marvellous blend of Malak and Maa Saheb, came running in.

'Come, Maa Saheb,' she said, compassionately and holding her mother's hand helped her get up.

Maa Saheb looked unsteady, as if she was going to fall. Putting her hand on Sarala's shoulder, she turned abruptly, leading herself back into perhaps even gloomier recesses of the Chhota Ghar.

'Sarala, we are Malati and Kamala, Surekha's sisters and we would like to be your friends,' Malati said as they left the room, fully prepared for rejection. If Sarala was feeling resentful of them, she did not show it. She displayed a young girl's curiosity and friendliness which spoke through her melancholy eyes.

'I will put Maa Saheb to bed and come back to talk to you,' she said and asked Bhasker to offer them some drinks and sweets. She spoke like the lady of the house, not just a daughter.

The girls sat on a velvet settee. A servant brought them cool pink rose sherbet in two silver tumblers and some sweet milky pedas. They felt guilty enjoying Surekha's sawat's hospitality.

'So, you girls don't want to get married I heard you say. So different rules for different daughters! Are you stepdaughters, by any chance? Ha ha! Did Surekha go to school?' Bhasker asked sarcastically.

'No, but she knows how to read, write, and count. And she can sing abhangs of Sant Tukaram and read and recite stories from the Mahabharata, Ramayana, and Puranas. Ayee has also trained her to be a good wife to Vilas Rao,' Kamala said defensively.

'Well, well. Let us see how well trained she is to be Vilas Rao's wife. She does not have to cook or clean here or work on the farm. He is an aristocrat, you understand. She has to rise to his level and be able to be a malkin—the mistress of this wada—and supervise the staff. Most of all, she has to manage his moods and bear his cruelty. Look what he has done to Maa Saheb, who is from a blue-blooded aristocratic family in her own right. What is she reduced to?'

He stopped as Sarala returned to the living room.

6
KRISHNA'S TULSI

'Let us go out to the garden,' Sarala said. It seemed as though she wanted to escape the prison of the Chhota Ghar and her jailer, Bhasker Kaka, who seemed at the same time to be a resident uncle and father to her.

The three girls walked out to the tulsi garden in front of the house. An early spring breeze was spreading the fragrance of the tulsi shrubs—young goddesses clothed in green and purple. The exotic lychee trees were breaking out into flowers of a kind Malati and Kamala had not seen before—little fairies wearing spiky dresses and dancing in clusters.

In the daylight, Sarala looked more like the fourteen-year-old that she was. As they walked around, they introduced themselves, told their story and confessed to being amazed by Vaishali and Vilas Rao's Amrit Wada—Home of the Nectar of Immortality. Sarala listened intently without once interrupting them until Kamala realized they were monopolizing the conversation and said, 'Sorry, Sarala. We are so happy and excited to meet you that we have not given you a chance to speak. Do tell us about yourself.'

Sarala smiled shyly and said, 'It's OK. I have not spoken to girls like you before. I mostly meet the daughters of the royal family and courtiers from time to time. So, this is a welcome break.'

'What about school? You must have fancy schools here in Vaishali, not the simple ones in sheds like ours in Ratnagiri,' Malati said.

'Well, I have tutors come every day to teach me Hindi, English, mathematics, and history, and I do give exams—I have passed the ninth grade—but without going to school. Yes, I am a bright student.'

'That's marvellous! You are spared the five-mile trudge, the caning, and the bullying in school. You learn everything in the comfort of your home,' Kamala said, almost enviously.

Sarala's eyes lit up for a moment, and then they dimmed.

'Kumbhanachya dusryabajula gavat nehami hirwagaar disto,' she said. 'The grass always looks greener on the other side of the fence, but it is not, Kamala. Truth is I really yearn to go to school, meet girls and boys of my age, and enjoy conversations, even if they are punctuated with fights and taunts. There is something to be said for being pebbles in a running stream, rubbing against each other and being smoothened by the friction. I see and live the world through my teachers and the many dais here and Bhasker Kaka, not through my own eyes and senses,' she explained, like a grown-up.

'OK, let's change places,' Malati said to her, half-laughing, half-serious.

'Wait, wait, not so fast. We have not talked about your parents and mine, have we? Your parents seem to love each other and love you enough, to defy custom. Look at me. Maa Saheb loves me with all her heart and soul. But she can't be a complete mother, can she? She lives in two worlds—one with me and my father and one with Lord Krishna to whom she is married. You see the tulsi plants here. On every Krishna Ekadashi my mother, like Vrinda—tulsi of the legends—gets married to Sri Krishna, whom she considers her true husband.'

'Oh, that's like living in a dream,' Kamala said kindly. 'Does Malak know? Does she allow him entry into that world?' she asked.

'Well, he knows this world of Maa Saheb with Sri Krishna exists. He does not understand it and labels it madness. That is why he left her,' said Sarala bitterly.

'But is he cruel to your mother as Bhasker Kaka implied?' Malati persisted.

'Don't listen to Bhasker Kaka. He is too protective of Maa Saheb and judges Malak harshly. Look, when we used to live in the wada with Malak, Maa Saheb did get fits and to stop her from harming herself he needed to tame her. Doctors even advised that she be put in a lunatic asylum, but Malak refused and shifted us to the Chhota Ghar—to minimize any provocation that would unsettle her. Now we have a nurse who takes care of her and Bhasker Kaka is always around to supervise,' Sarala explained, much to their relief.

'And is he a good father to you?' asked Kamala.

'He is—as much as a man in his position can be. He does visit us once a week. Provides fully for our well-being, talks to my teachers about my progress. But yes, that's not enough for me. I wish sometimes that he would scold me, even beat me—anything to show he really cares,' Sarala confessed.

'Arey Dewa! I feel sorry for all you have gone through. Hope things will be better,' Kamala said holding her hand.

'I don't think they will be better. Now that Malak is getting married again. He will push Maa Saheb more into her world of divine madness and I will be even more conflicted—hanging like King Trishanku between heaven and earth,' Sarala said.

'Well then, like Trishanku, you will be blessed to live with the stars! Don't worry, we will tell our Surekhatai, who is not much older than you, to be your friend and to look out for you,' Malati said reassuringly.

Sarala's friendly face flipped into an angry scowl. Her Cupid bow lips twisted up in disapproval. Her eyes suddenly flashed beams of animosity.

'Che! Che! She is going to be Maa Saheb's sawat and my stepmother. Why will she befriend me? It's against the law of nature. I will have to find my own way of navigating between my mother's heaven and Malak's new earth,' Sarala exclaimed to the girls' chagrin.

They rushed to tell Surekha about Maa Saheb and Sarala. She was with Badi Dai and Chhoti Dai, who were massaging her with oil and applying turmeric paste before her bath. They stood unnoticed at the entrance of the large open-to-the-sky bathroom enclosed with curtains in the zenana. The toothless Badi Dai explained to Surekha what she must do as an obedient and devoted wife as she massaged her.

'Don't be scared, nor defiant. Be respectful,' she said

'Is there something to be scared of? Malak told me he will not hurt me. I will obey him, but what will he do and ask me to do?' Surekha asked apprehensively. Her eyes fluttering, her mouth half open to drink in the droplets of wisdom from the spring of the dais.

'Oh my lado. You are going to be his wife, not his mistress, so you don't make the first move. Wait for him to call you, touch you, guide you,' Badi Dai said, with a wink.

'To do what?' asked Surekha.

Chhoti Dai, opened her red, betel stained-mouth wide in surprise.

'Didn't your mother tell you anything about Malak, huh?' she asked.

'How could she? She does not know him,' replied Surekha.

'Agabai! The bride is so innocent! What shall we do, Rama?' exclaimed Badi Dai, striking her forehead in frustration.

Both the dais burst out laughing, pouring warm water on Surekha's glistening body from a copper vessel.

Surekha looked embarrassed.

'Oh please, please, Badi Dai, tell me. I cannot risk ignorance and Malak's displeasure. Ayee only told me that I must make my husband happy and give him no reason to leave me for another. So please tell me what I must do to gain Malak's favour,' Surekha pleaded.

Badi Dai's old, rheumy eyes twinkled and the creases around them deepened, as she laughed again and began her lesson with gusto.

'You must know about Radha–Krishna's cosmic love play which is meant to teach us humans how a man and a woman embrace each other to show love and become one in body and soul,' Badi Dai said.

'You are the Radha to Malak's Krishna,' Chhoti Dai continued. 'He will touch you, play with your clothes and ornaments, and then with your body. Don't be eager yourself and it is OK to be shy. But when he signals that he wants to enter your body, remove your clothes, and give in to him easily. It should be your pleasure and duty. You may hurt at first, but don't show it. Later, you too will be part of the love play and enjoy it.'

Surekha blushed and asked, 'When will this love play begin?'

'On your nuptial night, day after tomorrow,' the dais said in unison.

Kamala and Malati looked at each other, a little embarrassed.

'Let us go before we are caught eavesdropping,' Kamala whispered.

So, they waited until Surekha came to her room to tell her excitedly about their meeting with Maa Saheb and Sarala. Surekha was fascinated but nervous.

Surekha panicked and wondered whether Maa Saheb has indeed some special powers of divine madness. What if there was a curse on Malak's whole clan! She wondered whether she should meet Maa Saheb and disarm her but worried if Malak would disapprove.

The girls asked her not to worry and assured her they would make friends on Surekha's behalf with Sarala and through her win Maa Saheb over, so she did not curse her. It was not Surekha's fault that she was Malak's second wife. He wanted it, and it was right that she should seek Maa Sahab's blessings too.

The wedding day arrived. Surekha was transformed from a fifteen going on sixteen maiden into the lady wife to be of the stately Malak. The slivers of her girlish calves peeped furtively through the dignified folds of a gold bordered, green Paithani sari. Her matching brocade blouse contoured the full breasts of a grown woman but her self-conscious pull at her padar to hide them and her unlined swan neck gave away her tender age. The brilliance of the gem studded wedding jewellery gifted by Malak could not smother the radiance of four moons emanating from her baby smooth skin.

Her fish-shaped eyes, though boldly kohl rimmed, sparkled with childish delight. Her delicate champa bud nose, refused to be weighed down by the snail-shaped pearl and ruby nath. Her closed rose petal lips, perfectly placed in her oval face, spoke to poise and serenity, but opened and spread themselves into a toothy, nervous giggle at the slightest provocation. Her womanly ambada bun at the back of her head could barely hide her fulsome braids so used to dangling on the sides of her head. The glory of jasmine hair garlands drew the final halo of white light around Surekha though, turning her from a farmer's teenage daughter into a Bride Goddess of the Manor.

Malak made an effort to look younger than usual in deference to his child–woman bride while retaining a regal mien. The girls were pleasantly surprised to see that he had shaved off his beard but kept a neat moustache. He wore tight pyjamas but with a nobleman's fitting long brocade coat. Perched on his head was a nifty golden turban with a playful, fanlike tura. But he did not omit a pearl and sapphire turban ornament, its royal blue highlighting his authoritative grey eyes.

Malati and Kamala were introduced to Vaishali's great tradition of attar when they tested the distinct perfumes: Malak and Surekha applied on their skin and clothes—he, the earthy and overpowering musk and she, the soft and sweet rose.

They stood together in the flower-bedecked pavilion with plantain trees and brass water pitchers placed at the four corners. With the Fire God as witness, they performed the wedding rituals. No longer divided by status, age, and region—they looked as if the heavens had indeed paired them together.

The priest proceeded to the antarpaat ceremony, where he held up a sheet of cloth between the two to the chanting of the auspicious mangalashtakas. He then removed the cloth and they garlanded each other, commanded by the gods to be joined in a lifelong union. Suddenly, Malati remembered what Maa Saheb had said about the antarpaat coming back between her and Malak, never to be lifted again, their union annulled.

Baba had tears in his eyes as Surekha went through these life-transforming rituals with calm and dignity. Baba performed the kanyadan ceremony, 'giving away' his daughter to Malak. Through this most merit-earning ritual, Baba was thereby assured a place in heaven! The couple performed the saptapadi, around the sacred fire. Malak got up to put the mangalsutra—sacred black and gold necklace—on Surekha.

Just then, there was a small commotion as a richly dressed Maa Saheb walked towards the wedding pavilion with Sarala, Bhasker Kaka, and her nurse in tow.

'Stop, I am coming,' called out Maa Saheb.

Surekha looked questioningly towards her. The usually calm and confident Malak appeared puzzled and unsure. But he soon collected himself, went to Maa Saheb, held her hand, and brought her to the pavilion.

'Let me do the ritual of handing over that mangalsutra to you to put around the new bride's neck. That way the transfer of my union with you to her will be complete and I will be free to be in union with my Krishna,' she said.

Surprised murmuring rippled through the hall.

Malak looked at the wedding guests and said, 'Please be quiet. We are in the midst of a sacred wedding ceremony.'

He gave Maa Saheb the mangalsutra. She ritually handed it back to him to the reciting of mantras. He put it around a bewildered Surekha's neck. She touched Maa Saheb's feet and asked for her blessing. Maa Saheb was taken aback.

She looked at Malak and said, 'Who am I to give blessings? The Goddess of the Hill Temple must bless this union. She is a good child you chose,' she said and left with her entourage.

Maa Saheb walked deliberately towards her Chhota Ghar, to celebrate her freedom from Malak and her union with her true husband, Krishna—one who would never leave her for another.

7

LIFTING THE WEDDING VEIL

Kamala and Malati were a little frightened for Surekha after Bhasker Kaka's remark about Malak's 'cruelty' and the dais' instructions to her. They decided to keep a watch on Surekha on her nuptial night and be her pathrakhins—protectors. So, before the bride and groom were led into the nuptial chamber, the girls ran to position themselves near the window behind the bamboo curtains in the adjoining terrace so that they could see through without being seen.

They soon heard footsteps and saw Surekha and Malak walk in—he leading with a swagger and she following meekly, taking in her surroundings.

Surekha stood looking uncertain of her place in her new husband's inner domain and twirled her sari padar around her fingers, like the first time she had met him. Malak asked Surekha to sit down. She sat gingerly on the edge of a chair, and rocked herself back and forth.

'Not there. Here, on the bed next to me,' he commanded. She obeyed reluctantly.

'Don't be scared. I won't eat you up,' said Malak with a laugh.

'What a thing to say, Papi,' Malati whispered to Kamala.

'He is only trying to lighten the mood and make her feel comfortable,' Kamala explained.

He gently lifted up her face and abruptly said, 'Remove all this jewellery. You don't need it now. You are a jewel yourself.'

She obeyed.

Surekha was still shy, smiling but not looking Malak in the eye.

'Now get rid of your blouse and sari,' he instructed. She sat there frozen.

'See, you don't have to feel shy. I'm your husband. Didn't the ladies tell you about the love play you must do as a wife?' he asked, impatiently.

Surekha nodded and whispered, 'But I don't know how.'

'Don't worry. I will guide you. See, I am removing my clothes too,' he said.

So, she plucked up courage, unknotted her blouse, and pulled loose her nine-yard sari, but shyly covered herself with the padar, did not let it go, and stood there trembling.

'All right,' said Malak, firmly pulling down the mosquito net around the four-poster bed.

He removed his turban, achkan, and his pajamas, but kept his muslin shirt on. The girls had never seen Baba with just a shirt on. They could not help but giggle at the sight of Malak's hairy legs and the outline of his body through the muslin shirt.

'Now, he is going to play games as the dais had predicted,' Kamala whispered.

'Shhshh,' said Malati, not wanting to betray their presence at this delicate moment.

The girls were mesmerized by Malak's play. He lifted Surekha like the child that she was and laid her down on the bed. He moved inside the net. They could only dimly see his hands rubbing her breasts and thighs then he climbed on top of her and their bodies seemed to join into one.

'See, now the antarapaat has been removed between them—beyond symbols,' murmured Kamala.

The old carved bed, inherited from Malak's father, creaked and the canopy of net swayed from side to side. There was a cry of pain from Surekha, but it was brief and stifled. Her protectors, Kamala and Malati, did not dare to go to her rescue. The love play seemed to be over. They were shocked to see Malak emerge out of the net, flushed and serious—all tenderness gone.

'Go and wash up and sleep on the other bed prepared for you,' he said gruffly.

She stumbled up, tears in her eyes, gathered her trailing sari, and clutched her blouse in her crossed arms trying to cover her breasts and bare legs.

'Why is Malak upset? What has Akka done wrong? Why is she crying?' Malati asked Kamala.

'I don't understand how he hurt her or how she offended him,' Kamala said helplessly.

Malak put on his nightclothes and came back to his bed. Surekha too dressed herself and quietly lay down on her new bed. He was soon snoring. She closed her eyes. Did she sleep? They didn't wait to find out; they slunk away, sheepish and aware that they had been in forbidden territory with no purpose served.

Baba was pacing up and down in front of their room when they returned.

'Where were you?' he asked angrily. They made a convincing excuse of savouring their last meal before they left for Ratnagiri.

The next morning, they quickly got ready, gathered their shiny new belongings and their old ones into a bundle, ready to leave, and ran to look for Surekha, dreading a confrontation with a surly Malak. But as they climbed the bannistered staircase, they saw Surekha coming down smiling with Malak, all richly dressed for another ceremony.

'Oh look, there they are—your sprightly sisters! Playing lukachhupi—hide and seek—in my wada? Ha ha! Looking for your Akka? She is now forever hidden under my angarakha! You will only find her when you look for me,' Malak said with a mischievous smile.

He was a different man this morning! Surekha smiled shyly too, and the girls smiled back in relief.

'Malak, we came to ask Surekhatai if she will join us in our last game of lukachhupi before we leave today. After we go, you can play lukachhupi with each other to your hearts' content,' Malati said cheekily, holding Surekha's hand.

'Yes, Malak. We have much more seeking than hiding to do—to find ourselves most of all, don't we?' said Kamala, emboldened to speak up too—showing off her wisdom.

'Your sisters are audacious, engaging in saval-jawab and arguing, even with me! Have you taught them to do that or have you learnt from them?' Malak asked Surekha in jest.

She smiled apologetically on her sisters' behalf.

'Oh no, Surekhatai is not like us. Ayee has taught her to be very polite and decorous,' Kamala said quickly.

'OK girls, come and join the breakfast ceremony. I hear Malati is a khadad—always tempted by food,' Malak said.

Malati was embarrassed but delighted to partake of another feast.

As they sat down after the chanting of mantras to enjoy the spread, there was a sudden murmur and Maa Saheb entered, with a nervous Sarala trying to hold her back. Unlike at the wedding pavilion the day before, Malak turned red with anger, but was coldly polite.

'Oh ho! Kay jhala, Savitri? Sarala, she should not be straining herself. Where is her nurse and Bhasker? Call them.'

Sarala apologized. But, Surekha got up quickly and went across to touch her feet.

'Bara, bara, sada saubhagyavati bhava. May you always be blessed with your husband and give Malak the seven sons that he desires,' Maa Saheb said, touching her head in benediction.

Bhasker Kaka and the nurse arrived. Malak looked reproachfully at them and turned to Maa Saheb and said, 'Ata apan ja Savitri. This is not the place for you to be. You have your own wada and temple. Leave the new bride alone. I will still visit you as I used to, and we will take care of Sarala,' he said firmly.

'All right! So, I am banished from here forever, is it?' Maa Saheb asked, almost pitifully, her face twitching.

'You have been gone from here for a long time, Savitri, well before Surekha came in as my wife and the new malkin. You have your own Krishna to worship and occupy you, have you not? Now, Bhasker, make sure Maa Saheb follows the norms I have set around here and you and the nurse take good care of her. I will make sure she has every comfort she needs,' Malak ordered.

Bhasker Kaka and the nurse coaxed Maa Saheb to leave. A crestfallen Maa Saheb clicked-clocked her way out of there in her wooden kadavas reserved for her worship. Malati almost felt sorry for her, but as the dais said, there could not be two swords in one scabbard and there could not be two malkins in one wada. So, she was happy for Surekha that the ground rules had been laid down in front of everybody, including Baba.

'And, Sarala baal, you are welcome to come in whenever you want to meet your stepmother, Chhoti Ma,' said Malak to Sarala with unusual gentleness.

Malati and Kamala held their breaths to see how Sarala would react. To their delight, Surekha went to Sarala and said 'Come, Sarala, let us embrace. I am not old enough to be your mother, but I can be your maitrin—your friend forever.'

Sarala looked taken aback, but did not resist the embrace. Neither did she respond. She sat down, but got up soon after the meal and touching Malak's feet, she ran away without a glance at any of the rest.

Baba, who had been silent throughout, turned to Malak and said, 'Javai Raja, amhi dhanya jhalo! We are so fortunate you chose Surekha as your wife. I am satisfied that you will treat her well and with respect and together you will overcome all difficulties. Surekha's sanskar, her upbringing, is to respect elders like Savitribai, and she will be a good companion and elder sister to Sarala.'

'Madhav Rao, thank you for giving me your daughter's hand. She is safe here. I expect her to follow her wifely duties, and not get into rivalries and conflicts. She should bear me sons to pave my path to heaven and I will be happy. I need peace of mind to do my duty by our Maharaja to whom I owe everything,' Malak said as he took their leave and left for the court.

When Malati and Kamala expressed concerns about Maa Saheb avenging the seeming insult to her, Surekha told them she was capable of handling everything as a 'woman of the world' and asked them to focus on helping Ayee now that she was not there.

Their journey back from Vaishali seemed unending—a reflection of how far they had travelled to marry Surekha off to Malak. Long stretches of green, yellow, and brown fields were spread out like Ayee's gudadi patchwork quilts, as they sped past villages and towns. Occasionally, they caught a glimpse of the cupolas, minarets, and spires of Hindu temples, mosques, and churches, shimmering in the sun or traced by silver moonlight in the night, proudly rising above and looking down at the scattered, humble settlements filled with people in awe of their gods.

At last, they reached Ratnagiri. Ayee was standing at the door of their home, smiling. The girls eagerly embraced her and couldn't wait to tell her stories about Surekha's wedding and her new life in Vilas Rao's wada.

Ayee welcomed them in rhyme.

Welcome home my dearest travellers,
Who left me yearning to be with the revellers,
You lived the wedding dream with joy and laughter
Much pomp, colour, and ceremony after!
I pined to be there from my solitary perch here
Constantly imagining the festive atmosphere!
Now that you are at last back with me,
Be my Sanjaya who could from afar see,
Like to blind King Dhritarashtra do relate
Be my eyes and ears, my senses exhilarate

Describe to me everything you've done and seen
So I can vividly envision the Vaishali scene.

'Ayee, of course, we will. Don't be impatient,' Malati teased, smiling at her.

'Of course, I'm impatient. You don't know what it is to be trapped here and not being there for celebrations of Surekha's all important wedding. Wait till I leave you all to go to a truly luminous world where you cannot reach me.'

'Don't ever do that, Ayee, we will never leave you alone again. We too missed you throughout and every time we saw something marvellous, we would think how delighted you would be. Now listen: it was as if a king and queen were getting married and Surekhatai was looking her part. The ceremonies were so grand and they had so many royal and British guests. Surekhatai now lives in a big palace like wada and has so many dais and servants to take care of her,' Kamala recounted, the pools of her sparkling eyes replaying in reflection, the spectacular Vaishali drama for Ayee.

'And, Ayee, she does not have to do any housework! She can while her time away wearing crisp Chanderi saris and gem-studded gold jewellery, meeting court and English ladies. And, of course, feeding her birds!' Malati added.

'So, my darling Surekha is well ensconced in her new grihasti? Rajyachi Rani! A queen to her king. I am ecstatic that she is happy,' Ayee said joyfully.

Ayee's brow was soon knitted up with worry about the dangers that may waylay Surekha in her new journey towards marital bliss. Did she have premonitions too, like Maa Saheb, wondered the girls.

'How is her sawat taking it? Did the mother–daughter duo behave well?' she asked.

'Oh, they joined the ceremonies and Savitribai gave her blessings to Surekha. And Sarala, the stepdaughter, has become friends with Malati and Papi and our large hearted Surekha has embraced her as a friend. So, you don't worry at all. Just continue with your prayers for her well-being,' Baba hastened to reassure Ayee before Malati and Kamala revealed their anxieties.

'Well, I am happy to hear that. And how is our Javai Raja behaving?' Ayee asked.

'Oh, he is such a gracious host. He gave us all rich clothes to wear and we enjoyed a veritable feast every day. He defended Baba when his own sister looked down on us all and made her leave the wedding house!' Kamala informed.

'Well, if you want to know whether he is taking Surekha's side and drawing boundaries between Maa Saheb and his new life with Surekha, yes, he seems to be doing that. Rest is up to Surekha to manage and how she reaches out to Maa Sahab and Sarala. She understands the need to do that,' Baba explained.

'It will also depend on her destiny—her bhagya,' said Ayee with a sigh.

'Now, now, enough brooding over Surekha. Focus on your well-being. Have you been resting, eating well, and taking my tonics? Let us now make sure you have a safe and comfortable birthing,' said Baba.

'Yes, yes. Ambutai ensured that. Now that you are back, I feel doubly strong,' Ayee said, donning her usual shawl of resilience to cover her bosom of ill health and discomfort.

'Kamala and Malati will help you with housework and Ambutai will look after you,' Baba said, sitting her down firmly.

'Ayee, I have even learnt how to make rajsi dishes of chicken and fish from Maharaj cook. They will make you strong!' Malati declared with a flourish of her hand, as if wielding a ladle.

'Ha ha! All you have learnt is to salivate at the sight of his delicacies and to eat like the glutton Pandava, Bhim,' teased Kamala.

'Ayee, bagha ga. Papi is calling me names,' Malati complained, blowing out her cheeks in pique and rolling her eyes at Kamala.

'At least I did not call you the demon Bakasur, who had an eating contest with Bhim!' Kamala laughed.

It gave Malati a good excuse to hug Ayee and hide her face in her sari that now covered the taut balloon of her stomach.

'Ayee, I can hear the baby's heartbeat,' she exclaimed.

'Well, watch out! The baby will kick you,' Kamala teased again.

8

A PASSAGE TO HEAVEN

After eating the simple meal Ambutai had cooked, Baba sent Kamala and Malati off to their room to sleep, so he could devote himself to Ayee's care. Kamala and Malati slept soundly in their own beds after a long time. Being back with Ayee was its own lullaby.

However, late that night, they heard distant sounds of Ayee moaning in pain, Baba making soothing sounds, people moving around with pots and pans. But they were too sleepy to wake up fully. The girls only rushed out of bed when they heard screams and Ambutai's wailing in the early morning.

Ayee and Baba were not in the house. Ayee had not come to them with her usual wake-up song—a bhoopali of Krishna-Gopala in her melodious voice.

> *Uthi Gopalji jayee dhenukade*
> *Lopali he nishi mand jahala shashi*
> *Wake up oh Krishna Gopala*
> *Go tend to your favourite cows*
> *See your cowherd friends beckon*
> *Eager to meet in pastures together*
> *The moon has become mellow*
> *The night has succumbed to light*
> *The rising sun bids you awake*
> *For your cosmic play to make*

Nor had she offered them a glass of fresh frothy milk straight from their cow Vaidehi's udders. Something was going on in the courtyard.

The girls rushed out into the courtyard. They saw Ayee lying on a reed mat. Instead of her famed patchwork quilt splashed with the green of the mango leaves and yellow of its fruit, the blue of the sky and the brown of the earth, she had chosen to cover herself with the white foam of the ocean. Her baby bulge had disappeared—so the baby must have arrived! She looked beautiful, even angelic. All she needed were wings. Her curly hair was in wet coils from having had a bath. To wash off the Red River perhaps. Her face showed no trace of pain. Brave always! There was even a smile! She was saying: see I have given your Baba a son and you a brother after all.

Malati came close to Ayee and called out to her. The one who would say 'Hoye! Aale ga!' to any call from her daughters, any time of day and night, did not reply. Kamala started singing Gopala's wake-up song—improvising the lyrics.

Uthi Uthi! Ayee! Ayee!
Kuthe geli tu majhi mai?

Ayee continued to sleep peacefully. Those eyes that always looked out for them were shut. Malati shook her. Feather light, soft and warm Ayee, who walked ever so briskly—*turu, turu, turu*—had become heavy and immovable like a cold stone statue of the Mother Goddess. Giving benediction without responding.

They looked around. A group of women from the neighbourhood had gathered and were sitting cross-legged on mats, their padars over their heads, whispering to each other and looking sombrely at Ayee. For the first time, they noticed that Baba was seated on a mat close by, his head bowed, looking dazed, holding what looked like a newborn baby in his arms, wrapped in a quilt Ayee had stitched just like the ones she had made for countless babies in their village. The baby started to cry. Ambutai took the baby from their reluctant Baba and asked the girls to follow her into the house.

'What's happened to our Ayee, Ambutai?' Kamala asked anxiously.

Malati just looked at Ambutai in terrified silence waiting for her answer.

'Now, now, you are big girls, so I have to tell you the truth. Your Ayee has been called away by Yamaraj and she has given you a baby brother,' Ambutai said.

'If we do penance like Savitri did for Satyavan, can we bring Ayee back from Yamaraj?' Malati asked hopefully.

'Yamaraj is unrelenting when he decides he wants to take someone away, like my husband. But you may get your mother back if your Baba wants, but she may not look like your Ayee,' Ambutai said, not looking the girls in the eye, instead gazing down at their baby brother, who was suckling at her breast.

'Ambutai is lying. Dead people don't come back. If they do, they only come as ghosts,' Kamala cried out and the sisters held on to each other tightly.

Their worst nightmare had come to pass. They broke into loud sobs, gasping for breath in between, their bodies heaving and writhing in indescribable pain—*chhat pat, chhat pat, chhat pat*. Malati felt like a fish freshly caught and netted out of the water, landing on the fisherman's prickly wicker basket, gasping for air.

Baba had no time that cursed day to talk and explain things to the girls. He had to take care of Ayee's funeral ceremonies. He wanted to hold on to Ayee's body for a day more, but the community priest forbade any delay.

'The prana has gone out of her body. You have to give fire to her body today to release her from the bondage of life and death and from the cycle of rebirth,' he explained.

Bhausaheb, who came in just at that time, embraced Baba and advised him. 'Madhav Rao, we all know your unusual attachment to your wife. But, for her sake, you have to let her go. If you keep a stale body in the house for long, it's not good for your newborn son and your young daughters too. Take it from a Brahmin.'

'What if Pratibha's atma refuses to leave your house? She will haunt it forever,' Ambutai had the last word.

'Well if there is even one grain of truth in that, I cannot risk hurting Pratibha's journey to heaven, can I? My selfishness has killed her. Now, I cannot give in to my desire to hold on to her earthly body and imprison her soul,' Baba said with resignation.

'She was a woman who earned a lot of punya from her good deeds. Be consoled in that she will go straight to heaven,' Bhausaheb said with unusual compassion and turning to Ambutai told her authoritatively, 'you had better nurture the newborn for our Madhav Rao.'

Ambutai looked at him in a strange way and said, 'Of course, I will take care of the baby as I am taking care of our own Bala.'

Bhausaheb left abruptly.

Baba returned home in the evening after consigning Ayee's body to the flames. Kamala and Malati were inconsolable.

'Baba must it not hurt for her flesh to be singed like that by fire?' Malati asked.

Baba embraced them for the first time since Ayee's death. They all cried together—even Baba. The Maratha warrior had lost his armour of bravery—at least for the moment.

'My children, once the prana goes out of the body, the body feels nothing. Only the soul remains and is liberated by the purifying flames of Agni Deva. Did you not study in your Bhagavad Gita lessons about the indestructibility of the soul? Lord Krishna tells Arjuna that the soul is not pierced by any weapon, nor burnt by any fire, nor is it dried by the wind, nor feels any pain or regret. So, your Ayee is transformed into a soul and she roams the heavens, free and happy. She will look down on us and she would want you to be happy.' Baba, calm and collected at last, was consoling himself as much as his daughters.

He looked at Ambutai, who was holding the newborn baby in her arms. 'Ambutai, could you please take care of the baby until I make arrangements for his care?' he requested her.

'But, of course, Madhav Rao. I owe my life and my own son's life to you and Pratibhatai. But for you two, I would have been consigned to a life of derision and isolation. You fought with the village council to let me live with dignity even though I was a widow. This is a small way I can repay your debt,' Ambutai said with feeling.

'It's I who am grateful to you. You have been a sister to Pratibha through thick and thin and now for her sake you are taking care of my children. I need some time to reorder my life and put together a semblance of a home for the girls and my son,' Baba said, his eyes once again welling up with tears.

'Baba, what shall we call our brother?' Malati asked, childishly trying to divert his attention to his long-awaited son.

'Your Ayee, before taking her last breath, was so happy that she had at last been able to gift me a son and heir. She asked me to call him Govind after Lord Krishna, but to save him from the evil eye, she said to call him Dhondu or stone. Your Ayee also asked that you both should have a life of freedom. I swear by her cherished memory that like a sea lion, I will repel the attacks from the sharks in our community and resist marrying you two motherless girls off until you finish college!' Baba said.

In the months that followed, Baba, who had so far been so full of energy, became more and more despondent. At times, he seemed to push his children away, rather than drawing them into his circle of affection. Kamala thought it was because he wanted to spare them the circle of sorrow he had drawn around himself. Just when they needed a soft presence to replace Ayee's, he seemed to be hardening himself.

Life without Ayee, was like trying to put a shattered clay pot together. Too many pieces just didn't fit together, some were broken beyond gluing and others unrecognizable. Baba, the chief potter, seemed to be the most broken of all and in no state to fix it. No more smearing his hands with the mud. No kneading and shaping the clay, let alone moulding it to near perfection on life's wobbly wheel and glazing it to perfection in a furnace.

His beloved orchards and farms stood neglected. He said he was vaidya no more, since he could not even save his beloved Pratibha. He seemed to look at Govind, with indifference, almost accusing the baby of taking his wife away from him. He could not find the words to talk to the girls—so emptied out was he of love and purpose.

Kamala helped Ambutai with the baby and the hitherto playful Malati got to work in the house any which way she could. Khandoba was now working indoors, no enemies to fight but the silences and the sorrow that assailed Baba's home.

He went to Baba from time to time and asked for instructions, hoping to rouse Baba's instinct for survival, for action on his farms and orchards. But unlike the mango wars Khandoba had fought, he had no weapon, no sling and clay bullets, no visible enemy to hit. The unseen enemy of Baba's grief could not be tackled with his war craft.

Almost a year passed. Baba was still in a stupor. The girls had meanwhile resumed school. Govind was growing up and crawling around. They received letters from Surekha telling them how well she was doing and that was a source of happiness for them. She wrote to say that she had had a baby girl, Veena. She wanted to bring her over. Baba hurriedly replied telling her not to come. Surekha responded by urging him to leave Ratnagiri and come to Vaishali, take possession of the ten villages gifted by Malak. He would then be closer to her and start a new life. She even offered to be Govind's and the girls' Little Mother!

This letter shook up Baba. He immediately gathered Kamala, Malati, Ambutai, and Khandoba around him and shared his deepest thoughts with them.

'I am ashamed,' he confessed. 'Whether prompted by Malak or on her own, my seventeen-year-old daughter has shown more maturity and resilience than her cowardly father. Grief had immobilized me, making me turn inwards, instead of reaching out to you girls, and even neglect my newborn son. I have been untrue to my dearest Pratibha and to the promises I made to her. I must wake up and become a karma yogi and take some tough decisions for us all.'

'Yes, Baba, we need to have you back with us. We have been adrift all these days,' said Kamala, who had become, as Ambutai said, the elder in the family.

'You all know that Surekha has invited us to move to Guna near Vaishali. I think a change of scene now would be good for all of us. I will sell my Ratnagiri orchards and farms and turn those lands gifted by Malak to gold, repay his debt, and come to terms with my eternal loss, if possible. But I cannot do it alone. Khandoba, will you and some of your assistants, who have the skills to make the transformation in Guna, accompany me with your families? I will give you, and them, land and homes, and a share of the produce we grow.'

Khandoba immediately agreed.

Baba turned to Ambutai and asked whether she could accompany them to take care of Govind.

'Well, as you know people expect you to take me as your second wife. That way, I could be a mother to your children and my son will get a father,' Ambutai revealed a desire she had been harbouring for long.

'Ambubai!' Baba exclaimed. 'I hope nothing in my behaviour gave you the idea that I was leading you on to that role in my life.'

'No, no. As a widow I have no right to expect to remarry. Whereas, of course, you as a householder cannot be without a wife. Since you are such an enlightened man and a follower of Maharishi Karve, I thought you will agree to marry me for your children's sake,' Ambutai cleverly put forward her condition for accompanying them while appealing to the social reformer in Baba.

'Although Pratibha has left her earthly body, she will always be with me. Know this, I will never replace her or marry another woman. I know you will give my children the canopy of a mother's love. But, for me, it's too big a price to pay. We will make different arrangements for Govind. As for the girls, I have a unique plan for them,' Baba said, quite categorically.

Ambutai looked downcast.

The girls didn't know what to feel, whose side to take.

9
THE CASTAWAYS

Govind was put in the care of Dayabai—Khandoba's wife. Ambutai left with her baby, Bala, in haste, without even saying goodbye. The next day, Baba took the girls with him to meet Sadashiv Pandit. He explained how he needed to change his karmabhoomi, his arena of action, and go to Guna, be near Surekha to start a new life.

'Panditji, I promised Pratibha that I will put them on the path of celibate scholarship, like boys, and reject child marriage or child motherhood. You showed me the way once. Show me again. A gurukul—boarding school—where girls can safely stay and study away from home. I believe in Maharshi Karve's message for all fathers—the real kanyadan is when you dedicate your daughter to Goddess Saraswati before you give her away to any man in marriage. I want my girls to not only finish high school, but maybe go to college as well,' Baba said.

Sadashiv Pandit was taken aback and asked how Baba had got to know about Maharishi Karve. Baba recalled how the Maharishi's disciple had come preaching in the market some years ago and while others dismissively said 'Chhe! Chhe!' Baba had imbibed the Maharishi's wisdom validated by the scriptures.

'I am amazed by you. You have fought a veritable crusade for girls' education not only by preaching to others, but by making a living example of your own daughters. So, I will help you,' said Panditji.

The girls gaped at their father. He wanted to send them away from the shade of his protective umbrella!

'I don't think such a gurukul exists, Papi,' Malati whispered to Kamala.

But Panditji said, 'Very well then, I advise you to go to Indore, one of the princely Maratha states of the Central Province. There is an orphanage and boarding school for girls inspired by the large-hearted Queen Ahilyabai Holkar, which is still flourishing.'

'But how can I send my children to an orphanage while I am alive?' Baba asked. 'What will Pratibha think of me? Will the girls forgive me?'

Panditji was quiet for a moment. The girls were tongue-tied, hoping desperately that Baba would give up the idea.

After some reflection, Baba himself said, 'But they are half orphans already. So, my wife in heaven and the girls will also understand that this is the best for them. The best way is the hardest, Sant Tukaram said. "And this is a pilgrim's path".'

'Spoken like a pandit,' Sadashiv Pandit said admiringly. Turning to the girls he recalled another abhang of Sant Tukaram: 'Shuddh beeja poti, phale rasal gomati. From the purest of seeds, do you get the most wholesome, juicy, and beautiful of fruits. There is no seed better than that of learning and this is what your father is sowing for you.'

Baba seemed recharged. The girls felt as if the earth of Ratnagiri was shaking and had opened up right under their feet to swallow them into her belly.

Khandoba was waiting with their bullock cart looking very disturbed.

'What happened Khandoba? Speak up,' Baba asked impatiently.

'I found one of our carts at the edge of the forest leading up to the Kajali River. And guess who I found in it? Ambutai's son Bala, wrapped in a bundle. It was his crying that led me to the cart,' said Khandoba.

'Well, it's a good thing that the baby is safe. Hope he is in Dayabai's custody,' said Baba.

'Yes Malak. But I did not find Ambutai anywhere. I followed the track; it led me to the riverbank, where I saw some clothes that Daya says belong to Ambutai.'

'Arrey deva re', Kamala exclaimed. 'She must have drowned!'

'Now, now. Don't let your imagination run wild. Which mother—that too a widow—would leave her baby and commit suicide. I am sure she will come back to fetch him. If not, Govind will have a companion in little Bala. Maybe that's what Ambutai wanted.' Baba tried to reassure the girls, but his knitted brows and pursed lips betrayed his concern that she may indeed have taken her life in desperation.

That night Malati dreamt an Ambutai version of the legendary Ganga–River Goddess–King Shantanu story. Because of Brahma's curse, Ambutai wanted to consign her son to the river and Baba stopped her! Baba did not ask any forbidden question, though he had given a 'forbidden answer' to her question. So, she left her son behind as punishment, even as she chose to drown herself in the Kajali River to become a legend herself!

As they stared at a parting from Baba and Ratnagiri, Malati realized the real meaning of Maa Saheb's predictions about them. They had lost their dearest one—Ayee; they had gained baby Govind in their lives, and they were going to part from their family! And they were not getting married but going into extended celibate scholarship!

Baba plunged into selling his beloved mango orchards and farms. He sent messages to Malak and Surekha that he was ready to move to Guna. He sought Malak's help with the girls' admission into Ahilya Ashram. Surprisingly, Malak approved the plan and immediately finalized their admission.

Since Ahilya Ashram had some day scholars from rich families attending the school too, the authorities agreed to give admission to rich Malak's poor, half-orphan sisters-in-law. The girls did not know whether to laugh or cry. Clever Kamala pleaded with Baba, to reconsider his decision about getting someone as their stepmother.

'You will always have one mother. Besides, stepmothers are bound to mistreat stepchildren. You know the story of Dhruva,' he said firmly.

'But, Baba, we are now grown-up enough, and like Dhruva, with Lord Vishnu's blessing, we could ward off any harm caused by a stepmother,' Malati pleaded.

'Caught you, Kamala and Malati! You can't say you are too young to go to the ashram, but old enough to deal with the machinations of a stepmother! Start preparing for your journey to Ahilya Ashram,' instructed Baba playfully.

The girls had barely survived the near boat wreck of Ayee's death and now they were careening towards crash landing onto a desolate shore. When Ayee used to talk about destiny, had she ever thought of theirs as castaways in an orphanage? They thought not. And Malati and Kamala despaired.

The girls understood what it is to go to an ashram gurukul when Baba took them to the Ratnagiri market to buy regulation clothes. Four sets of rough cotton parkar polka in green and blue, thick cotton nine-yard saris and blouses, full-sleeve jackets made of quilted cloth for winter and two pairs of footwear completed their wardrobe! Baba forbade them to take any fancy clothes.

Dayabai helped them pack their modest belongings into two small tin trunks. Khandoba got them fresh durries, a thick quilt, and a pillow each. These were rolled together into two neat bundles in a casement hold-all. That's all it took to gather and transfer their life to a strange new destination.

As they headed to the Ratnagiri station with their baggage, they bade goodbye to their beloved earthen home, with its red tiled sloping roof, long emptied of its soul since Ayee had left them. Shikha, Bela, Lasya, and Sulu, their playmates of the hours stolen away from school, were silently standing by the wayside, waving goodbye. Their arms seemed to draw arcs of friendship in the air. Their cow Vaidehi mooed and their goats bleated them farewell. Even the dogs, whom they had raced with, and alley cats whom they had secretly given scraps of food or donas of milks, ran after their cart as if this was the last time they would see them. The mango groves were without fruit, but the mango flowers seemed to waft their fragrance carelessly in their direction.

From atop their branches, the koels lanced their song at the departing girls—*Kuhu! Kuhu! Kuhu!* It was not the beginning of monsoon.

'Hey Kamala! Do you think the koels are giving us a message of hope or warning us that like Sati Parvati, we too will be condemned to live a thousand years imprisoned in a koel's form at the dreaded ashram?' Malati whispered to Kamala.

'Don't be dramatic. The koels are just saying goodbye. We—you and I—will be our own selves in the ashram, whatever happens,' Kamala replied smiling reassuringly.

The bullock cart with Baba and the girls driven by Khandoba passed the village square. Bhausaheb was sitting among a clutch of men smoking the communal hookah under the village banyan tree.

When he saw them, he called out and asked where Baba was taking the girls.

Khandoba slowed down the cart and Baba hesitated for a moment, then said with pride, 'I am going to send them to the best girls' school in India. As Pratibha wanted!'

'But why? Surely, they could continue in the present school? Nobody was molesting them there!' Bhausaheb said, smiling conspiratorially at his companions and taking a long drag at the hookah—its *gad, gad, gad* sound almost taunting Baba.

He had tried in vain to persuade Baba to marry the girls off to his friend's sons in a nearby town.

'Because a school can never be the best if there are only two girls in a class full of boys! That school is best where girls have their day and say,' said Baba, flashing back a smile as they moved on.

To Malati's surprise, Bhika was waiting by the roadside with some boys from the village. He waved for them to stop. He held out a book to Malati.

'This is a going-away present from us boys—chants of Sri Hanuman. Although Hanuman is worshipped by celibate scholars–brahmacharis and boys, you will need his help since you are setting out to be balika brahmacharins, is it not? I know girls are not supposed to worship Hanuman, but then you are more like boys, right?' said Bhika, smiling.

Malati couldn't tell if he was being facetious or genuine! She hesitated to accept the gift.

'Take it, Malati. It is a peace offering, and yes, Hanuman is a protector of all balika brahmacharins as well,' Baba encouraged her.

Malati took the book and respectfully touched her forehead to it.

'And there is no taboo to girls worshipping Hanuman, for men and boys worship goddesses too, don't they, Bhika?' Baba added. Bhika nodded.

'Practise your wrestling well, Bhika, I will come back and give you a tough fight and a bloody nose the next time I am here,' Malati blurted out. Both he and Malati laughed, much to Baba and Kamala's amusement.

At the station, it was time to say goodbye to Khandoba and the girls were in tears. They held his hand tightly.

'We will miss you, Khandoba Kaka. Thank you for being our protector and for indulging us and not tattling on us to Baba and Ayee. Please take care of Baba, Govind, and Bala,' Kamala and Malati said by turns.

The big burly man, not accustomed to baring his emotions, especially before his master, burst into copious tears. His shoulders heaved; his chest convulsed. His flared nose and outsized ears quivered and his face twisted like a sculpture gone wrong—an avatar of Khandoba the girls had never seen before. Khandoba gathered all his courage to make one last appeal on the girls' behalf to Baba.

'Malak, these girls are too young and raw from their mother's death to cope with what goes on in orphanages. I know, because I ran away from one myself,' he said.

'Khandoba, this is a boarding school, not an orphanage. They will treat the girls better than here if they were to be married. I would not send them otherwise,' Baba assured him.

'You both look after each other. Good thing about your new school is that I won't have to drag you for five long miles!' said Khandoba to the girls; smiling through his tears.

They boarded the train. Malati was distracted, albeit fleetingly, by the marvel of the train going faster and faster, from standing still to rocketing along. They stared until Khandoba and the station dissolved into the landscape of Ratnagiri, left behind among the mango orchards of their childhood.

The journey to Indore seemed endless. They talked to Baba, trying to dissuade him from leaving Ratnagiri. Baba let them prattle on till he couldn't take it any more and said, 'Bara bara, ata chup raha. I know Khandoba was right being concerned about sending you both away at the tender ages of twelve and thirteen! From the affection of a home and a cosy little village town like Ratnagiri, you are being sent to an impersonal and tough city orphanage and school. And here I am, locked in a train compartment with you, drained of my iron resolve and wondering if I am doing the right thing by you,' Baba bared his heart at last.

'Baba, we will make the best of it,' Kamala the Wise assured him, instead of pushing him to relent and change his mind.

'We are ready to go into battle, Baba, and succeed,' Malati said, her martial spirit rising up.

'No. No. I don't need you to fight. All I want is for you to follow the rules of celibate scholarship, study well, and shine. Imagine that you are in a real gurukul—an ashram of the sages. Austerity and simplicity will be your way of life. The other girls there will be your new family.'

Then he held up the example of the great Maharani Ahilyabai Holkar who ruled the Malwa state, fought on the battlefield, and built a prosperous and compassionate queendom.

'And she was better, wiser in statecraft, more skilled and valiant on the battlefield and more just and committed to the welfare of her people than the men—her father-in-law, her husband, and her generals. She also foresaw the designs of the British and warned the peshwas against their machinations. Let her be your ideal,' Baba exhorted. The girls were momentarily fired up and forgot their cloying self-pity.

Their train finally chugged to a halt at the Indore railway station. It was overflowing with a stream of passengers trying to pour down on the platform and jostling into a whirlpool with the river of those trying to embark. Railway officials were pompously shouting instructions. Loved ones coming to receive passengers outnumbered the passengers themselves. There was no loved one to receive the girls. Instead, their loved one had come to leave them behind.

They managed to get off the train with their luggage. Malati held Baba's and Kamala's hands firmly as they stood on the platform, a lonely trio in the milling crowd. They hailed a tonga outside.

This city was like Vaishali with magnificent palaces and wadas, temples with delicately carved shikharas and marble facades, elegant stone homes and tree-lined streets. The girls' spirits lifted.

'Baba, this too is a mayanagari like Vaishali. I think I am going to like it here,' Malati exclaimed enthusiastically, not wishing to be left behind in her stoicism.

Baba smiled and said, 'Well, I told you this is the best school in the best city of the best maharani of India! Just the right place to groom you into someone great! Not just housewives.'

The tongawalla smiled and said, 'Yes, we are lucky to have Maharani Ahilyabai as our ideal. But it is difficult to manage the ambitions of my wife at home. Ha ha!'

Baba was not amused.

10

DESTINATION ASHRAM

They soon arrived at a big pink mansion. 'Look Malati look! It is like a palace except that there are no resplendent kings and queens. No caparisoned elephants and splendid horse carriages. No turbaned retinue, decoratively standing about the palace grounds. Only little princesses like us of all ages in simple clothes and leafy tiaras—playing, shouting, squealing, and running on either side of this long, semi-circular driveway!' Kamala exclaimed at the sight of the ashram to lift Malati's mood. Malati was not amused at the caricature drawn but could not help smiling as she noticed how the princesses seemed to freeze into a giant tableau as they stopped to watch with friendly interest the horse cart with two 'new princesses' trot into their seemingly happy realm.

Kamala and Malati's momentary cheer soon turned to despondency at the thought of their imminent parting from Baba. They quietly unloaded their luggage and walked into the imposing lobby with Baba.

A tall watchman-cum-receptionist with a turned-up moustache and a beard that seemed to cover most of his jaw and cheeks, got up to greet them from behind an oversized desk. Baba asked to see the headmistress, Sarojatai Bhandarkar.

'And who may I say you are? Is she expecting you?' he asked, barely audible through the forest of hair around his mouth.

He looked Baba up and down as if assessing whether he was worthy of being given access to the high and mighty principal. Baba's rough dhoti, shirt, sandals, and coat obviously didn't impress him. Nor did the girls' simple dresses and humble baggage. What did he expect them to bring—Shivaji Maharaja's treasure chest?

'Yes, I think she knows I am bringing my two daughters for admission to the ashram. My name is Madhav Rao Desai. I have been sent by Sadashiv Pandit from Ratnagiri,' Baba said.

'Well, I don't have any reference here,' he said dismissively, flipping through a well-thumbed register.

'Please check the reference of Sardar Vilas Rao from Vaishali. He is my son-in-law,' Baba said patiently.

'Oh, sir! Why didn't you say so before? Come with me. My name is Sudhakar,' he said, looking at them with new respect and leading them up a flight of stairs to the first floor.

'So, status matters, even in the ashram. That too to this forest-faced durban! Huh!' whispered Kamala to Malati. Malati laughed softly as Sudhakar glared at her.

They were ushered into a well-furnished room with faded green velvet curtains and sofas. A plump lady with a motherly face smiled at them.

'She seems kind enough,' Malati whispered to Kamala.

'Ya, ya, come in, Madhav Rao, Malati, Kamala,' Sarojatai said, as they hesitated at the door. 'Please sit.'

They sat silently on the chairs in front of her desk. Baba found it difficult to talk to a woman in authority. In Ratnagiri there was no woman in the village council, not even a teacher.

'Panditji told me your story, and Vilas Rao from Vaishali also endorsed your request. But I want you to see for yourself what Ahilya Ashram is like, so that you go into this with your eyes open. This school is mostly for abandoned or orphaned girls. These two have a wonderful father like you. So, unless they, and you, agree with and like what Ahilya Ashram is all about, it is best you return with the girls now. Once they are in, this is a one-way street and you have to sign a document that puts them in our custody till they finish schooling,' Sarojatai explained.

Baba looked at the girls. They did not dare to say anything. 'I have taken this decision with open eyes and meeting you has convinced me it is the right one. I will sign the document handing over the charge of my daughters to you,' he said without hesitation. 'I would like to return to Ratnagiri now. I am leaving a deposit of two hundred rupees to take care of anything else that may be required.'

'You don't have to pay anything, Madhav Rao. This is an orphanage-cum-school and only day scholars pay fees, since they come mostly from rich families,' Sarojatai said, handing back the money.

'It is true that I am not a rich man but these girls are only half orphans, so I don't want to deprive the real orphans of their place. So please accept this humble contribution, I will regularly pay some amount,' Baba said and left the money on the table.

'All right, if that makes you feel better. I will ask the cashier to enter this donation into our books. I admire your sense of dignity,' Sarojatai said. The girls smiled proudly.

Baba turned to them to say goodbye. It was too soon. Desperate to prolong his stay, Malati asked him when they would see him again. Sarojatai, who was called Maji by the girls in Ahilya Ashram, replied that they would see Baba in six months and that they could write letters to him meanwhile. And then, with a quick lift of his arm and a kiss on their foreheads, Baba was gone.

∽

Maji walked round to Kamala and Malati and placed her hands on their heads as if in benediction. 'Don't look so forlorn. You are unlucky to lose your mother, but blessed to have a father who has dared to change the rules of the universe for his daughters. You must live up to his expectations and not give him reason to regret the choices he has made for you,' she said.

Kamala and Malati nodded, comforted by Maji's words.

Malati said, 'My Baba did not ever beat us. Will the teachers cane us? Are we only going to study or we will get playtime?'

'Don't worry. No caning for diligent students. There will be some new subjects and books to study. But you will get plenty of playtime. Didn't you see the girls playing outside when you came in? Remember though, no play during study time and no study during playtime,' she warned.

Maji then called the warden, Champatai. She was thin, dark, and manly, her nine-yard sari the only giveaway of her being a woman and no resemblance to the fragrant flower after which she was named.

'Come with me, pick up your trunks. The durban will bring your bedding,' she ordered them, not a crinkle of a smile on her concave cheeks.

They meekly followed Champatai to another part of the school with several halls, watched by what seemed to be hundreds of pairs of eyes. The sea of girls and the expanse of the spaces intimidated them. Champatai stopped in front of Hall 7 and opened the door. It was the size of Baba's whole house. It had clean stone floors. Chatai matting was laid out, row after row with beddings on top. The durban brought in their hold-alls and they put down their trunks. Champatai then introduced them to the Hall Monitor Shaila and left.

Malati would never forget the moment when Shaila, a fair, light-eyed, serious looking girl of Kamala's age, greeted them. Malati and Kamala felt that they had known her from their previous birth, as they told her later.

'Ya, ya! Welcome, you new Lotus Buds, to Ahilya Ashram and Hall 7. I will be your guide. I will tell you everything that goes on here and what is expected of you. OK, first things first. What are your names?' she asked.

'Malati and Kamala,' they replied in unison.

'Well, here I will give you another name—because this is your rebirth into a new life and avatar,' she declared.

She studied them both, as if reading a book. 'I will call you Chhabi—a perfect picture, Malati. It's sweet sounding and captures your aura,' she said.

Malati did not like the way Shaila disrobed her of her name and identity. She also knew she couldn't begin her first day by opposing a monitor.

She smiled and said, 'I like it. But do I get to keep my original name, too?

'Yes, of course. The teachers and Maji will still call you Malati, but all the girls will call you Chhabi. You can let this be a secret name among us, under my rule,' she laughed.

'I have two names already. Papi and Kamala. I don't want a third. You can choose one,' Kamala said firmly.

'I don't like your insolence, but I will tolerate it only this time! Papi it shall be!' Shaila replied and they all laughed.

'OK, girls, let me tell you your daily schedule. Wake up at 5 a.m., have a cold-water bath, both winter and summer, wash and dry your clothes daily. Then prayers, followed by breakfast. Classes the whole day, punctuated by lunch, "drill", and "lezim" in the playground, dinner at 7, study and lights out at 8.30. And then we do buzzing,' Shaila rattled off the daily routine.

'Maji told us we get playtime too. You know we used to play games with boys in our school and village,' Malati said to her with a superior air.

'Yes, playtime is after study time in the afternoon. You were with boys in school?' Shaila asked, her eyes wide open with amazement and a little envy.

'Yes, of course. We were the only girls in a school full of boys and it feels strange now to be in a school with no boys and only girls!' Kamala explained.

Malati related the whole school story and boasted about defeating Bhika in a wrestling match.

'Enough, dear Chhabi! God gives us one or the other by turns! We used to long to have more girls join our school. Our father tried in vain. Now here we are at last, where we want to be—with other girls.' Kamala explained.

But Shaila was not to be bested by anyone.

'Indeed. I see you come here after some unusual experiences and stories to tell. I have some too. By the way, the school has music lessons for those gifted like me. I learn Hindustani and English style of music and also play the harmonium.'

Kamala and Malati were impressed and said almost together, 'You are so talented. We can't imagine matching up to you!'

Just then, a loud bell rang.

'It's dinner time. Let's go,' Shaila said, and they followed her into the dining hall, resigned to be in her custody!

Malati was full of anticipation. The dining room was cheerful enough with beautiful, if faded, paintings of the three goddesses, Lakshmi, Saraswati, and Parvati, on the walls.

'They say Maharani Ahilyabai wanted them to inspire us and smile down at us Lotus Buds—her name for the orphans. Maji must have told you how the ashram seeks to be the sun, the wind, and the water to nurture us, the Lotus Buds, into fragrant flowers,' Shaila explained with a sarcastic smile.

'Like this,' she held up both her hands, palms facing each other, fingers pressed together in the conical shape of a lotus bud. Then she slowly opened her fingers to mimic the unfurling of the petals into a round, layered lotus flower. She pretended to smell the lotus, appreciating the fragrance, 'Aha....'

Malati liked the idea. She looked up at the pictures of goddesses.

'But if we become lotus flowers, the goddesses will descend and sit upon us! Ayeega!' she exclaimed in all earnestness.

'Crushed, no doubt,' Shaila replied coolly and they burst out laughing.

'Don't make fun of the goddesses,' Kamala said sternly.

'Or of the Lotus Buds,' added Shaila, winking at Malati.

They sat on mats and kept their designated metal plates and bowls on the ground. The cook's assistants came with giant bowls of food. They doled out what seemed to Malati small amounts of watery dal, turmeric flavoured cauliflower and potato curry, boiled rice, yoghurt and two pieces of chapattis. A roundel of condensed milk sweet was the only redeeming part of the unappetizing meal.

'Don't they ever serve fish curry or spicy chicken?' Malati asked, ignoring Kamala's squeeze of her hand.

'Issh! All you ever get here is grass and chaff. So, eat that and think of all the juicy and flavoured delicacies you have ever had. You will enjoy your meal not knowing the difference,' Shaila joked. 'We orphans, of course, know no better,' she added ruefully.

'You'd better eat your dinner or you'll be a very hungry tiger at night,' Kamala advised Malati.

'The food is much better on the cook's good days. But, they say he has a shrew for a wife and whenever she is nasty to him, he is indifferent in the kitchen,' Shaila explained.

'And does he cook well when his wife is good to him?' asked Kamala mischievously.

'No, only when she goes away to her mother's house and threatens never to come back,' Shaila replied.

They all laughed. The meal suddenly exuded an aroma and taste that even the ashram cook on his good days could not perhaps invoke. Malati gobbled up everything on her plate with gusto, wiping it clean with her fingers.

After dinner, Shaila led them back to Hall 7 to unpack their trunks and settle down to sleep for the night. As they entered the hall, the twenty girls in the dormitory came up to greet them with an affectionate hug. Shaila introduced them to all.

'By the way, they are not real orphans. They have a father, but no mother and he sent them to be here with us. Let's welcome them with a special session of honey bee buzzing in our best hall. Its Number 7 because the legend goes that Ahilyabai, who was a scholar of Sanskrit and Hinduism began her school around it and signifies the onset of creation—in which Purusha, or the original cosmic being, was offered by the gods to create the universe and also the human race—you and me,' Shaila said.

'Oh really? If Purusha created the universe, why is it women who give birth and grow the human race?' Malati wondered.

'Good question, Chhabi. Look, Prakriti is the woman principle of nature, who by accepting Purusha, creates us humans!' Shaila replied with even greater wisdom than Kamala.

'So, without us women, Purusha can't create anything,' Kamala inferred.

'Then why is it that women, who are but Prakriti incarnate, treated like the fifth caste, and Purusha, the men, rule?' Malati wanted to know.

'You are right. We are lucky we have no contest with boys in the ashram. Our contest is among ourselves,' Shaila said and ordered them to go to bed.

11
THRIVING WITH SLOW POISON

The girls of Hall 7 lay down on their mattresses, pretending to be asleep. Champatai came and put out the lights. Within minutes of her leaving, they were buzzing, as Shaila had promised. One by one, each girl introduced herself with her story and sang. How sweet and gossamer soft were their whispered songs! Each shimmered in the half darkness of silence.

Each girl without exception, began her story with the prologue, 'When I was discovered in the ashram', to show that she was a foundling, an orphan. The girls said this without self-pity, almost as a badge of honour. They then embellished it with imaginary stories about who their parents were and why they were abandoned.

'I lost my mother at birth. My rich merchant father had to sail to far-off lands. He was shipwrecked, and the dai in whose care he left me abandoned me in the nurturing basket of the ashram, a talisman amulet of silver tied around my neck. My father will come back some day, drawn to me by the magical amulet and loaded with riches to reclaim me,' Meera said with a happy smile and sang a song about ships and voyages that end with a reunion.

Of all the stories told that night Malati's favourite one was that told by Swapna.

'When I was a baby, my parents, who were mystic poets, were compelled to jump into the confluence of the Chambal and Kshipra rivers to atone for their transgressions and gain spiritual merit so that I, their daughter becomes a miracle maker when I turn fifteen.' Swapna then sang an abhang of the thirteenth century young saint poetess Muktabai, the sister of Warkari saint Dnyaneshwar. Kamala and Malati were bewitched by the refrain of her song.

Mungi Udaali Aakashi
Teene Gilale Suryashi
The ant flies into the sky,
She swallows the sun.
Another miracle!

> *A barren woman begets a son.*
> *A scorpion burrows down to the nether realms*
> *And Shesha, the snake king, bows his head at its feet.*
> *A fly gives birth to a hawk*
> *Muktabai sees all!*
> *Muktabai laughs!*

'All right, now Papi and Chhabi, introduce yourselves and sing a song together,' Shaila commanded.

Kamala asked Malati to prove the family talent for spinning a yarn.

'We come from Ratnagiri. Our mother was an apsara—heavenly nymph, who dared to fall in love with a mere mortal—our father. For this infraction, the king of gods, Indra cursed her and ordained that the moment she gives birth to a son, she will have to leave Baba and go back to heaven. So, my parents were happy when they only had daughters. The moment a son was born, our mother had to leave us. After her death, Baba heard an akashvani, from the sky. It told Baba to take care of his son in his home, but to send his daughters to the ashram of the great queen of Indore. So, here we are,' Malati finished with a flourish.

Now they looked at each other, Kamala and Malati, wondering which song would impress Shaila and their hall mates, which tune would ever so gently break the transparent sheath of quietude that enveloped them now. The crickets outside beat them to it. *Thit-thit-thit-thit-thit,* their irrepressible ditty trapezed through the windows and raised the tempo of their hall mates' anticipation, the irises of their eyes sparking, their nostrils gently flaring and narrowing, letting their breaths speak for them during intervals between the stories and the songs. Finally, Kamala got the courage and holding Malati's hand in reassurance, sang Ayee's favourite abhang of Sant Tukaram.

Malati followed Kamala's melodious lead in a slightly baritone voice and kept the beat by deftly clucking her tongue.

> *Sadhuni vachanag khati tola tola*
> *Anikane dolani na pahave*
> *Sadhuni bhujanga dharitil hati,*
> *Anike kampti dekhoniya.*
> *Behold the sage unperturbed*
> *Grasping a snake in hand,*

Drinks its poison
Slowly! Drop by drop!
And the sage thrives
While onlookers tremble with fear.
And can't even bear to see
The impossible becomes possible
Only with sincere effort and practice
Says Tukaram

All went quiet when they stopped. And then a gentle clapping!

'You have been accepted! And you chose the right abhanga. In this ashram it is all about being able to digest slow poison and survive, and if possible, thrive,' declared Shaila with a wry smile.

Malati and Kamala embraced her and thanked everybody.

'Shaila! Shaila! Shaila!' There was a soft chorus demanding Shaila's story and song.

'OK! OK! Sh sh! I was born in a Brahmin family that was attached to the Khajarana temple. My father became the head priest at a young age. When I was but a baby, another jealous Brahmin, who had not been selected for the post, plotted to kill my parents. Anticipating his enemy's attack, my father brought me to the ashram and left me in its safe custody. My parents never came back to pick me up. A new priest took charge at the temple!' Shaila said, without emotion.

'Oh, I'm so sorry,' Malati said.

'We are not to feel sorry for anyone here. We are now Lotus Buds, able to stand on our own stems supported by the collective roots of the ashram,' Shaila said dryly.

Then she sprang a surprise. She sang an English song. On popular demand.

This was a first for Malati and Kamala. Although they had learnt English in school, they had never sung English songs.

Shaila said the song expressed an orphan's yearning for a home and that she had learnt it from the English teacher, Miss Crawford, who said it came from America—a land that was even farther away than England.

Oh, give me a home, where the buffaloes roam,
And the deer and the antelope play,
Where seldom is heard,

A discouraging word,
And the skies are not cloudy all day.
Home, Home, Sweet Home.

Malati clapped lustily when Shaila stopped. Shaila's bright cat eyes glimmered with a faraway look. A wave of homesickness made Malati and Kamala too pine for the home that they had left behind. But the one who never uttered a discouraging word—their Ayee—was gone. So, it was not a really sweet home any more, they consoled themselves.

'OK. Now off to sleep everybody,' Shaila commanded and lay down herself.

Malati and Kamala were exhausted and slept instantly. But Muktabai came to Malati in her dream and laughed. 'What miracle have I done that you are laughing at me?' Malati asked. 'Or are you mocking me because for now I am but an ant, learning to crawl on the earth of the ashram.' And she woke up to the clanging of the morning bell.

Malati and Kamala rushed to have their baths, put on new regulation parkar polka, and presented themselves before their guide. After hungrily eating their breakfast, Shaila took them to their sixth-grade classroom.

The classroom had wide benches to seat thirty girls. Shaila introduced them to their class teacher, Miss Salve—a slim, good-looking, nine-yard sari wearing young lady, and a graduate of the same school. They took their seats right in front, as directed by her. The maths, Sanskrit, science, and Hindi classes went way above their heads, the standard being far higher than that of their village school. So, Maji arranged for them to have extra tuitions.

As for English, they had studied it in Pandit Sadashiv's class. But now they would have to 'twist their tongues' and 'break their pens' at quite another level to learn this language of power. It was like inducing a rebirth to learn the spellings, the pronunciation, and grammar, and then putting it all together in fluent speech and writing.

They were overawed that their English teacher was a white Englishwoman, Miss Crawford. They worried that unlike other students who had imbibed it since they were foundlings, they would struggle with its alien nature. As the classes progressed however, Kamala and

Malati both fell in love with her and with the English language and literature she taught and embodied.

Miss Crawford was pretty, with light brown eyes, red lips, pink cheeks, and brown hair streaked with gold. She reminded them of Mary, the mother of Jesus Christ they had seen in the coloured pictures that the missionaries from Goya sometimes distributed in Ratnagiri, and which Malati and Kamala avidly collected and hid away in a bamboo box. Not wanting to be caught worshipping foreign goddesses!

Miss Crawford was kind and gentle, even affectionate. She recited English poetry and sang English songs. Her special classes made the girls feel that it had been worth coming to the ashram just to be with her and they vied with each other for her appreciation. They wondered whether the English always had this effect on Indians. Was that why Indian rulers handed over their kingdoms to them?

They would never know, for they were already under British rule. And themselves under the English goddess's spell. Who better to ask than Shaila, their resident guide?

Shaila laughed with derision. 'Miss Crawford is no goddess. She is the daughter of an English soldier who had worked for the Maharaja as adviser and almost betrayed him to the British. The Maharaja found out, confronted him, and he fell at the Maharaja's feet. Forgiven by the magnanimous Hindu ruler, he pledged the services of his daughter to Ahilya Ashram. Actually, she had run away with a Rajput, disappeared for a year and then suddenly came back, without any explanation. Wake up. Your Miss Crawford is not worth worshipping, nor is her race honourable. Remember, they are ultimately mlechchhas—the impure ones,' said Shaila.

Shaila's story about Miss Crawford made Malati feel even more sympathetic towards her. Poor woman! She did not seem to be bitter and was so good to even those from the backwaters like them. In an effort to evoke her sympathy, Malati told her that they were half orphans and mourned their mother's loss.

She smiled and said, 'Oh! That's like me. My mother too died when I was your age and I was brought up by a dai and my father. That's why I like to work here.'

So much for Shaila's bonded labour story! The girls wrote letters to Baba and received prompt replies. Malati wanted to complain to him about the cold-water baths, the unbearable burden of studying, the occasional caning that she was prone to receive for work not done, not getting enough or good food, and missing home. But Kamala did not allow her.

'What is the point of telling Baba that? He will only think we are weaklings, unable to cope with our inescapable circumstances.'

Kamala had suddenly grown up and become Malati's protector and guide. She kept hotheaded Malati out of schoolyard brawls or dining hall quarrels. She reined in her mischief and made her concentrate on her studies, reminding her of the purpose of their being at the ashram. She washed her clothes when Malati felt unable to put her hand into freezing water, as the weather became increasingly cold. The cold bit into them in the early mornings and nights. They warmed themselves by luxuriating in the thoughts of their much-anticipated visit to Vaishali.

They were relieved when the school closed for winter holidays at last and Baba arrived to take them to Vaishali. Malati felt privileged, for once. She could escape the ashram, even if only for a month. Most of the girls had nowhere to go. Only the company of each other and of their imaginary relatives and friends from exotic kingdoms to amuse them.

'Genuine orphans, poor things,' Malati said sympathetically to Kamala.

'Don't say that. We are part of them now. Just because we can get away to a better life at home for a short while, does not mean that we are superior to them. In some ways, they are better off. They won't be unhappy when school reopens, because they would not have known any better. How terrible we will feel coming back from a grand holiday in Vaishali,' scolded Kamala.

So, guiltily Malati went to each of their friends and asked them what they would like her to bring for them from Vaishali. Bead necklaces, golden glass bangles, miniature dolls, and toy kitchen things, pictures of beautiful people, statues of gods and goddesses, saffron-flavoured milk sweets—all the things that were either unavailable or a rarity in the ashram.

'Bara, bara! I will ask Baba and Akka to get these for you,' Malati promised with a smile, proud that she was in a place to give to others.

Baba arrived on time, looking leaner and more sun burnt, but as handsome and sturdy as always. He made polite inquires of Maji about their progress and conduct and thanked her. They got into the waiting tonga and set off for Indore railway station to catch the train to Vaishali.

'So, girls, how have you been? Kamala, you look pale and very serious. Malati—you seem bubbly as ever, but your plump cheeks have sunken in somewhat. I suppose with all that they make you do and not eating home food and your motherless existence to boot, there has to be that effect,' Baba asked questions and answered them himself.

'Yes, Baba, but we are fit and strong,' the girls replied.

'So, what have you learnt, apart from Hindi and maths? How much English do you know now? Say something in English to impress me, let's see how good that English mem is in teaching a farmer's daughters her language.'

'How do you do, Baba?' Malati asked.

'I know that phrase—my Gora saheb buyers use it,' Baba said, smiling.

'It is sunny today,' Malati said looking out of the train window at the sun-soaked fields, assuming that Baba would not understand.

'But winter rains coming soon,' he replied in broken English, laughing.

'We'll teach you English, Baba, then you can go back to Ratnagiri to become a tehsildar or a collector,' Malati said.

In Ratnagiri people used to say that it was enough to know the Gore saheb's language to become high officials.

'I'd rather that you two become collectors. Would you like that?' Baba said.

'Women don't become collectors, Baba,' replied Kamala.

'Nothing can stop you, see what the nationalist leaders are saying,' Baba replied. He then told them how leaders, especially Mahatma Gandhi, were demanding freedom from British rule while saying that we must free our women too and make them equal partners in the freedom struggle. They may even come preaching to the princely state of Indore or to Vaishali. When Kamala asked how they could join the freedom fighters, Baba replied: 'No, no. You don't need to do anything except study for now. Knowledge is the weapon you must learn to use. That's what the British did. When the time comes, you will find a way to contribute.'

They asked him about Desaikheda, his new settlement in Guna.

'Malak has given me virgin lands and I have had to cultivate them from scratch and I still have a long way to go. So, it is best that you girls stay in the ashram and go to Vaishali instead of coming to unsettled Desaikheda. Your father's new work in progress is not suitable for you yet.'

'We know, but it would have been nice to be a pioneer like you, founding villages, building homes and schools, and planting trees and tilling the fields. Ayee always used to say there is rare pleasure in building something from nothing, growing plants from seeds,' Kamala said.

'Yes, I want you to be pioneers too, but on a different frontier. You will build new roads that will lead other girls to an elevated place, though getting there may be hard,' Baba said patting them on their backs.

12
THE REUNION

'Baba, how is Bala? Any news about Ambutai?' Malati asked. Baba suddenly looked grim. He told them that when Ambutai was permitted to stay on due to Baba's advocacy despite being a widow, Bhausaheb had exploited her and lived with her secretly. He threatened to exile her if she resisted. So, Bala was really Bhausaheb's son. When she confronted him and asked to be taken as his second wife, he refused to acknowledge any relationship with her or Bala. He even threatened to kill them if she ever gave any hint of this to anyone.

'Oh, that is why Ambutai referred to Bala as "our baby" when Bhausaheb came to condole!' Kamala recalled. This revelation prompted the girls to share their suspicion that Ambutai wanted Ayee to die so she could marry Baba. He dismissed that idea and instead saw Ambutai as Bhausaheb's victim who took her own life in desperation when Baba too rejected her.

'I don't know if my decision would have been any different had I known the truth and whether I would have confronted Bhausaheb's demon,' Baba said.

'But now that you know, and everyone knows, why don't you hand over Bala to Bhausaheb? Why should you have to bring him up?' asked Kamala.

'Because Ambutai took care of Govind and both of you during a critical time in our lives and she helped Ayee. Bhausaheb may well cast him into the river—an unwanted child! Maybe that's why she left Bala in my bullock cart,' Baba said compassionately.

They reached Vaishali station in the morning. Malati's mouth watered at the sight of the cauldrons of frothy almond and saffron flavoured milk and the slurry of golden-brown halwa swimming in ghee at the station stall, and she asked Baba for a treat. Baba readily agreed.

How pleasurable to the tongue was the halwa—granular texture, yet soft and smooth, full bodied yet delicately silken, spreading a layer of abiding sweetness, the perfume of cardamom rising up to thrill her nostrils! And oh, the rush of delight when the hot saffron milk swirled around her mouth in a blast, tickling her taste buds!

'Baba, this is what heavenly amrit must be like! Reminds me of what we have missed!' Malati said looking both happy and wistful.

'Oh, Chhabi, stop it. I have told you that the joy of finding something anew only comes when it has been lost in the first place,' said Kamala.

'I agree,' said Malati, as she wiped off the last grains of the halwa with her fingers and gulped down the last drop of milk from the kulhad.

'Hey, are you going to eat the kulhad and the dona too? Let go!' teased Kamala.

'OK, I'll leave that to the cows. But can I have some more?' Malati asked Baba.

'Oh Chhabi! Are you going to empty out the poor vendor's stall and leave the other travellers hungry?' Kamala couldn't stop teasing Malati.

Malati blushed and hid her face in Baba's wool jacket, its rough fibres pricking her cheeks.

'Malati, you are with your Baba and you can ask for anything. And why are you calling her Chhabi?' he asked Kamala.

'Oh, our Hall 7 monitor, Shaila, has given her a new name to be used amongst us ashram girls. Because we are reborn at the ashram. Chhabi does fit her cuteness and liveliness!' Kamala replied.

'It sure does fit her. And were you renamed Papi?' Baba asked, laughing.

The girls liked this: Baba with his indulgence and light-hearted banter. He clearly seemed like a man reborn himself.

'No, Baba. My pet name, Papi, has been accepted by Shaila!'

'Well, I must say, seeing you whole and intact, happy and growing in every possible way is a big load off my shoulders. I am glad I chose this way,' he said with satisfaction.

They headed towards Malak's wada in his carriage They fell silent as the two majestic horses, their black manes flying, clip-clopped along the paved roads of Vaishali, their neighing piercing their ears from time to time. Fat drops of winter rain fell on the canvas stretched over the passenger seats with a *pat, pat, pat, pat* insistence, to accompany Kamala and Malati's rain song.

Yere yere pausa, tula deto paisa
Pausa ala motha, paisa nighala khota.

Rain oh rain do come down
For your pains I'll give you a paisa coin
The rain did come pouring down
But alas my coin turned out to be fake.

'No, no,' Baba said smiling, his white, even teeth showing through his thick moustache. 'Winter rains are not like the monsoon rains. They come reluctantly and run away quickly, so you have to bait them with real money, like this,' he said throwing a coin into the air and singing staccato.

Yere yere pausa, tula deto paisa
Paus ala bara paisa nighala khara.

Rain oh rain do come down
For your pains I'll give you a paisa coin
The rains did come pouring down
This time my coin was real for sure.

Surekha was waiting to welcome them at the majestic carved wooden door of Amrit Wada with baby Veena in her arms. Veena was like an English baby—fair, with Malak's grey eyes and Surekha's fetching smile. Surekha had put on weight, she looked more grown-up, and confident, unlike the frightened sparrow of a bride they had left behind nearly two years ago. She was Prakriti now to Malak's Purusha and growing his race! Malati thought that she must have learnt to play love games with Malak as the dais had instructed. She smiled to herself.

'And what is making my Malati smile?' asked Surekha.

Malati quickly invented another reason for her smile.

Kamala eyed Malati suspiciously, almost divining what was passing through her head and pinched her. It was uncanny, how the two had begun to think alike and even read each other's minds.

Malak came down to greet and meet Baba and the girls. He was charming to Kamala and Malati, taking interest in their life at the ashram. He spoke to them in Hindi and English to test them.

'See how good the school is. You girls have picked up new languages so quickly. Now you can teach your Akka, too, so that she can converse with the ladies of the court in Hindi and English and not be tongue-tied,' Malak said to the girls.

'Surekha's vocation in life is to be a good wife and mother,' said Baba, rising to his first-born's defence. 'Her sisters are studying for a different purpose. Maybe, when Surekha finishes with childbearing and her duties as a housewife, she too can afford the luxury of learning languages and mixing with the elite ladies here.'

Malak frowned. Baba realized that he had overstepped his maryada as a father-in-law and said, 'As the father of a married girl, I know I have relinquished my rights to you, Vilas Rao, and as her swami you can demand anything of Surekha.'

Malak turned red, but replied calmly and deliberately, 'As my wife, I give her all respect and bestow dignity. But she has some social duties to perform on my behalf too. I have enough dais to take care of Veena and other children that will come, and servants to cook and clean. Remember, she is no longer a farmer's daughter. She is the state minister's wife in Vaishali.'

The girls did not like Baba's abject surrender and tried to break the awkwardness of the moment. They offered to teach Surekha English and Hindi in return for learning abhangs and Puranas from Surekha. Surekha readily agreed.

Malak smiled. Baba sought his permission to leave the next day expressing gratitude for inviting the girls to spend their vacation with them.

'They are Surekha's sisters and will always be welcome in Vilas Rao's wada,' said Malak graciously and left for the royal court.

'You have given the gift of our precious Akka to him. Why should a girl's father be so apologetic about staying at his daughter's house?' Malati said, pouting.

'I can't keep taking advantage of Malak's graciousness. It takes time to change the ways of the world. Each must do their bit—one girl, one woman, one man, one fight, and one small change at a time! Surekha, listen to your husband, but stand up to him gently but firmly if you feel there is injustice. I will always stand by you,' Baba affirmed.

The girls settled in their room and lay down with pleasure on beds with indulgently plump mattresses and warm, purple velvet quilts that regaled their skin with their silky-smooth feel and tickled them with their furry pile by turns!

'Papi! Isn't this heaven! I have already forgotten the cold that seeps into our bones through the thin mattress on the floor at the ashram. Ahh!' Malati sighed with pleasure, as she lay spreadeagled on the bed but felt she was flying.

Kamala smiled. 'Savour the luxury of this moment, Miss Chhabi! We have been caught in so many mayajaals spread by the divine hunter that I don't know which net of circumstances is real and which one is an illusion and where he is taking us next,' she said.

'Ah yes! When we meet those we have parted from, an illusion is created that they will never leave us again. Until the next time we are left behind, alone once more. We were so happy to meet Baba yesterday and he would be gone tomorrow!'

Malati sighed.

English and Hindi lessons with Surekha gave them a chance to spend time with her and look below the surface of her 'all is well' world. They asked her how she felt about having a second baby the dais told them was on the way.

'I am fine. This is my destiny. To be a mother to Malak's daughters and sons. We are all well looked after. Unlike Ayee I had an English doctor to help deliver Veena, not a midwife,' Surekha informed them.

Surekha made it her mission to indulge her sisters like she would her own daughters, and in ways Ayee would have done, had she the means. She gave the girls clothes and shoes as gurudakshina for her language lessons.

Malak gave Surekha whatever she asked for and thrust upon her clothes and jewellery she did not even ask for. They witnessed how Malak celebrated Surekha by setting up a sari festival to select new saris for her personally.

A well-known Chanderi sari vendor with a flair for dramatic salesmanship came to the wada and set up a stage. Whirls of nine-yard saris of all colours with dazzling and delicately patterned silk and gold borders were his eloquent actors. Each sari was embellished with unique medallions, flowers, and paisley designs, sprinkled all over the translucent fabric like stars in the sky. Then he, a master ventriloquist, made each sari come alive and speak a sing-song dialogue.

Blushing Gulabi Chanderi am I
Specially woven for you to tie,
My master weaver for your love did vie
Give it your regard, do not feel shy.
I, Hirwi Chanderi am one of a kind
Am so green, spun fresh from the weaver's mind
No other can make this design any more
Its creator died even as to its uniqueness he swore.
I, Neeli Chanderi was coveted by the queen
I could not let her wear it though she was keen
Wanted to save my blue Krishna self only for you to treasure
Told her I would make another sari for her pleasure.

Each of the Chanderi 'sari actors' were pleated to display their fall and flow and caressing Surekha's face with their padars, each exclaimed 'see how I add lustre to you'.

'Che che! What are you saying! You saris don't add to my wife's splendour, she gives you beauty and purpose!' Malak said proudly as Surekha blushed.

Malati and Kamala watched with joy, and a bit of envy, this drama and the tidy pile of saris that Malak finally bought.

'Avadalana tumhala?' Malak asked Surekha, smiling.

She smiled back shyly and said, 'Issh. Do you have any doubt? I love them.' Then she used Ayee's favourite line, 'I must have done some good in my past life to deserve a generous husband like you.'

Malak turned to the girls and said, 'Indulge, indulge you two, in Vilas Rao's ashram! You will inherit some of these riches soon enough.'

One afternoon the girls asked Surekha about Sarala and Maa Saheb. Her beautiful face clouded up for a moment. 'Maa Saheb's "divine madness" ebbs and flows. She is frustrated in that cage of her own making and with the external world which she can't control, so she blames Malak, and now me,' Surekha mused.

'And Sarala? She is so bright and beautiful. Yet she is burdened with being her mother's keeper, instead of living like a young, carefree girl with wings,' Malati remarked.

Surekha informed them that Sarala did come to meet both Malak and her regularly and that she was more a friend than an enemy. But, in her heart, Sarala did resent her mother's sawat. Surekha tried to be supportive of her regardless, and Malak kept up his relations with them the same as before. She never accompanied Malak to his meetings with Maa Saheb and did not talk to him when he returned in an agitated state.

As for Sarala's future, they were getting proposals for her marriage. She was not keen, but Malak said she had studied enough. Surekha supported whatever he thought; her only request was that Sarala should be married off only when he found the right match, not to anyone who came along, simply because it was that time of her life, or that she was a burden on him.

Many well-placed families were wary of Maa Saheb's reputation of madness and unfairly stigmatized Sarala. When Surekha tried to vouch for her sanity and brilliance, they accused Surekha of trying to pass off a 'flawed bride-to-be' just to get rid of a stepdaughter from her life. The only proposals were from Maratha families eyeing Malak's money or from boys with problems. Malak was quite worried.

'Arey, deva! I feel so bad for Sarala. Akka, they say when God makes you suffer too much, does he then not compensate for it in some other way?' Malati wondered aloud.

'It should be like that. But can that which is given as a boon be of equal value to that of any loss and suffering? How can God ever compensate us for losing Ayee? Or Sarala for her childhood and now her womanhood being lost in the shadows of her mother's divine madness?' Surekha replied.

Just then, baby Veena woke up and started crying. Malati and Kamala took turns to calm her but only when Surekha held her close to her bosom, did Veena smile. They understood then, how mothers naturally cull the primal heartbeats of their firstborns while still in their wombs, so they can resonate with each other long after babies cease to feel the rush of their mother's life-giving Red River in their veins.

13
PROPHECIES

Engrossed in the little baby, the sisters inadvertently walked into Maa Saheb's tulsi garden. Maa Saheb came straight towards them and tapped Surekha's bent head in benediction and smiled at Veena.

'This is the first time I have seen your firstborn. She is exceptionally beautiful,' Maa Saheb said.

Then, gazing at Veena's grey eyes, she prophesied, 'This child is going to do something exceptional that no one has done before, earn name and fame. But she will also bring much sorrow to you and Malak.'

'Oh, Maa Saheb, she is only a baby. Don't look into her future and make disturbing prophesies,' pleaded Surekha.

'And as for you. Look me in the eye,' Maa Saheb was relentless.

Surekha tried to look away but those kohl-dipped eyes seemed irresistible. Ma Saheb chanted mantras, swaying and shaking in a trance.

'My Devi Mata will bless you, will give you sons and riches for many years. But Veena and your husband will be the cause of your death,' Maa Saheb predicted.

'Don't curse me, Maa Saheb. I did no harm to you. Instead, I have been Sarala's well-wisher, her friend, and join Malak in planning a bright future for her,' pleaded Surekha.

'This is just Devi Mata's warning you can act upon and try to avert a disaster,' she replied.

'As for my Sarala, she will find her own way to sunshine all right. Whatever you claim, which stepmother can wish her stepdaughter well?' she said and laughed a febrile laugh, her ribcage vibrating with the effort. The spirit then went out of her.

Bhasker Kaka led her home. The girls turned back to the Bada Ghar, quite shaken themselves. Surekha trembled too.

'Akka, Maa Saheb is either a real oracle and Devi Ma actually possesses her and gives her divine vision, or she has some black magic power to curse and cause harm,' Malati said fearfully.

'No Malati. She tries to get into people's minds. Akka, you forget this and stay away from her. Avoid the fear of the future that such things stir up in our minds. I for one want to be pleasantly surprised by the good things that happen and not worry about the bad things that will happen anyway!' Kamala tried to reassure Surekha.

'If we start piecing together the prophesies, she made about Papi and me the last time we were here it all came true and not in the benign way I had interpreted it,' Malati reminded her.

'Malati, stop! It's just a coincidence. And in any case, no mortal being has the power to change or shape another person's destiny!' Kamala said.

'It was no more than a chance meeting and she got a divine vision. At least she predicted some exceptional achievements for Veena and some good years for me with many sons that I will bear. That gives me enough time on this earth. How much more can a woman ask!' Surekha philosophized.

'Ignore the bad things she said about Malak. He is so good to you,' said Kamala. They were all becoming admirers of Malak. Soon, it will be that in their universe, Malak could do no wrong!

The girls prayed there and then that Maa Saheb's dismal prophesies are proven false while the favourable ones come true.

Sarala came visiting the next day. She had grown taller. Her doe eyes sparkled, her heart shaped face throbbed to a new smile, her long neck and filled out body had come together in incredible harmony.

They greeted and complimented each other warmly.

'You look like a heroine from a Kalidasa play!' Kamala gushed, showing off her newly acquired knowledge of Sanskrit literature.

'Oh, to fit into that mould, I will have to be more rounded everywhere! And remember the Sanskrit saying: "Shodase varshe kanya gardhabi apsara bhavet!" Even a girl who is as ugly as a donkey, is beautiful at sixteen!' said Sarala self-deprecatingly.

'Your Akka has been good to me and I think I am beginning to like her and trust her,' Sarala said.

'Well, it is good for you two to be there for each other!' said Kamala.

They began to form a close friendship with Sarala. They spent time with her, shared secrets, read the books she recommended, and explored the wada and its environs. They could feel a new lightness of spirit in her—an awareness of her own beauty and inner strength, from becoming learned and scintillating. It must take a lot to cut away the chains of darkness with which Maa Saheb and Bhasker Kaka had unwittingly tied her down all these years.

She told the girls that she was writing a novel in English.

'My novel is about the subterranean world of amrit wada—the patal lok—a world of dense secrets. The thrill lies in lifting the veil slowly to reveal their beautiful or ghastly faces. For now, my English teacher Robert Butler is editing it. Although he is beholden to the British Resident, he is sympathetic to Indians,' Sarala explained.

When they asked to meet Mr Butler, she demurred.

'I keep my real world separate from the world of imagination and literature that I inhabit with him. The gods and goddesses of Greek mythology fascinate me. So, in my novel, I become Persephone, the beautiful young goddess of vegetation and flowers—akin to our Phulrani! Hades, the king of the netherworld and her uncle, falls in love with her. He carries her away to his kingdom and she becomes the queen of the netherworld,' Sarala told them.

'So, who rescues her?' Malati asked, her curiosity rising.

'Persephone's mother, Demeter, searches for her all over and wreaks havoc till her father, Zeus, forces Hades to let her return to earth. But King Hades plays a trick, and Persephone has to spend six months on earth and six months in the netherworld. Like Persephone, I too inhabit two worlds, but I do not follow seasons. I traverse these two worlds every day. Chhota Ghar is my netherworld and Bada Ghar is where I come up to breathe and be with my father!' Sarala explained. 'Maa Saheb is both, a prisoner and the imprisoner! But I know she will one day play her part of Demeter,' Sarala concluded.

'Who plays Hades? And does Robert figure in the story?' Malati asked.

'That is for you to guess and read when my novel is completed. I tell stories within the story about crime and punishment, reprieve and retribution of the "mound people" whose unmarked tombs are in Amrit Wada. They arise and confide in me,' Sarala explained further.

Malati demanded to see those tombs.

Sarala took them to the tombs and they listened to and visualized the tales of the tomb people—mostly women—through their Persephone's words and eyes!

'Behold the Sly Slave, who, ministering to her masters day and night, steals their treasures and boldly escapes to a land of freedom. But how does she end up in these tombs? Betrayed by her co-slave, who was jealous of her, her master hounded her, brought her back, and tortured her to death. Look!' Sarala held up pieces of bones that looked too small to belong to a grown human and Malati could not stop herself from saying so!

'Oh, Malati. Slaves were often starved, so they remained dwarfs.'

Another day they heard another fantastical story, this time told as a puzzle:

Why is this daring damsel in distress?
She ran away with her lover, no less.
She is the daughter who dishonour brought
Outraged by the outcast union she wrought
Punished for loving beyond the limit
In death both remain joined in spirit.

'Look how the skeletons of their hands are clasped together!' Kamala remarked, astounded.

The tomb that horrified them the most was a mass grave.

'Some women members of the clan were foolish enough to blackmail the head of the family. They were buried alive. I, Persephone, as a descendant of the lords and ladies of Vaishali, knowing what it is to be a victim of tyranny and fate, shall liberate these tomb people by cremating their remains to the chant of mantras. To ensure that their tormentors get punished in other ways and in other worlds!' Sarala declared grandly as a finale.

Later, although bound by secrecy, the girls discreetly verified all these stories with the dais.

Badi Dai laughed and said, 'Kai sangte? Which mounds? Skeletons and victims? You are hallucinating in Sarala's company—and in the daytime too!'

'Maybe we are. But let us show you,' Malati said confidently.

So, one morning they went quietly with the dais to the homes of the tomb people. They dug gently like Sarala, seeking out the bones under the loose earth. They found nothing.

'See, we told you. It is Sarala's illusion. No wonder people think Sarala has a streak of divine madness too. You had better not get infected!' said Badi Dai.

They did not confront Sarala but did insist on meeting Mr Butler, wanting to be sure that he actually existed! She finally relented and they accosted him before he entered the Chhota Ghar for her lessons. He was tall, picture-book handsome with a thin moustache, and a sensitive face. Sarala introduced them to him, her eyes dancing playfully.

'Oh! Nice to meet you. I did not know your stepmother had sisters who go to an English school and appreciate Greek mythology!' Robert said.

'Nice to meet you too, sir. We learn English language and literature from an Englishwoman, Miss Crawford,' Kamala explained proudly.

'And we love her!' Malati piped up.

Robert and Sarala exchanged a smiling glance.

'It's good to love your English teacher. You can learn the language of the heart faster. We English are irresistible, are we not? We conquer hearts just as we have your land!' Robert said, laughing.

When Sarala told Robert she wanted to share her novel with the girls he said it was still incomplete.

'See you later and give my best to Miss Crawford. Who knows, we may meet some day. For the British, India is a small world!' And they both went into the Chhota Ghar.

Malati and Kamala furiously read up on Greek mythology and Persephone. They were left wondering whether a Hindu goddess could ever become a Greek one.

Malak had been very preoccupied lately and the girls had not seen him much. Surekha said there was a big crisis brewing in the Vaishali government and a feud going on with the British Resident. As finance minister, he was in the centre of it. There were rumours that Malak may even lose his job.

One day, Malati and Kamala went to the market to pick up gifts for their friends. They visited the shop of a famous bangle seller near the main chowk as directed by Surekha. They were selecting their gifts from rows and rows of colorful bangles and bracelets in crystalline glass and shiny gold and silver painted ones with girlish delight, when they overheard heated exchanges. These seemed to come from a tea stall partly hidden by a decorative, trellised awning of the fine leaves, and pale green fruit bunches of giant, shady neem trees. A gathering of men was drinking tea with a young man in a dhoti and kurta at the centre, who was holding forth with great passion.

'Dear friends. You are looking at a "do top government" of the Maharaja and the British. First, they sent our young men as cannon fodder to fight in the British World War—3,000 dead from this city alone. What did we get as reward, but the dead bodies of our brothers and sons? Tell me?'

There was a roar of 'shunya—nothing, not even gratitude or honours' from the audience.

'Now they are going to fire the biggest projectile ever from their double barrel cannon to ruin both the farmers in our villages and the traders and artisans who are the lifeblood of commerce by taxing both like never before,' he continued.

'You watch out. The British want to fleece and impoverish our people and our Maharaja is an accomplice and slave to their diktats to enrich his treasury so he can build more palaces for himself while our people starve and struggle to make ends meet.'

There were murmurs of protest from some loyalists of the Maharaja in the group. 'Don't spread rumours like that, Pravesh Babu. This is not true. Our Maharaja cares for the people. He would not do anything to harm them. What can he do if the British Super Raja here holds a sword to his neck?'

The girls moved out to hear Pravesh's reply, deaf to the bangle seller asking them impatiently to either choose or leave.

'Then he has no right to rule if he can't protect the interests of the people. I have it from the staff of the Finance Minister himself. They will announce it soon. That is why you must join the freedom movement and give a fitting reply. We have already spread the word on what we have to do. Saam, daam, danda, bhed—every means we must use. Don't be cowed down or you will be mowed down!' Pravesh warned.

The girls went closer to get a good look at Pravesh and caught a fleeting glimpse of his bearded face, fleshy lips, and big black eyes blazing with determination to do or die! He soon disappeared into the melee of the bazar. They returned to the shop, picked up their bangles, and headed home to report to Surekha. A worried Malak summoned them. Malati told him exactly what they had heard, almost mimicking Pravesh.

'Though only thirteen–fourteen years old, you have your minds and ears tuned to listen and understand what is important even when you are selecting trinkets and don't miss any nuance. You two make good guptachar spies!' Malak said appreciatively

Malak rushed to the court and asked to have an audience with the Maharaja alone so that any moles of the British Resident would not listen in and thwart his plan.

'Maharaj, I have been pleading with you not to increase taxes any further on the ill-intentioned advice of the British Resident. We cannot tax our people beyond what our farmers, traders, and artisans can bear. I have reliable information from our spies that both the violent revolutionaries and the Congress Party agents are exploiting the disaffection among the Vaishali population about previous tax increases, and now somehow, they have information that we are going to impose additional cesses. There is already a call to action given by some groups. Believe me; if you lose the peoples' trust and respect, it won't be long before the British take Vaishali over for direct rule. Your Majesty, you are very wise and persuasive. Please evade this arrow and convince the Resident that such a move will boomerang on the British themselves and fan the fire of the freedom movement! They need the maharajas as shields against the ire of awakened masses!'

The Maharaja was convinced.

'You leave it to me. Please pass an order to slightly increase the personal allowance that I give to the Resident. That's all. And Vilas Rao, I value your "neither fear nor favour" advice.'

Malak returned to the wada in the evening quite relieved, even elated. Later Malati and Kamala saw and recognized the bangle seller from the shop going up to meet Malak. Malak must have got some special bangles on the quiet for Surekha as a surprise, they surmised!

Malak did a shake-up in the Revenue Department but Pravesh Babu was still at large. When Surekha asked Malak why he was not being arrested he said, reflectively, 'We need the Praveshs of the world to keep everybody on the straight and narrow path! It is a cruel choice people like me are asked to make. Between the comfort of keeping my privilege and the risk of losing it all and more for Bharat Mata. I pray to Lord Shiva to give me the wisdom to choose well.'

14
THE SÉANCE

The next morning, Kamala woke up at dawn complaining of severe pain in her stomach. A big red stain on her skirt and on the sheet frightened Malati and Kamala both.

'Are you getting the Red River gift too? Are going to have a baby like Ayee and Akka? You don't even have a husband!' Malati cried out.

Kamala hid her terror and feigned casualness saying, 'Just another discomfort we girls have to put up with.'

Kamala had to go through the torturous rituals of puberty in the Vaishali household. She was put in a separate, dark room with a mat to sleep on, given soft muslin rags to soak up the smelly blood, which came thick and fast the first few days. Bland meals were left outside her room, because she was considered impure during her periods.

Malati felt sorry for Kamala and for herself in anticipation, and could not stay away. She stole into her room and brought her gossip from other wadas that the stable boy reported; the most dramatic and noisy quarrel between Badi Dai and Chhoti Dai; Malak's latest gifts to Surekha. She also smuggled in delicious morsels of Maharaj's dishes, but Kamala was in no mood to eat much.

On the fifth day, Kamala was allowed to have a bath and given shiny new clothes and made to perform a puja. She even got gold earrings from Malak—her first piece of jewellery. Malati told Kamala that she wished that she would come of age quickly and in Vaishali.

'The stench, the pain, and imagine the additional work this would mean at the ashram,' warned Kamala. So, Malati closed her eyes and wished her first wish away.

A day before they were to leave, Sarala invited them to meet a priest who could summon their favourite person's ghost.

'I don't believe in bhut–pret,' said Kamala with an air of superiority.

Malati threw her arms around her.

'Well if it is fake, then let's go and prove Sarala wrong and have some fun. If it is true, then would you not like to summon Ayee's ghost and talk to her?' Malati asked.

Kamala was moved enough to kiss the curls off Malati's forehead.

'Since when has my innocent sister learnt such tricks of persuasion? OK. You rascal, let's go.'

Just as the big ball of the orange sun had begun to sink behind the hill, the three girls began climbing towards the temple. Kamala and Malati held hands, just in case their disbelief turned to faith. They were surprised to see that the temple was a humble, small structure, much like the roadside village shrines of Konkan, rugged like the stone speckled landscape around it. Inside the sanctum sanctorum was a large stone statue of a goddess. Her eyes were fish-shaped and painted over with black soot—like Maa Saheb's. Malati was not sure that she found the goddess beautiful, but brushed away such blasphemous thoughts lest the goddess's vaguely carved four arms come down on erring humans like her. Malati asked why, if goddesses are so powerful, they needed to have more than two arms. They could move the world with a finger! She must have wondered aloud because Kamala hushed her up and asked her to pray.

The girls stood before the deity quietly, heads bent in veneration. Malati noticed the deity's big rough feet covered with red vermilion dotted in by hundreds of worshippers. Malati remembered the three goddesses Baba said they should always worship in their minds and actions—Lakshmi, Saraswati, and Parvati. How were the goddesses so powerful, so serene, so, all knowing. They were women too. Why could they not be like the goddesses, they had asked him many times.

'Your life should be a struggle to be like them,' Baba had told them. 'Learned and accomplished like Saraswati, happy and full of shree—good fortune—like Lakshmi, and strong like Parvati or Shakti.'

'But how can mere girls like us be goddesses? Destiny decides our lives, doesn't it?' Kamala had asked.

'You have to make friends with destiny. The important thing is to believe in the goddesses and in your innate ability to be like them. Then, in time, their light and glory will reflect on you,' Baba had said.

'But others, especially boys and men, could pull us down,' Kamala had persisted.

'But there are men like me, who will help you conquer your destiny and be like the goddesses. Believe! Believe! My daughters,' Baba had urged.

Now, as Malati remembered his words, she felt a wave of belief come upon her. The formless, fish-eyed goddess became beautiful.

They walked up behind the temple and there, seated on a log of wood, was the Ghostman. Malati was relieved to see that he was a young Brahmin priest, no matted locks of Shiva nor a trident ready to fly out in anger, nor the band of ghosts, accompanying him.

Sarala took out a cloth bag, emptied its contents, and set it around a pile of twigs for the séance. A bottle of mustard oil, camphor tablets, grains of rice, a sheaf of betel leaves, a hairy brown coconut, some coins, and marigold flowers. The priest lit the twigs into a fire as pathetic as he himself looked in that role. He drizzled the mustard oil on it. A yellow smoke with a pungent smell rose and enveloped them, scratching their throats. He started chanting mantras softly to summon the bhutatmas—ghostly souls!

'There are some mantras to drive away the bad ghosts, but also to summon the good ones. You both want to call your mother, isn't it?' he asked with a knowing look.

Even Kamala was impressed by his prescience, until she noticed Sarala's triumphant smile and realized that the Ghostman's divination was courtesy Sarala!

So, they sat down for the séance, a little sceptical. Not expecting miracles here.

'OK, now close your eyes and think of your mother, envision her, feel her close to you, and prepare what you will say to her when she comes,' the Ghostman said.

'Pratibha, bha, bha, bha. Yaga! Yaga! Yaga! I have opened the door for you to meet your daughters,' he intoned.

Kamala and Malati closed their eyes and concentrated on Ayee's second coming to earth, in an alien country, away from her beloved Konkan. It was becoming cold, but Malati shivered because she felt Ayee's presence, her soft touch, the fragrance of freshly churned butter from her hands, her soft, luminous face bending to kiss her. Malati moved her lips but found her tongue stuck to the roof of her mouth, her mind empty. She had become a chakora bird, starved of her Ayee's love in the day of all these years of parting, and now that in this much awaited night when her Ayee's moon had risen before her, she could sup in her moonbeam, but did not know how.

She was desperate now. She pleaded with Ayee to unlock her tongue.

'Ayee, Ayee. Have you come back for good? Did the fire hurt you? What is it like in heaven? Did you meet all your babies that had gone before you? They say that in heaven, people have no hunger, no thirst. You only drink Amrit, the nectar of immortality. You look like an apsara, your sari has grown silver wings. Ask God to allow you to come to us, perhaps just for holidays. Better still, please visit us in Ahilya Ashram. We need you there the most to give us boons. Papi and I are now in grade six. We speak English like the Gori mems. You know Surekhatai has a baby—Veena. She has your smile. Come to hold her. Govind is without a mother too. Baba refused to get him a stepmother. At least God should now have pity on us all and send you back.' The chakora had supped on the moonbeam—jumbling everything up, as the words came out in a torrent.

Ayee smiled away the answers, waving her flower hands around Malati's face in blessing.

'Why don't you speak, Ayee?' Malati asked.

But, Ayee was walking away, her small, pretty feet turned backwards so Malati could not follow her!

'Malati! Kamala!'

Was that Ayee speaking at last?

No. Malati and Kamala jerked open their eyes. Their names were being called out from a distance. Alas! It was Chhoti Dai, come to look for them and to tell them that Baba had come to take them to Indore.

'I met Ayee. I spoke to her. She was saying something to me when she heard our names being called. If we go away now, I won't be able to see her any more,' Malati pleaded urgently.

'You will. But you must go now or I will be in trouble with Malak,' said the Ghostman and ran down the hill.

The three girls walked briskly to Amrit Wada.

'So, did you meet your mother's ghost too?' Sarala asked Kamala.

'Maybe,' said Kamala, unwilling to admit her failure to 'meet' Ayee. She wondered whether, unlike Malati, she just did not yoke her willpower—icchashakti—to the acute longing for her dear departed Ayee forcing her to come back from the other world and manifest herself.

'Where were you girls?' Baba asked touching their cheeks lightly and holding his palms atop their heads in blessing. They bent over and touched his feet, Vaishali style, but Baba moved back displeased.

'Oh no! Girls don't touch their father's feet. They are like goddesses, holy to men, whether they be fathers or brothers or husbands,' he said.

'Baba, just ten days ago I had been declared untouchable. And now you are saying girls are sacred?' Kamala said a little angrily.

'You are even more sacred than before as nature's preparation for your role as mother has begun. But no marriage for long so guard yourself well,' Baba said reassuringly. He gave them a big box of sesame laddoos.

'And I have put together all your gifts. So, treat your friends to your heart's content,' Surekha said handing them a bulging bag.

The next morning, they bid farewell to Surekha. Sarala declared that they were now part of her family.

'We would not have enjoyed our stay here and learnt so much without you,' Kamala responded.

'You also taught me to count my blessings—including that of my mother,' Sarala said.

'Well, you showed us our mother even if for a fleeting moment,' Malati whispered.

Malak came to say goodbye and Kamala thanked him for his guidance and pampering.

'Well, Madhav Rao, you have bright girls here, and you have chosen their paths wisely,' remarked Malak with a smile.

∽

Back at the ashram, there was much excitement for the first few days—handing out gifts to friends in instalments to heighten their suspense and prolong their pleasure; teaching new abhangs, telling them stories of Vaishali's denizens, dead and alive; tales of love, hate, revenge, the war of gods and goddesses from Greek mythology, about the British stranglehold on Vaishali and Indore, and the rise of the freedom movement—all these swapped at honeybee buzzing time, evading detection from killjoy Champatai.

Kamala and Malati plunged back into the spartan ways of the ashram. But Malati often grumbled about the cold-water baths and bland ashram food and threatened to run back to Vaishali. Kamala laughed away the discomfort, dared her to run away, pointing out that nothing would make Baba change his mind. On the contrary, Malati will be viewed as a coward. Malati hated Kamala's cool wisdom at such times. She had a way of robbing Malati of her sense of martyrdom in suffering the hardships while also scotching any incipient rebellion in her against their ashram stay.

But soon, Ganapati, the mouse-riding, modak-eating god Malati worshipped, smiled upon her. A new girl, Maji's niece, Chandra, joined the ashram as a day scholar. The only child of rich Prarthana Samaj, social reformer, doting parents, Chandra became their classmate and Malati's best friend from the moment they met each other.

She was a slim, sharp featured girl with Malati's brown complexion. She had short hair like the English mems—a novelty in the ashram. When Malati and Papi had to wash their long thick hair once a week and braid them every day, they were tempted to take a pair of scissors through them and unburden themselves. So, they were rather envious of Chandra's bob cut.

'Chhabi, you are the sister I never had. I feel as if I have always known you. I am charmed by your big dancing eyes and spontaneous sense of play and fun,' Chandra said.

Malati warmly reciprocated the feeling.

Malati was sometimes overwhelmed by Chandra's obsession with her—kissing her plump cheeks, wrapping her thick black ringlets around her fingers, and swinging them back and forth, impulsively drawing her close to her in embrace. She insisted on holding her hand when they were outside the classroom, showing her off as a proud possession, a rare doll. Malati did bask in the warmth of her friendship, delighted that it marked her out as someone special, to be envied by other less fortunate girls.

And then, Chandra's generosity to her 'touched her tongue and stomach' as Kamala caustically noted. Chandra shared her tiffin from home with Malati and soon she started bringing double the quantity of food.

Malati's friendship with Chandra became the talk of the ashram. 'They are like Lord Krishna and his impoverished friend, Sudama. Chandra brings delicacies for Chhabi from home, whilst she herself eats the humble peeth poha that is Chhabi's share of the ashram food,' a classmate said spitefully.

Kamala's confessed to Malati that she was beginning to feel left out and did not know how to insert herself gracefully into their dukdi which had a no intruders sign up.

'As my sister and protector, you are part of us, not intruder,' Malati replied.

'Oh! So, you two have become us and I am the add-on!' Kamala exclaimed.

'No. I complained to Ayee about my hard life here. So, she sent Chandra to ease my pain.'

'You, cheeky girl!' exclaimed Kamala with a laugh and lightly slapped Malati.

'Papi, can't we become a tikdi, a cosy threesome?' Malati pleaded with her.

Kamala smiled away the recrimination.

'Well, Malati. I have a dukdi with Shaila. We have so much in common—reading forbidden books in the library, joint music lessons, and secret chats near the lotus pond. Shaila and I now stick to each other like flies stick to jaggery,' she confessed.

'Who is the jaggery and who is the fly?' Malati asked jokingly.

'Difficult to say!' Kamala replied with a grin.

'It is my turn to feel left out!' Malati exclaimed. They were at ease now and often got together as a foursome!

One day, Champatai, the warden, summoned them to the auditorium along with some twenty girls of all ages from other classes and halls. The girls wondered whether they were in trouble. When Champatai announced that she had been put in charge of organizing the annual Krishna Leela dance drama to celebrate Lord Krishna's birth anniversary and that she, along with other teachers, was going to choose the performers from among the students, they whooped with excitement.

They were surprised that Maji had chosen Champatai to be incharge of an artistic project like that, but 'Maji knows best' was their motto! After the tests, Champatai went into a huddle with the other selectors and finally announced that Janhavi, the eldest and tallest among them, would play Krishna. Maitreyi was to be Radha, Krishna's consort, much to Shaila's disappointment. She did get an important part though, that of Rukmini, Krishna's wife. Kamala was chosen to be Yashoda, Krishna's mother, and lead singer. Chandra would act as Krishna's father, Nand. Others made up the chorus of family members, friends, and foes of Krishna. And Malati was the sutradhar holding the dance drama together. As Champatai explained 'sutra dhaaryati yaha saha sutradhar—the one who holds the strings is the puppeteer—like the great puppeteer above!'

15

KRISHNA LEELA AND SHITALA MATA

'Girls, practice and put your heart and soul into this and play your parts to reflect the divinity of it all,' Champatai exhorted them.

They shouted 'Yes we will' in unison except Shaila who stayed back to demand the role of Radha. She did elicit a promise to make Rukmini's part bigger and include more dancing and dialogue. The girls agreed that Shaila was way more qualified to be Radha, but advised her to outshine Maitreyi as Rukmini.

'You get to be the wife, not just a girlfriend of Krishna!' Malati joked in consolation.

On the day of the performance, the auditorium was festooned with paper buntings. The stage had a pastoral backdrop showing rolling meadows, the Jamuna River, the Govardhan hill in the farthest horizon, cows, deer, and peacocks in the Vrindavan forest closer to the eye—all painted on the cloth by the ashram art students. The Holkar queen herself and the princesses were chief guests.

Malati, dressed in a man's regal costume and a gold turban, strutted on to the stage and set the dance drama rolling in as stentorian a voice as she could muster. 'Your Royal Highnesses, Maharani and rajkumaris, yajaman and yajamanin, welcome to this Krishna Leela brought to you by the students and teachers of Ahilya Ashram. We transport you all on the chariot of song, dance, and drama to the time, place, and story of Lord Krishna from his childhood to when he became the saviour of the kingdom of Mathura and then, the king of Dwarka. Revel, dear rasikas, in the celebration of his avatar as the cosmic musician, dancer, and lover to Radha and husband to Rukmini,' she said in a sing-song, bard-like tone and tenor, her voice cresting and falling to the accompaniment of sitar music.

She introduced each character as they appeared to the *dhap dhap dhap* of the tabla and the show began. Kamala played Mother Yashoda to the hilt—she had practice big sistering Malati! She and Shaila sang tunefully and in harmony. Chandra, as Nand, looked fatherly enough with her bob cut, a false beard and moustache, and a put-on gruff voice, occasionally giving way to a girly squeak. The play continued without a flaw, until they reached the part where Radha was to make an entry. Maitreyi, who a while ago had been waiting in the wings all beautifully dressed as Radha, had disappeared.

There was an awkward pause. Malati remembered Ayee's sobriquet for her, Malati Yukti—the improviser. She had to do something to retrieve the situation. 'Our Radha has disappeared,' she announced with a sombre, worried look and then smiled and said: 'What do you expect from her? She is Maya—illusion, is she not? So, she will appear to you only if you actually believe in her love as Krishna did!' She babbled on whatever came to her mind from Shaila's stories on Radha–Krishna and her Bhagavad Gita lessons. How unique and sublime their love was, how they are but two in one, and what the meaning of this phase of Krishna's life was for his later role as the Maharathi—the Great Charioteer—and the Creator of the Song Divine—the Bhagavad Gita. To her surprise, the audience listened in rapt attention.

Meanwhile backstage, Champatai and the teachers hunted frantically for Maitreyi. Finally, she was found unconscious on the floor of the bathroom and was carried off to the medical room.

'Our Krishna Leela cannot be interrupted. Let the show go on!' Maji ordered. Champatai was upset and red-faced.

'But there can be no Krishna Leela without Radha,' she cried, wringing her hands.

Shaila, who was all dressed for Rukmini's part came forward cockily, claiming she knew the part well and that after all there was a Radha in all of them. Champatai agreed with alacrity.

'OK, let's go on. Malati, announce the next act of the play,' said Maji, and all the actors lined up.

The audience watched with delight and generously applauded, as Shaila as Radha and Janhavi as Krishna, with a peacock feather topped tinsel crown, enacted the Raas Leela, the dance of cosmic love between Krishna and Radha. No one noticed that Shaila was not the original Radha.

They ended the performance to a standing ovation. The queen and the princesses patted and congratulated all the actors. The Queen even complimented Malati on so eloquently playing the role of a sutradhar and her instant wit that saved the day!

A few days after their triumphant performance, Shaila gathered the four of them together in the garden after classes. 'Hey girls, do you know Champatai is in big trouble over what happened in Hall 1 where the warden sleeps,' she announced almost gleefully.

Kamala expressed surprise that Champatai slept in the hall and not in her cottage with her husband.

'Husband? Does she not look like a man herself?' Malati remarked.

Everyone laughed. But Malati remembered that Ayee used to tell them not to make fun of peoples' looks, as everyone had been created in God's beautiful image, and felt a little ashamed.

'Well, I intend to snoop and find out what ails Champatai,' said Shaila.

Soon after, Malati went alone to check up on Maitreyi in Hall 1 without telling anyone. Maitreyi still looked pale and unwell. Malati asked how she was. She put her off by saying she needed to rest.

'Look, please tell me what happened that day and I will leave,' Malati persisted.

'Well, I was perfectly well until I drank some water. I felt stomach cramps so I rushed to the bathroom and that's all I remember, OK! Next thing, I wake up in our doctor's clinic. My water pitcher was lying there. Anyone could have put in something to knock me out,' Maitreyi said calmly.

'Well, Maitreyi, I am sorry you missed playing Radha. You are the best. I am glad Shaila was there. Otherwise, the play would have been a disaster, and as sutradhar, that would have been a tragedy for me!' Malati said grandly.

'Oh that! Shaila had been rehearsing my part more than I had. She is born ready to play Radha to any Krishna. We have grown up together. God forbid if you are in the way of anything she wants!' Maitreyi replied bitterly. Maitreyi's good girl act seemed to be slipping. Maitreyi smiled at Malati's discomfiture.

Malati offered her a box of sweets from Chandra.

'Thanks, but no thanks. You all are Shaila's friends. What if you are her agent?' Maitreyi said.

'I am leaving the sweets for you. If you don't trust me, give them to a cat you don't like meowing around.'

Malati and Kamala's time at the ashram seemed to race by.

It was like a rustic swing they had in Ratnagiri. Its jute ropes pricked their hands and the hard wooden seat was uncomfortable in the beginning. But after a few days of swinging on it, as Baba had predicted, it became miraculously comfortable! Also, initially Baba had pushed the swing for them, and then they were on their own, their feet and body learning to kick up the momentum.

'I guess it's about getting used to the strange, to the needle pricks and thorns, about overpowering the difficult and achieving the impossible and being happy whatever happens,' Malati said pensively.

'Malati, what is happiness? Is happiness a placid sense of stability and contentment, devoid of the thrill of fear? Or is it about alternating between the depths of anguish and the peaks of elation? Do we get most pleasure in realizing our own aspirations? Or living up to someone else's? Is your disappointment at your being denied your cherished dreams greater that the thrill of receiving other unexpected boons delivered to your doorstep?' Kamala asked.

'I think happiness is all of this and more. I know you say that anyone can buy my happiness for a paisa—so low is my threshold. But I do heed Maji's injunction to have the "unhappy ambition" of doing something way beyond my capacity or circumstance. Like Muktabai's ant, scorpion, housefly, and barren woman who have the audacity to try to make miracles, whether I succeed or not,' Malati replied.

Malati and Kamala soon discovered that before happiness came survival. Shitala Mata—the goddess of smallpox, the mother of all contagious diseases—came to Indore as a curse but which Shaila fervently believed, must be stoically accepted as a gift.

Maji dismissed the Shitala Mata belief as superstition to justify helplessness in the face of an implacable enemy. The moment she heard that Shitala was invading, she took swift steps to insulate the ashram. Teachers, dais, and cooks were locked in or out. Day scholars like Chandra were kept out—a severe privation for Malati.

However, stories from outside the gate could not be locked out. They heard from across walls and gates how a visitor to the Khajarana temple who stayed at a nearby dharmashala was suspected to have brought the pestilence from as far away as Kashmir, infecting the pujaris and other devotees. And it spread in a conflagration to other parts of the city making people sick, pockmarked, and even blind and raining death in certain crowded quarters of the city. A conflict reportedly broke out between the Maharaja and the British Resident on how to deal with what was becoming an epidemic, engulfing more and more localities.

The Maharaja wanted to respect the sentiment of his subjects—even the most educated of whom seemed to believe in some kind of divine agency of the disease, wanting to rely on traditional ways of coping with if not averting it, and resented the aggressive way in which the British wanted to hound out, isolate, and stigmatize those infected. They heard tragicomic tales of how families played clever hide-and-seek games with the initial 'search and take out' teams of the government. They dug underground bunkers, broke up walls to create recessed spaces, hid in trunks and cupboards or in storage beds.

Some patients nearing death were secreted away to nearby villages for proper funeral rites, which the authorities had forbidden to limit the spread of infection. Food and other essential things had to be smuggled between the city and surrounding villages. Streets and bazaars were deserted during the day but came alive when people came out brazenly under the cover of darkness to buy and sell and go about their life and business as they were accustomed to, each presuming they have Vishnu's shield that Mata Shitala could not penetrate.

Under British pressure the Maharaja announced punishment for those patients and their families evading detection, treatment, and inoculation. However, at the same time, reward for those volunteering to surrender themselves and report on others under the grip of Mata Shitala. No one could say whether any of these steps stopped her inexorable conquest of the kingdom, but when Shitala Mata breached the ashram fortress, the inmates knew this was her last frontier.

As a vindicated Shaila declared, 'Shitala is a goddess for a reason. She is unstoppable, all pervading. She travels on the back of the wind and is in the air we breathe as life threatening specks of disease. She immerses herself in the water we drink and courses through our body fluids. She jumps from person to person like a bhutatma. Just coming face to face with the one she possesses, gives Shitala an opening to make another conquest. The goddess must be propitiated with puja, cooling holy water, neem paste, and turmeric applied to those afflicted. Getting treated by English medicine would only anger Shitala Mata.'

The inmates were ever more frightened by Shaila's portrayal and lived daily with the dread of her afflicting one of them suddenly and then spreading amongst all like wildfire. They were afraid to go to sleep, terrified to wake up. What if? And who next will become a pockmarked victim unto death or if she survives, be ostracized and left to suffer alone.

Maji reprimanded Shaila about her fear-rousing proselytization, assembled the Lotus Buds to counter Shaila's sermons of surrender to the goddess. 'This is a disease—not any goddess. Our defence is to stay clean, be vigilant, and report immediately when you or your friends get symptoms. Don't be scared. We will not abandon you, but help you to recover. Don't believe that magical charms or prayers alone will protect you. You have to take all necessary inoculations and medicines. Stay strong. There will be a few cases that can get bad and then and only then we are in goddess's hands,' she added, partially surrendering to irrational faith after all.

At first, when the cases were just a few, Malati tried to fight Shaila's insistence on inevitability and mocked her. 'Shaila, you remind me of Sant Tukaram saying to the good Lord Vithoba, "It is our faith that makes thee a God." You seem to invest godliness in a mere disease with your faith!'

'Oh, you wait till you see what happens. As a real orphan I cannot but make Vithoba of every disaster or benediction,' answered Shaila convincingly.

Mata Shitala's first serious victim was none other than the brawny Janhavi. Shaila persuaded Malati and Kamala to visit Janhavi arguing that they had all been inoculated. As usual, she loved to court danger and pose as a super human but Malati could hear her heart go *dhaunk dhaunk*! They sneaked into Janhavi's isolation room. Janhavi was lying alone—moaning and tossing, breathing hard, in distress. She saw them and managed a wan smile when she saw the marigold flowers they had brought as offering.

'Hey girls, are you not supposed to stay away from me?' she asked.

'Nothing can stop us from seeing you. How are you?' said Shaila, cheerily.

'My head is splitting and I am burning up, can I have some water?' Janhavi requested.

She quaffed down the water proffered by Shaila, squirming with discomfort and scratching herself uncontrollably. Shitala's handwriting was all over her face, neck, and arms. White, suppurating, and bumpy pustules around red patches seemed like Mata's many angry eyes, watching them and shooting out vajras—deadly thunderbolts.

Malati involuntarily shivered and moved away. Janhavi sensed the panic in their faces, dew of sweat on their foreheads.

'You are crazy to come here. Champatai will be here soon, and if you get caught you will...' she could not complete her sentence.

Shaila brushed off Janhavi's warning. Kamala asked if they could get anything to comfort her—always the Good Angel to Shaila's Curious, if not Dark Angel.

'No. You can tell me whether they think I am going to die. The doctor does not tell me anything,' she said sadly.

'Don't worry, you will recover. How did you get it is Mata's mystery since you were among those inoculated?' Shaila assured and questioned at the same time.

'It is my bad luck, I guess. Or the sin of conspiring with my Rukmini against my original Radha,' she said and looked accusingly at Shaila.

'What are you saying? You are my Krishna, Janhavi! You will rise from this as another avatar. We tough orphans will fight off the Mata even as we worship her!' Shaila said quickly.

Malati could barely control her tears as Janhavi closed her eyes and told them to go. They looked at each other helplessly and slunk away.

'Poor Janhavi is delirious, talking nonsense! That must mean her end is near,' Shaila announced callously.

'Don't say that!' Malati cried out. 'She will surely recover.'

A few days later, Shaila was proved right. They got the devastating news that Janhavi had passed away. The first time Malati had come face to face with death was when Ayee was taken away from her. But Janhavi's and some other deaths of Lotus Buds stabbed her heart with a different cut. Yamaraj did not spare they who had a whole life ahead to flower.

'My Krishna gone! I am forlorn and lost. Is he not supposed to be immortal? O Mata Shitala, you should have taken his original Radha away instead,' Shaila sobbed on Kamala's shoulder.

'As a God-fearing girl you should not say such things!' Kamala admonished her.

'I am religious, but not God-fearing! I do question him. If he had to choose, he should have chosen the more deserving one, is it not?' Shaila retorted to their utter shock.

'Don't carry your Krishna Leela rivalry too far, Shaila. You got to play Radha after all. You won. Now be magnanimous. We don't know who wins in the end in these made-up contests. Let go!' counselled Kamala, obviously disturbed and angry.

'Dear Papi, Maitreyi has been my rival for Maji's and Champatai's attention ever since we came here as babies. In the classroom and outside it,' Shaila said, her eyes burning.

'See, Shaila, Maitreyi seems at peace. Why are you agitated?' Kamala asked.

'Maji and Champatai came in together and meant everything to us Lotus Buds. Maitreyi pretended to be a kind person before them but did cruel things to me. Tried to look better than me and made me look grasping and uncaring,' Shaila responded. Malati was tempted to show her the mirror then and there, but held back.

Kamala reminded her of Shitala Mata circling around them and told her to savour the boon of life and not insult it by wishing others ill.

16

WHATEVER WILL BE WILL BE

It seemed an eternity before the siege of Shitala Mata was lifted and the ashram limped slowly back to what it was before. The foursome got off lightly. For Malati life became normal when Chandra finally came back. They embraced each other as Lord Rama did when he reunited with his brother Bharata after fourteen years in exile! Was there a story of two sisters meeting after a long separation in the epics or did noble human emotions get seen through men's eyes alone, wondered Malati and Chandra!

Maji ramped up their classes to make up for the disruption caused by the Mata Shitala interlude. The quartet immersed themselves in studies. Miss Crawford had taken a few months off, gone to England, and only returned after the epidemic was over. Malati and Kamala were glad to have her back. They had missed her and no other English teacher could take her place in their hearts and minds.

Meanwhile, they had read English books beyond their tenth grade and ages of fifteen to sixteen years to dazzle her with their mastery over the English language and their passion for English literature.

Miss Crawford began by asking them to recite passages from books she had recommended and to relate them to their own lived experience in some way—'Life as Literature Game' she called it. Malati and Kamala had selected some favourite passages—and made a special notebook to give her. They put up their hands so they could read from it.

Malati's first pick was, 'The fault, dear Brutus, is not in our stars but in ourselves,' from *Julius Caesar* by Shakespeare.

'Miss Crawford, we often blame fate for bad things that happen to us as an excuse to shift blame from our own actions. But sometimes the blame does lie with our stars! We lost our mother not because of anything we did wrong. It was the fault of our stars, was it not?' Malati asked her. Miss Crawford agreed.

'I have had the weakness, and have still the weakness, to wish you to know with what a sudden mastery you kindled in me, heap of ashes that I am, into fire from *A Tale of Two Cities* by Charles Dickens. You,

Miss Crawford, have kindled the fire of love in us—heap of ashes that we were—for English language and literature,' Malati said with a flourish.

'Oh, you are no heap of ashes, but I am happy to have made your fire burn brighter,' Miss Crawford said.

'Tell the Wind and the Fire to stop, not me from *A Tale of Two Cities* by Charles Dickens. We are determined to go on our difficult path and do something extraordinary—no one can stop us,' Malati was unstoppable.

'Indeed. May the wind be at your back and the fire within you roaring,' Miss Crawford said.

'Any man's death diminishes me, because I am involved in mankind, and therefore never send to know for whom the bell tolls, for it tolls for thee: John Donne, Meditation XVII,' Kamala went a notch higher than Malati. 'When the smallpox epidemic hit Indore, we thought we were safe in the ashram. Soon, we were all affected. The bell indeed tolled for all of us.'

'Yes, so sad,' Miss Crawford, said.

'We are not the same persons this year, as last, nor are those we love. It is a happy chance, if we, changing, continue to love a changed person from *Of Human Bondage* by Somerset Maugham. We, your admirers, are not the same persons you left last year, and you too would have changed. We are hoping that by a happy chance, you continue to love the changed persons we are, as we love the changed you!' explained Kamala.

'Yes, I do,' said Miss Crawford.

Malati could not stop herself from raising her hand to have the last word. 'When I think what life is and how seldom love is answered by love, it is one of the moments for which the world was made from *A Room with a View* by E. M. Forster. It is indeed the moment that you return to us in love, Miss Crawford, for which the world was made,' she said with a flourish.

And everyone clapped, as did Miss Crawford. She looked at them with a special glance of affection and singled them out for praise.

'Girls, I have deep attachment to you all and the ashram, hence I came back. I had gone with much idealism to England to stay but realized I don't belong there any more nor did I ever.'

When they gushed about the love filled 'literary' reunion they had with Miss Crawford, Shaila was cynical.

'Don't be under any illusion she came back for you girls. England is not kind to single women returnees who have erred. So, stop talking about loving your teachers. It may be mistaken for something unnatural and you will be in trouble like Champatai,' Shaila warned.

'What do you mean?' Kamala asked.

'Well, Maji has been told and students like me have given evidence that Champatai has been misusing her position and "loving" some girls for years,' Shaila explained.

'So maybe favouritism is not fair to other girls, but nothing wrong with that!' Malati asserted.

'Oh, Chhabi! You are such an innocent little girl! All your reading of Greek and Hindu mythology has taught you nothing,' Shaila said scornfully.

'All they have taught me is that you can have love between women, but their bodies cannot unite,' Malati insisted on the truth, as she knew it.

'Have you forgotten that Athena's owls were women transformed? Aphrodite's lovers included women. Bhagiratha, the legendary king, whose penance brought the Ganga River was born from the love and union of two queens,' Shaila said, emphasizing that the unnatural is natural for some.

'So, what made you keep quiet all this while, and why did you tell on her now?' Kamala asked.

'Because I mistakenly thought I was the only one. But when I saw Maitreyi become her favourite, I realized I was wrong not to tell all,' Shaila replied unashamedly.

Malati, Kamala, and Chandra were shocked. A few days later they heard from Maji's office that Champatai had left the ashram because she wanted to rejoin her family in nearby Dewas. Malati and Kamala liked to believe Maji's story. For, if they believed Shaila's, it shattered their idea of who Shaila was in too many ways for them to retain their friendship with her, besides bringing the venerable Maji's character into question.

One of the tests that Maji had devised for girls to take before they graduated to the final year of school was the 'bhula bhulaiyya pariksha' or the labyrinth test. The 'bhula bhulaiyya' was made of tall kamini shrubs in one corner of the ashram. The girls saw this forbidden area every day from afar with a 'pleasant dread' of knowing that they would have to pass this difficult hurdle sooner or later. They also knew that many had failed the test. The time had come now and Maji called them and explained its significance.

'Girls! The labyrinth in our Hindu tradition is a symbol of wholeness. The circle and the spiral together evoke a meandering but purposeful path that turns on itself several times; but there is only one way to the centre, it represents a journey to your own centre and back out into the world. You must walk single-mindedly on the right path in the bhula bhulaiyya meditating on your purpose, come out of it within the hour allotted to you, and record your thoughts and conclusions. I will then judge whether you are ready to go from this centre out into the world next year and onto your next centre.'

It looked simple enough to Malati, Kamala, Shaila, and Chandra given that the wooded area of the bhula bhulaiyya was not very large to cover and they already knew their purpose was to go to college as the next step and eventually take up pioneering careers. True, the dilemma was about choosing to be teachers and educationists like Maji or social reformers like Ramabai Ranade and Savitribai Phule or freedom fighters like Annie Besant and Sarojini Naidu.

At the other end of the wishes-spectrum, they debated between having a Krishna-like lover to their Radha or a customary marriage. Shaila, Kamala, and Malati insisted on dreaming 'of a Radha–Krishna like cosmic and carnal love'. Chandra pointed out in vain that Radha and Krishna as lovers were flawed and their relationship was unreal and doomed. As for the the spiritual purpose, they were all satisfied that they kept their pact with God to remember him and his teachings often enough between their day-to-day duties, to earn the required merit in this world and the next!

On the appointed day, the ninth graders assembled for the labyrinth test. When her turn came, Malati entered through a leafy arch at the entry point, navigating gingerly at first through rather stifling narrow passages, marked by dense, twice taller than her, kamini shrub 'walls'. She soon strode forth more confidently, pushing aside aggressive branches that bent forward to arrest her progress, jumping over its many trunks that sat astride the trail. She tried to meditate on her life, past and present, and to imagine her future.

Instead, she got lost in the twists and turns of the bhula bhulaiyya and its many distractions. The auspicious *hu hu hu ti ti ti* chant of the saffron bodied Brahminy mynahs visiting from nearby temples inspired her, just as the ominous *caw cu caw cu* of the black crows flying across, dampened her enthusiasm. The shuffling of invisible people's feet comforted her, while the sounds of scurrying animals and the faint hissing of serpents gliding through the thickets, startled her. The lemony scent of the white kamini flowers intoxicated her, but she barely escaped being stung by the swarming bees they attracted. Familiar voices urged her to take a particular turn here and strangers from a yet unseen future warned against dangers ahead and fuelled hesitation there.

After some false turns, backtracking a few times, and forcing her mind to concentrate, she finally reached the centre marked by a stone statue of Ganesh—the God of new beginnings. Once there, she finally found the undistracted time to 'go into herself' to 'seek' her worldly and spiritual purpose. She chanted Om, disclosed her desires, and sought direction. The only advice she got from Lord Ganesh was that it was too early to 'find and meet' her purpose, but she was on the right path, the quest should go on! She had to struggle even harder to get out of the centre back to the world outside and when she finally saw the exit arch of the bhul bhulaiyya, she heaved a sigh of relief. As if she had achieved something merely in her being able to exit!

In her report, Malati noted how thrilled she was by her journey, humbled by her 'discovery', and eager to explore further her purpose in this world and beyond. Kamala, Shaila, Chandra, and others also went through the test. When they finally submitted their reports and met Maji, she told them that though no one had excelled because their reports were thin on the spiritual purpose, she was happy that almost everyone had stated their intention to do something purposeful in the world besides marriage. They had passed the test and were deemed ready to go on to finding their new centre next year after graduation. She did not remark on the Radha–Krishna romance purpose because, expectedly, none had dared to bare this to Maji! They were taken aback when Maji complimented Malati on the honesty of her admission that she had not yet 'found' any of her purposes, but listed many that were on the horizon.

When Baba arrived to pick them up after two long years, Maji told him that Malati and Kamala had done very well in their studies and that he had every reason to be proud of them.

'But you must never allow them to be satisfied with themselves. Nor should you be. If they have to reach for the sun, how can you be content with their circling the moon? I believe, they can do better.'

Baba agreed. She informed him how they had survived the smallpox epidemic. Baba was shocked and protested about being kept in the dark. Maji silenced him by reminding him that he had signed off on their responsibility to her. She went on to tell Baba about their brilliant performance in the Krishna Leela. Kamala and Malati beamed at the praise. When Baba looked uncomfortable, Maji explained its significance.

'Drama, music, and dance will gain dignity, if there is a purpose attached to them. You want them to be Savitribai and Ramabai—the social reformers and freedom fighters, I hear. You need oratory and acting skills to convince people to change their mind. In the freedom movement, they need to awaken the masses with patriotic songs. So, rejoice at their accomplishments!'

Baba got up and folded his hands.

'I thank you for nurturing my daughters in every way. They have garnered all kinds of skills for the transformation they will bring in themselves and in others.'

The girls left for Vaishali truly elated. On the way, they caught up with Baba's news about his work in constant progress—Desaikheda. In Vaishali, Malak and Surekha had had a second child—their first son, Vishnu. All, even Maa Saheb, were feting Surekha. There was to be a big celebratory jalsa—a dance and music performance with the royals in attendance. They reached just in time for it.

Surekha helped them get ready for the jalsa and gave them her silk saris and brocade blouses, but Baba put his foot down when she offered them her gold jewellery to wear. 'Let them be the celibate scholars they are meant to be. As it is, all these fine clothes can turn their heads and make them vain,' he said firmly. So, Sarala came around with fresh flower jewellery of sweet-smelling jasmine like Radha was seen wearing in the calendar picture that hung on their wall in Ratnagiri. She also put the shringar of lip colour and kohl on them—a first.

There were no mirrors in the ashram. The best the girls could do was to look fleetingly at their reflections in the still lotus pond.

So, when they saw themselves in the mirror in Vaishali, they were thrilled. Malati and Kamala could not recognize the alluring Mohinis gazing back at them. Gone were the plain looking, dowdy ashram girls, accustomed to wearing coarse, regulation clothes.

That she was not tall, alas, like Sarala and Surekha, nor fair like them and Kamala did not seem to matter any more, Malati told herself as she preened before the mirror. And not only because, as Sarala had disarmingly claimed when Kamala had remarked how beautiful she was, that at sixteen years of age, even a female donkey looks like an apsara. Malati suddenly realized that she fitted the description of many apsaras of Hindu epics in the way her body was being sculpted into curves, and how her face and features were being chiselled to complement her glazed earthen complexion. If that was not enough, she reckoned that her thick long tresses tamed into a braid and impossible ringlets bouncing playfully on her forehead and cheeks would certainly turn heads towards her at the jalsa. She always knew she had large, 'speaking eyes' as Chandra had said, but the kohl lining gave them a new magnetism. Malati did like this avatar of herself—the goddess rising!

17
PLEASURE LADIES AND FIREFLIES

Baba was all 'suited and booted' for the jalsa. He wore a long tunic, tight pajamas, and golden brocade turban. With his sun-baked swarthy complexion, sharp features, and a handlebar moustache, he looked an unlikely but handsome nobleman of the Vaishali court. Malak personally came to make sure that he was comfortable in his new clothes and role.

Kamala and Malati were very proud of Baba. How much he had accomplished since the time of Surekha's wedding, when he was thought unfit to be in the same room with the royal family. Today he was a host of honour, as Surekha said. The arrival of his first grandson was auspicious for Baba too!

Malak greeted the girls with affectionate pats on their heads. 'I am glad my guptchars are back at a time when they may be even more needed for spying,' he joked in a whisper.

'We are always ready to serve,' Malati said self-importantly. Baba beamed with pride.

They had overheard some passengers in the train saying that Vaishali had become quite a revolutionary hotbed and a 'rainbow' of nationalist groups from directly British ruled states, some of them in disguise, were coming there to organize and regroup to launch actions against the British. Baba feared that there must be duress on the Maharaja and Malak from the British Resident to crack down on nationalists in the state. The girls entered Amrit Wada expecting to drink some of the patriotic amrit being churned out of Vaishali's samudra.

As Malati and Kamala were getting ready for the jalsa, they asked Sarala whether she had a beau and whether he would also be at the jalsa.

'Not so fast,' said she, mischievously. 'First, you have to tell me all about yourselves.'

'You know the ashram is like a nunnery—a manless world. So, all we do is fantasize about the godly men like Krishna we want to love,' Malati replied.

Sarala's brow shot up in a sardonic arch, the opposite corner of her lip scrunched down. 'Oh! The blue-bodied, yellow loincloth wearing Krishna with a peacock feather crown? Good luck finding the exact fit, and even if you find him, will he not marry another woman like Krishna did?'

Like Chandra, Sarala squelched their Krishna fantasies with the heavy pestle of her logic.

'As for me, I have more than two on the horizon—God can't make up His mind,' she said laughing wryly.

The girls asked her about Robert. 'We were truly in love. Bhasker Kaka found us in an embrace one day and tattled to Malak who would not brook my marrying a much older man—neither rich, nor aristocratic, and a possible British spy. I dared not elope with him because we would be hounded down by the British and Malak together!'

'Malak must have exploded!' Kamala exclaimed.

'Well, I told Malak I liked Robert and wanted to marry him but that Robert had shown no interest. I did not want Robert to get into trouble and lose his job. Why should he be punished for loving me? Malak was furious, but he did not want a scandal, He just called Robert and told him that his services were not needed any more. Robert understood,' Sarala said sadly.

'So now what happens to your Persephone book?' Malati asked.

'Well, it is still being written, but Robert will no longer be my ally in my escape from the netherworld. Meanwhile, Malak is looking for a husband for me. I have told Malak that I don't want to get married unless the groom's side accepts me for who I am—an educated woman, the daughter of a mother who is blessed with a divine gift, and a brilliant father anchored in the real world. And Chhoti Ma supports me there.'

When asked about her second beau, Sarala replied, 'I can't share his identity with you. Besides, because he is on a patriotic mission, he can't be distracted into marriage and hence is more unattainable.'

Now Malati and Kamala were even more intrigued. Malati saluted her, started singing 'Vande Mataram' and marched to it to tease her.

'All you need to know is that I have now become passionate about ridding Vaishali and India of the British Raj and will help him in my own way, whatever it takes—saam, daam, danda, bhed,' Sarala declared.

Saam daam danda bhed! Who else had said this? Malati strained to remember. It was Pravesh Babu, the mysterious young freedom fighter they had seen and heard at the tea stall, egging people to adopt all means possible including force to overthrow both the Maharaja and British rule! How could the daughter of a minister in Maharaja's government be in love with one who was seeking to wage a war against the state? Malati and Kamala exchanged shocked glances but said nothing. They had never told Sarala about Pravesh Babu, and the bangle shop incident and how they had tipped off Malak just in time to save the day for him.

'So, have you at least found out whether he is a Congress Party, Hindu Mahasabha, or the Hindustan Republican Association activist? Better tell Malak as it could endanger him,' advised Malati.

'I can't say anything. I have taken an oath to secrecy on a flame,' said Sarala and showed them a taper burn—skin still raw and peeling on her right palm. So, she had gone far enough in this. Malati decided that she and Kamala would follow Sarala to her trysts to save her from herself. If they could.

Before they could ask her any more questions, Sarala gave a final tweak to their saris and the three debutantes trooped down to the venue of the jalsa dressed to entice, to see, but also to be seen by young men and their mothers as prospective brides. Tall, turbaned durbans welcomed the guests. Surekha and Sarala greeted and welcomed the ladies and ushered them to the zenana.

The sounding of bugles by the buglers of the Royal Army heralded the Maharaja's arrival at the wada. Malak received him and his splendid entourage with utmost courtesy, bowing low. Baba was standing beside Malak who introduced him to the Maharaja as a pioneer, nurturing new settlements in a deserted and dacoit infested part of Vaishali kingdom and doing invaluable service for the people there. The Maharaja conveyed his appreciation.

Baba replied with a curtesy, 'I am blessed that Vilas Rao here and you, your Royal Highness, see me as a worthy stakeholder in your own mission of providing Ram Rajya to the people of Vaishali.'

Cries of 'Maharaj ki Jai ho' rent the air. The avuncular Maharaja sat down on the mattress. Three Englishmen invited by Malak turned up with their wives. The British Resident had excused himself as he was travelling to an emergency conference of British

Residents of Princely States—on the growing menace of anti-British revolutionaries.

Sarala whispered a running commentary throughout the jalsa. The British had their own caste system based on birth and money and the officials at the jalsa were not aristocracy, she claimed. The Maharaja and Malak indulged them because they had superior knowledge about guns, warfare, and machines that eased the lives of Indians. They were clever at spreading their religion and beliefs around. So, Indians had to know their secrets and prove to them our cultural superiority.

'Till such time as we are able to defeat them through the Gandhian method of non-cooperation,' Kamala said loftily.

'How can we defeat such insidious conquerors without shield and sword, cannon, or guns?' Malati said presenting the revolutionary Savarkar's view.

'If you ask me, we are going to need both,' said Sarala.

The girls felt the eyes of the young noblemen at the jalsa upon them. Perhaps drinking in the beauty of sophisticated Sarala but they too could be hovering in the periphery of the young men's covetous vision!

Bearers in red and white uniforms served wine and whisky to the men and mild sherbet shots to the ladies. The Englishwomen and some noble ladies asked for wine. Silver bowls of finger snacks were passed around. The singers cleared their throats and the harmonium player, sitarist, flautist, and tabla players tuned their instruments. Sonabai, the charming, middle-aged mistress of ceremonies appeared, wearing a rich Banarasi silk sari, her head heavily adorned with jewellery masquerading as hair.

'Excellencies, ladies, and gentlemen, welcome to this magnificent jalsa hosted by Sardar Vilas Rao to celebrate the arrival of his son and heir, Vishnu Rao, and to share the joy with his sovereign king and his friends. Please join me in congratulating Surekha Sahiba for bringing this much-awaited gift to Vilas Rao. I salute and pay tribute to the Maharaja—he of the Sun dynasty and of eternal grandeur. I call on all present to derive the utmost rasa from the recitals of music and dance this evening.'

The musicians began the recital. The girls had heard folk music in Ratnagiri, the lilting songs of the fishermen, the devotional singing of the wandering minstrels, the cheeky tamasha and lavani dialogue-in-song and dance that came whirling to even their backwater village and town. Their musical training had begun in the ashram. But the music they heard at the jalsa seemed what the mystics called Anhadnaad—the sound of the Pure Supreme Being!

The English ladies seemed bored. The court ladies kept up the appearance of polite interest. The menfolk were clearly impressed, punctuating each stanza of thumri or ghazal with shouts of 'wah! wah!'

Just then, a dai came into the zenana and called Sarala out. Was Sarala taking advantage of the jalsa to arrange a tryst with her patriot? No. Sarala looked distressed and went out abruptly. The jalsa was so novel and entertaining and Surekhatai needed them to be there to help with the English guests that they did not go to check on her.

Sonabai introduced three young dancers, each distinct. The oldest of the three, Ketakibai, was a dusky, sharp featured Maratha lavani dancer, dressed in a nine-yard sari with a gold belt showing off her tiny waist. As she danced, her rounded high buttocks and shapely legs shook tantalizingly before the patrons. She occasionally fanned out her sari padar and held it up to frame her expressive face and darting eyes. Sonabai joined in the dance towards the end.

'Look at this Sonabai! She has no shame, The way she jiggles her plump body at her age, her flabby flesh going *thul thul thul!*' exclaimed the wife of the Minister for Security.

'They say she was quite a sensation in her time,' Surekha commented, to Malati's delight. She had learnt to engage in gossip after all. Sarala had said that it is the first step to making friends in these circles.

'Don't we know? Our husbands are still great fans of hers. Yes, we have to admit that the ruins proclaim that the edifice was a majestic one,' said the Minister of Welfare's wife.

Sonabai introduced the Kathak dancer, Aminabai. She wore a gold bodice over a sheer white muslin frock through which the contours of pajama clad thighs and legs, peered in and out naughtily. Her agile feet moved swiftly to the beat of the tabla as she pirouetted in whirls with giddying precision.

Her ankle bells sculpted their own sonorous patterns with aplomb—*jhan jhan jhanak jhanak jhanak jhan.* The noblewomen watched hawk-like as Aminabai took every opportunity to 'arrest' the men with her eyes, neck and hand gestures, with the thrust of her nippled breasts, and the gyrating of her waist and hips!

'These Muslim girls are brought up to please their men, so that their husbands don't take multiple wives,' said the Defence Minister's wife contemptuously.

'But even Ketakibai, swung her hips suggestively towards the men and winked under the pretence of telling an erotic lavani story. And our Hindu noblemen too take other wives when they tire of us and our childbearing,' said the Culture Minister's wife. She checked herself as she realized that the hostess herself was a second wife.

'They say these women have special ways of avoiding pregnancies. They know how to give and take pleasure with men. We just lie down and surrender our bodies to them passively. We are not supposed to show any enjoyment or do anything ourselves to enhance our pleasure,' the Welfare Minister's wife complained.

Surekha looked at her sisters, embarrassed. They whispered to her not to worry, as they already knew. She smiled and turned her attention to her guests and their not so noble talk!

'In the old days, royal courtesans like Amrapali used to coach even princesses and queens in the art of love. Igniting the carnal fire, awakening the kama—the libido in each part of the body, from the ears, neck, and breast to the arms and legs and everything in between!' the Public Works Minister's wife piped in.

'But if we do that, our men will think we have learnt these from some unseen paramour and are harlots,' the young, third wife of a nobleman conjectured petulantly.

'Whenever our men are in heat and come atop us with force, they are fresh from these pleasure ladies, still intoxicated by their acrobatics and guiles. You can only hope to earn merit in this birth—so that you are born a man in your next. Then yours is the choice!' declared the Interior Minister's wife, salaciously.

For the finale, Gulabibai, the third dancer, joined the other two dancers to perform the lattu or pinwheel dance. It became another contest between the frenzied pinwheelers gyrating and crisscrossing without crashing and harpooning with their come-hither glances, their men rasikas, besotted lattus themselves, spinning more from the intoxication of the pleasure ladies than wine.

'The way the men are getting aroused, I wish I was in the witches' place, how thrilling it would be to be desired rather than just taken,' said the third wife of a nobleman.

'Hey,' cautioned the Welfare Minister's 'profound' wife, 'men may admire their artistry and enjoy their bodies, but they treat them as fallen women. They are fireflies—they have to burn themselves out to emit light. Shining now, forgotten the next moment.'

18

AGNIKANKAN—THE BRANDED OATH

Sarala returned just in time to join the jalsa dinner. She, Kamala, and Malati were seated next to Savita, the Indian wife of the Englishman who worked in the Royal Treasury. Malati asked her questions about what it was like to be married to an Englishman.

'Oh, I am happy and lucky to be married to him without having to convert to Christianity. He allows me to follow my own customs and dress, and he loves India,' she said.

Malati nudged Sarala and whispered to her, 'Here is your role model if Robert is still your man, not Pravesh!'

'What do you mean? How do you know Pravesh?' Sarala hissed.

Now Kamala came to Malati's rescue and told Sarala how they had heard Pravesh speak.

Sarala relaxed. 'Will talk later,' she said.

After dinner, the girls walked Sarala to the Chhota Ghar.

Malati suddenly asked, 'Would you have liked to be a pleasure lady?'

Kamala said 'no' so quickly, as if she was afraid she would say yes. 'Silly girl! We are not, and we cannot be them,' Kamala retorted, her face turning red!

'But, oh, how I would like to wear their costumes and jewellery! But face it, we can't be them, because we don't have their beauty or their talent,' Malati said dreamily.

'But I am sure Sarala will have none of that now. She will don the saffron sari of a freedom fighter and sacrifice everything for her Pravesh Babu,' Malati teased her.

'You know earlier, I would rather have been a Pleasure Lady and a firefly, than an extinguished first wife,' Sarala said. 'But now, my aim is to don a saffron sari for my beloved Bharat, and before I burn out like a firefly in patriotic duty, I will set the forest of the British empire on fire!' Sarala declared solemnly.

Malati and Kamala then asked Sarala why she had to leave the jalsa.

'Maa Saheb heard about the jalsa from Bhasker Kaka. She was agitated and wanted to attend. So, I had to calm her down. I didn't want her to embarrass herself by coming there!' Sarala explained.

'We agree. Maa Saheb is at a higher plane of consciousness and only those who understand that should meet her,' Kamala said.

Sarala smiled. 'You know, for a stepmother's sisters, you are really compassionate beings! I am fortunate to have Chhoti Ma and you both as my friends!'

As the girls neared the Vrindavan gardens, they saw a shadowy figure of a man in white near the Chhota Ghar, but when they approached, he was gone!

The Chhota Ghar, swamped as it was by more than its usual inky darkness, only allowed shafts of light to run out from niggardly slits. Malati pulled Sarala's arm and touched the scar of her illuminated, flame-singed palm lovingly. Then puckering her lips, blew over it *fu, fu, fu, fu*, pretending to cool the Agnikankan—the branded oath.

'Your break-up with Robert should not lead you in rebound, to throw yourself into the firestorm of the freedom movement on a romantic whim. It has serious implications for your Baba Saheb. Tell us what's really going on,' Malati said.

'I can't tell you. I owe no one an explanation. It's my life, my choice after all,' Sarala said and pulled her hand away from Malati's grasp and vanished into the Chhota Ghar.

Malati and Kamala decided to hide behind some tulsi pots to see if the visitor who had slunk away earlier came back. Sure enough, after some time, the same man came back, made a night owl-like sound—*yeee hi hi hi hi*, and waited outside patiently.

They saw Sarala run out barefooted and give him a silken pouch saying, 'This is all I can offer at this time. Hope you will use it well for your noble cause. Jai Hind!'

The man bowed and said, 'Thank you, Devi. You can yourself come to our adda and see how your donation helps. The address is on this slip. See you tomorrow at three in the afternoon,' he said. When a band of light briefly caught him, the girls realized he was not Pravesh.

Just as Sarala rushed back, Bhasker Kaka accosted her at the door. They overheard a loud altercation between the two. 'Who are you meeting at this time of night, young lady? I saw you talking to a man. You are getting out of control. The water of your deceptions is now flowing above my head. I will have to report you to Malak first thing tomorrow morning.'

'Do your damndest,' said Sarala sharply and pushed him aside to go in. They heard the banging of doors.

Malati and Kamala reflected on their friend 'Persephone Sarala' who sought 'love extraordinary'—that which would vicariously enhance her own achievement. It ended up being unrequited, reflecting instead on her inadequacy or her fate as she interpreted it at different moments.

Changing the sombre mood of their reflections, Kamala planted a kiss on Malati's forehead and said, 'We did feel like heavenly nymphs today, though no divine lovers came to us. Now sleep, little angel, as they will only come to us in our dreams—for now.'

The next morning brought shocking news. Bhasker Kaka had passed away! Kamala and Malati rushed to commiserate with Maa Saheb and Sarala. They were never admirers of Bhasker Kaka. His mocking tone and his barely veiled resentment about Malak marrying Surekha had not endeared him to them. They had always wondered whether he was a protector—pathrakha—and benign presence for Maa Saheb as he claimed, or an agent provocateur in Malak's first marriage, as the dais made him out to be.

The bigger mystery was what had he been to Sarala. He had perhaps been an uncle who had watched over her as she grew up, tossed around in the maelstrom of Maa Saheb's tumultuous relationship with Malak, a guide and anchor in the separate, sometimes dark, sometimes radiant world of her mother's divine madness.

Recently, Sarala seemed to have outgrown him. She had made friends with Surekha against Bhasker Kaka's inclination. Sarala was now exploring the limits of her freedom to fall in love with a man of her choice, whether Robert or the mystery man, Patriot. Bhasker Kaka had disapproved and become a sneak, a betrayer. Even a tormentor? A Hades Persephone had wanted to escape forever from?

When they arrived at the Chhota Ghar, Maa Saheb was sitting still, emotionless, next to Bhasker Kaka's body, which was on a bier. It was covered with a white sheet, but his face was visible. How peaceful he looked, even smiling, ready for his last journey to the netherworld.

Sarala stood beside Maa Saheb, looking grave but serene. The dais and staff of the Chhota Ghar and Bada Ghar were there to bid him farewell. In death let no one be reviled they seemed to announce.

The girls went to Maa Saheb, touched her feet and expressed their condolences.

'I did not see this coming. My Mata did not show this to me. I have lost my power!' she said mournfully, but shed no tears. Sarala put her arms around her mother.

'Nobody, not even the Mata, can foresee everything. Her universe is too big to capture everything about every being. Remember you told me that yourself?' she said consolingly.

'Yes, but he was not just any being. He was my pathrakha. He gave up his family to be with me, watch my back and yours!' Maa Saheb lamented.

'Yes, he was noble in his sacrifice, and both you and I are grateful for that. But maybe there was something in the karma of his past life, that made him sin in his present life.'

Sarala spoke in riddles! Usually, one paid for the sins of one's past life by having to suffer in this one, despite being virtuous. Not the other way round.

Malak arrived with his secretary, bowed to Maa Saheb in condolence. He bowed before Bhasker Kaka's body and threw flower petals on it.

'We will arrange for an honourable cremation and funeral ceremony for him—the least we can do for the services he has rendered to us and to this family,' Malak announced and turned to Maa Saheb and Sarala.

'We will get another housekeeper. Sarala won't be here for long. For she must get married sooner rather than later, is it not, Savitri?'

Maa Saheb looked dazed for a moment and then said, 'Yes, yes. That's what I see in the future, but I could be wrong!' Sarala immediately shot down the idea of a new housekeeper, left her mother's side, and went to embrace Malak. With Bhasker Kaka—the 'father' forced upon her by fate and now removed from the scene—was Sarala feeling free to reclaim her real father, her Baba Saheb from the Malak she was taught to revere but not love? Malak was taken by surprise at this display of affection, but he did not push her away.

He patted her on the back and took her to Maa Saheb and said, 'Savitri, don't worry. I will take care of everything and be your pathrakha!'

'Now let the departed be taken to his everlasting abode. Sarala, take your mother to her room and stay with her,' he added authoritatively and left as suddenly as he had come.

As the girls were leaving the Vrindavan tulsi garden, they heard some dais and Bhasker Kaka's valet talking.

'I can't believe he died so suddenly due to natural causes. I had taken his meal to him last night, and he was his usual self, ordering me around. No sign of any malady,' the valet said.

Malati grabbed Kamala's hand and they quietly stopped to listen.

'Well, when I went to his room this morning, I found it strange that he was still sleeping, his face was blue and his chest was not moving, I rushed to call the nurse. She came, felt his pulse, and declared him dead,' the valet continued.

'Well, he was not the most popular person was he, your boss? Always bitter, always suspicious!' one of the dais commented.

'Anyway, it's a big loss for Maa Saheb. As for our Princess Sarala—it is a big release. She was fighting a lot with him recently. Remember last night?' the valet speculated.

The pallbearers brought Bhasker Kaka's body out to take it for cremation. Malati could not but turn back to see the face of the dead man. Was it really blue? In the sharp rays of the sun outside, and from a distance, alas she could not be sure.

'Don't ever go there!' said Kamala, following Malati's eyes. 'We will never know, and even if we do, what can we do?'

They went straight to Surekha and Baba and told them everything they had seen and heard the night before and that day.

'Surekha baal, you be your gracious self to Sarala and her mother. Keep an eye on Sarala though. No harm should come to you or Veena or your children,' advised Baba.

'I will take care, Baba. Sarala knows I am her supporter. Malak never liked Bhasker Kaka anyway but am glad he is ensuring him a dignified send-off,' Surekha said.

'Should you not find out what revolutionary activity Sarala is involved in? It could endanger Malak,' Malati suggested. She got permission from Surekha to surveil Sarala. That afternoon, Malati and Kamala accompanied by Surekha's trusted maid, followed a plainly dressed Sarala deep into the gullies of Vaishali in an ordinary carriage. They kept a safe distance and hoped they wouldn't get lost and checkmated in Sarala's chess of subterfuge!

After meandering and taking unexpected turns and twists, Sarala stopped at what looked like a sari shop in the famous Sanskar bazaar district. The young man who had met her the night before, received her warmly and they went in, closing the door behind them. Malati and Kamala went to the back lanes to check on Sarala's whereabouts. They passed by rows of windowless sheds with closed doors. They hid behind a cart parked in the lane to see if any door opened.

When they had almost given up, the doors of three of the sheds opened suddenly. They spotted Malak's bangle seller coming out of one of the doors and looking around to check if anyone was watching. He then whistled, and a swarm of loaders poured raw rice over earthenware pots arranged like laddoos on top of buckets and ranged bangles in cardboard boxes. This 'festive' cargo was then loaded onto handcarts and covered with canvas. Thelawallas plied the carts out of the lane on to their destinations.

Malati and Kamala were in a dilemma. Malati persuaded Kamala to confront the bangle seller rather than leave unseen.

'Hey girls, you are trespassing. You seem to have lost your way and come to the wrong place. Please leave at once,' the bangle seller said rudely.

'Maybe you are at the wrong place. Should you not be at the bangle shop or at Amrit Wada of Sardar Vilas Rao,' Malati countered cheekily. The bangle seller was left speechless—recognizing them now as the sisters-in-law of Malak who had come to his bangle shop.

Malati, on an impulse rushed to where the bangle seller was standing and tried to force entry through the open door of the shed. The bangle seller barred her with his outstretched arms but couldn't stop her from looking into the workshop, foundry, and storehouse rolled into one busy arms beehive inside the cavernous shed.

Sinewy blacksmiths were forging axes and swords, melting metal in blazing furnaces, beating them into shape and attaching handles. In another corner, some young men were engrossed in assembling bombs and explosives, following instructions pasted on the wall. Pistols and guns were stuffed into stretched-to-the-limit gunny bags waiting to be stitched shut.

The girls were horrified. So, this was the preparation for an insurrection against the 'two cannon government of the Maharaja and the British' that Pravesh had called for!

19

MUD IN THE LOTUS POND

'Arre, Deva! This is treason! Are you plotting violence against the Maharaja? Does Malak know?' Malati demanded.

'No, we are absolutely loyal to the Maharaja. You girls must leave immediately and not breathe a word of this to anyone or you will put Malak Vilas Rao in danger,' the bangle seller warned.

'Where is Sarala? We saw her entering the sari shop,' Malati pressed on. 'We hope she is not involved in all this.'

'Who is Sarala? I don't know her,' he said and went into the shed banging the door shut on them.

They went back to their carriage. Sarala soon emerged from the sari shop this time accompanied by Pravesh! They left unseen by Sarala and reported everything to Baba and Surekha who swore the girls to secrecy. Surekha assured them she would inform Malak so he could crack down on the revolutionaries. Most importantly, she would ensure that Malak ended Sarala's entanglement with Pravesh and his gang.

The day they were to leave for Bombay, they went to say goodbye to Sarala. They asked her about Pravesh. 'He has disappeared from Vaishali and my life too. My brother revolutionaries have freed me from my oath and pleaded with me to stay away to avoid raising suspicion. So, here I am, thwarted in my quest for doing something meaningful in love and for a worthy cause—the liberation of Mother India!' she said dolefully.

On the way back, Baba shared his misgivings on the girls' experiences in Vaishali and worried that they would have felt tempted to quit studying, opt for a decadent lifestyle, and marry some wasted princeling.

'Baba, which girl is not dazzled by the glitter and glamour of royal living. But rest assured, we saw enough to value what we have,' Malati assured him.

As soon as they returned to Ahilya Ashram, they began preparations for their Intermediate exams. It was during one of these study sessions that Malati made a discovery about Chandra that almost destroyed their friendship. Chandra told them that she was going to church so could not join them on Sundays. The girls joked about her propitiating the Allah of Muslims too.

'Don't joke about it. My parents believe in taking what is best in Christianity and using it to improve our sick Hindu society,' said Chandra seriously.

They stared at her in shocked silence. Shaila could not believe that Chandra was a Christian and she, the all-knowing, did not know. Malati was aghast that Chandra had kept it a secret from her best friend for so long. In the ashram they did study the New Testament as part of their English course and sacred Hindu texts like the Bhagavad Gita. Their teachers and staff were Hindu, except Miss Crawford.

Their Assembly prayer was what Shaila called the 'Orphan's Plea' to an anonymous, stubbornly uncaring God!

Twameva mata cha pita twameva
Twameva bandhusch sakha twameva
Twameva vidya dravinam twameva
Twameva sarwam mam deva deva

You truly are my mother, my father, and my brother
You truly are my friend, my knowledge, and my wealth
You truly are my all, O God of gods supreme.

'Are you upset that I did not tell you about it? I had good reason. In Ahilya Ashram, religion is irrelevant. When a baby orphan is dropped into the palna and the bell rung, do we know for which God the bell rings! Papi and Chhabi came here with some religious moorings. Shaila, do you know whether your parents were Hindu? Moreover, does my having Christian beliefs change who I am?' asked Chandra, smiling mysteriously.

Malati, couldn't explain her irrational feelings of betrayal. She did not reassure Chandra who then got up and walked away without a word. They did not remonstrate, unable or unwilling to stop her.

Shaila, urged Malati to use her charm and pacify Chandra. Malati tried all her tricks to woo Chandra back. Nothing worked. Then, on Kamala's advice, the girls completed the ritual of 'rusna-manavna'—being upset and making up—when Malati quoted from the Bible, Proverbs 17.9. 'Whoever would foster love, covers over an offence, but whoever repeats the matter, separates close friends.'

Malati then asked Chandra, 'Is that what you want—to separate forever?' Chandra smiled benignly and quoting from the Gospel of Saint Luke 6.37 said, 'Do not judge and you will not be judged. Do not condemn, for you will not be condemned. Forgive, and you will be forgiven.'

Encouraged, Malati put forward her cheek to be kissed. Chandra slapped her cheek playfully and banged her bob cut head twice against Malati's braid-covered one in a gesture of reconciliation. They grasped each other's hands with newfound camaraderie, stronger than ever for having been nearly lost.

The temporary rupture with Chandra ignited in Malati an intense curiosity about the religious origins and inclinations of her classmates in the ashram—the denominations of those very gods who had tossed these girls into orphanhood. Shaila, her first subject, knew everything about everyone, but no one knew who she was. Had she come with any signs of her parentage? Beyond the fable Shaila had knitted about her father being a murdered Khajrana temple head priest?

Shaila deflected all queries about her past. 'I am a Hindu palna orphan. Am I not fair as a Brahmin and drawn to Lord Vishnu by my inborn vasanas?' she asserted. She read the Hindu scriptures intently and could even discourse with the erudite Sanskrit teacher on the Bhagavad Gita. As always, Malati had no option but to believe Shaila.

In the midst of it all, they got the awful news that Miss Crawford's father had died of pneumonia. Malati and Kamala decided to pay a secret condolence visit to the 'temple' of their English goddess but it seemed Shaila had beaten them to it. As they approached the door of the whitewashed cottage, they heard loud voices and crying. Then Shaila burst out of the door, red-eyed, her long black hair loose, wild, and unkempt.

'Go! Go! Go to that Gori mem of yours! She is a hard-hearted, self-centered mlechchha! For me, she is the Raktabeeja demon whom, I as Kali shall spear and slowly drink the blood of!' Shaila announced ferociously, on seeing them, and ran away.

What happened, they wondered, and vowed to comfort Miss Crawford and not allow her to be more upset by their intrusion. They knocked on the door nervously and entered Miss Crawford's living room. They could scarcely recognize the gracious lady they knew in the woman they saw crouched before a table with her father's photograph on it. Miss Crawford was sobbing uncontrollably and looked pale and old. She took no notice of them.

'We are sorry, miss, to hear about your father's death. We are concerned about you,' Kamala murmured awkwardly.

It seemed to be ages before Miss Crawford raised her head and walked up to them.

'I am fond of you two and you are also Shaila's closest friends. If you are really concerned about me, dears, then go and talk to your friend. I have just discovered that Shaila is my daughter. My father only told me on his deathbed that he had lied to me about the death of my baby—the symbol of my ill-fated marriage to Pratap—and had secretly given the baby to the ashram and made me work here, so that I could watch over her,' she said at length.

'Oh, that is marvellous for Shaila!' said Malati almost enviously.

'And for me! But Shaila thinks that either I hate Pratap or that I succumbed to pressure from my father not to acknowledge her. Either way, I stand condemned in her eyes,' Miss Crawford said.

'It is a big shock for her. To grow up for seventeen years thinking, she is an orphan and then to discover that she has a British mother—one she knows closely, but only as a teacher. Once it sinks in, she will, I am sure, be overjoyed to have a real mother, that too, one such as you,' Kamala said sincerely.

Miss Crawford put her arms around them and unashamedly let herself cry clean, hot tears of hope. Malati wiped her tears with her sari padar.

'Hope of paradise regained for me and for her,' she said, laughing through the stream now flowing down her cheeks. 'You two! Mothers in India hold out their saris to their children to comfort them or wipe their tears away. And you are mothering me! Now go get my daughter back, little mothers,' she commanded.

Malati and Kamala could not find Shaila anywhere. Kamala remembered that she and Shaila loved to visit the lotus pond, behind the palace, and they both ran there.

A pair of swans was gliding serenely between the languid, fan-like leaves that lay flat on their ribbed backs, brushing against the pale green and pink, upright and arrogant tapered buds, gazing down their graceful necks at the blushing whirls of lotus flowers, expansive, with sunny, yellow hearts.

Shaila and Kamala used this place as a getaway because it was so peaceful. They loved to sit and gossip or just watch the pantomime of the swans and the lotuses against the setting sun. And sure enough, Shaila was there. Not on the bench beside the pond, but in it, wading towards its deep centre.

'Shaila, stop! Why are you going to the forbidden mayavi kendra—the centre of dangerous illusions—of our lotus pond?' Kamala called out.

Shaila turned around sharply. Her eyes were maniacal. She did not seem to see or hear Kamala and kept wading on. The startled swans edged away from this invasion of their playground, wings aflutter. A litany of complaints issued forth from their orange beaks—*beep-honk, beep-honk beep-honk.*

The girls had no idea that this transparent, crystal-clear water hid so much mud and slime in its belly. As Shaila waded through the water, she stirred it all to the surface. The fan leaves twirled and wound themselves around her legs and arms, squandering their wealth of liquid pearls into the pond. As an offering to Goddess Shaila. She took no notice.

A shawl of dark brown, muddy water soon draped Shaila's waist and then her shoulders. Her delicate face was level with the lotus flowers. But she was not smiling like them. She was deaf to the voices of the girls calling out to her. Kamala panicked and jumped into the pond.

'Shaila, talk to me, to Papi, your best friend! Even if you are angry with Miss Crawford—and I can understand that—why are you punishing yourself? You are too intelligent to do that,' Kamala urged.

'I know that. But I want to deny her a daughter the way she denied me a mother all these years!' Shaila shouted back.

'You don't have to acknowledge her or go with her. That is the way to deny her,' Kamala the Wise tried to inveigle Shaila with her arguments into coming out of the pond.

'How can I face my ashram mates, huh? I carry the shame of my rejection at birth, not by an unknown parent, but a mlechchha mother who was here with us all the time and did not claim me. Better the muddy water above my head than being alive and covered with the slime of indignity,' she cried, pain and anger throbbing in her voice.

'Dearest Shaila! Come back! I will have to drown with you as I cannot swim.' Papi sounded desperate enough.

'Go away, Papi. I know you come as your beloved English teacher's envoy! Tell her to drown in the pond of mud too, if she truly cares for me, as she claims!'

The sludge was now rising up to Shaila's determined chin.

Kamala asked Malati to fetch the durban. Malati ran as fast as she could. When she returned with him, Kamala and Shaila were locked in a tussle and it seemed that Shaila was dragging Kamala into the whirlpool of dark, clammy waters. Both of them bobbed up and down, struggling to keep aloft.

'Shaila is no longer fighting me,' Kamala shouted out. 'We both want to come ashore, but are being pulled down and can't lift ourselves out!'

'Oh my God! It's the dal dal—the mysterious quagmire in that part of the lake. They say a spirit that lives there pulls those who dare to go and disturb it. Stay as you are, keep your head turned upwards and move your feet as if you are cycling. Chant your prayers! I will pull you both out,' the durban shouted out to them.

Malati and the durban waded in towards them with two long sticks, which they extended, to Shaila and Kamala to hold tight as they pulled them out with all their might. Shaila and Kamala broke free and waded out of the quagmire.

All of them looked like molten sculptures of slime. Shaila had swallowed some muddy water and was rushed to the clinic, while Kamala and Malati went off to wash and change before going to see her. Maji was with Shaila, her face still determined, her usually bright eyes overcast with bitterness.

The all-knowing Maji held Shaila's hand gently in her own and said, 'My child, you have always been special to me and to the ashram. More beautiful, more talented, more loved. Ask these girls if they didn't think so and envy you for it. It was because I knew that you are Miss Crawford's daughter. I swear that she was unaware of this. I was helpless as both the Colonel and the Maharaja swore me to secrecy. Your accepting Miss Crawford as your mother will not force you to give up Hindu beliefs nor to become a Christian. Don't you remember your favourite verse from the Bhagavad Gita about assuming new lives, casting away old ones like worn-out clothes?'

'I don't want to believe in that verse ever again. It is used to justify anything and everything that fate does to disembody us, dissemble us! Miss Crawford will always remain what she made herself out to be—the foreign English teacher who didn't have the guts to spare me my orphaned existence,' she said, her face contorted in anger and sorrow.

'All right. Do you believe me—your Maji—or not?'

Shaila softened a little. 'She wants me to go to England with her. I have always hated the British. I'd rather live an orphan, but in my own country,' she sobbed. 'Moreover, if I were to accept her as my mother and go with her, I and she too, will be misfits.'

'I am proud of your power of reasoning and take credit for it. Let's take one step at a time. Accept her as your mother, show forgiveness and reconcile, then we can persuade her to stay on here.'

'Am I becoming such a burden to you and the ashram that you want to unload me on to Miss Crawford?' asked Shaila.

'Frankly, yes,' said Maji, matter-of-factly, refusing to rise to the bait. 'After you pass your Intermediate, there is no place for you here except as a teacher, whenever there is a vacancy. You have to make way for other palna entrants who have to be given shelter and brought up to your level.'

'Then get me a job somewhere else or get me married to some decent Hindu. I'd rather keep my worn-out, but comfortable clothes on, than be naked in my new dharmaless incarnation.'

20
STARDUST

The following week, studies and special classes overwhelmed Kamala and Malati. Miss Crawford was still not back. So, they decided to go to see her and suggested that she arrange a reunion between Shaila and Pratap. The English rose had wilted, worry lines appearing on her like cracks in the sandal paste markings on a Brahmin priest's forehead. Her golden-brown hair looked faded and limp, its lustre lost.

'We were married in a temple. He was called away suddenly by his father in Bilaspur and he never returned. I was heartbroken. I don't know where he is—alive or dead. She has to accept me alone, as I am, or not at all. I am giving her time till after her Intermediate exams,' Miss Crawford said firmly.

The exams came and went peacefully at the ashram. Thirty girls were tested for the rigour of their training and their own dedication and intelligence. Kamala, Shaila, and Malati managed to get a high first division while Chandra missed it by a whisker. Every one of the thirty girls passed; Maji beamed with pride at her unfailing record.

Maharani Chandravati presided over the simple but moving graduation ceremony. The graduates wore peacock blue, gold-bordered saris—a graduation and farewell gift from the Maharani. Pointed satin caps crowned their braided heads. They suddenly felt and looked like grown women.

The Maharani addressed the graduating students with the ease of an eloquent orator.

> This class of 1925 graduating from our ashram will always be special. Those who go into the forest first, have to hack down the trees and thorny bushes. Grapple with dangerous animals. Clear the way. Make it safe for others that follow. We will be watching you all very carefully. You have to cut down the trees of prejudice blocking your way. The demons of exploitation—you must defeat. The new fertile fields of fulfilment you have to create for women.

The students clapped. These words of the Maharani sprinkled some stardust of dignity on to naturally diffident, young women orphans, unsure of their future. For a moment, they were elated that they could well become stars, not just planets in the new 'solar systems' emerging in India that Maji often referred to.

> Know that it will be a long time before you come close to being regarded equal to men. But show them that you are truly their shakti and power. That it is for their own good that you should stand up, and stand up tall. The ashram inspired by the great Maharani Ahilyabai is meant to instil in you the confidence that you can navigate the world on your own now, be self-reliant! So, I wish you all the very best. Outside these gates, only our prayers are with you. Go and spread enlightenment to other girls.

When the Maharani ended her speech with an exhortation to being on their own, the graduates relapsed into sallow insecurity. As if, the stardust blew itself into grey, gritty, ash clouds.

'How can the Maharani leave us in the lurch? Can't the ashram arrange jobs for us or get us married? Most of us have nowhere to go,' whispered some of the orphans.

Maji addressed these concerns in her speech.

> The Maharani in her infinite kindness has agreed that the ashram will help graduates find jobs as teachers. Those who want to study further will be given guidance. You can stay here for another two months. You must know that we have changed you, but not the injustice in the world. No one from good families will come to pick a bride from amongst girls with no family background. Begging them to marry you goes against the self-respect we have taught you. Maybe you will meet your life partners—the enlightened ones, when you study further or take up jobs.

Most of the girls were reassured only partially by what Maji said. Kamala and Malati were worried more for the others than for themselves. They had their Baba and Malak as their guides who had plans for them to join college, like Chandra. The other girls did not.

It was time for Kamala and Malati to wind up their life in Ahilya Ashram and prepare for the next yuga. They couldn't believe they had spent five years here! They came as simple village girls and they were going out as educated and self-aware young women. It was not as Sant Tukaram said: 'When one looks into the mirror, it seems as if one is looking at a different object, yet one is looking at oneself.' The image and the object had both been transformed. They were seeing a different Malati and a different Kamala, whichever mirror they looked into!

Malati would have loved to go to Ratnagiri and proudly present themselves as high school graduates! Especially to Bhika—the sarpanch's son. To show him that they had neither become good wives nor were they under any man's thumb! They had earned a fate better than most girls and even boys!

But for now, Kamala and Malati had an unfulfilled promise to keep—to bring together Shaila and her mother.

'With her, never. With my father, wherever he is, yes,' Shaila said. 'She can't get me to meet my father because she murdered him!'

Kamala told her not to believe in such scurrilous stories and shame the victim that Miss Crawford was. But Shaila would not be persuaded.

Malati and Kamala were thus unable to give gurudakshina to Miss Crawford. They were happy that at least she had agreed to stay back in India on Maji's persuasion for now, and would try to win over her daughter. Shaila meanwhile seemed to be getting her earlier energy and magnetism back.

On the last day, when they went to say their goodbye to Miss Crawford, they found her cottage empty and locked. They turned around disappointed. Shaila came up suddenly from behind them, smiled beatifically, and said, 'Your efforts are not in vain, dear Papi and Chhabi. She did pay her dues as a mother. She left her flesh and blood here in India to be reunited with her father someday. She vacated her chair as English teacher. You can visit me, dear friends, in this cottage—my new home as the new English teacher at the ashram!' and she opened the lock of the cottage door.

ꕤ

Baba arrived at the ashram, to take the girls away for good. This leaving was like no other. The ashram had become so much a part of them that outside it they would feel naked and exposed. They once again harked back to Sant Tukaram: 'I am the Brook that has merged into the river. My Country is now the whole Universe.' They would have liked to celebrate their arrival into that universe. But it was a bit too intimidating!

Maji suggested to Baba that Malati and Kamala follow Chandra in joining Elphinstone College in Mumbai and she would make recommendations for their scholarships. Baba readily agreed. The girls touched her feet with respect and gratitude as they said farewell.

The girls were excited to finally go to Desaikheda and visit Baba's 'life project', to meet their brother and the larger family they had parted from so long ago. However, Malati expressed some anxiety about their going to Bombay—a totally strange place, knowing no one.

'Bombay is a Marathi-speaking place and safer for girls than cities in Central India. Malak has a representative there and you at least know Chandra. Yes, unlike the ashram, your teachers will be mostly men and you will be among a handful of girls in a classroom full of boys. You be careful about the city-bred boys who will try to inveigle you into disgrace. So, keep your distance to safeguard your chastity. You are on a different, more difficult, but ultimately more rewarding, path,' Baba warned.

Boys! Kamala and Malati had not had time to consider that Elphinstone College would have teachers and students their age other than those in saris or skirts. Baba had just reminded them that in classrooms and canteens, in libraries and playgrounds, they would be jostling with those wearing dhotis and pants. They hoped that unlike Bhika, their classmates would be knowledge hungry, fresh-faced, and as curious about them as the girls were about the boys. It would be a wonderful change from the women only monotony of the ashram. The lurking dangers added to their exhilaration.

'Being with men will test our willpower further and our conquest over kama will be the greater,' whispered Kamala, always one to find a clever excuse for being attracted to forbidden things.

'But you have self-control, I don't. I can't say that the sheer novelty of being in the company of boys will not turn my head,' Malati worried.

'Ha, ha! You can resist anything except food! And you can't eat handsome men, can you?' Kamala joked.

Kamala told Baba that their aspiration to be freedom fighters might be side-tracked just when the movement was gathering force. Bombay, they heard, was becoming an epicentre.

'Concentrate on your mission of studies, girls. The freedom struggle will go on for decades. The mighty British are not going to give us freedom so easily or so quickly. So, you can always contribute after your education is complete. Let the men make the sacrifice. They have enjoyed the privilege of education for long.'

Their train, the Storm Queen, flashed past quilted fields and toy towns. Around evening, she surrendered herself to the Chambal ravines. It was home to the dreaded dacoits that struck terror even in the bravest hearts of Guna. Their terrain—beehad—was forbidding. Smooth-faced sandstone mountains rose steep and dense, chasing the Chambal River on its labyrinthine course. Here in the scrub forests and hills, the dacoits ingeniously carved hideouts in the rocky landscape, lured the police and rivals to breach their fortresses, only to meet with treacherous death.

The ascending full moon lit up the rivers and gorges into crisscrossing patterns of silver ribbons. As they admired the breathtaking views, Baba warned, 'But don't go by Chambal River's beauty and the innocent glances cast by the moonlight on the water. The river is the true ally of the dacoits, becoming their quickest escape path and sanctuary, while she tosses their pursuers unkindly into her churning belly!'

'Baba, these tall shadows on our side, are they cast by the sentinel hills or the dacoits? Do they ride horses that run faster than the trains?' Malati asked gingerly.

'Heavens forbid,' said Baba. 'They may well be the shadows that rouse fear before the dacoits themselves arrive.'

In Vaishali, Malati and Kamala had heard many stories about the dacoits. Badi Dai, the supreme storyteller, made them out to be romantic heroes; pious, Shiva and Shakti worshipping men and women, driven to dacoity by poverty and injustice.

Ah, yes! She claimed to know one or two gangs led by women, too— the glorious Rani Lakshmi Bais of the Chambal. True descendants of Arjun and Queen Premila in martial arts, they were incredibly brave and had disdain for their own lives. The male dakus were the saviours from rapacious landlords or high caste tormentors and rapists.

Chhoti Dai, of course, would have none of this glorification of ruthless killers, backstabbing cowards, and petty thieves, looting rich and poor alike. Nor of the hauntingly beautiful beehads of Chambal, for they were inhabited by malevolent spirits. She recounted the story of Draupadi, the Pandava queen, cursing the Chambal River for being a mute spectator when her husband Yudhishthira wagered her and his cousin Dushashana dishonoured her. For Chhoti Dai, the dakus were debauches and rapists themselves, from whose lustful eyes good men hid their wives and daughters.

'I swear on my late husband that I have myself seen how unrepentant these dakus are about taking other people's lives. I pray every day that the British sahebs and our Maharaja will together crush them like ants. Only then will my liver be calm,' she would say with vehemence.

More than her wanting to prove her archrival Badi Dai wrong, her misgivings were borne of the personal tragedy of her husband dying in a dacoit raid on their village, leaving her a young widow.

The train suddenly came to a stop with a lurch. They looked out of the windows in surprise. There were nowhere near any station. Then came the sound of horse hooves striking on the parallel footpath—*clippety clop clippety clop clippety clip*. The dreaded dacoits had materialized from those shadows! Baba looked out of the window and tried to hide his precious young daughters with his blanket.

But Malati could not keep herself covered and threw the blanket away as she heard a dacoit shout: 'Attention everybody, nobody is to move. Do as we tell you.'

There were gasps of fear, but no one dared to even whisper. They could now see some passengers being pulled out of the train by the dacoits.

'Have mercy on us,' the passengers pleaded, as the dacoits' swords grazed their necks. The girls shuddered.

'Spare our husbands,' begged terror-stricken wives, pulling away their husbands from the grip of the dacoits. Children started crying.

'Will you give your money or shall I cut off your hands, gouge your eyes out, or make you lame for life?' they heard one of the dacoits threaten a passenger.

They must have carried out their threats, at least in part, as some passengers who saw the butchery from their compartment, looked horrified and screamed. One woman turned and vomited onto the floor of the compartment. Grains of just-eaten rice and dal in blobs of yellow, splattered on the floor. The foul stench of terror rose in a spiral to hang in the air.

'Now is there anyone else foolish enough to follow their example?' a dacoit asked.

The girls shivered uncontrollably. They tried to get some courage from what Miss Crawford had said once—enemies arouse fear to take away hope and deny righteous victories. So, we should be brave and pray. Malati recited a hymn to Lord Hanuman—the disaster-averting god.

Four dacoits entered their compartment. Everybody froze, their eyes fixed on the ruffians. Unnaturally tall, the dacoits' fierce eyes glowed through the black chadar covering their heads and faces.

The dacoits were looking for a potential wealthy target—a moneylender or landlord—hiding amongst the largely poor, village folks. They picked out two potbellied men who looked like traders. As they got up to meekly follow the dacoits, they shook like palm trees in a storm, their dhotis flapping and seats wet.

'Please stop!' Baba said loudly. 'These people are poor like us. If they have any money, they can part with it. Don't kill them.'

21
BABA'S RIGHTEOUS EMPIRE

Malati and Kamala could not believe their ears. Why was Baba being so foolhardy?

A dacoit rushed towards him and caught him by his neck. The girls clung to Baba and tried to push away the dacoit.

'Who are you to talk to our leader like that? You and your daughters here will be dealt with first,' he said viciously.

'I am Madhav Rao Desai, the maha sarpanch of Desaikheda in Guna. If you operate in that area, you know me and know that we are neither rich, nor do we wish to fight you. So, leave us alone and let these people be,' Baba said looking them in the eye.

'Since you have given your address, you will hear from us soon,' said the leader of the band, signalling to the dacoit who had caught hold of Baba, to let him go.

The two traders quickly emptied out their pockets and shoes of a few silver coins and prostrated themselves before the dacoits. They were lucky to get away with only light sword gashes on their backs, thanks to Baba.

The dacoits melted into the darkness that enveloped the ravines when the full moon retreated behind dark clouds, as if on cue. The conductors and guards, who had mysteriously disappeared during the confrontation, reappeared. They picked up the dead and wounded like they were collecting luggage that was left behind.

The Storm Queen resumed her journey pretending that nothing had happened to stop her in her tracks. The girls had been shocked into silence by the encounter with the dacoits and Baba's brash intervention. The soothing movement of the train now helped them compose themselves to question Baba.

'It's like when a man facing a snake or a tiger will invite an attack if he shows fear or tries to harm them. But, if they see that he is not aggressive or fearful, they will go their own way. It's the same with these dacoits,' Baba said.

'Dacoits are robbers and murderers without the animal code of honour! So, we were lucky to escape their wrath now, but they may yet come after you and us!' Kamala said, still agitated.

'I can't solve the problem for the entire region, but I try to protect my villages by arming them. They will never negotiate with us, if they think we have no alternative but to submit to their tyranny. I told them that we will provide some food but they should not loot or pillage, and we can't give any money nor shelter them during their hide-and-seek with the authorities. I have given information and advice to Vilas Rao too to help the authorities tackle this menace,' Baba explained.

'Lucky if they will keep the pact,' Malati said, unconvinced. 'Also, if you don't help the authorities to catch them, how will they ever manage to end dacoity?'

Baba was silent for a moment.

'There is a difference between a short-term truce and long-term victory in war,' he said thoughtfully.

They reached Guna station. A less muscular and much older Khandoba received them warmly.

'Ya! ya! Welcome you goddesses of Indore!' He surveyed them from head to toe, his face wreathed in smiles.

'You young ladies have to be fed well—with chicken, wheat, butter, and milk, so you are strong before you go on another expedition,' he said.

Kamala and Malati looked at each other and giggled.

'Is that your way of showing us affection? Fattening us, huh!' asked Kamala.

Khandoba noticed the tension on Baba's face, looked around and saw that some dead bodies and wounded passengers were being taken off the train amid the wailing of bereaved families.

'Arre Bappa! So, the dacoits struck, hoye? Are you OK?' he asked them.

'Nothing like a brush with the dacoits of Chambal to make you stronger,' he added, trying to lighten the mood.

The journey to Desaikheda in a bullock cart on the bumpiest of dirt roads shook them—*gat gat gat gat*—like water gurgling in an earthen pot. Through the dust clouds enwrapping them, they saw stretches of green and mustard yellow farmlands and scattered villages with humble thatched huts and brick houses huddled together in intermittent, convivial clusters. A while later, Baba's large brick, two-storeyed house with its sturdy red tiled roof, greeted them. A little boy in pajamas and shirt stood at the door.

'That's Govind,' Baba said with pride. The girls waved excitedly. He waved back shyly.

They got off and embraced Govind. Baba, in a rare gesture of affection, put his arms around all three of them.

'Baba, what have my tais brought for me from Indore?' asked Govind, still too shy to talk directly to his long-lost sisters. Baba interjected.

'Your tais have brought that for you which you don't get in the bazaar or village fair—knowledge,' Baba said, sensing the girls' embarrassment.

'Can I play with it, especially when my playmates run around and I can't catch up with them?' Govind said referring to his limp from an earlier dacoit attack Baba had not told them about.

'Yes, of course. It is something you get from books and from those like your tais blessed by Goddess Saraswati. You sit on your swing in the courtyard and just read and listen,' Baba said. Later, Baba asked them to teach him sports, tell him stories, and get him to be bookworms like them!

Malati asked about Bala. Baba told them about the 'Ambutai miracle'. She, who had been given up for dead, turned up to claim Bala a month ago. After Bhausaheb fobbed her off with money on the condition that she leave the village for good, she set the scene for her apparent suicide. She cleverly deposited Bala with Baba, knowing he would look after him. She then went all the way to Hingne, near Poona, where Baba had once told her Maharishi Karve had a widows' home. The gods at last smiled on her. She not only got shelter there but also learnt tailoring and ran a tailor's shop there. Once she felt confident that she could support Bala on her own, she came back to claim him.

'What a story of redemption! But how did Bala take this revelation?' Malati asked.

'Bala, who was only seven when Ambutai returned, was crushed to know I was not his real father and resented his mother for abandoning him. But she explained that if she had gone to Hingne with an illegitimate baby, she feared being denied shelter. Anyway, Bala is where he belongs. Assured of a good upbringing. She also vowed to restore Bala to his real father,' Baba said.

Later, as a climax to the Ambutai story they heard that Bhausaheb had been stabbed to death near his house by an unknown killer. The girls wondered whether it was natural justice meted out to Bhausaheb by random fate in someone else's guise, or it was punishment for spurning another overture by Ambutai! As Khandoba said cryptically, you can rebuff a hapless widow, but not the incarnation of Goddess Shakti Durga!

Kamala and Malati had barely settled down to rest and relax in their home after being in exile for several years, when Baba alerted them to their 'holiday mission'.

He explained how he had tried to live down the ignominy he had suffered when he took up the cause of girls going to school in Ratnagiri. Malati and Kamala as his Intermediate-pass daughters who would soon be going to Elphinstone College as pioneers, were his revenge on the small minds of the Ratnagiri panchayat and those ignorant men and women who failed to see light. Along with that, all these years he had been preparing the ground for making Desaikheda a model for girls going to school along with boys. He had made much progress in blowing holes in the outdated and warped logic of the villagers there of keeping women and girls bereft of Ma Saraswati's benediction. However he still faced some residual resistance. So, while they were still there, he planned to convene a maha panchayat of all villages under him and convinced them to send their daughters to the Saraswati Vidya Mandir. 'Remember, this we can't fail and I want you to campaign with me in the villages to create a wave. In particular, I want the oldest matriarch, Ajibai, and all of the womenfolk on our side. In selecting candidates to stand for elections to the maha panchayat I had made sure that each of them sends their daughter to school. But Ajibai's son is an influential councillor and is too much under the sway of his mother and I don't want even a single dissenter. So, get to work while I coax the panchayat councillors into compliance with saam daam danda bhed!' Baba declared and laughed conspiratorially.

They heard from Khandoba how Baba deployed Kautilyan tactics. Some councillors were offered much coveted land or grazing rights, cattle sheds, and new ploughs to replace broken ones, free treatment of their sick family members, winter clothes and bedding, farming tools and seeds as inducement. Equally the more recalcitrant ones were threatened with cancellation of their 'illegal' land deeds and denial of access to common facilities like village water sources and community halls and temples. Some even faced the withdrawl of the guns and swords issued to them as leaders of the village defence forces. Some were given 'inside information' on how some others were conspiring against them and promised support in their property disputes and power games.

Meanwhile, Malati and Kamala went from house to house to try to befriend the women and girls in the villages who confessed their eagerness to meet people like them bearing such exciting experiences. They told them stories of their ashram life—the good and the bad. And how they were headed to new adventures in Bombay as equals with the Gora sahebs and elite Indian men and boys!

They distributed little 'parcels of knowledge' including stories from the Hindu epics to get them interested in reading and writing and then broached the subject of the mothers of girls supporting the Saraswati Vidya Mandir resolution that was to be taken up and passed at the maha panchayat.

The mothers' reactions were mixed. Some protested that this would deprive them of the helping hands of their daughters in housework and caring for younger siblings while others cited tradition and custom. But slowly and surely, they convinced most mothers that their daughters deserved a better life than they had had, away from the hazards and pain of child marriage and child motherhood and enjoying the benefits of going through a celibate scholarship and play, enlightenment, and fun phase of life, just like boys.

Most importantly, the village girls themselves hankered after the miracle of going to school. Malati and Kamala assured them that their husbands and fathers were agreeable, but wanted them to make a strong demand so they could have the honour of bequeathing this gift to them. They therefore agreed on a game plan.

The village girls soon began to hero worship Kamala and Malati and demanded to be taught all the things they had learnt at the ashram. Each day a new topic was covered in history and geography, maths and Sanskrit, Marathi, and even English. Song and dance, poetry and lezium, hu tu tu and seven tiles became the marvellous moments of enjoyment between them. They were however least impressed when

Malati and Kamala boasted that they will someday join the freedom movement.

'So, you are going to be like the dacoits who claim to be fighting for freedom! Will you be able to wield lathis and lances, swords, and guns?' they asked with newly learnt logic, leaving Malati and Kamala speechless.

Ajibai's was quite another mountain to climb. They saw in her a likeness of Chandrabai who had failed the Jijabai test in Ratnagiri. Ajibai had made sure that the young girls from her large brood, stayed clear of any contamination spread by Baba and his school. Now she kept a hawk's eye on his daughters' movements, to pre-empt any conversion of the village women to his cause.

The girls tried to engage her by seeking her wisdom on everyday matters—how to cook halwa and saag, how to milk the cow, how to make the best dung cakes for fuel, how to sew and embroider, and weave wicker baskets while sharing their experiences of Krishna Leela performances or Shitala Mata's visitation at the ashram. The girls recognized that ensnaring her into changing her mindset was crucial but taking down a brasspot full of beliefs, which she had carried for so many years on her head, would require quite another ruse.

One day, when Kamala and Malati were playing badminton in the open field where boys normally played gulli danda and kabaddi, a crowd of girls and boys gathered. The girls showed Govind how to play badminton with racquets and shuttlecock across a makeshift net set up by stringing an old nine-yard sari on two poles dug into the ground.

The chase after the bird soon became a leap to freedom for the young girls who were watching. One by one, they tried to hit the flying bird, with much giggling and to shouts of encouragement when they did manage to hit it and boos when the racquet missed it.

Hearing the happy squealing, Ajibai appeared and saw with her dimming vision the young girls of Desaikheda chasing a silly feathered toy.

'Hey, you shameless girls!' she cried out angrily. 'Have you forgotten your household responsibilities? Your padars are slipping from your heads and exposing your shoulders! Kali Yuga—the dark age of sin—has arrived! The sarpanch should not allow his daughters to defile the whole pond of our life of dharma.'

The embarrassed village girls quickly withdrew from the improvised court, their padars hastily covering their shoulders. But Kamala and Malati played on with their padars tightly wound around their waist, riding on the udan khatola—the flying machine—of their cloth shoes to catch the bird in flight. On Malati's signalling, the girls suddenly mobbed Ajibai, put a racquet into her hand and held a shuttlecock to its head. Zing! It flew towards Malati's side of the court and she returned the serve. Ajibai seized the racquet and hit the shuttlecock back to everyone's surprise. Malati was too shocked to hit it back. There was a roar of delight from the onlookers. They clapped and declared victory for Ajibai who too was pleased, though she tried to hide it. Malati embraced her and shouted 'Jai ho Ajibai!'

From that moment, Malati and Kamala became friends with Ajibai. Though still wary of girls being unbound wantonly and taking delight in what she regarded as unwomanly sports and being diverted from housework into studies, she seemed to realize at last that she may lose authority if she denies these freedoms at least to the unmarried girls. As Khandoba pointed out, Ajibai was too proud and set in her ways like yoghurt from creamy milk to put her authority behind Baba's Saraswati Girls' mission. But her opposition was silenced as that of her son as they discovered on the day of reckoning.

The maha panchayat was held in the cool time of dusk under another wisdom bestowing banyan tree, its trunk clear of the gnarled roots coming up, unlike in Ratnagiri. Over a hundred sarpanches and panches of Baba's villages sat purposefully on a newly built, enormous brick platform. Malati and Kamala had not seen such a large multitude of villagers—men on one side and women on the other—sitting patiently on square reed mats each brought along, unfurled and spread on the flattened dusty ground.

Baba called the meeting to order. He first announced the dedication of the Saraswati Vidya Mandir as the first middle school in the area to the people of Desaikheda to thunderous clapping, cheers of *olu olu holu* and 'Jai Shiv Shanker, Jai Ganesh, Jai Vishnu' from the men and boys and well-rehearsed chants of 'Jai Bhavani! Jai Saraswati! Jai Lakshmi!' from the women and girls! Baba picked up on that.

'Did you hear that? The women and girls of our villages see this Vidya Mandir as the vastu—dwelling—of the three goddesses. They demand to be blessed by them and I have consulted widely among the councillors of all villages. It is decided that we will open the doors of the Vidya Mandir to both girls and boys and you will be duty bound to send both your sons and daughters to school from next week,' Baba announced.

The women and girls clapped wildly, not afraid of their men who too were soon shamed into joining them. The councillors shouted their assent. Ajibai and her councillor son gave theirs in absentia.

3

The sound of horses neighing to high heavens followed by loud altercations just outside their house, roused Malati and Kamala early one morning. They ran to the window. The dacoits who had threatened Baba in the train were at the gate. The girls were rooted to the spot and watched fearfully from behind the bamboo curtains.

Chief Sardar Maan Singh was on horseback. He wore a plumed khaki turban, black sleeveless jacket, and narrow pajamas. Square silver amulets were tied with coiled, thick, black thread around his neck and his muscled arms. To ward off which evil eye when theirs was the most evil of all, thought Malati.

The Sardar had a bright red trident mark on his forehead. Badi Dai's Shiva worshipper! The Sardar proudly carried his many scars, one still fresh, raised, red and snarling, slashed across his left temple. A warning to adversaries of many a skirmish survived and won.

And then his eyes! What did these dacoits eat that made their eyes glow like embers? Even more overawing than the big, rusty, wood handled rifle that the Sardar carried or the glinting swords the others brandished. Through the bushel of the beard and moustache—now no longer covered by a chadar, the faces of all the dacoits glowered.

'Madhav Rao, you said that you will work with us and not against us! But you have broken your word! Our Sardar is unhappy,' one of them said loudly to Baba.

'I have faithfully followed our compact of friendly coexistence,' Baba replied.

'You don't have a choice,' said the Sardar.

'We always have choices, don't we?' said Baba coolly.

'Oh, yes? What would you do otherwise?' asked the Sardar, coming up to Baba on his horse and holding his gun aloft menacingly.

'Oh, there are a hundred ways we can refuse to cooperate and even imperil you. We can refuse to give you sustenance for starters,' Baba retorted.

'And risk your villages being burnt or crops destroyed?' challenged the Sardar.

'That will be self-defeating. You know the saying—even the wet log burns with the dry log when you set it on fire. You will die hungry if there are no crops to feed you, if our homes are burnt, our villages devastated. You live because we live and work. You live off us. If we are not there, who will you lord over or hold hostage with the authorities?' Baba replied unfazed.

The Sardar was silent for a minute. The two men glared fiercely at each other.

'Remember we are nomadic. We are not dependent only on Desaikheda,' the Sardar asserted.

'Yes, but if you don't show grace, you have no shred of moral authority. You are already outlaws with the authorities. You will become harami in people's eyes—devoid of any legitimacy,' Baba retorted.

'How dare you swear at our Sardar? You are now playing beyond your—league. We will finish you here and now,' one of the dacoits said, whipping out his sword and holding it to Baba's back. Baba was unarmed but did not flinch.

22

DANGEROUS ENCOUNTERS

Malati and Kamala ran down the stairs and against all injunctions to the contrary, picked up the short stout sticks hanging at the entrance, hid them behind their backs, covered with their padars and rushed out into the courtyard. 'Please don't harm Baba,' they pleaded and approached the three dacoits meekly to Baba's consternation. Before the dacoits could respond, Malati swung her stick in a lightning lathi–lezium move she had learnt at the ashram, and hit the dacoit threatening Baba and he fell to the ground. Kamala swung at the second dacoit who was so surprised by the attack that his sword clattered down too.

'Oh, so you have taught your daughters subterfuge to attack us in the guise of appealing for mercy, eh!' said the Sardar. The two dacoits got up, picked up their swords, and turned towards the girls. The Sardar himself dismounted from his horse and walked towards Baba. 'Back off from my master and don't touch the girls. I will shoot your Sardar dead, do you hear me?' Khandoba shouted as he rushed up and held a gun to the Sardar's head. From nowhere, ten members of the village defence force converged with swords and guns.

Suddenly, the ferocity died out of the dacoit's eyes. The Sardar ordered his men to stand down.

'I tell you again, your power comes from our tolerance. Don't breach its banks. Otherwise, the floods of our righteous indignation will swallow you,' Baba said steadily looking the Sardar in the eye.

The Sardar seemed to wake up as if from a trance. 'I see that you are arming yourself against us. This is a direct challenge that may not go unanswered,' he warned Baba looking at Khandoba and the other veers.

'We have a village protection force. It is purely defensive and not directed against anyone. There are many bands that roam this region, not only yours, although you claim this to be your catchment area!' Baba said.

'Aha! If you don't submit to our authority, you will not live to see the devastation we will cause,' the Sardar sounded ominous.

'Oh Sardar! Since you seem to be a sensible leader, claiming to fight the injustice of landlords and the oppression of authorities, your enmity should not be with our peaceful, hardworking, mostly poor villagers. There is no surplus to loot. Only enough for us to share with grace. Not yours to claim by right,' Baba said firmly, but patiently.

The Sardar's face contorted with anger—his brows descended onto his eyes, his hairy nostrils flared open, and his lips twisted into a scowl. 'You can't escape our claws with your clever talk, Madhav Rao, nor outgun us forever,' he threatened.

'Well, if that is the language you want to speak, remember, the villagers know exactly where you live, which gangs are your enemies. The authorities in Vaishali are keeping an eye on you, too. We can win against you without using the swords and firepower we too have acquired,' Baba asserted.

The Sardar looked at him resentfully, but with grudging respect. As he turned around to leave, in an attempt to reassert his lost authority, he fired shots in the air, lashed the horse harder than needed, extracting an annoyed snort, and led his men out of Desaikheda. Baba thanked Khandoba for his heroic rescue and lauded Malati and Kamala for their timely intervention. But he worried that their direct exposure to the dacoits made it unsafe for the girls to stay on or ever return again! Little Govind had already paid a price.

By the end of the girl's stay, Govind had recovered from his injury and was running around. He did well in studies and appeared to be a natural kathakar, holding his peers spellbound! He wanted his sisters to take him along to Bombay to study.

'Govind, you could go once you finish school in Guna. But then, unlike them, you have the responsibility of carrying forward the Desai family line and farming tradition—father to son. Will you protect the villagers against the dacoits?' Baba asked him.

'Yes, I will,' said Govind, the chosen one, proudly.

Baba and the girls briefly stopped at Vaishali to meet Surekha and take Malak's blessings. The girls were eager to see Sarala, who was now married to a nephew of the Maharaja—Abhimanyu. The boy's family had approached Malak for her hand. He was well above even Malak's family status—rich and royal—and she could live close to her mother. Her in-laws appreciated that she was educated and able to engage with the British and other royal ladies! She was becoming an asset to her father-in-law too in the management of their estates. Abhimanyu was not as engaged.

The girls met Sarala very warmly. Within minutes however, she opened her 'memory box of discontent' pulling out one complaint after another against Abhimanyu.

'All my ideas of romance and love and of my becoming someone extraordinary were cast into the sacrificial fire of our marriage,' Sarala declared dramatically.

'Abhimanyu, my husband, does not take to my body with passion nor speak to me with love like Robert nor is he a hero driven by a noble cause like Pravesh Babu, both of whom were made to disappear from my life by Malak,' Sarala said.

'You can either be a nobleman or work for a noble cause, not both,' Malati joked.

'But seriously, our expectations about romance spring from what we read in mythology, in Kalidasa's plays or English novels. We know that everyday relationships are imperfect yet we delude ourselves. Don't start with that expectation in a marriage arranged in heaven and not willed by you,' Kamala advised.

'Just imagine Abhimanyu to be your Krishna. You will feel like a Radha and find passion in him,' Malati said reassuringly.

Their gratuitous advice stung Sarala. 'So say the girls who have practically grown up as nuns, who have had no acquaintance, let alone any bodily or emotional dalliance with any man.'

The girls threw up their hands and smiled sheepishly. She was right.

Malati changed track and said, 'I can't imagine that a learned man of his lineage will not passionately fall in love with a young and beautiful wife with an aura of her own like you. You combine both a wife and mistress in you!' They all laughed.

They congratulated her on her managing her father-in-law's estates.

'Yes. I don't think my mother-in-law is very happy about that, but I don't care. Anyway, now tell me about you. I heard you passed your Intermediate brilliantly. Congratulations. Where to now?' Sarala asked.

Malati told her all about their next destination. A flicker of envy passed over Sarala's beautiful face. Then she smiled and said, 'I am the goddess of good fortune. I bless you. May you find the best men to romance in Bombay, even as you do a bit of studying on the side!'

Malati asked to go to see Maa Saheb and seek her blessings before they left on an uncharted journey the next day.

The Chhota Ghar was surprisingly bright. The curtains were open, sunlight streaming in. There were flowers in silver vases and a Krishna temple had sprung up in an alcove of the living room. The furniture was new and plush. Maa Saheb remained faithful to her ancient, regal couch. Lean and wasted as ever, but much lifted in spirit, she sat there beaming and transformed. With Hades now banished to the real netherworld, her daughter's life in the glory of its spring, Goddess Demeter seemed happy, almost human. They wished her well.

She welcomed her beloved daughter with a smile they had never seen before. In some strange way, she even welcomed her sawat's sisters warmly. 'Come, come, baal. Come, you sisters. See, your friend has got married and found her Krishna. Remember, I had told you I see a bright future for her? Abhimanyu is a good man. He will take care of her,' she said.

'Maa Saheb, it's more that I take care of him,' said Sarala, playfully.

'You, girl. You had better be careful with that attitude. I know you get it from me. Look where it got me!' she said, with a tinge of sadness.

The girls sat on the new sofas and waited for her attention to turn to them. The spools of sandalwood incense spun out the threads of an ethereal fragrance and hinted at Maa Saheb's inhaling loving kindness and inner peace with it. Which comes first? They could not say. The pungent fumes of burnt camphor billowed, whispering that Maa Saheb was healing but still needed to emerge crystal pure from her past. Either way, in her new alcove temple, her white marble Krishna was smiling. Pleased with her worship.

They looked at her expectantly to pronounce on their future. She seemed to go into a trance. Finally, she opened her eyes. Malati earnestly gazed back at her, ready to accept whatever she had to foresee.

'Last time I was afraid I had lost my divine intuition. It's come back! Malati, your bravery will be tested like never before. You and Kamala will be in a big city and feel rudderless but will soon grow well into your new avatars. You will both meet young men—but marriage is very, very far away. I see a lot of turmoil and tough times in between,' she said.

'Come, let my Krishna himself bless you,' she said, leading them to the alcove.

The girls prostrated themselves before the smiling Krishna. When they rose up, Maa Saheb was gone.

When Malak came home that evening, the girls went to see him, prepared for some questioning, but much affirmation.

He welcomed them warmly and said, 'I am pleased and displeased you both have passed your Intermediate exams with distinction.'

They were puzzled.

'If you had not done well, I would have had a good excuse to marry you off to good Maratha grooms. But you are on track to go to Elphinstone College. Don't disappoint your Baba, who has put so much faith in you. I have people there who will support you but also keep a watch on you!'

The girls smiled and said, 'We will not disappoint you and Baba.'

'Malak, we want to thank you for encouraging us. And we only got through the ashram because we had the haven of Vilas Rao's wada. Akka has been our little Ayee,' Malati said earnestly.

'Oh, you have become so big that you are now recounting favours and thanking me. Leave that to Surekha and your Baba,' Malak said graciously with a laugh. 'Look, Bombay is a big place. You must be careful. Have you learnt some wrestling or self-defence?'

'Malati and Kamala used their lathi–lezim move to defend me against the dacoits in Desaikheda,' Baba said proudly.

'I am ready to brandish other weapons too including for fighting the British,' Malati said self-importantly.

'I don't want any of us from the family to be involved in any anti-British activity. Is that understood? You will endanger us here and yourself there,' Malak said. The girls nodded.

23

BECOMING ELPHINSTONIANS

The grand Victoria Station welcomed them to famed Bombay. Noisy, sweaty masses of brown people rushed out of steaming trains onto the wide streets of Bombay. Malati and Kamala gazed in wonder at the impressive, high-ceilinged glass, iron and brick building. The imposing facade of the station, its splendid stone dome, turrets, and pointed arches, a fine mix of Indo-British architecture, they were told.

The poorer passengers left by foot, tonga, or cycle rickshaw for their hovels. The white sahebs and their mems—and there were more of them than the girls had ever laid eyes upon—smartly walked past them into magnificent Victoria carriages that put to shame the wobbly tongas of Indore and even Vaishali. They looked at the motor cars in wonder as a privileged few proudly slipped into chauffeur driven ones.

The Vaishali Maharaja's Bombay representative Arjun Dev received them at the station. Baba was relieved to have a guide in this bewildering new place. He took them in a Victoria to the Maharaja's guest house to rest and prepare for their meeting next day with the principal of Elphinstone College, Principal Hamil, an Englishman who would determine their destiny.

As Malati and Kamala stood on the seashore near the guest house, they pensivly watched the mighty sun dim his orange lamp in the sky in gentle preparation for darkness. In that fantastical pink, purple, and blue light, they spied the waves rushing in with shells gathered from the sea's bosom in white lace-edged cups, squandering them on to the Juhu Beach. Malati remembered Ayee telling them as little girls in Ratnagiri to steal the sea's bounty of shells at the sacred sunset hour and listen to them—they speak to you, they recite mantras in your trusting ears, she said. But alas, all the girls could hear at that time was the simple percussion of the ancient sea creatures the shells carried within them—*dhingana, dhin dhin dhingana, dhingana!*

Now in 1925, as young women of seventeen–eighteen years bracing for the most trying period of their lives, they picked up the seashells again—the fan-shaped shell, the spiral cone, the sundial, the cowrie, and yes the unmistakable, trumpet conch shell of Lord Vishnu. This time they did hear the mantras and found the clues to the music of their future—the *shh shh shh* of calm, the *gad gad gad* of ebullience, the *hush hasha hasha* of power, the *dhadak dashak dhak* of affirmation, and the *aahom aahom aahom* sound of benediction. Malati and Kamala felt a surge of confidence, the ebbing of fear.

After dinner, that night, Baba, Arjun, and the girls discussed ways to approach their meeting with the Elphinstone College principal.

'I have had many occasions in life, when I have had to deal with people in authority from an unequal position. My son-in-law as a powerful benefactor, intellectually superior persons like Pandit Sadashiv and Maji, or physically intimidating ones like the dacoits, I had to put up with the racial arrogance of the Gora sahebs, even when I knew we are from a superior civilization. Your English principal tomorrow, your Indian and English professors, and your urbane Bombaykar men classmates will pose similar problems for you,' Baba said.

Kamala and Malati felt intimidated by his preface until Baba smiled and advised, 'Be confident of who you are. Only circumstances differentiate you from others and put them in superior positions. Use your brains, courage, effort, and ingenuity—to change the circumstance enough for you to be in a comfortable place. With your teachers, you can show your mettle and you will be recognized as exceptional. With your peers, nothing is as magnetic as empathy. Forgive small trespasses. Deter bullies by showing they will pay a price for every blow they strike and that like Shivaji you will hit with a retractable waghnakh—a tiger claw—if you don't have cannons.'

'How do we deal with the British?' Kamala asked.

'Be proud heirs to our Indian heritage. At the same time, admire and learn all that is good about the British—their ideas, their science, and their ways of ruling. Eventually, when India becomes free, you can use these learnings to great effect,' Baba counselled.

'Ho Baba,' said Kamala and Malati, the mantras of the seashells still combating the devilish crabs of doubt trying to climb back.

Malati could hardly sleep that night. Tossing and turning in her bed, waking up with the spark of a clever repartee, tormented by the dread of being tongue-tied at a crucial moment, rehearsing her dialogue with the principal and summoning all the gods of the English language to carry her through this imminent ordeal.

The next morning, they got ready and Arjun took them in a Victoria to the college. He pointed to its Gothic-Indian building with the bust of the main funder Rustomji Cowasjee on its facade, the magnificent frontage, the bell tower, and the galleries looking out into the Victoria gardens and the fine detailing in brick and stone. They gawked at the wonders. Passers-by looked at them in amusement and one of them joked: 'Aho! No amrit drops are going to fall from heaven into your mouths but flies could!'

Malati felt as if the veins in her forehead would burst. Her face was drenched in sweat. She tried to wipe it off with her sari padar, but the droplets promptly reappeared threatening to form rivulets. Kamala too was sweating, and their blouses clung to their bodies, not all of it due to the warm sea air of Bombay. Their nine-yard saris stuck to their wet calves, making a flip-flap sound as they walked. Even swift-footed Malati could barely keep pace with Baba and Arjun.

Before they realized it, they stood outside the principal's office and were led immediately in by a liveried peon. No time to compose themselves. An electric fan whirled above their heads, its breeze reviving them a little. A red faced, tall, plump man, Principal Hamil quickly appraised his visitors. He greeted Baba and asked Arjun to translate for him.

'I can do that, sir,' Malati said with a sudden rush of self-belief.

'OK, sure. Please translate faithfully and without blushing when I praise you girls,' Hamil said, kindly.

'Yes, sir, and if I do blush at your praise, you will not detect it on me!' Malati replied, smiling shyly.

'Madhav Rao, I am happy to have brilliant girl students like your daughters admitted to Elphinstone College. We are trying to encourage more Indian women to go for higher education and be torchbearers of social reform,' Hamil said.

Baba expressed gratitude and told him about how passionate he was about girls' education and his work in Guna.

'Yes, I have heard that and I congratulate you for seeking to spread this "contagion" of education. Well, your good deeds will resonate in your daughters' successes and well-being,' Hamil said with genuine respect, showing no disdain for this ordinary farmer in his homespun dhoti, shirt, cap, and rough leather sandals.

'As promised, I have arranged for them to be given a scholarship to cover tuition and living expenses. You know this is going to be a co-educational environment. I am sure you young ladies will be sensible, careful, and worldly wise. Are you ready?' Hamil asked.

The girls nodded enthusiastically, not wanting to admit feeling scared.

'Yes, sir. We will stay on our own, be careful, and adapt quickly. We feel privileged to be able to study in this premier college, be pioneers, and do you proud,' Malati rushed to repeat quickly what she had rehearsed, before the principal changed his mind about them.

'We have been well prepared in the ashram school for the rigours of studying here,' Kamala added confidently.

'That's the way, that's the spirit,' Hamil said, looking pleased.

'I am grateful to you, sir, and to the British for giving a mere farmer's daughters a chance to study in your fine institution and for supporting women's education in India,' Baba said effusively.

'They have earned it. Best of luck, young ladies,' Hamil said graciously.

Kamala and Malati bowed, joined their hands in a namaskar, thanked him again, and returned to the guest house, elated and uneasy at the same time, about their new incarnation as Elphinstonians!

Arjun found them paying guest accommodation in Girgaon at the home of a childless Brahmin couple in their thirties, Hema and Mohan Agashe. They would give them three meals a day and a furnished room with an attached bathroom to stay in. It had a separate entrance and a small terrace overlooking the city. They could not have asked for more.

Baba was uneasy, but Arjun said he could vouch for the Agashes being cultured and honest. Hema Kaki and Mohan Kaka—they asked the girls to call them that—further endeared themselves to him by pledging that they would treat them like their nieces. This was such a quick sewing of relationships between strangers that the girls wondered whether the stitches would give way at the slightest stretch and pull. For now, their assurance was good enough for Baba, and their house was walking distance from their college. So, they moved into the Agashe home. Baba saw Malati and Kamala through another difficult parting.

On the first day of college, as the girls made their way on the path they had memorized, they noticed a young man—handsome, bespectacled, wearing an elegant dhoti and shirt—following them. They wanted to shake him off by taking wrong turns, but Kamala was afraid that they would get lost themselves. So, they walked on, pretending to ignore him.

When they reached the gates of the college and entered, to their surprise their stalker followed them right into their classroom. It was a class of thirty with seven girls. The stalker seated himself just behind them, unconcerned about Malati's withering gaze.

Professor Seal, a red-faced Irishman and professor of history walked into the classroom and introduced himself. He then asked the students to introduce themselves.

Before the first person could answer, Malati impetuously raised her hand and said, 'Sir, I am Malati Desai, I come from Ahilya Ashram School in Indore. I passed my Intermediate in the first division and I love history.'

'Good to know, Malati. But it was not your turn yet to speak,' Professor Seal interrupted her a little sternly. 'Anyway, you can finish now, but in future please follow the order in which you are asked.'

Malati was flustered, but continued her plea.

'Sorry, sir, but I chose to speak out of turn because I wanted to complain about this young man sitting behind me. He has been stalking us all the way from Girgaon to here,' Malati asserted.

There was a hushed silence as if they were watching a ghost pass by! Professor Seal looked amused and said, 'Mr Stalker, would you like to introduce yourself and explain why, on the very first day of college, you gave chase to these pretty young ladies from Girgaon to the classroom?'

'Professor, good morning. I am Guru Kopikar. I am a student in your class, as you can vouch from your attendance register. I live in Saraswat Colony in Gamdevi. I did not intend to follow these ladies, but they crossed my path when I turned onto the road at Girgaon. I was simply walking to college, too, and happened to be behind them,' Guru said and in an instant, he became the hero and Malati looked foolish.

Everyone laughed. Malati was red-faced, almost in tears. Professor Seal asked Malati to apologize to Guru.

Before Malati could get herself to do that, Guru said, 'You do not have to apologize, Miss Desai. It's not your fault. How could you know that this stranger following you was not only a fellow Elphinstonian, but a classmate? You are new to Bombay. It's probably the first time that you two are setting out on your own.'

'OK, that's a gallant young man. You are off the hook, Malati. Just a tip for the future. I know, as young women in a new city you must be vigilant but you must not brand young men as stalkers without checking. And by the way, all girls and boys here in Elphinstone College are allowed to talk to and befriend each other,' said Professor Seal, with a twinkle in his eyes.

'Why must he be magnanimous? Why couldn't he have acted the injured party? Instead, he made himself look wronged and noble and me a peevish, misguided complainant!' Malati said to Kamala later.

'Don't be perverse. He seems to be a man of good character. Considerate, seeing the other's perspective and not putting his ego first. We should be grateful to him for being gracious despite our gross misunderstanding of him. Next time he meets and strikes up a conversation you should apologize to him,' Kamala advised.

After classes, they returned to their new home famished. Hema Kaki was waiting for them and immediately served them a simple and delicious meal of dal, roti, and vegetable curry.

'So, how was your day? Did you like your new college? How are the boys in your class and the Englishmen teachers?' she asked, conspiratorially looking around even though Mohan Kaka was not at home. They answered all her questions and told her about the Guru incident.

'Oh my God. You girls are bold, haan! To get up like that and accuse him in front of the professor! Look, I have never been to a college, I am eighth pass though—don't forget—but it's good to send a message on the first day that you are no nonsense and nirbheek, fearless girls!' she said gleefully.

Malati already liked her and felt she was going to be a friend and counsellor. She was a great cook too. They loved her vegetable curries and dal and soft rotis brushed with ghee. No meat or fish though, as they were vegetarian Brahmins.

Mohan Kaka, a dapper, light-eyed, tall, slim man worked in a British company and was mostly out, working odd hours. He did not have his meals with them. He was aloof, but not unfriendly.

Baba had said wherever you are, compare your place with what was worse before and you will like what you have now and you will be happy. So, it was for Malati and Kamala. The food and their lodging were a great improvement indeed. Their spacious room had two proper string beds with soft mattresses, clean sheets and pillows, and a study table. They did not have to sleep on the floor and they discovered that cold-water baths were a boon, because Bombay did not have a real winter!

Getting to know their professors—mostly Britons—was like crossing rivers of understanding every day! They were delighted and honoured to learn that their English literature teacher was the brother of the famous humourist and writer P. G. Wodehouse. Only the mathematics, Marathi, Sanskrit, and philosophy professors were Indians.

Pandit Shiv Shanker, their Sanskrit professor, called the girls the Auspicious Seven Devis of the BA first year class. All professors tended to nurture them like Baba took care of his delicate medicinal plants. They were concerned perhaps that the girls may be unable to withstand the academic rigour and quit. The girls liked the extra attention but worried that the boys may feel jealous. They even heard them murmur that the girl students were being 'romanced' by the professors. They decided to ignore the gossip.

'But you, Chhabi! You have to be careful not to show adulation as you used to do with Miss Crawford. It may be misinterpreted,' Chandra warned Malati, sniggering.

'Sadly, they are too old for us to romance!' Malati sighed!

∞

One morning, a few weeks later, Malati and Kamala found Guru walking behind them again. He kept a respectful distance and then walked past them. It was clear that he wanted them to come up to him and talk. Neither Guru nor Malati initiated the conversation so Kamala came forward.

'Guru, good morning! Maybe you should walk with us so it does not appear that you are following us, or worse, that we are chasing you!'

'Well, I have no problem as long as Malati does not accuse me of being too forward!'

They all laughed and broke the bowl of awkwardness with a smash.

'I am sorry about that. My fault.'

Malati tendered her apology and they opened the window—not yet a door—to get to know each other.

24

GETTING ACQUAINTED

Guru told them that he lived with his father, brother, and stepmother close to their flat. He was born in Kumta, but grew up in Bombay. This was his city. He went to St. Xavier's Missionary School. He came from a family of lawyers from both his father's and mother's side.

He was fascinated by Kamala and Malati's life story.

'You are real pioneers. I have great respect for your father. He chose the harder road to travel. You know, we have something tragic in common—we lost our mothers whilst they, and we, were still very young. I share your father's revulsion against early marriage and motherhood. I think that killed my dear mother too a year ago,' he said with empathy.

Guru's voice trembled with emotion and his eyes were moist. He appeared to be a sensitive and gentle soul. But then, who would not be emotional, fresh from the tragic, untimely loss of a beloved mother. Six years on, though still hurting, Malati sometimes felt guilty that the pain of Ayee's loss was gradually transforming into flashes of happy memories of time spent with her, not away from her.

'So, sorry for your loss. Our Baba refused to marry again as he felt that a stepmother is by nature callous. Now we look back and thank God and Baba for making that choice,' Kamala said.

'Well, we shall see about my stepmother. She is very young—just three years older to me, so I find it difficult to call her Ayee. She is naturally overwhelmed. So, far she is all right,' he said.

'Look, ladies. I know you are new to Bombay, to studying with boys and mostly British teachers. I too went to an all-boys' school. I have no sisters. So sometimes, I am unaware of how you ladies feel and see things differently from us boys,' Guru said, smiling.

Malati noticed the dimples on his cheeks for the first time making him even more likable. It seemed to Malati that their lives were mirror images to some extent. But he had the privilege of being a Bombaykar.

'And yes, Bombay—the heart of the British Raj, beats to a different pulse from the one we are used to. So, we have much to adjust to apart from academics,' Malati confessed.

'So, do count on me to help you make sense of this new world of boys and girls, of Britons and Indians that we are entering together. Also, I would like to learn from you both,' Guru said with an avuncular air, but also with humility.

They smiled. 'Sure, we are happy to start a knowledge exchange!'

'Good. And I guess there could be nothing better than our walking to and from college as a "moving class".'

'Whenever possible,' replied Kamala, not wanting to commit.

Malati wondered whether it was commonplace that a young man, a total stranger, should bond instantly with two young women from another community and share thoughts and feelings so openly?

Maybe people here intermingled with each other easily across the age-old fault lines of conqueror and conquered, Brahmin or Kshatriya, of being born to a farmer or a lawyer, in Ratnagiri village or the mega city of Bombay, of being women and men—meeting simply as human beings. If that was so, Malati was happy to be in Bombay.

They walked on engrossed in conversation and arrived at the college gates with a new spring in their steps. They still sat apart, but the distance between them as classmates had dissolved.

Malati looked forward to their classes with Pandit Shiv Shanker. He was a consummate boatman ferrying them back on the River of Time to the banks of the classical era of Sanskrit literature. That day, he recited verses from Kalidasa's lyrical play *Meghdootam*—the Cloud Messenger—with clarity and ardour, his voice rising and falling in a quaint, sing-song way.

Malati was completely enraptured and closed her eyes, imagining herself to be the exiled demigod yaksha, pining for his beloved, and travelling with *Meghdootam* over the lands of Bharatvarsha that he so poetically evoked.

'Malati! Are you sleeping?' Panditji's voice startled her out of her reverie.

'No, sir. On the contrary. I was deriving true rasa from your wonderful recitation, the darkness of my closed eyes a perfect backdrop for the vividness of sights, sounds, aromas, and feelings your Kalidasa evoked,' Malati explained with candour.

'Oh! If that is so, which stanza captivated you? Can you also read to

me the stanza following that?' Panditji said, sceptical her explanation.
'Sure, sir,' Malati replied and started reciting.

Twamasar prasabhita vanopallavam sadhu moordhrna

When weary and tired,
You travel along, Oh Cloud!
Rest atop the Amrakuta Mountain
Gladly will he accept
You unburdening yourself
For how can he forget
Your rain that doused his forest fires
The poor and humble
Remember and repay
Each favour, each debt,
All the more then, that one
So exalted will show gratitude

Panditji was taken aback, not so much because Malati proved she was actually listening to him, but that she had memorized it in just one hearing.

'That's surprising! Have you studied Kalidasa's *Meghdootam* before?' he asked.

'No, sir,' Malati said and went on to read the next stanza.

Chhano pantaha parinat fal dhyoti biha kan namre

Oh Cloud! As you move on
Like braids of oiled hair
To the Summit of the Amrakuta Mountain
And mango groves bursting with fruit,
Cover His girth
Heavenly couples passing by
Will imagine that they see
The Earth's own breasts
With dark nipples in the centre
Surrounded by the pale gold of the rest

Malati finished reading, blushed, and sat down. Pandit Shiv Shanker asked everyone to clap and said, 'Malati, that's for your recall, clear pronunciation, and diction. You have a love for Sanskrit, don't you?' he asked.

'Yes, sir, I do. And Kalidasa, I like the most—for he is the Shakespeare of Sanskrit literature,' Malati replied.

'It's the other way around Malati. Shakespeare is the Kalidasa of Europe. Kalidasa came first and his legacy is unmatched. Don't forget, he is the bard of the mother of all Indo-European languages,' said Panditji with pride.

'Yes, sir. We tend to use the British standard for judging our own treasures,' Malati was contrite. Panditji was pleased.

Malati was happy that after her embarrassment on the first day with Guru, she had redeemed herself in the eyes of her classmates, if not yet in the eyes of of Professor Seal.

Professor Wodehouse came in next and he introduced them to the rich and profound heritage of Shakespeare. He picked *Hamlet* as their course book, which the girls had read on their own to impress Miss Crawford. So, they looked forward to this literary trip of reading one of Shakespeare's greatest tragedies—half remembered, half fresh!

Professor Wodehouse started by asking them to recite any passage they knew. Guru recited the most well-known passage from the play with operatic passion:

> To be, or not to be, that is the question:
> Whether 'tis nobler in the mind to suffer
> The slings and arrows of outrageous fortune,
> Or to take arms against a sea of troubles
> And by opposing, end them.

This soliloquy of the Prince of Denmark had always resonated with Kamala and Malati too. Like Guru and Hamlet, they had also borne the slings and arrows of outrageous fortune and lost a parent. Guru had a stepmother to match Hamlet's stepfather! Though thankfully, there the similarity ended.

'I really enjoyed how you turned the tables on Pandit Shiv Shanker. And then, you amazed the whole class with your recitation after hearing the passage just once. You have a gift!' said Guru to Malati admiringly, when they were returning home that evening.

'Oh that! I am a born parrot!' Malati said modestly. 'You recited the iconic speech from *Hamlet* very well, too.'

Guru insisted on seeing them to their house. Hema Kaki was waiting at the door and smiled at him. He greeted her and introduced himself. The girls hurriedly said goodbye and thanked him, signalling that he should leave.

Hema Kaki laughed and asked in a voice loud enough for him to hear, 'So, is this the young man who you accused of following you? Oho! He looks a sajjan—a good man. And he is handsome too—such noble features, broad forehead, big eyes, arched lips, golden complexion, slim and tall. And his dimpled smile, uff! His glasses make him look like a writer.'

'Hema Kaki! The way you talk will make Mohan Kaka jealous,' Malati teased her.

'Oh, he will desire me and value me more if I appreciate other men!' she said coquettishly, her face flushed pink and her eyes rolling with mirth.

'Who are you, Hema Kaki? So full of life and sparkling bright!' Kamala said, teasing her.

'I tell you, if I had been able to go to college like you, I would have done justice to it. But, of course, I can do that through you two—my daughters now!' she said.

At every mealtime, when Mohan Kaka was not back from work, Hema Kaki came into her own.

'Hey, girls. Listen. Let's make a deal. I will serve you a delicacy every day in exchange for an anecdote or two about your college! And you must teach me English so I can talk to Mohan Kaka's British colleagues' wives,' she said.

'It's a deal,' the girls said, licking the raw jackfruit curry off their fingers.

'I have no children to show off, nor am I beautiful, but this way I can make your Mohan Kaka proud of me,' she said.

'Hema Kaki, but you are so beautiful!' Malati said.

Hema Kaki kissed Malati's forehead. 'See, that is why I love you girls.'

Mohan Kaka came in just then, greeted them formally, and asked whether they were comfortable.

'Yes, thank you. Hema Kaki is taking such good care of us,' Kamala said.

'I am sure! She has nothing better to do!' he said with a touch of sarcasm.

'Don't say that, Mohan Kaka. She does so much work in the house and takes care of you,' Malati rose to her defence.

'Oh, so you have converted these college-going girls into your pathrakhins, have you?' he said, a little menace in his voice.

The light went out of Hema Kaki's face.

'They befriend me. I am looking after them,' she explained, stung by the pathrakhin reference.

'Mohan Kaka, she is the best hostess, and we have adjusted to Bombay only because we can come back to your home. We are grateful to you too, for hosting us and being so enlightened,' Kamala the Wise rose to the occasion to diffuse the tension.

Mohan Kaka relaxed, and beaming said, 'Well, I work for the British, you know. So, I am liberal about women's education. Others may not have allowed single girls to stay in their homes like this.'

'Thank you, Mohan Kaka,' the girls said in unison and headed upstairs. Not all may be well in this paradise, the girls thought.

∽

It was almost a year since the girls had come to Bombay and to Elphinstone College. Their friendship with Guru continued but they made friends with other boys in their class too.

On the sports field, Chandra and Malati partnered with Vivek and Shyam—the Kaul twins—in badminton. The twins were champion players but deigned to play with the girls—the only two sportswomen in class. After all, the sight of girls wearing saris tucked tightly around their waists, prancing around on the badminton court gave them the triple pleasure of doing a novel thing, a mild contest, and a spectator sport! Kamala joked that they thought they could defeat Malati easily on the court, while they could not defeat her in the classroom where she outperformed them. Malati practised hard, so that one day she would beat them on the court too.

Guru was no sportsman and after class went to the library or to the drama society. When Malati criticized him, Kamala said with a grin, 'Not everyone has a talent for sports. He is an intellectual like me. He really loves plays, and I hear he is trying to stage a play in the college. We could get roles in it!'

Since coming to Bombay, they had read Marathi novels and plays and had heard so much about the vibrant theatre scene there. Men played women's roles and wore bangles, literally. It was rather brave of them. It took a strong man to surrender the male ego, did it not? To transform into a woman—considered a lesser being—even for a few hours a day.

Malati was very curious to see a play where this transformation was on display.

'Your Mohan Kaka is an aficionado of musical plays but he says decent women don't go to see plays,' Hema Kaki told them.

'Why? Are they afraid we will fall in love with the men who act as women or we will catch men rasikas falling in love with the nata-nayikas?' Malati asked, sarcastically.

Hema Kaki laughed. Malati promised she would take Hema Kaki to see a musical play with Mohan Kaka. Hema Kaki hugged her.

'Oh, I love you bold and crazy girls. It might just work,' Hema Kaki said.

Later, when they were alone, Kamala admonished Malati. 'How can you raise false expectations in the poor woman? I get a nasty feeling that her husband bullies her more because she is childless. I am quite suspicious about his job that keeps him away from the house for such long hours and late into the night.'

'She is so good to us. Let's ask for Guru's help,' said Malati.

'Oh Malati, you are a kind troublemaker,' Kamala exclaimed.

As soon as they met Guru, Malati made the request, and saw a glint in his eye behind his spectacles. A spark had been lit in him.

'Well, the reigning king, or should I say queen, of Marathi Sangeet Natak, these days is Bal Gandharva—the Celestial Singer. He transforms seamlessly into every woman character he plays.'

'Are there no women actors in plays?' Kamala asked.

'No, respectable women don't join men's theatre. There are some all-women theatre groups. But the crowds go there only to ogle at women and to be in a closed space with women other than their wives, sisters, or mothers. My father forbade me to attend lest I set up liaisons with the actresses. Ha, ha,' Guru explained.

'OK, so please please get us to see Bal Gandharva's plays for Hema Kaki's sake,' Malati pleaded.

'I suspect, Malati, you are more eager to go yourself. I will do it,' Guru replied, looking at her searchingly.

A few days later, Guru brought his friend Arvind whose father had a stake in Gandharva Natya Mandali to meet them. He suggested that he could smuggle them in and make them sit at the back.

'But why should we be smuggled into the theatre like contraband goods? Women audiences should make it more profitable for them. We can set a trend. After all, we have heard that Bal Gandharva has set trends in clothes, jewellery, and social mores. It would help in making Bal Gandharva known beyond existing rasika circles,' Kamala argued. Beneath the veneer of an aesthete, Arvind was a shrewd businessman, and he instantly bought their idea.

25

THE CELESTIAL SINGER

Kamala and Malati rushed home in great excitement to tell Hema Kaki that she should get ready to attend the *Ekach Pyala* play the next evening. Kamala used her tact to persuade Mohan Kaka to join them for the show, arguing that they would only go if Mohan Kaka introduced them to the cultural heart and soul of Bombay.

Hema Kaki cleverly feigned ignorance and said, 'But how can I go? There is so much to do at home.'

'Nonsense, Hema. We will all go if the girls are so keen. After all, we owe it to them as their guardians,' Mohan Kaka said.

Malati was delighted but also nervous about this adventure. Kamala asked her to be confident that everything will go according to plan. She joked that Malati was more excited about being a pioneering woman rasika than enjoying Bal Gandharva's music.

The next day, they rushed home after class and found Hema Kaki all dressed up in her best silk paithani sari, jewellery, and jasmine gajra. They dressed up themselves. Guru arrived to accompany them. He complimented Hema Kaki on her radiant look and the girls on their being transformed into Bombay ladies!

'Bal Gandharva may ask you to come up on stage and sing,' he said earnestly.

'Agabai! I can't sing and Papi is out of practice,' Malati fretted.

Guru laughed. 'I was only teasing you.'

Mohan Kaka failed to show up. They reached the theatre just in time and Arvind received them, looked at them with approval, and ushered them straight to the front row. They would be in Bal Gandharva's line of vision!

Hema Kaki was wide-eyed with excitement at being the only women in the theatre and wondered whether the drama company would be forced to throw them out. Malati assured her that since they had been given a pride of place, no one would want to disrupt the event.

She kept looking at the door for Mohan Kaka. Despite this, Malati suspected that she seemed to be quite happy that he was not there to make her feel less than herself and enjoying the freedom. Guru sat next to Malati. He seemed as excited as they did, having broken through a wall.

The men in the audience stared at them. It was as if they too were 'staged' as Guru noted, but thankfully, there were no protests, only polite curiosity. Many men were on their own and others came with their friends. The lighting was subtle with flares on the sides; the audience was in half darkness, except those in the front rows like them. The silken curtains opened. The play began. Bal Gandharva the illusionist spread his web of maya right before their credulous eyes.

The fervent contest between the half-woman and half-man incarnated in the fused being of the Ardhanarishwar, enthralled Malati and Kamala from the very first scene when Bal Gandharva appeared as Sindhu, a middle-class housewife. His muscular body vied with the graceful flow of his Maheshwari cotton sari with its reversible bugdi border, its padar casually flung across his wide shoulders. This even as he delicately twisted its edge with a demure, sideways glance at the uncaring 'husband'.

The sleeves of his checked 'khan blouse' seductively clasped his firm biceps when he held up his hand heavenwards, seeking the benediction that never came. As he touched his padded breasts to express Sindhu's heartache, his tall erect form seemed to melt away like the hearts of his rasikas. His long manly strides across the stage, jostled with his consciously cultivated, nubile, feminine gait.

His powdered pale face caught Sindhu's sorrow, his cheeks nevertheless bloomed with the rouge of rapturous suffering. His painted lips parted in both pain and song. The crystalline pools of his kohl lined eyes, beseeched pitifully even as the kunku dot on his forehead confessed to Sindhu's lifelong bondage in marriage—come what may.

The wig with a round bun ensured that the irrepressible fuzz on his face and assertive thick eyebrows had no chance of betraying his masculinity and dominance. His deep, powerful voice sounded incongruous sometimes when he spoke for the meek Sindhu, but when he sang her songs of hope, he believably sublimated them into celestial notes.

The artifice of his cross-dressing was only one part of the maya he created—that of a loving, all sacrificing wife of Sudhakar who was spurred by his evil friend Teliram towards self-destruction. In her unquestioning submission to a deeply flawed husband as her supreme master and destiny, Sindhu came through as a tragic hero, fighting until the end with her faith and fate! Paradoxically, the songs by Bal Gandharva, just lifted them out of the sense of despair Sindhu's condition invoked.

Kashiya taju padala, mum shubhaga shubh padala.
Narak hi ghor saha kanta, ho swarg mala aata—

How can I, as his wife,
Leave my husband's sacred and auspicious feet.
When I am with him,
Hell is bearable and seems like heaven to me.

As Bal Gandharva sang the signature song joyfully, the incongruity of an insensate, inebriated Sudhakar, oblivious to the suffering he was causing his wife and yet inspiring such devotion from her, did not seem to disturb the rasikas present, except the newest ones.

After several encores, the play ended at midnight to thunderous applause. Guru was crying.

Malati turned to him with a smile and said, 'Hey, Guru, don't waste your tears on this make-believe tragedy.'

'At moments like this, I see my mother in every woman who suffers or dies. See, Malati, look around you at other men—I am not alone,' he said.

'You know, Guru, I have no sympathy for a woman who thinks being submissive and long suffering is a supreme virtue! Why should Sindhu be glorifying her sorry state as heaven?' Malati asked Guru.

He was taken aback by her questioning.

'You see the Indian wife is so dependent on her husband, she has no way out if he is trapped in hell himself. Moreover, it is a testament to her strength of character that she stays steadfast to him,' he replied.

'But being subservient is her weakness not strength—never mind Bal Gandharva's edifying Sindhu act,' Malati asserted.

Before he could answer, Arvind came to take them backstage to meet Bal Gandharva. They were delighted to meet the maestro in person. He smiled at them indulgently and said, 'So you are my first women rasikas. Did you derive rasa as much as the men did?'

'Your singing was divine, Guruji, and, of course, your acting transported me to another world,' Kamala gushed.

'And how did Sindhu's story inspire you?' he asked.

'Too tragic for me. Sindhu should have been more of a Durga.

I would like to see your more happy and assertive avatars,' Malati dared to say.

He looked surprised. 'Of course. Come and see other, more happy plays and those with a social message like Sangeet Sharda on widow remarriage. We will open my plays to women from now on,' he said.

Malati clapped her hands in glee like a little girl and then blushed when Bal Gandharva patted her head.

Hema Kaki too was emboldened to speak. 'I can't believe I am in your presence. It seems like a dream! You are a true Celestial Singer!' Hema Kaki bent to touch his feet in respect.

He moved back. 'No no. My rasikas are the ones I bow to,' he beamed at her and folded his hands. 'Your patronage is my reward.'

When they trooped out of the theatre, Mohan Kaka was waiting for them. He apologized and explained that he could not get away from work and asked how they had reached the theatre. He looked at Hema Kaki who was still basking in the afterglow of watching Bal Gandharva on stage and meeting the maestro in person.

Hema Kaki explained it all and said they had kept a seat vacant for him till the end.

'Oh, looks like you enjoyed it even though it's a tragedy!' he said.

They introduced Guru to him.

'As their local guardian, I must know who they are befriending,' he said and proceeded to shoot a quiverful of questions at him—who he was, what family and caste, where he lived, etc. He looked impressed when Guru, unfazed, answered all his questions.

'Oh, so you are a Brahmin! Like me. So, what are you doing befriending these Kshatriya girls?'

'Well, how is a Brahmin like you their Kaka and local guardian?'

Mohan Kaka laughed. 'You and I are going to get on very well. You seem to be an intellectual, a rasika like me, and a witty Brahmin, and we are now connected to each other by our association with these two splendid Maratha ladies. I will take it from here and escort the three ladies home in a Victoria.'

They thanked Guru profusely and went with Mohan Kaka on a Victoria ride of Bombay at night—or rather in that bewitching hour when it is neither night nor dawn yet! The sight of a Bombay half-asleep in darkened buildings and half-awake on its lamp-lit streets, capped the excitement of that memorable evening.

They barely spoke on the way back, each of them for their own reasons. Mohan Kaka probably felt his redundancy now. Hema Kaki was trying to suppress, not express her happiness, just in case Mohan Kaka scorched it with his sarcasm. Kamala and Malati savoured their little victory on behalf of Hema Kaki in silence.

'OK, ladies. We are home,' Mohan Kaka broke the silence.

'Thank you, Mohan Kaka. We missed you at the play. Hope you will take us there another time!' Kamala said tactfully, to allay his resentment towards them all.

Mohan Kaka looked pleased and said, 'Well, I will definitely treat you to another happier play.'

The girls bid them goodnight, went up to their rooms, and fell asleep instantly.

When they came down the next morning, Hema Kaki was not there. Strangely, Mohan Kaka served them their breakfast. He explained that she was not well, resting, and was not to be disturbed and that he did not encourage such outings for her because she could not take the exertion well.

Guru joined the girls on their walk to college. They were still suffused with the pleasure of their once-in-a-lifetime experience.

'I am glad you enjoyed the play! But I am a little worried about your Mohan Kaka. He is a deep one! He did not turn up and praised you two while looking at his wife to make her joy evaporate! I feel sorry for Hema Kaki,' Guru said.

Malati told him about Hema Kaki not appearing for breakfast that morning.

'They have been married for years. We have only just arrived, so let us not rush to judge them or their marriage,' Kamala said sagely as always.

Malati however requested Guru to check whether Mohan Kaka worked at the Britannia Company and where he went after office.

When they returned home, Hema Kaki, to their pleasant surprise, was singing a Bal Gandharva song.

'Hema Kaki, what a wonderful voice you have!' Malati exclaimed.

'Don't you girls praise me! Don't make me so brave and carefree that I will fly and sing like a kokila bird and risk having my wings cut, my neck twisted, my voice silenced,' she said.

'What do you mean, Hema Kaki?' they asked puzzled.

'My heart will burst if I don't tell you something I have kept secret all this while,' she said. 'I used to be a well-known singer in Pooe. Your Mohan Kaka heard me sing and fell in love with me. I ran away with him, we came to Bombay and got married.'

'Oh, I knew such a wonderful voice must belong to a trained singer!' said Kamala. 'Why did you give it up?'

Hema Kaki then explained that Mohan Kaka had made it a condition to their marriage to hide her identity as he was a Brahmin and she was not. Coming from a singing community, she would be looked down upon. She confessed to secretly practising her singing but she was not allowed to sing to Mohan Kaka as he was afraid it would make him change his mind. What a travesty of love and talent this was, thought Malati.

They noticed that her pink face had traces of redness and she had bruises on her arms. She followed their gaze and covered her arms with her sari. Kamala grabbed her arm to examine it.

'Don't hide or glorify your pain. Don't be a Sindhu!' Malati chided her.

'It's my entire fault. I should not have left the house and re-entered that world of music. I was carried away, Malati. So, when we returned, I couldn't help asking your Kaka whether I could start practising my music again. He exploded. He said he did not want me to slip into ignominy again. Well, he was a bit rough with me,' she finally confessed.

They felt enraged. All they could do for now was to embrace her and put a balm on her wounded psyche.

Mohan Kaka came home early for a change and had dinner with them. There was an uneasy silence at first. He was all praise for Hema Kaki's cooking though and awkwardly tried to humour her.

Malati asked Mohan Kaka about his day, and he explained how the British were demanding masters, but recognized and rewarded merit and hard work. He always tried to show them that Indians were not indolent shirkers but that meant Hema Kaki had to stay alone for long hours. He was glad that she now had the girls' company.

He then informed them that Arjun had asked him for a report on how the girls had been doing in studies and other activities. When they assured him that they were doing well in studies, sports, and music, he suddenly asked, 'Staying out of man trouble, I hope?'

'Kaka, we study with men, play sports with them. They are no trouble. We are no trouble to them either,' Malati joked in response.

'You are going to give them a brilliant report, are you not, just as we are going to give a good report about you to Arjun and our brother-in-law. They hold you in high regard!' Malati added putting on her most innocent face and looking at Hema Kaki.

'Of course. It works both ways,' he agreed.

The girls made sure that secretly they built Hema Kaki's confidence by encouraging her to practise singing regularly, dig out her vast repertoire of bhakti geet, natya sangeet, thumri, and ghazals so she could be ready for the stage. They held out the hope of finding an impresario who would enable her to reach large audiences of rasikas—which was vital, as she said, to rediscovering her muse.

Guru was not surprised when they told him about their discovery.

'While you three ladies were engrossed in watching the play, I was looking at each of you. Malati was hungrily absorbing everything as a pure rasika. Kamala was engaging as a student of music. And Hema Kaki was singing along tunefully under her breath. Now it adds up. She is an original celestial singer herself.'

∽

A few days later, Guru came to Malati and Kamala very excited and informed them that while it was true that Mohan Kaka worked in a senior position in the Brittania Company he was spotted visiting a satyagrahi's house after work every day, possibly to do some clandestine work. The girls were surprised but exclaimed that Britannia was a perfect cover!

The girls took Guru home and got Hema Kaki to sing a Sangeet Saubhadra song, 'Priye Paha', Lord Krishna's ode to his wife Satyabhama after a night of cajoling. She instantly obliged.

Priye paha ratricha samaya saruni
Yeta Usha kaal ha

Oh, look dearest! How the Night has passed
And the Queen of Dawn has arrived
How forgetting the world's joys and sorrows
We had all gone to sleep
On waking up,
They come back to claim us.

26

SUNFLOWER FACES THE SUN

Guru, a seasoned rasik, was very impressed with Hema Kaki's singing.

'Hema Kaki, your voice should not be stifled within the four walls of this house. It must please the ears and storm the hearts and minds of rasikas everywhere. You have to cross the threshold of your home and climb onto the stage in the world outside. I will ask Arvind to help and persuade Mohan Kaka,' he said.

Hema Kaki smiled a hesitant assent, fear still writ large in her eyes. Just as Guru was about to leave, Mohan Kaka arrived unexpectedly. Hema Kaki got up hastily. Picking up her tanpura, she scurried inside. He looked both puzzled and annoyed.

'What is this "ghost of singing" that you have stuffed into Hema's head?' he asked the girls in a stern voice.

'Mohan Kaka, with due respect, if music is the reason you fell in love with her, why don't you let her sing? Hema Kaki's gayaki, her singing talent, is not a ghost to be exorcised. It is a divine sunflower to be nurtured and allowed to face the sun of audience appreciation,' Malati said.

'Yes, Kaka. She has been faithful to your love by bearing the darkness of silence, denying herself and you the sunlight of music. Why? Nobody here knows where she comes from or who she is. You have already given her a new name. She can sing for plays or give concerts with your guidance,' Kamala pressed on.

'These days even respectable ladies from Brahmin families are giving performances and I could ask my friend to introduce her to some impresarios,' added Guru.

They expected a volcanic eruption in response. Instead, Mohan Kaka was quiet and looked thoughtful.

After a moment he called out: 'Hema!'

Hema Kaki came running, flustered and apologetic, and stood before him, head bowed, bracing for a death sentence on her singing aspirations.

'Well, this moment had to come. I was holding back a dam burst from Hema for far too long. So, in the form of these girls, Goddess Saraswati is opening the dams and commanding you to unleash your musical talent. Prepare yourself. I will do what I can, and Guru, please do ask your friends to help,' Mohan Kaka said with a sigh.

A sigh of relief, or of worry? Malati wondered.

Malati impulsively took Hema Kaki's and Mohan Kaka's hands and brought them together. Kamala and Malati covered them in a collective embrace, leaving both of them embarrassed and Guru amused.

Guru followed up with Arvind and they introduced her to some natya mandalis. Hema Kaki was launched as a rediscovered artist as Hirabai—diamond—mined by Mohan Kaka. She played the role of Subhadra in the *Saubhadra* play enacted by a women's natya mandali. She went to Bal Gandharva to seek his blessings, and was thrilled when he asked her to sing his favourite song. She sang the first two lines, but he stopped her.

'Wah, Hirabai. But for me mere good is not perfection! Crackle with the betrayal Subhadra feels towards the shawl, which she personifies and accuses of being an arasik—lacking all aesthetic sensibility. You have to radiate emotion and Subhadra's longing for Arjun when you sing!' he said.

Hirabai sang with a new passion:

Arasik kiti ha shela, agabai!
Hya sunder tanu la soduni ala......

Oh my friend,
How I have resented this unaesthetic shawl
That I had presented to my beloved Arjun
How could it bear to part from his pristine body
I shall now punish it
By locking it away
For I want the cursed, cruel drape
To be out of my sight forever

'That's like my acolyte! Go forth and be fulfilled!' Bal Gandharva said.

'I promise to do that, Guru Dev. You have inspired me to sing again!'

Mohan Kaka weaned himself away for a while from the world

he traversed between his British boss and his swadeshi friends. He spent more time with his rediscovery, Hirabai. He had a new respect for her.

Malati was very grateful to Guru and praised him to his face for the first time.

'Guru, thank you, for what you did for Hema Kaki. I see that your friendships are very deep and heartfelt.'

'Well, that's the least I can do. I don't have much to give. No money, no treats, just a caring heart, a willing ear, and sincere counsel when friends need it. My friends know that the favours I ask of them are also based on a shared passion—for poetry, music, drama, or just human bonding,' Guru replied, and added, 'but you are a do-gooder, too, Malati. Those you love and care for, you are loyal to them and go out of your way to help. I admire your boldness, the way you speak up and advocate for people and causes without fear or guile.'

Malati tried not to be pleasantly disrupted by Guru's affectionate gaze and his praise of her. But an effervescent Hema Kaki rushed to join the conversation.

'I agree. Don't you also like her ingenuity in spotting a story behind people as she did in my case?' asked Hema Kaki.

'Of course! And the way she spins a yarn and the amusingly graphic details with which she enacts people's idiosyncrasies and mannerisms! Have you seen her imitate our professors? Or some of our classmates!' said Guru.

'Yes! But don't think she does not imitate you....' Hema Kaki teased.

'Hema Kaki stop!' Malati cried.

'Why? Guru should know how you bring out his bookish approach, gullibility, sentimentality, and avoidance of sports in your imitation of him,' Hema Kaki said mischievously.

Guru's smile vanished and he turned to Malati and said, 'Well it's better that than being insensitive, cold and aloof, blunt and opinionated, strong-willed and obstinate, like you sometimes are!'

Hema Kaki realized she had incited a storm. 'Hey Guru, she also sprays the perfume of praise from her attardaan on you, haan! Just as you drizzle yours on her! One thing I know for sure. Both of you seem to simmer with vivacity when you are with each other! I even detect a tremor—*val val val*—of the heart when you try to meet each other every day!'

Malati and Guru both looked bashful and Guru murmured, 'Well as long as our faults and oddities do not cloud out our endearing qualities in each other's estimation!'

Kamala who was watching this exchange later remarked to Malati, 'Hema Kaki is right about Guru and you. I have noticed how he singles you out for praise and indulgently smiles at me every time he does so.'

'Well, you are a witness, participant, and mediator sometimes, in all that happens between Guru and me, which anyway is not much beyond words and glances. I could, however, turn around and complain that I am not as "included" in your friendship with Ram,' Malati responded.

Kamala was indeed getting close to Ram, the slightly built Kokansatha Brahmin boy with a brooding demeanour. If he did not wear a dhoti and a puneri cap, he could have passed for an Englishman with his fair skin and grey blue eyes. Trade with Europe had been going on for centuries along India's west coast and he joked that he was a living symbol of the intermingling that happened!

Their friendship was blossoming as they engaged in intellectual discourses over philosophy. They made an ideal pair—the delicate, fair-skinned, slim, and petite Kamala complementing him perfectly.

'So, Papi, you and Ram seem to have struck a chord. I suppose it is easy to bond by seeking answers to the purpose of our existence and the nature of the universe itself,' Malati teased her.

'I must admit to a passion for philosophy, and none better than Ram to understand and expound on it, in all its glorious complexity,' Kamala admitted. 'When we are together, we are often in a trance. In the company of the greats of Western, Hindu, and Buddhist philosophers—Socrates, Aristotle, Descartes, Kant, Nietzsche, Yagnavalkiya, Shankaracharya, Rishi Kapila, and the Buddha—we have stimulating debates,' she said.

'Are you elevating Ram to their level? Well, I must grant that he is brilliant and no one in class can match his philosophical insights. On the other hand, if anyone can don the mantle of Gargi and Maitreyi—women philosophers of Vedic India, who could contest men in philosophical debates—it is you. One path, two destinations reached!' Malati remarked looking into her eyes.

'What do you mean? For me it is only my love for philosophy, not the philosopher!' she replied, laughing.

'For now. But not for long will you be able to separate them. For I detect a cold flame burning between you and Ram fuelled by philosophy, but now drawing from the passion of the flesh too. His grey blue eyes reflecting themselves in your brown ones. The arrows of your arguments colliding in mid-air with a zing, breaking and falling to the ground in a philosophical recreation of the Mahabharata battles. Your lips turned up in triumphant smiles for points won, but at times for points lost to win hearts!' Malati asserted.

Kamala waved Malati off, pretending to take this teasing lightly. But in her heart, she knew it was all true.

For both Kamala and Malati, however, these were early days with Ram and Guru. They told themselves that they were too young, too inexperienced in the ways of young men and of Bombay. In keeping with Baba's injunctions on 'abstinence' from men and marriage, they did not want anyone to read much into this.

Moreover, as Hema Kaki acknowledged, Malati and Kamala were no sunflowers needing to face the sun of Guru and Ram. They were spinning out from the nebula of their new universe, becoming sun disks to send forth their own light.

Malati soon got busy with sports. She had badminton practice with Chandra and the Kashmiri brothers after class and had been in good form, mostly due to the inspiration of her ebullient partner, Shyam. Chandra's enthusiasm came from her increasing affection for the other brother, Vivek. Vivek was her doubles partner and their post-game strategy sessions were getting more and more intense.

One evening, Mohan Kaka came home in great agitation and told the girls about the botched Kakori train robbery carried out by HRA revolutionaries on 9 August 1925 and how in the questioning of those arrested, the Central Provinces, and specifically the Vaishali–Guna connection, was revealed. Apparently, many of those involved, including Ram Prasad Bismil and Ashfaqallah Khan, had stayed in Guna area and drawn resources, including arms, bombs, and money from there for their revolutionary activities. Some said they may have hatched the conspiracy there too and that revolutionaries may still be hiding there.

'I hope it does not lead to any retaliatory and punitive action against the Maharaja of Vaishali and your brother-in-law—his trusted minister—by the British. The sword of annexation by the British always looms over their heads, but they are capable of worse!' said Mohan Kaka.

The girls did not reveal what they knew but scanned the photos of those arrested in the Kakori case in the newspapers. They were alarmed to spot the bangle seller and Pravesh Babu though they seemed to have to have gone by other names. They were fearful for Malak now.

Bombay was also heating up, with Gandhiji's Non-cooperation Movement, gathering traction. They did get restless when they came across freedom fighters—young men and women who wore khadi, espoused swadeshi and swarajya, distributed pamphlets, and canvassed them to join. They were however compelled to follow Malak's injunctions to stay away—for now.

Meanwhile Guru's home life was becoming more dismal. When Malati and Kamala asked him why he looked particularly depressed one day, he poured out his grievances against his stepmother, Mai. After the tragedy of his mother's death, his father, Appa's sisters, were cruel to him and his brother Ganesh, starved them, and even branded Ganesh's hands with hot tongs when he asked for more food. But they were not prepared for what came in the form of their new mother.

He had initially empathized with her but when she went out of her way to target Guru and poison his father's mind against his sons, he had revulsion for her. He wondered what made Appa blind and uncaring about the torture Mai was subjecting them to. Guru knew Appa as a self-absorbed lawyer intellectual, but he could not accuse him of being passionate about his stepmother.

Malati interjected mischievously that not getting enough passion from her older husband may be Mai's problem. Guru looked curiously at her and agreed. He confessed that Mai resented Guru's not warming up to her. That is why he took care to lock his room at all times to give no excuse to her to create misunderstanding between him and Appa.

'How do you counter her misbehaviour?' Malati asked.

'Each issue is a different battlefield. During our meals, we made sure that our father eats with us. I taught my brother to eat a mouthful of rice and curry and ask for some more curry, because the rice was too dry. Once she gave more dal and curry, he asked for more rice because it was too wet and runny! So, she finally gave up the extra labour and started serving us ample amounts from the beginning,' recounted Guru.

They all laughed, but Malati felt sorry.

He disclosed that once or twice Mai had tried to argue that Guru was 'a grown horse' and could do with less 'grazing' to which Appa had quipped that he should be fed more kulith—horse gram soup—for all the running around and brainwork he did. When Malati noted that Appa perhaps considered him a high-performance racehorse as his first-born son, Guru admitted that his father wanted him to become a lawyer like him.

Guru further revealed that Ganesh looked for ways to ingratiate himself with Mai, so he could be at least spared harsh treatment. Mai made him spy on Guru. So, he fed Ganesh harmless pieces of information to pass onto her!

Listening to Guru's woes about his stepmother made Malati and Kamala think that the malefic power to destroy seemed to be greater and more to be feared, than the power to spawn love and togetherness was to be coveted!

27
THE EXALTED BOMBAY COMPANY

As newly-minted, one-year-old Bombaykars, Malati and Kamala had barely scratched the surface of the many-splendoured Bombay society. Their social circle was limited to the Agashes and their friends—which not surprisingly were a select few from the Britannia Company or from among closet freedom fighters. The girls had to be careful in mingling with them. In college, they made friends, but none, neither Guru nor the Kaul twins and not even Chandra had called them home or to social gatherings to introduce them to their families and friends, let alone to icons of the times—British or Indian—they had boasted about knowing.

They were disappointed that Chandra—someone who was one of their best friends, a bridge to their past and who knew their worth, had not deemed it necessary to initiate them into the rituals of more sophisticated and elite social circles of a city she called her own. Maybe, they were not ready for the 'social fire test' and Chandra did not want to embarrass them and herself, they reasoned. Remembering what Baba had told them about dealing with those seemingly superior in their life in Bombay, they patted themselves on the back for making as much of a social leap as they already had.

They were therefore pleasantly surprised and felt vindicated when Chandra invited them to her home for a social gathering before they left for Vaishali and came with Vivek in her motor car to pick them up! Hema Kaki and Mohan Kaka were overawed to be introduced to Chandra, the daughter of eminent Prarthana Samaj affiliated Bhandarkar family and Vivek, a judge's son—from an elite part of the girls' social circle.

Chandra stoked their interest even more when she announced that among the guests would be Jehangir Petit, music lover, patriot, mill owner, Mahatma Gandhi devotee, and philanthropist. Malati had told Hema Kaki earlier how he had funded the Bombay Symphony Orchestra that had just been launched by London-trained German conductor, Edward Behr bringing together local Indians to play in the orchestra 'of the people and by the people'.

Chandra had boasted about attending its brilliant first performance at the famous Excelsior Theatre in Bombay. Behr was looking to encourage experiments in fusing Western and Indian music in the future. Hema Kaki lost no time in requesting the girls to take up her musical launch with Mr Petit and Chandra told Malati to do so at their forthcoming lunch.

'Oh! And I have a bigger surprise for you both. You will meet someone you would never have dreamt of meeting,' Chandra said.

'The freedom fighter of two continents, though not born Indian, she wants to be reincarnated as one in her next life. Named the avatara of Saraswati, she combines spiritualism with politics and became the first woman president of the Indian National Congress.'

'I can't believe it. Our heroine and goddess, Annie Besant?' Malati exclaimed, jumping up and down, clapping her hands!

They got into Chandra's shiny, big Wolseley. 'Meet the perfect 10 motor car,' Chandra said.

'Am more than pleased to meet this wonder. Do you know it is a first for us—sitting in this handsome black and silver motor car, with its biscuit leather and wood interiors; to be seen in it, be framed by this epochal abstract art of steel and glass in a welter of geometric shapes—the squares, the rectangles, the arches! Surely a novel, "moving experience",' Malati said, quite carried away.

'Chhabi, you invest art and life into a mere machine!' Chandra teased her.

'I don't agree. Abstract art, even cubism, has been inspired by these modern inventions of cars, planes, and telephones. Is it not a "new way of seeing", about surprise, about disturbing the well-worn ideas of aesthetics?' Malati explained.

Vivek finally spoke up.

'As a young man, I do see art as life and life as art in a car! Besides fine engineering taking us places, smoothly and faster!'

'I see the car more as a moving art exhibit, with pictures of things we pass by, getting framed by its windows,' said Kamala, grinning at Malati.

'Bagh han, Papi, you are making fun of me!' Malati cried petulantly.

'No, on the contrary, I am justifying both yours and Chandra's perceptions according to philosopher Kant that since the senses do not think, but understanding does, both sensibility—aesthetic—and understanding—logic—must come together!'

All three of them looked at Kamala in awe.

Vivek sat in front with the chauffeur and the girls sat in the back—holding hands like old times. Kamala and Malati were brimming over with anticipation, a little nervous, about how to conduct themselves in such 'exalted Bombay Company'. Chandra felt the sweat on their hands.

'Aga bai! There is no reason to be nervous. It's my home you are coming to,' she said reassuringly.

'In Indore, remember, we used to welcome you into our home—the ashram. You were the guests! Now, the roles are reversed,' Malati replied smiling.

The car stopped in front of the magnificent Windsor multistorey, seaside building. They got out of the car and entered the grand lobby. Shyam was at the entrance waiting to receive them.

'Welcome! I missed you, Malati. How are you?' Shyam asked.

'We are fine. Good to see you all here,' Malati replied.

A beautifully carved iron and wood elevator lifted them effortlessly and landed them on the third floor, right in front of the apartment. Then the cage opened and set them free!

Kamala agreed with Malati that this too was an amalgam of aesthetics as art and logic as utility. 'We feel elevated! The moving cage—another first we had not reckoned with,' Malati said beaming.

Shyam and Vivek exchanged glances. Malati imagined the brothers must regard them as yokels. She shrugged.

Chandra pressed the doorbell. A liveried servant opened the door. Surprisingly the furniture and decor of the spacious apartment they entered was proudly swadeshi. Acclimatized to Bombay's humid heat, not aping cold London's aristocracy. Who wants damp, musty velvet drapes, dusty wool carpets or rusty brass and blackening silver decorations, they seemed to say.

The sofas congregated in a lotus formation on cool inlay work stone floors in the large living room to greet the former Lotus Buds from the ashram, inviting them to cogitate and meditate. The upholstery of blue khadi cloth with motifs of conch shells evoked the home's proximity to the sea. Parrot blue and green Poona saris pretended to drape the windows, looking the other way as the errant sea breeze billowed and rustled through their fine meshes. They also turned and twisted naughtily to allow tantalizing glimpses of the sun speckled waters outside. Large Radha Krishna paintings on walls defied self-proclaimed Hindu sceptic Chandra's preference for pictures of Jesus Christ.

Chandra's tall and elegant parents with an aura of warmth and cordiality came up to greet the girls.

'So, you are the sisters Chandra never had! The beloved and rumbustious Chhabi and the wise and calm Papi we have heard so much about, but were not allowed to actually meet,' said Rupa aunty, almost complaining.

'It's the school that did not allow us to bring the boarders home, Mama,' Chandra said to dispel the impression that she had been embarrassed about them.

'We are happy to finally meet. Congratulations. I believe you both are outstanding in studies. Very creditable for girls with your background,' said Gopal uncle.

'Baba, they are ashram orphans no more but sisters-in-law of a minister from Vaishali. They have seen it all and studied on their own in Bombay for a year. They are more astute than perhaps I am!' Chandra again interceded.

The girls were amused that she contradicted her parents with the authority of 'an only child empress'.

'And now meet the great woman leader of all times, and freedom fighter of two continents, Annie Besant,' said Chandra steering them to the sofa at the centre where she sat beaming at them. Her spiritual radiance and political charisma seemed to wipe away the years from Annie's face. Her 'boy cut' mass of wavy silver hair shouted 'wisdom!' from her crown top. She wore a long-sleeved Western style blouse combined effortlessly with a white cotton sari, reflecting her Irish and Indian duality. She seemed painted in the contrasting colours of serenity and animation.

Seated next to her was a swarthy, handsome young man, with a prominent nose, high forehead, and large penetrating eyes. Two shocks of hair stood like sentinels on either side of his head. They guessed he was the 'philosopher son' with Messianic potential whom she had adopted—Jiddu Krishnamurti. Nurtured by the Theosophists as the head of the 'Order of the Star of the East' to prepare for the coming of a world teacher, he had been making waves.

Jehangir Petit, was there too. He wore the traditional dress and cap of the Parsi community. His exceptionally large ears spoke of his receptivity to music and to the 'far bugles of the freedom movement' as Chandra had described to Malati. His elegant wife in her cream georgette sari with delicately embroidered pink roses on it, had the air of a gracious patroness. Chandra's father introduced them to each diginitary as shining examples of how education takes you places.

'We are great admirers of yours, madam. Whenever there were difficulties in our journey, we were inspired by women like you to push ourselves to the farthest. Your fearless advocacy on women's and girls' rights, including on birth control is so badly needed in India and is a powerful tool for transformation. We salute you for ceaselessly exerting yourself for India's freedom,' Malati said, her face tingling to Annie's intense gaze.

'You educated Indian girls are the wellspring of my life's mission now. The right kind of education is the arrow of Rama—one solution for all that ails India and Indians. My work for India's freedom also includes attaining the two freedoms simultaneously—you cannot have a free India if her women are shackled by ignorance and by men,' Annie Besant replied.

Kamala shared their guilt about studying in college when other young people were joining the freedom movement.

'Look, we need women to be empowered first to help galvanize the freedom movement. You finish your education, and then you must contribute with the capabilities you have acquired,' she said echoing Baba's admonition.

The Petits were very gracious and complimented them, living up to their 'progressive' reputation.

'You are the kind of young women I want my schools to produce! Bravo. I see you are admirers of Annie Besant, as you should be. But I would urge you to support Gandhiji's satyagraha and swadeshi movements and attend his public meetings without formally joining them. All streams lead to the ocean of independence and you should not be hesitant or exclusive in swelling them,' Mr Petit advised them with a mischievous glance at Annie.

'OK, so you are siding with Gandhi—go on! Tell them to take to the streets, break the law, provoke the police, and resort to arson! Has the Chauri Chaura incident not shown that it is difficult to control a flood if the embankments of restraint are broken down?' she asked.

'Annie, all I am asking them is to support all non-violent movements!' Mr Petit clarified.

'They can do one better! You girls go and teach at the Banaras Hindu University I have founded with Madan Mohan Malaviya, after you finish college here. That will be a more lasting contribution than pamphlets, marches, and protests,' Annie suggested.

'We may have to learn to do both—teach and protest!' Malati declared to their amusement.

At lunch, Kamala was seated next to Jiddu Krishnamurti. He told her about the life changing 'mystical experience' he had in Ojai, California, some three years ago and how he now lived in a state of 'benediction', embracing the 'sacredness', and the 'otherness'.

Malati was intrigued to note some tension between Annie and her 'son'. Chandra whispered that Jiddu was becoming a bit too independent of his Theosophy mentors after that 'cataclysmic spiritual experience'. But for Kamala, this discourse with Jiddu, was equally 'life-changing'. If Ram had not already captured her philosophical soul, she might well have drowned in the deep oceans of Jiddu's eyes—the window to his immanence, as Chandra later teased her.

Malati did not forget to ask Mr Petit's help in launching Hema Kaki on the big stage.

'You don't miss any chance to advance your purpose do you, young lady?' Mr Petit said.

'It's my nature. If I care for someone and I feel her talent deserves high patronage such as yours, I am not afraid to ask,' Malati said defiantly, and Chandra laughed.

'See, Jehangir uncle, she is truly my soulmate. Clear like the blue sky. No clouds to hide behind. You have to give her credit for that, for her persistence and sincerity. And it's not anything she is asking for herself. You should consider it!' Chandra pleaded on Malati's behalf. He relented and asked Chandra to meet Pestonji in his office to follow up. Malati was delighted and profusely thanked them both.

Shyam, who had been watching Malati intently, invited her to the balcony to get a sea view. They stepped out together and he pointed to the unending belts of shimmering beaches, the new tall buildings in the distance that broke the horizon where the sun drenched, sparkling seawaters met the bluest of blue skies.

'So, I hear you are going to join our tennis group next year. Will see more of you then on the courts! We should see more of each other off the courts too,' Shyam said. She was not sure whether the searchlights of his eyes or the sun glitter reflecting from the sea were blinding her.

Malati blinked and turned her head to observe him at close quarters for the first time. She had played with him on the same side of the court for ten months. But she had been busy chasing the shuttlecock and looking out for shots and volleys from Chandra and Vivek, rather than directing her gaze at Shyam.

Now he stood next to her, two of them undisturbed on the balcony, watching flocks of squawking seagulls chasing each other in the skies, their wings mimicking the flared skirts of the pirouetting Kathak dancer she had seen in Vaishali, at one moment, and maddeningly descending to seesaw on the waves, at another. And Shyam was saying they should meet off court! Malati unabashedly appraised him as a man would a woman. A tall, fair, well-built young man, with an eagle nose, big hooded eyes, and fleshy pink lips stared back at her.

'Where do we have the spare time?' Malati replied.

'Chandra and Vivek are close, and you and I could be too. It was I who suggested we invite you and Kamala today,' Shyam slipped in an obligation on Malati.

'Oh, that's nice of you to think of us. It's been an unforgettable encounter with our hero, Annie Besant,' Malati replied.

'You know why I like you and find you attractive? It is your fresh and full of wonder and anything-is-possible attitude to everything. When you were admiring the "cage" coming up, you thought Vivek and I were ridiculing you. On the contrary, we were appreciating you and forcing ourselves to look anew at what we take for granted,' he said.

Malati thanked him.

'And what is it you like about me?' he asked.

'Your unreturnable serves and shots on the badminton court, your athletic body that makes you an ace sportsman, and your friendly manner,' said Malati promptly.

'I hope you will get to like other things about me, too, especially my good heart!' he said smiling.

'So where do you live?' Malati tried changing the topic.

'Oh, nearby. My father is a judge in the Bombay High court as you know,' he said with a touch of pride.

'Yes, that's amazing! My father is a farmer and a vaidya. He founded a whole settlement of villages in Guna,' Malati said with equal pride.

They were called in as the other guests were leaving.

Malati touched Annie Besant's feet and asked for her blessings. She embraced them both and said, 'You have my blessings! I see a very bright future for you in whatever you do. Choose well and be someone in your own right, always!'

28
THE STAR OF MY MOTHERLAND

Shyam insisted on escorting the girls' home. 'This is Shyam Kaul, our classmate and my badminton partner in college,' Malati said to Mohan Kaka and Hema Kaki.

'Are you not going to say I am more than that,' Shyam asked Malati provocatively.

'What more?' Malati demanded, 'That your father is a judge?'

'No, no. That I am a friend,' he said and laughed.

'Pleased to meet you and your brother. I am so happy our nieces keep such exalted company,' said Mohan Kaka.

'Kaka, he is not exalted. He is not a judge. He is a student like us!' Malati asserted.

'I am exalted all right. I am a Brahmin, my father is a judge, and I am of the superior species—that of men! Right, Kaka?' Shyam laughed, teasing Malati, knowing how strongly she felt about women being superior, not just equal!

Kaka looked at her and said with mock humility, 'I cannot agree with you Shyam, when these two goddesses are around! I bow to them. If you want to be friends, learn to bow to the devis too!'

'Hema Kaki, your fan and admirer, Malati, is unstoppable! She took up your case with Mr Petit for sponsorship, even at the cost of annoying him,' Shyam told her before Malati could say anything.

Malati told her that she had kept her promise to Hema Kaki and it was agreed that Mr Pestonji would meet and test Hirabai—the singing sensation along with her manager Mohan Kaka, and Chandra would facilitate.

Hema Kaki was overjoyed. She embraced Malati in gratitude.

Later, when Hema Kaki was in the kitchen, Mohan Kaka explained to Malati that he was worried about Jehangir Petit asking Hema Kaki for favours in return for patronage. Malati vouched for Mr Petit having no ulterior motive. Yes, he wanted to make history, doing things no one had done before; that was the only satisfaction and profit he sought. He was a selfless supporter of Mahatma Gandhi and she supposed that Mohan Kaka should empathize with him since he was himself so inclined. She disclosed that they had found out about Mohan Kaka's own patriotic activities and his going to the house of a satyagrahi after work.

Mohan Kaka was forced to admit to his nationalist affiliations, but clarified that he was not a Congress supporter. He was fighting for Akhand Bharat—a follower of Veer Savarkar—the original votary of taking to arms to rid India of British colonialism. He recognized that Veer Savarkar had since changed tack and instead become the foremost advocate of Hindutva and the Hindu Mahasabha, setting up a branch in Ratnagiri, after his release from a ten-year exile in the Andamans. Mohan Kaka wanted to be faithful to Savarkar's original revolutionary strategy. The girls offered to help him in his patriotic activities.

'I don't know what you as women can do in our movement. Moreover, I have promises to keep—to your father and Arjun's master Vilas Rao—and to my collaborators, especially after the Kakori tragedy. That means you must not know what I do and you must have no part in it,' Mohan spoke emphatically. They gave up and promised not to mention this even to Guru.

Hema Kaki returned to the living room. Mohan Kaka told her that they should not rush to meet Pestonji and that he would not accompany her. She was upset. Whenever a meeting with promoters came up, there was palpable tension between Mohan Kaka and Hema Kaki. They did not argue, scold, or shout. But Kaki's tightly clenched teeth, her quivering pink lips and puffed cheeks held in a spate of unexpressed feelings. Her chubby hands moved scissor-like, jangling her bangles, lifting pots and pans and banging them *phatak-phitak* on the floor, opening and shutting cupboards to have an idle chit-chat with her wardrobe, and swilling hot tea from the cup she put before Kaka, calculated to make his favourite Britannia biscuits in the saucer soggy. Every movement proclaimed that all she wanted to do was go onto the stage yet another time and sing out her soul.

The girls had learnt to read Kaka's stern look, his bushy eyebrows raised in an arc, his clamped jaws and determined chin—all part of his armoury to fight off any weakening before Kaki's emotional onslaught. He refused to look at Kaki at such times, in case he was moved to give in to her unspoken wish. Instead, cat-like, he slurped the spilt tea from the saucer with the gooey biscuit. He then shut himself off into a tent of English newspapers or Marathi nationalist publications that always sat side by side on the rack. Like his conflicted loyalties!

Beyond ensuring that Kaki did not become vulnerable to unscrupulous touts, the girls suspected that Kaka feared she might outgrow her role as his wife and become untethered from him, especially because they had no children. Despite these tensions, Hirabai had done quite well, singing solo and widening her repertoire to enchant audiences beyond the Marathi rasikas.

When Guru dropped in the following day, Hema Kaki, as always, fussed around him, offering him snacks and some 'delectable gossip' about the girls' visit to Chandra's house. Guru's face clouded and he said with a bit of irritation, 'Hema Kaki, are you telling me this to make me jealous?'

'Well, are you? If so, then I have succeeded in my purpose,' she said mischievously. 'You better watch out for the Kaul brothers. There is competition there.'

'They were in exalted company,' added Kaka.

'Yes, But I think the others are lucky to be in our Kamala's and Malati's exalted company?' Guru said with a smile.

'Oh ho! You are in a generous mood. We don't deny that we are equally exalted—potentially!' Malati said, smiling too.

Guru took the girls aside and told them that Mahatma Gandhi was in town and staying near his house on Laburnum Road in Mani Bhavan from where he had unleashed many cascades of the freedom movement to pressure the British. Guru had secretly attended one of his early morning meetings. One of Gandhiji's aide, Chhagan Bhai had encouraged him to form an informal cell to spread the Congress's nationalistic messages in Elphinstone College and beyond.

'Will you help me?' he asked.

Malati and Kamala demurred.

'I don't expect you to give speeches or distribute pamphlets or join protests. But let's stage a play and use that to mobilize our fellow Elphinstonians to form their own patriotic cells. We can attend public meetings and encourage others to do so, and write under pseudonyms for the *Young India* journal. You could write about educated young women's perspective on British rule, national movement, and about Bombay as a hub of it.'

The girls readily agreed since it would not violate their pact with

Malak and Baba. When they returned, they found Kaka in deep conversation with some young men in his courtyard. They presumed that he was conferring with his freedom fighter team. Hema Kaki told them to wait in the living room until they left.

Mohan Kaka quickly dismissed them, came, and sat down with Malati, Kamala, and Guru. They shared their plans of discreetly supporting Gandhi's satyagraha movement fully expecting him to be displeased. Instead, he coolly invited them to what he called a Bharat Manthan Baithak at the end of which they could choose which stream of the freedom movement to join.

'Look! Since I came here years ago, I have seen the rivers of different communities and castes joining the sea of Bombaykars—spanning all trades and professions, from the dock and mill workers to the sailors, from lawyers and accountants to clerks and administrators. It is this manthan of Savarkar's Hindu Ocean here in Bombay that will bequeath the amrit of Bharat's freedom,' Kaka said.

'And people like us come here to fulfil new kind of dreams—to get higher education and callings and a larger stage. Each one of us can reinvent ourselves, unrecognizable from what we were! Wear the chola of patriotism and contribute to the manthan, the great churning,' said Malati, getting into the spirit.

'Indeed. Bombay is truly the crucible of an emerging new aspirational India, and beats to the rhythm of the many drums of the freedom movement,' Kamala commented loftily.

'But the question I ask myself often is that unlike most previous conquerors, the British have remained alien, never become one with the people of the land. So, will that be their strength or weakness? And will this manthan succeed against them?' Malati wondered.

'Strength, because nearly three lakh Britons in a country of over twenty crores are invisible to the vast majority of people. So, most don't know or care about who their upstream exploiters are, for their immediate oppressors are familiar Indians—the landlord, the petty babus, and tehsildars, moneylenders, lawyers, police, factory owners, and managers. That is the strength of the British and that's what we are up against,' Mohan Kaka said.

'Also, the churning of the Hindu Ocean is incomplete. High-caste Hindus, have been guilty of keeping the low castes out of their temples and homes, so this exclusion of Indians by the British is not new to them. That is why we need to unite all castes into one Hindu Rashtra and abolish untouchability and discrimination to drive out the British,' Kamala said eliciting approving looks from Kaka.

'Well don't forget the babu classes, the army of Macaulay's Westernized collaborators like us, now feel the racial injustice of British rule acutely. They are restless and have the most will for freedom. And that's what the Congress Party also seeks to tap. The British need them to be their instruments of governance, but they could, and are turning the tables on them if they don't change things like Indians not being able to join the ICS on equal terms. My father testifies to the discrimination Indian lawyers and litigants alike face in the courts. There is no equality before the law here!' Guru interjected vehemently.

'But I am optimistic, because they are not Sri Krishna to hold up their mountain of an empire on a mere thumb. To hold sway over such a large discontented mass of people, who have been awakened and unified as they are getting under Mahatma Gandhi. That is the weakness of the British Raj and our strength,' Malati said optimistically.

'Don't waste your time and effort with Gandhi. Veer Savarkar is the real messiah of unity. He asserted that Hindu is one who regards and owns this Bharat Bhoomi—this land from the Indus to the seas—as his Fatherland as well as holy land, whatever form of religion or worship he may follow. It is this bond of Hindutva, without discrimination of caste or sect, which will act as a glue. Not separating each community within Hinduism like Gandhi and his Congress Party are doing. Also left to them and their gradualism, we will never reach our goal. Waging a true war of independence, by whatever means possible, including force, is the only way the British will leave. The Congress unfortunately is led by cowardly Western educated leaders who just want to pole vault themselves into prominence and power,' Mohan Kaka asserted.

'But then, how do we ensure that the wily British—a lesser civilization who had subjected us to the shame of being outgunned, divided, and conquered—do not use the same ruses again?' asked Malati.

'Our former rulers—the Muslims are playing into British hands and creating disunity. So, unless we Hindus unite against them, and isolate and enfeeble them, we will not succeed in throwing the British out,' said Kaka almost fiercely.

'Should we not ensure that the Muslims do not get pushed into becoming Jaichands and are instead part of our Akhand Bharat project,' Malati persisted.

'Exactly, unless we co-opt them, we may be far away from ejecting the British and closer to a big Hindu–Muslim divide. Is it not the wild elephant, which the freedom movement votaries have to tame, Kaka? And is it not what Mahatma Gandhi is trying to do?' Guru chimed in.

Mohan Kaka had had enough it seemed. He abruptly asked the girls which stream they wanted to join and both Kamala and Malati fearlessly told him that they would follow Mahatma Gandhi, whose non-violent way they thought, was the only way.

Kaka glared at Malati, Kamala, and Guru, took a pinch of snuff from a rectangular silver snuffbox and snorted it out into a cloud of foul-smelling brown dust. He then got up and dismissed them saying, 'You represent the namby-pamby youth who are getting subverted by British education to support their B-team that Gandhi is leading. You will see that force has to be met with force.'

∽

Guru invited Kamala and Malati to join him for a walk by the sea. The moment they reached the beach, Malati took off her sandals, dangled them in her hand, tucked her ochre sari, and ran a zigzag path on the sand, scrunching its silky grains under her bare feet, leaving her small footprints in the wet sand. She competed with the drama of the white plumed egrets circling above them, the stork-billed kingfisher with its fiery red bill and flamboyant blue dress dashing past, and the flute like call of the golden yellow oriole amidst the clumps of trees and bushes nearby. Her hair flew wildly in the sea breeze. Kamala and Guru laughed indulgently at Malati's playfulness and the unruly picture she made.

'Come on. Let's run a race,' she called out.

Kamala refused as the sand and pebbles would prick her soles. Guru said he would keep Kamala company. 'Anyway, I am no Shyam to be your partner in sports,' he added wryly.

Malati ran back to them panting. Guru looked at her transfixed, as she lifted her shapely hands and twisted her vagrant hair back into an obedient knot. He instantly recited a poem by Richard Lovelace to describe her curly black hair in flight!

Let it fly as unconfined.
As its calm ravisher, the wind,
Who hath left his darling th' East,
To wanton o'er that spicy nest.
Every tress must be confest
But neatly tangled at the best;
Like a clue of black thread,
Most excellently ravelled....

'Look who is showing off!' Malati called out, trying to hide her shyness.

'You are guilty of inspiring this poetic recall!' Guru said, gazing at her dreamily, almost as if Kamala was not there.

Kamala smiled and looked away, allowing Guru and Malati to draw an unseen awning of togetherness over their heads.

'Let's at least walk, you lazy ones, if you can't run!' Malati said to break the spell.

They walked towards the black rocks that walled off the sea from the winding road. There they sat down to watch the waves crash against the hard, grooved surfaces of the rocks with full fury. Slowly, but surely, they did seem to erode and break the mighty rock. They were not sure whether the waves had the force of the militant revolutionaries or what Mohan Kaka called gradualists under Mahatma Gandhi, but both together seemed capable of chipping away the rock of the formidable British empire. The three of them looked at each other in silence, reading from the same patriotic songbook of hope!

Kamala started singing—Ne Majhshi ne, the anthem to their Motherland that Veer Savarkar had written when he was in Brighton nearly twenty years ago. Though, she was still in chains, it roused in them the strength to continue to believe in his aspiration. Guru and Malati joined Kamala in singing lustily to the insistent drumbeat of the waves.

Nabhee nakshatre bahut ek pari pyaaraa,
Maj Bharat bhoomichaa taaraa
There are many stars in the firmament,
But there is only one that is beloved to me.
The star of my Motherland—Bharat!

29

METAMORPHOSIS

As they walked back, Malati told Guru how she looked forward to reuniting with Baba shortly and for him to be surprised happily by the changes in them as liberated young women.

'Well, I can testify to the changes,' he said. 'From the insecure young girl straight out of an ashram, who complained about me to the young lady who lords over not only me, but other boys too in college, who has all the professors admiring her scholarly abilities and has Mohan Kaka and Hema Kaki wrapped around her fingers—it's a kayakalp—an extraordinary transformation,' declared Guru.

The girls had indeed felt that they lived, studied, played, and socialized in a small but expanding, cocoon of the baffling big city of Bombay. It demanded continuous spinning by them—the silkworms—shedding off the casings they came with and renewing them with known and unknown silken threads spun from daily experiences.

'The past year has been an intellectual and metaphysical kayakalp for me too in college including because of my friendship with you both,' Guru claimed.

'But unlike you, we have had to adjust to the field of action being, what was hitherto a man's world, with our college as its locus. Your Mai and our Akka have the conventional wisdom of generations of mothers to guide them. We have no such lantern as we intrepid intruders stride into your world,' Kamala said.

'You are no intruders. You have melded into our masculine realm, if there is such a thing,' said Guru.

'But we would like to shape it too and make you men more like us!' Malati exclaimed.

'You are succeeding. Look at me,' Guru said, disarmingly.

'Well, you are a rare champion. See what some of our other classmates say or do. They make us feel as if we are having to constantly respond to Saint Muktabai's call to us crawling ants to dare to fly up into the sky, making it our own new territory and even dare to swallow the sun,' Malati said.

Guru contested her claim.

'Don't diminish yourselves, even to make your achievements appear greater. You both are no ants. You were birds with strong wings already skimming the skies when you came here, and now you have had to fly ever higher. So, describe to me your flight path differently!'

Malati repeated what she had often told herself as her aims—learning new subjects and ideas at levels of complexity that only men so far were privileged to access; meeting and interacting with men—Indian and British professors and classmates who had no kinship to them; having a vocation besides marriage and children. Maybe, to be someone recognized as Malati or Kamala—not always as someone's daughter, wife, sister, or mother. And finally, to strike a blow for winning the battle of the sexes!

Guru endorsed those aims but added, 'Arre! This caricature about power division among the sexes is overdrawn. Look how a twenty-year-old woman in my home is lording over us men. Mai is like a monkey given the charge of guarding the family shrine with all the offerings laid out before her. Instead of guarding it, she gobbles up the offerings, crushes the flowers, and knocks down the oil lamps, wreaking havoc.'

'Well, she is an exception. Kafka's *Metamorphosis*, a craze these days in literary philosophical circles, holds a mirror to Mai's behaviour. Mai looks like a Kafkaesque metamorphosis into Grete, the cruel, uncaring young woman,' Kamala said.

Guru sighed his assent.

It struck Guru that he liked spending time with the girls as if it was the natural thing to do. He was never conscious that they were young women, except when a sudden flash of their feminity hit him and then he only remembered poetry. 'I find you as intellectually engaging and stimulating as my men friends, perhaps, even more so,' Guru confessed.

'The feeling is mutual,' Kamala said.

'OK, then do you feel the same with Ram and the Kaul brothers,' Guru asked, smiling mischievously.

'With Ram, I share a passion for philosophical debate and I think Malati has a healthy sports partnership with Shyam. Vivek is our best friend Chandra's partner. Different strings of our tutari vibrate to different notes,' Kamala replied.

At a debate organized at Elphinstone College on social reform and British rule, Professor Seal had claimed that without British advocacy and support, the kite of Indian women's liberation would not have flown at all and that after all, injustices against women survived all other empires. So, when Malati recalled that, Guru had to point out that the British had not set a good example. There were no British women leaders in any positions of power in India.

'Oh! Their preaching women's emancipation for Indians is to show how they are morally superior!' Guru exclaimed.

'Then we Indians should prove our moral superiority by showing how we ourselves value women,' Malati retorted as they entered Mohan Kaka's house.

They found Mohan Kaka waiting for them, his lips pressed and fists clenched something they had not witnessed before. He sat them down after Guru left and in a raised voice, scolded them for being away until late at night. He accused them of betraying not only the Ratnagiri heritage of Veer Savarkar but also Malak's trust by pursuing a deviant political path, misguided by Guru. He demanded to know what their relationship was with Guru.

'Guru is a classmate and a friend who has been very good and helpful to you both as well, isn't he?' Malati replied.

'People do favours in this city to serve their own purpose. These educated men deceive you by seemingly admiring you for your intellect or the way you hit the shuttlecock. All they are after is to enjoy you like bees craving the nectar of flowers. Do you understand me?' said Kaka.

'We are tough young women of the world, no wallflowers for craven bees. If Guru had any ill intentions, I would put him to the ground in a minute. Although much shorter than him, I am stronger. See my wrist, Kaka?' Malati replied brandishing her solid wrists in the air.

'As for Guru's misguiding us to support Mahatma Gandhi's stream of freedom movement, we respect Veer Savarkar and his Hindutva vision, but would you or Malak want us to take to arms to drive the British out? We offered to join you but you said women couldn't do anything. Malak too asked us to refrain from any overt activism and we don't plan on joining any picketing or protests as yet,' explained Kamala and promised not to mention Mohan Kaka's own activism to Baba.

When Hema Kaki tried to intercede, Mohan Kaka turned on her, accusing her of encouraging the girls to cross boundaries so she could herself have the licence to do so.

'Kaka, we did nothing wrong with Guru,' Malati affirmed.

'Oh, he knows that. We followed you last evening,' confessed Hema Kaki, sarcastically.

'How can I vouch for them to Malak if I don't personally keep an eye on them as their protector?' Kaka explained, looking at Hema Kaki with exasperation.

'They are girls of good character and very strong resolve. They will never do anything wrong,' averred Kaki.

'A thief acting as witness to a robber! If I had not lifted you from the cesspit you were in, you would not be wearing a respectable garb today. Don't let the little success you have had in singing go to your head. I can bring you down in a moment and send you back where you came from, whenever I want,' Mohan Kaka responded with a mean spiritedness the girls did not expect of him.

'How cruel of you, Mohan Kaka. We thought you love our Kaki. She is pure Prakriti to your Purusha!' Malati said before she could stop herself.

Emboldened by the girls' support, Hema Kaki pulled herself up into a Goddess Kali, her orange sari aflame with rage. Her plump body went into an unlikely tremble, her eyes welled up, but tears did not flow. Then the Goddess's volcano erupted in full exuberance, the molten lava of words seemed to gush from her mouth and flow down in streams through her tongue in aiming to turn the Mahishasur demon of Mohan Kaka to ash!

'I should never have believed you when you brought me here and assured that we are going to put my past behind us. I was better off where I was. I at least had the freedom to sing! You are now making my singing career a big concession from you. Don't you dare suspect me of infidelity to you. Otherwise....'

'Otherwise, what will you do?' Kaka demanded, somewhat subdued.

'Exactly what you are threatening to do to me—go back to my previous hell of a life and bring it here, to Bombay,' Hema Kaki said defiantly.

'Being with these girls has made you reckless!' he hissed and picked up his office satchel and marched out of the house in a huff.

'Everything is lost!' Hema Kaki gasped, the Kali in her rapidly deflated. She sank to the ground, crying inconsolably. Malati and Kamala rushed to comfort her.

The showdown with Mohan Kaka was a moment of truth for the girls. The wheels of their life in Bombay rested and moved on the axle of the Agashes providing them a harmonious home. Malati felt particularly guilty for the storm. It was probably because the girls had not lived in a proper home with parents for the last seven years and had dealt with everything in Bombay on their own terms. Their hosts were an uncommon couple too, and their moth and flame dalliance, was not easy to be around, without being singed a little.

They apologized to Hema Kaki on Mohan Kaka's behalf, as much as on their own, and counselled her to forgive his offensive outbursts, make amends for his sake, and for her own. Selfishly, they didn't want Kaka to insinuate to Baba that they are 'wanton young women' or that they were actively engaged in the satyagraha movement against his advice and thwart their near idyllic progress in college.

As it was, Malati had been guilty of some indiscretion in college for which, in different circumstances, she could have been suspended. Just before the college closed for the holidays, during their English literature class, Professor Wodehouse read out O'Shaughnessy's *Ode* as a finale to the year's poetry reading 'expedition'. Although the poem so patently celebrated the glory of the Victorian era and its imperialistic ambition, English nationhood, and race, he asked the class to interpret it as if they were feeling and living the poem as young Indians would.

Guru promptly responded.

'Though we the Indian students here may be "wandering by lone sea breakers", "sitting by desolate streams", we have enough civilizational inspiration to be "making our own music, dreaming our own dreams". Despite being born and raised as subject citizens, as our minds and horizons open, we have a growing belief that, "yet, we are the movers and shakers of the world forever" in a new India.'

Professor Wodehouse lauded what to Malati seemed a restrained, if not a tame reply. She expressed herself far more candidly: 'Sir, I would like to dip it into the colours of Indian nationhood—the saffron of sacrifice, the green of prosperity, the white of harmony and purity that our freedom fighters have evoked. Though we young Indians may appear to be "world losers and world forsakers", the evocation of "each age is a dream that is dying" is about the death of British imperial glory that I desire and forcsee happening soon.

We are eager to welcome an age "that is coming to birth"—that of freedom for India from British rule and the rebirth of all Indians and their civilization.'

She said almost uncaring about the import of her baring her patriotic feelings before a British professor in an Elphinstone College class.

The usually good-humoured Professor Wodehouse was wide-eyed and red-faced with embarrassment, and her classmates were stunned into silence. He asked her to see him after class. No one else dared to repeat Malati's 'patriotic mistake'.

'Miss Desai, how could you make such an error of judgement? I, as a liberal, grant you your freedom of thought, but under the circumstances of you and your country being under British rule, you do not have the luxury to oppose the British Raj—at least not in public. I am letting you off with a warning, but there will not be a second chance,' Professor Wodehouse warned her when she went to meet him after class.

'I am not sorry for my thoughts; and I do thank you for encouraging us to think freely. Yes, if I have caused you any problem—and I know some of our loyalist classmates could report this to the principal—I apologize, sir. I will henceforth be careful,' Malati replied, her hands folded in half repentance.

Malati and Kamala had come to believe that they were living in Bombay at a time when everything was being turned inside out and upside down the improbable Muktabai way. It was as if the small, sweet elaichi bananas, grew with their ivory coloured, fragrant, sweet, pulpy flesh outside, enveloping their thin, yellow, blotchy skin inside. It was as if the Indian tiger had come out of the forest, and sat supping with brown coolies at the starched linen covered table in the Gymkhana Club of Bombay, being served by British sahebs in red and white uniforms doubling over to please the natives. It was as if the frail Indian ascetic with nothing but the sword of his soul force, the shield of his khadi loincloth, and the cannon fire of the Indian masses, was breaching the iron and stone battlements of the great British empire, riding on the waves of his tremulous voice. They cherished their freedom to become part of this miracle making—even if as a tiny particle! They did not want to lose that privilege.

SMOKE AND MIRRORS

Guru accosted Malati and accused her of being 'reckless'. Although he was proud of her courage, he counselled her to conserve their firepower for later, more effective, action. He promised that they would together do whatever best they could through other means. He asked her to choose her vehicle well to take India to 'destination freedom'.

'I like to believe that as we walk on this path. Goddess Saraswati sends her Serene Swan to take us to our destination of wisdom, Goddess Lakshmi sends her Lucky Owl to take us on an optimistic path, and Goddess Durga dispatches her Roaring Lion to give us power and determination to fight our life's and nation's battles to victory. I understand the need for discretion for now and I promise to be careful,' Malati assured Guru and then Kamala, who looked as if the world had come to an end.

Fortunately, for the girls, Mohan Kaka's mood became conciliatory with Malati, Kamala, and importantly Hema Kaki, before Baba and Arjun arrived.

Hema Kaki however was bent on pinning Mohan Kaka down to good behaviour in the future. 'Aaho, it's not so easy. How could you speak to me with such contempt that for some time I lost my swabhiman. It is these girls who helped me regain my self-respect. Don't ever do it again. Next time I will just leave, even if I invite hell to my and your doorstep.'

'It won't happen again. Do you want me to touch your feet? But you three must not also gang up on me!' he said calmly—a repentant angel rather than yesterday's spiteful demon whom Hema Kaki's Durga had turned to ash.

∽

The next morning, Baba and Arjun came to pick the girls up. He thanked the hosts for taking good care of them and for agreeing to keep them until they finish college.

As the girls left Bombay for Vaishali, they realized how time had grown wings and taken flight. They told Baba about their life, friends, including the men friends, great professors, what they were learning, sports, and their examination results. He was very pleased with everything they had achieved. Then they demanded to know all that was happening in Vaishali and Desaikheda. Baba turned towards them and Malati noticed a healing wound and a scar on the right side of his neck.

'Baba, were you hurt? Did the dacoits come again?' Malati asked touching the scar.

He pushed away her hand and said, 'It was an accident. Everything is fine in Desaikheda. Govind is growing up well. The real storm was and probably still is in Vaishali with your friend Sarala the troublemaker,' Baba sighed.

He explained how Surekha was caught between Sarala accusing Abhimanyu and Ramabai of harassing her and their levelling counter charges. He asked that as her friends, Malati and Kamala should verify the truth and find a solution, thus repaying their debt to Malak.

The girls concluded that there was never a dull or peaceful moment in Vaishali. And it was their friend Sarala's fate, or even her choice, to be in the vortex of that perennial storm; nay, she was the storm!

They were delighted to reunite with Surekha who now had three children. Veena looked like a beautiful seven-year-old English girl—not at all like their niece! Both her brothers, Vishnu and Vishal, were handsome toddler princes. They hugged them and held them close.

After settling into their room, they sat with Surekha on her carved wooden swing in the veranda.

'So, how has Bombay and college been for both of you?' Surekha asked. 'The new mantle sits well on you I see!' she said affectionately.

'You, Malak, and Vaishali prepared us well for our Bombay and college odyssey,' Kamala said earnestly.

Surekha smiled. Between Malati, the natural born storyteller, and Kamala, the philosophical commentator, they traversed the crowded terrain of their Bombay experience over the past year. At times, Surekha became an eagle soaring above the landscape of their lives, holding her wings outwards without flapping to get a steady, sweeping overview, her sharp, eagle eyes catching the tall trees and edifices of their achievements. At other times she switched to becoming a low flying sparrow, her wingbeats furiously kicking up momentum, discerning the tiniest detail, picking up the smallest grain of 'what happened to them' and 'what they did', snapping up the 'worms of their discomfort' with her beak, and swallowing them away like their Ayee would have done.

Surekha punctuated their narration with exclamations of concern, cheer, and admiration.

Aga Bai!
Kai Chhan!
Wah Wah!
Kasa kela tumhi doghani he?

In between, Veena too joined them, pretending to listen and interjecting with 'unbelievable maushis', allowing herself to be drenched but not drowned in their discourse!

Over a sumptuous lunch with the Maharaj's signature mutton curry and cauliflower stuffed parathas, succulent warm jalebis dripping with saffron infused syrup, topped by sticky fig sweets with mouth freshening spices of betel leaf paan, the girls asked Surekha about their friend Sarala. She grimaced, repeated what Baba had told them, and remarked that Sarala was causing the biggest turbulence in her household and that it was a case of the stepdaughter tormenting her stepmother.

'Sarala told us last time that she did not feel the passion with him. But we did not take her seriously, because she has a habit of belittling what she has and fantasizing about what could have been if only...' Kamala said.

'Well, it appears, as with royal families here, he may be addicted to afeem—opium—and hence, erratic in his behaviour. So that could inhibit passion,' Surekha admitted with a smile.

'Oh, as for Ramabai's complaint, every mother will say her son is a paragon of virtue—a Vishnu in flesh and blood. When the wife tries to reform her flawed son, she faults the daughter-in-law,' Malati pointed out.

Surekha informed them that Sarala's father-in-law Krishna Rao was supportive of her so far. But it had become a dangerous contest with Ramabai. And it had reached beyond Sarala's bedroom and her in-laws' wada to Malak and Surekha. Since they were kin of the Maharaja, she worried about repercussions in the court.

She had advised Ramabai that the elders should do nothing to queer the pitch in their marriage but the mother-in-law seemed unconvinced. She, therefore, wanted the girls to go and meet Sarala and get the full story, because with Surekha, Sarala instantly put on a sly smoke and mirrors show. She always assured her everything was fine between her and Abhimanyu and Krishna Rao and that Ramabai was jealous.

The girls went across on the sensitive mission with some trepidation. Sarala's wada was even better appointed than Malak's. Sarala came to receive them at the spectacular brass clad gate with the sun dynasty emblem embossed over it. Meant to dazzle nobodies like Malati and Kamala whose only family emblem could be a plough or Shushruta's mortar and pestle!

They embraced, appraised and complimented each other, and entered a cavernous hall. The very tall and well-built Abhimanyu was reading a book. He seemed so imposing behind an English green and gold leather covered table. He looked up and flashed a smile that lit up the room. The girls faulted Sarala for not feeling the passion!

Sarala introduced them warmly, without taking his name.

'We are happy to meet you at last! Last time we were here, Sarala did not allow us!' Malati said with a smile.

'Ah, that is Sarala for you. Those she loves, she holds them captive like me! And you, I believe,' he responded.

Malati tried to look carefully into his eyes to see if there was any sign of afeem addiction, but he looked alert and normal.

'You two are very different from your elder sister,' he said. 'I can't believe you have the same father! Sarala told me you went to an orphanage school and now live alone in Bombay and go to college there. Very brave! I admire that.'

'Well, if I had the chance, I would happily do that, too. Don't tempt me,' said Sarala.

'You could not live a day without all your comforts and retinue of servants, could you?' he said sardonically.

'You don't know me. I can live an ascetic's life, or even that of a freedom fighter on the run,' Sarala retorted and glanced at the girls meaningfully.

The girls talked a little about their adventures in Bombay and the freedom movement. He seemed very concerned about the Congress's attitude towards the princely states. He was alarmed by the capture of Pravesh and other revolutionaries from Vaishali in the Kakori case. The girls were not sure if Sarala looked uncomfortable with the way Abhimanyu was enjoying talking to them or with the mention of Pravesh.

'Are you going to monopolize the conversation with my friends? Come girls, let me show you around this legendary wada.'

'Ah! The estate of which you are the queen?' he said to Sarala, his face twisted into a sardonic smile. The charm evaporated.

'I am the crown princess, only because you are the crown prince. Your mother is the queen,' Sarala responded sweetly trying not to be sarcastic.

'Good, good. Go ahead and savour these luxuries while they last. Who knows, with the tide of the freedom movement rising, what will be the fate of the princely states and aristocrats like us and your father when the plebeians take over and the violence and anarchy of the revolutionaries rule the streets,' he said wryly and went back to his book.

Malati noted that he was reading Bal Gangadhar Tilak's magazine, *Kesari*—and other books by Tilak, including *Shrimad Bhagavad Gita Rahasya*, were on his desk. They too looked well-thumbed. She was impressed.

'Are you a follower of Tilak, our radical nationalist leader, labelled the father of Indian unrest for independence by the British? Or are you just an admirer of his conservative views on social reform and women's emancipation?' Malati couldn't resist provoking him.

'I am both. The only aspect of his teachings I am puzzled by, as a Maratha myself, is his zigzagging on the caste system and his anti-Maratha stance as a Brahmin,' he replied, smiling.

'I don't believe you are against women's education or their activities outside the home,' Malati persisted. 'You would not have married our friend, if that was so.'

'That's true. I am OK with women's education because that makes them interesting wives who can mix in high company. But not for them to work like men,' he said firmly.

'Well, Sarala is a well-educated wife with social charm, without the disadvantage of her working outside the home,' Malati said.

'Yes. But she is working in another way all right. I don't know which is worse. Well, you ladies enjoy your tour,' he said and abruptly ambled out of the hall.

They settled down to talk in the richly decorated living room with silver vases, birds and elephants. Large, gold framed paintings of Abhimanyu's ancestors hung on the walls and glared down on visitors. Their luxuriant beards and moustaches gave them a fierce look even as their lips were stretched in half formed smiles. Strangely, they brandished unsheathed swords in their raised right hands, their scabbards hanging disjointedly on the left side of the waist. Had they only been threatening potential enemies or sending messages through generations to the women of the family whose portraits were missing on the wall?

Sarala followed Malati's gaze and said, 'Ah! No portraits of Abhimanyu's women ancestors are on the wall because none were as beautiful and as intrepid as me! One day, you will see my portrait up there, in acknowledgement of my extraordinary and pioneering achievements!'

'We have no doubt you will make it to those walls. But I am sure you will not wave a sword, but a quill pen,' Malati joked.

'No, no! I will be brandishing a gun!' Sarala replied and made a gun shooting gesture. She then led them down an arched passage to the garden. A tall, plump lady wearing a green silk sari, gem-studded gold jewellery spilling all over her—ear, neck, chest, arms, and ankles too—shuffled and tinkled towards them. She was Ramabai. Sarala introduced them to her. She greeted the girls very warmly. 'Oh, so you are Surekha's sisters. How different each of you looks from the other! Same parents, I suppose?' she asked, barely hiding her curiosity.

'Yes, we are of the same father and mother. God made us with great finesse and care—each to be a distinct painting and sculpture!' Malati said quickly, before Ramabai remarked that Malati was the only brown-skinned one with impossibly curly hair, while both Surekha and Kamala were fair with sleek straight hair.

'I agree. All of you are beautiful in your own way. Now I remember, seeing you at the jalsa and enquiring about you for Abhimanyu. But was told you were headed to college in Bombay,' she said, glancing at an annoyed Sarala.

'Well, Sarala is very special to us and we hope you make her happy at this time,' Ramabai added as she went on her way.

They entered a well-tended garden with neat flower beds and topiary hedges. They sat on cushioned chairs. Liveried waiters served them sherbet and snacks. Sarala shooed them away and their conversation rolled.

'Abhimanyu seems a very good husband. Even Ramabai seems pleasant,' Kamala remarked.

'He is good except when under the influence of opium, he is unpredictable and insufferable. He is not violent but cruel with his words. And he is unable to make love to me as a man to a woman,' Sarala came straight to her chief grievance.

'It's OK if he does not pounce on you every day for love play. In any case, is it not the men who demand and have the hunger to enjoy a woman's body?' Malati teased.

'You supposedly modern women should know that Kautilya opined that women are twice as hungry for food than men and their desire for sex eight times more than that of men? Of course, he also said that women's astuteness is also double that of men and their courage six times!' Sarala said, showing off her scholarship to justify her own 'hunger'. When questioned by Kamala she promptly quoted the Sanskrit verse: strinam dvigunam aharo, kamasch ashta Guna Smita, anartam sahasa dosha swobhavyata.

'It is strange, but to be expected, that these verses of Kautilya which recognize the strengths and desires of women are never remembered, but all the demeaning things our thought leaders said about women are used by men to justify their superiority and dominance!' said Kamala.

'But Sarala, have you told him about your desires?' probed Malati.

'Yes. Used all the tricks of pleasure ladies, to arouse him. If there is no proper union of our bodies, there is neither the pleasure of kama nor the duty of procreation. Ramabai is now eager to have a grandson. So, she keeps taunting me and blaming me. I may, like my mother, become the discarded wife!' Sarala retorted bitterly.

31

HEIR TO THE ESTATE

Malati and Kamala felt that they had solved some part of the puzzle of the Sarala–Abhimanyu discord and had something tangible to report to Surekha after all.

'Maa Saheb is under the impression that I have found my happiness. And she is finally at peace, even happy. I want to keep up that illusion. Malak will say, it is your karma, find a way to cope with it. Ramabai did complain about me to Chhoti Ma. This is something unspeakable. I am glad I can talk to you and lighten my heart,' Surekha said.

Malati wondered if Krishna Rao could help clear her name but realized that a father would be even more reluctant to accept that his own son was not virile like a bull. It would be a blot on his own manhood, would it not? But Sarala seemed to have faith that he understands, and is sympathetic to her because of that and showed more affection than even Malak.

He was an ace equestrian and hunter, and had promised to teach her both these royal skills and take her for men's only shikars. Ramabai resented her closeness to Krishna Rao and the time he spent with her teaching these and the management of his estates.

'One day, like Maharani Ahilyabai, I will be heir to his estates, his "kingdom". Provided I fend off Ramabai's machinations,' Sarala said.

'How can Akka help you?' Kamala asked.

'By keeping Ramabai engaged and neutralized. And advocating my case with Malak, so he does not blame me. And, of course, not telling Maa Saheb about my misfortunes,' Sarala gave her wish list.

Sarala then remembered to turn the spotlight on Malati and Kamala's 'love life'.

'Have you found anyone who stirs you? In whose thought your body burns? Whose words spoken in admiration and love keep you awake at night?' She looked at them eagerly.

'No, Sarala. Sorry to disappoint you. We have many friends who are men but not lovers, because we are not at that stage yet,' Malati said with a dramatic sigh.

'Girls, this is not like casting a horoscope and saying that Venus is now favourably aspecting the seventh house, and you are going to get married in two years, and you wait for that moment. Since you girls have the freedom to meet young men—and I envy you for that—if you feel any surge of desire around them, then you have to let it move you towards a consummation, and get the stars to bless you.'

'We don't have that luxury. We have a goal, away from all this for the next few years. Our horoscope is already cast. But are you studying astrology?' Malati asked.

'I am learning astrology from the royal astrologer's young and "desirable son", under the pretext of learning Sanskrit scriptures—and that is the one thing I do that pleases Ramabai,' Sarala said. 'I am proud that I have inherited my mother's gift of premonitions. I study astrological science so people don't label it madness!' she said.

Malati recalled that Ayee was no fortune teller. But on the day before she died, she foresaw that she was going to a faraway, luminous land. So, there was in everyone a third eye, the ability to see beyond the every day and the present! It is only that some people had that as a constant and some mortals like them, just saw the future in a rare flash of foresight.

'Tell me what are people most afraid of? Of the future, of the unexpected happening to them. And if you can somehow help them get a preview of what is to come—more bad than good—they feel prepared. Assured. That's going to be my ultimate weapon—Brahmastra—in my battles here. I already practice it with Krishna Rao, and he goes by my predictions,' explained Sarala, the heir to her mother's divyadrishti and Krishna Rao's 'estate'.

And there came Krishna Rao, an older and bearded avatar of his handsome son. He did have the erect bearing, sinuous gait and that certain swagger of a rider, and the killer look and passion of a hunter. Malati now realized why he and Sarala bonded together. He probably saw in her the beauty and grace, and most of all, the spirit of a feral mare—straining at her leash, eager to gallop into the wild. Like a good rider, he set her free, yet tamed her, let her find her farthest horizons and yet brought her back to his stable.

Sarala brightened as soon as she saw him and rushed to touch his feet. He lifted her, held her shoulder just for a brief moment, and looking into her eyes said, 'No, no, your place is in our heart.'

'Rao Saheb, your blessings are the reason for my happiness here,' she responded with feeling—in marked contrast to the formal, sardonic exchanges between her and Abhimanyu, and the evident distrust between her and Ramabai.

'Sarala praises you so much and envies you your freedom to study and be on your own. Sarala dear, won't you offer them dinner?' he said graciously.

Kamala and Malati politely declined.

On the way back to Malak's wada, Kamala was pensive and silent. Malati wondered whether Sarala was weaving another of her victim-turning, avenger, the-wronged-woman-turning-Durga stories. And using all of them to good effect? Kamala was inclined to give her the benefit of the doubt for now.

Surekha looked particularly buoyed that evening.

'Ramabai was here just moments ago,' she said as soon as she saw the girls. 'She is very happy with Sarala. It's a big relief for everyone.'

Malati and Kamala looked at each other a little bewildered but told her the gist of their conversation and Sarala's requests. Surekha looked puzzled.

'She has no physical relations with Abhimanyu, he is not virile enough? That is strange, because Ramabai just gave me the good news that Sarala is pregnant! And I have told Malak as well!'

Malati and Kamala were stunned! What kind of games was Sarala playing? They may be considered educated with more exposure to the outside world than Sarala and hence expected to be worldly wise. But Sarala had a survivor's cunning. Like the stingray fish they had been warned against in Konkan, she instinctively sent out her venomous barbs, both against those she considered her predators, and those she eyed as her prey. They did not know whether they should judge her harshly for her pretenses, lies and worse, or accept them as her weapons of defence against presumed enemies. Anyway, at least for the moment, Ramabai was happy and would desist from blaming Surekha for brokering an unviable alliance.

Just then, Veena came running in and announced that she was starting her horse riding classes with her Baba Saheb. Surekha was, worried that she was too little, and could get thrown off the horse.

When Kamala assured that Veena was all set to be a pioneer woman equestrian in the family and explained that to Veena, she said, 'Oh, like you both? I want to follow you and go to college too.'

Malati was flattered that little girls of privilege like Veena looked up to her and Kamala as role models, despite their humble origins.

When Veena pranced away to play, Malati asked Surekha if Malak loved Veena as much as he loved his sons. That made Surekha laugh. 'He treats Veena as if she is his son and heir! The boys feel jealous!'

Surekha reminded Malati and Kamala of Ayee, feverishly, eternally busy. As if she was keen to prove her usefulness on this earth. As an incarnation of the nourishing Goddess Annapurna to her household, of the nurturing mother goddess to her children, of the shakti-giving goddess to her husband's ishwar! She waved away their suggestion that she rest and enjoy the luxury of being served by dais and servants and invoked Ayee's ideal of a good grihani—housewife. Surekha's eyes welled up as she recalled Ayee's exasperation at her indifference to motherly advice, and here she was fervently living it like worship.

They asked her about Malak and she confided that though strict, he cared for her. Surekha had almost died at childbirth when Vishnu was born and Malak was distressed. He had mellowed a lot thereafter. She feared him less now. He even joked with her and they talked about their life, their children. Amrit Wada was shrinking into a cosy hut like Baba's, built with the mud, tiles, and reed of their smiles and tears, their frustrations, and their hopes—and yes that indefinable devotional love. It was no longer just a luxurious wada full of duty-bound strangers.

'To paraphrase Sant Dnyaneshwar, I have now imbibed the elixir of experience to annihilate the division between the bound, the aspiring, and the released,' she said, wiping her tears and smiling. Malati and Kamala were moved by her emotional poise and embraced her.

When asked about the Maa Saheb, Sarala, and Malak equation, she admitted that she was at one time gullible to Sarala portraying herself a victim, and even hard-headed Malak often believed her. But she had learnt to cross-check everything Sarala claimed and Malak too trusted Surekha to deal with her. For now, it was a happy interlude and she wanted Malak to savour it.

As for Maa Saheb, Surekha said that she did see her sometimes, but she never went there with Malak, not wanting to impinge on their time together. She sent the children over at Maa Saheb's request sometimes. Maa Saheb did thank Surekha for finding Sarala a good, happy home.

The girls remarked that Surekha was now adept at Hindi and English languages and mixed with the noble ladies and the British ones with ease to become a social asset to Malak. Surekha followed Malak directions to navigate her relations with noble ladies, to avoid getting embroiled in the court rivalry and conspiracies that wives either carried forward or ignited. 'I don't pretend to be a jhan-jhanit gappa tappa—red hot gossip monger. My secret weapon is being a good listener and the court ladies spontaneously confide in me. I make some sympathetic interjections, laugh or ask leading questions, and they let loose a flood of information. Malak now asks me every day for a bulletin!' Surekha said, laughing.

That evening the girls met Malak in the big durbar hall.

'Arjun and your father tell me that you both are happy and doing very well in college, including in sports,' he said.

'All because of your support and that of Baba. Yes, Malak, I play badminton well but I don't do horse riding like Veena,' Malati said smiling.

'Ah that! You see, she is so bright and beautiful and a leader. All the royal children want to play with her. And since they go horse riding, she has to keep up,' he explained, his eyes lighting up. Then he suddenly looked serious and asked whether they were guarding their chastity since their Akka was planning to find high-class suitors for them without realizing that Malati and Kamala were not Sarala.

Baba's face fell. He agreed that no one from a high-class Sardar family would want to marry the daughters of a farmer from Konkan. Not everyone was a connoisseur like Malak. Because he had picked her, Surekha was probably dreaming for her sisters.

'No, no. I meant that none of these "high class men" would want to "handle" wives who are college graduates, "city spoilt" and exposed to other men constantly!' Malak clarified.

They all relaxed.

'You may have to settle for boys from other castes that you meet in college! Tell me if you have anyone in mind now,' Malak said, half-serious, half in jest, as if he knew something through Arjun.

'No, Malak, we don't,' Malati and Kamala said in unison.

32
THE WILFUL SNAKE GODDESS

'Girls, listen to me carefully. Mohan Agashe would have told you about how the British are carrying out an extensive investigation on the Vaishali–HRA links and networks after the Kakori case. Now erase everything from your memory about your visits here or you will endanger Maharaja and me. Also, to avoid any future complications, you must resist all temptation to join any stream of the freedom movement in Bombay,' Malak said. The girls meekly promised to comply.

They did not tell Malak about the play Guru meant to stage to mobilize patriotic opinion and form freedom cells in Elphinstone College, nor about their well appreciated contributions to the *Young India* journal and their intention to join Mahatma Gandhi's satyagraha movement. Nor did they share the truth about Mohan Kaka's nationalistic activities though they did not rule out Malak knowing about them. The girls were learning now that are many types of truths on the other side of a lie and that like Malak, they must learn to keep them in separate compartments.

They had heard that there was a growing wave of support for Gandhiji and the Vaishali Maharaja was wary but not unsympathetic. The Central Province, Nagpur in particular, was becoming a hub of the Hindu Mahasabha. The government was in a bind because it could not encourage protests, nor could it be insulated from what was happening around Vaishali in directly British ruled parts of the Central Province. Revolutionary activities, but also Vaishali boys joining the Congress, the Hindu Mahasabha, or the Muslim League were raising the hackles of the British Resident.

Malak suddenly asked them about Muslims in their class and warned against any matrimonial alliance with them. The British policy of divide and rule and separate electorates, the resulting polarization, and Hindu–Muslim riots were spilling over to infect even those like Malak who had been broad-minded. As he finally said goodbye, he wished them strength, discretion, and self-control.

Malati and Kamala had avoided visiting Maa Saheb, but they were obliged to answer her summons with Sarala in attendance. Maa Saheb seemed to be happier and lighter. Gone were the heavy brocades that proclaimed that she was to a wada born and that she remained its mistress—never mind that Amrit Wada's new mistress had installed herself effortlessly as the new deity and Maa Saheb's town crier was no more. The gem studded jewellery that weighed her down rather than lifted her frail, bird like body and highlighted her gaunt, angular features, rather than embellished her intrinsic beauty, were jettisoned. An ivory coloured Chanderi sari cast a cool, moonlight glow on her—enhancing her divine madness aura.

A brown rudraksh bead necklace adorned her long bony neck and cascaded down onto her neatly pleated padar, resting on her slender chest with aplomb. Rudraksh gold earrings made a perfect match. Fresh mogra flower bracelets encircled her thin wrists, spreading their fragrance when she lifted her arms in prayer. Sandalwood paste tilak on her forehead between her kohl-traced eyes showed she had gravitated to another plane of consciousness—closer to her Krishna.

'How do you like my new avatar ordained by Lord Krishna as his more sublimated lover and devotee especially since I am going to be a grandmother?' she asked, reclining as usual on her favourite couch, not a queen but commanding still.

'Did you see, my Sarala now lives like a queen and is everyone's favourite? No longer the castaway wife's daughter, who is quickly replaced by the new wife's children in her father's affection!' she said bitterly.

'But, Maa Saheb, that is not fair. Malak loves Sarala as much as he loves Veena or his sons! And both he and Akka are always looking after Sarala's best interest!' Malati asserted vehemently, shaking her head reproachfully, no longer overawed by Maa Saheb's divine madness.

'I have always said Malati that you are special, bold, and don't hesitate to say it as you see it, no matter what. I have to concede that your sister is the best friend I could have asked for. If only she was not my sawat! And mind you, no matter what riches and happiness she gives me and Sarala, she cannot be redeemed from the sin of being my sawat in my book of reckoning!' Maa Saheb replied.

'Maa Saheb, it is Akka who put Sarala in the happy place she is in today!' Kamala reminded her.

'No! It is Sarala's own merit and blessed destiny, not Surekha's charity,' Maa Saheb said arrogantly.

Sarala endorsed her mother's proposition.

'OK then if god forbid, Sarala has a problem in her husband's home, you will have to blame her and her destiny!' Malati said mockingly.

'What do you mean? Does she have a problem that she has not told me about?' Maa Saheb immediately asked, looking worried.

'No, no, Maa Saheb, she deserves the best,' Kamala retrieved the situation. Sarala looked distressed but said nothing.

'When she is blessed with our first grandson, she will make Malak proud. I will feel redeemed too, as I failed to give a son to Malak,' Maa Saheb said.

'Indeed Akka, believe me, will be the happiest,' Kamala lost no opportunity to promote goodwill for Surekha. Maa Saheb laughed derisively and changed the topic.

'When are you girls getting married? Has Malak kept some boys hidden in the pocket of his cape for you?' Maa Saheb asked, sarcastically.

'No, Maa Saheb, we wish to finish college and study further. I may become a lawyer!' Malati invented an ambition on the spot to rouse their jealousy.

'And Maa Saheb, we don't need Malak to find us husbands. In fact, we may already have found them. Do you still see visions? If so, you must see that,' Malati said, rising to the bait as righteous anger rose inside her about Maa Saheb's ingratitude towards Surekha and her mocking those who had invariably befriended Sarala and been respectful to her.

Maa Saheb suddenly got up from her couch, towered over them, and looking deep into their eyes, cast a light on their future.

'You both will face many hardships, not get married for a long time, nor live in luxury. Malati, don't be arrogant about your ability to become anybody you want. You will not reach your destination!' Maa Saheb declared as if she was willing it, summoning it! Sarala, the neophyte astrologer, agreed with Maa Saheb and smiled condescendingly.

Malati and Kamala hastily left the Chhota Ghar regretting having entered it. Sarala was right—there is nothing people fear more than dire predictions about their future. The mother–daughter duo had momentarily sucked all optimism out of them.

༄

That night the spectre of an Icchadhari, self-willed, shape shifting, Snake Goddess with a human face, a red and gold bridal veil on her hooded head, a nag mani gem on her forehead, rose before the mind's eye of Malati. The goddess's neckless, long, tubular body extended for several yards, its scales intermittently catching the rays of the silver moonlight.

She zigzagged her way through the shrubs of the Vrindavan gardens of the Chhota Ghar, onto the lychee orchards of the Bada Ghar. Then she moved onto the cobbled stone path and reached the steps of Malak's abode.

She paused, and then glided up the marble stairs—hoisting the front part of her body onto each step and then pulling the rest up into a coil. Again and again, till all the steps got swallowed up. Once on the landing, she stealthily moved towards Malak and Surekha's room, her laboured hissing and musky smell the only inkling of her advance. She stopped outside the window closest to the door, hitting the glass repeatedly with her tail.

'Malak, don't come out. Keep the door closed. Keep Akka safe and Veena and the boys out of the Snake Goddess's reach,' Malati shouted.

Malak did not hear Malati. He opened the door and asked sternly, 'Who is it?'

The Snake Goddess pulled herself up as high as she could, dropped her red veil, and lunged forward to strike Malak, her forked tongue flicking out.

'What are you doing, Sarala?' cried out Malak, and reeled back aghast!

'All I am doing is embracing you forever,' she said.

'Malati, stop screaming!' Kamala shouted and shook Malati, who woke up sweating. It was very early in the morning and still dark outside. Her heart pounded, skipping and jumping against the floors and walls of her chest at the memory of the Snake Goddess. She was wet with the perspiration of fear.

Kamala tried to make light of it. 'Let us not be like the mother–daughter duo. We have now seen their true colours. We enlightened women can't be gullible to the hocus pocus about ours, or Akka's, future being dark or the duo trying to pass off their ill will as divination. Moreover, they did not threaten Akka directly,' Malati was not reassured. The next day, they shared their anxieties with Surekha.

Surekha acknowledged the inherent insecurity and ingratitude of the mother–daughter duo. But she doubted they would deliberately harm her family. Malati was unconvinced. She recalled how Sarala claimed the privilege of being perpetually aggrieved and resentful towards Surekha as a stepdaughter, no matter how sincerely she did her duty as a good stepmother. Kamala worried that despite having her own husband, and a loving father-in-law, she was still obsessed with trying to be Malak's favourite.

Surekha determinedly gathered her padar tightly around her waist and said, 'You must know that I am your Akka, Malak's wife and woman of the world. I will line up enough tricks to thwart any sinister designs of the duo. I have not interacted with the crafty court ladies in vain.' She asked them not to tell Baba about all this as he had his own ordeals in Desaikheda with the dacoits. In a recent skirmish, Baba had got injured and two people of his village were killed. She assured them that Malak was helping quash this menace in Desaikheda and neighbouring areas.

Sarala paid a surprise visit to say goodbye to the startled girls as they were leaving and said, 'Dear friends I have some good news—I am going to be a mother soon! I am sure it's a boy and I am going to name him after Baba Saheb.'

'Oh, congratulations. Akka told us when we came back from your place. We were pleasantly surprised! And then your mother mentioned it too!' Malati said, mildly sarcastic.

She brazenly smiled at them. 'I guess you have reason to be confused!'

In the clear light of day, away from Maa Saheb's darkness, she again seemed worthy of their indulgence. The Snake Goddess was casting a spell.

Their Vaishali sojourns had shown the girls that it was common for women to undercut rather than reinforce each other—a perverse female bonding most typified in mother-in-law–daughter-in-law hustling contest. United by marriage and divided by a struggle to control both the son and husband. Sarala and Ramabai, were caught in another kind of power tussle altogether. Krishna Rao, not Abhimanyu, seemed to be the prize!

33
TWO SUITORS

Back in Bombay, Malati and Kamala went straight to Mohan Kaka's home and Baba returned by the evening train to Desaikheda. Hema Kaki was delighted to see them and even Kaka looked pleased. They asked Kaki about her singing assignments and things at home with Kaka.

'We are fine now. How can we not be? After all, we both gave up so much to be with each other!' she said, her face permeated with contentment.

'Oh, by the way, Guru had come by to inquire about you both—"when will your dear nieces be back?",' she imitated him perfectly.

'None of the others from among your fan club came asking—neither Ram nor Shyam! I guess for now, Guru is your Dhruva Tara, your Pole Star!' Hema Kaki laughed.

Guru was visibly happy to see them, as were Malati and Kamala to meet him.

Guru informed that much had happened in Bombay whilst they were away. The Kakori case had shown that the revolutionary movement was active in Bombay and in princely states like Vaishali too. He guessed that Malak and his colleagues would be fearing the revolutionaries, while living in islands of old-world inertia surrounded by the roiling sea of anti-British mass movement.

Malati was torn between keeping the secret of the revolutionary goings on in Vaishali right under Maharaja's and Malak's noses if not with their blessings and wanting to defend Vaishali's nationalistic credentials.

'Well, the people of Vaishali have shown themselves to be nationalists, if not revolutionaries!' she said.

Guru then wondered whether Mohan Kaka had any HRA links. They denied this vehemently, 'accusing' him instead of having the Veer Savarkar and Hindu Mahasabha blood in him.

'Bombay is in the forefront of change—politically and socially—and it's where the battle for freedom will be fought the hardest for all of India to see and emulate. So, what are you proposing to do about the play and using it for mobilizing our college youth?' Kamala asked Guru.

'I hope to stage *Satteche Gulam* by B. V. Warerkar. It is his latest play with the freedom for India, anti-British message conveyed so cleverly that the college authorities will give permission. We can organize 'charcha mandalis' around the play which will then be the nucleus of patriotic discussion groups to spread Gandhiji's message and recruit followers for the future,' Guru outlined his plan.

Guru pointed out that vernacular literature and theatre especially the Bengali and Marathi ones, were being used powerfully for mass mobilization. The British feared the pen of influential Marathi playwrights like Warerkar and poets like Balkavi and Yashwant, as much as the voice of political leaders like Savarkar and Tilak.

'Well, I hope you will give me a leading role in it! Warerkar's women characters are fully fleshed out, and not simply stick figures languishing in the shadows,' Malati remarked.

'Hey, Sutradhar Malati! You have to pass the acting test first not just be "appointed" the heroine!' Kamala admonished playfully.

'I, Sutradhar, will make sure to pull the right strings to earn the role, Papi,' Malati retorted.

'In real life there is no sutradhar. We are all tossed around in the storm of people and circumstances without any puppeteer manipulating the strings,' Guru said cynically. 'But that apart, I agree, Malati, you could try for the lead role.'

'Well, if you can be the director of the play, then I can be the heroine. We both are full of passion, signifying no experience!' Malati said cheekily.

'You both are rolling out chapattis and getting ready to eat them without lighting the stove. Go and get your permissions first, Guru,' Kamala remonstrated.

Guru already had Warerkar's permission to stage his play. He went on to secure the backing of their Marathi Professor Sukhtankar and the help of Professor Wodehouse, their most liberal teacher, to allow them to stage the first ever Marathi play in Elphinstone College. He argued that the British period of Indian history was the golden age in the efflorescence of Indian vernacular literature and that it would be a magnanimous gesture to allow a 'safe play' to be staged. The cultural committee cleared the script and the principal himself gave the final seal of approval.

After Maa Saheb had told Malati she would be thwarted in her ambition to be a lawyer, it had become an obsession and a primary goal in life for her. So, she waylaid Guru one day and asked whether he wanted to be a lawyer like his father.

'Yes, law is in my blood,' Guru replied.

'Well, what would you say if I told you that I too want to be a lawyer? Defy my heredity?' she asked provocatively.

Guru looked surprised, then smiled at Malati and said, 'You will make a great lawyer! You have a terrific memory—so facts and law, procedure and case jurisprudence, will be at your fingertips; you are logical and you argue fearlessly with the power of Goddess Vacha. You don't need law in your bloodline.'

'Thank you. That encourages me immensely. Unless you are making fun of me?' Malati said.

'How dare I? I have to survive through BA, then LLB, with you bossing over us all! As they say in my native place, Karvar, you can't live in the same river as the crocodile and court its enmity,' Guru replied.

'Am I as fearsome as a crocodile?' Malati demanded in mock anger.

'I am too scared to say yes! So, no, of course not!'

They all laughed.

'But seriously, I do dream of being among the first women lawyers in Bombay Presidency after I finish my BA,' Malati asserted. 'And fighting the cases of freedom fighters.'

Classes began in earnest and they all got busy. Nevertheless, Malati gave in to Chandra's persuasion and enrolled herself for tennis.

'Welcome back Malati. Now you better be on good terms with me, because I am the ultimate tennis champion and I can train you till you come up to our level,' Shyam said proudly.

Malati frowned and declared she would take lessons from a coach to come upto their level. Shyam then offered to supplement them and Malati accepted by flashing a conciliatory smile.

'That's better! Chandra you were right to be won over by her smile in the ashram! It is bewitching, especially when it comes like a ray of sunlight through the dark clouds and thunderstorm of her displeasure!' Shyam said smiling at Malati.

Her tennis adventure thus began with Chandra and gang. The next few months were consumed by studies and tennis practice. However, Malati could not forget her promise to take Kaki to meet Pestonji to secure a singing assignment since Mohan Kaka was hesitant. When they arrived at his impressive seaside office with Chandra, he welcomed them kindly, but was very professional and matter-of-fact. He asked Hema Kaki about her singing career before she started in Bombay, who she trained under and which gharana or musical atelier she belonged to.

These questions unnerved Hema Kaki. Malati sought Pestonji's indulgence, and they went into an adjoining meeting room for consultations. Hema Kaki's face was flushed and she was shaking uncontrollably as if Mother Earth was opening up to swallow her like Sita.

'Why must he ask about my past? I have left it behind,' she cried. 'He should ask me about my new singing career in Bombay. And I can sing for him here and now, or invite him to my next concert,' she said, wringing her hands.

Malati held her hands, pressed them in reassurance, and tried to calm her.

'Tell me what is troubling you about your past and then I can advise you how to present it to Pestonji,' Malati said.

Hema Kaki looked into her eyes guiltily, hesitated, and then confessed, 'I belong to the family of Shamshad Begum, the famous courtesan who owned a high-class kotha—many called it a glorified brothel—in Bombay. I know we told you a different story. I grew up in her kotha learning singing and dancing. I was trained by Ustad Salamat Ali Khan from the kirana gharana—one of the best.'

She began her confession with a sense of shame, but finished with a tinge of pride.

'Was he your father too?' Malati asked.

'Maybe. My mother never admitted or confirmed. So, you see why I cannot reveal this to Pestonji or anyone?'

'Pestonji is not interested in your parentage or religion or caste, only in your musical lineage,' Malati said.

They went back and Hema Kaki answered all questions of Pestonji. He was hooked, and asked her to sing samples of a traditional thumri, a bhajan, and a ghazal. Hirabai flawlessly sang songs in all three genres. Pestonji looked visibly impressed.

'Hirabai you really are talented—as if gayaki is in your blood. We will try to organize a big concert for you to present your full repertoire. Ask your manager to be in touch with me,' he said to their great delight. Hirabai thanked Malati and Chandra warmly.

'Well, if you did not have talent, no amount of advocacy would get you anywhere,' Chandra said graciously.

∞

Malati found herself attracted to both Guru and Shyam—polar opposites both! With Guru, she shared her passion for literature and drama. With Shyam it was her newfound love of tennis. With both, she tried hard to prove her true mettle, win their admiration, not only as a woman trying to do something different, but by excelling as 'one of them'.

She could not quite discern whether she was drawn to them because they gave wing to her flight or she wanted to fly so that she sparkled in their eyes! She had to be able to dance with them, not to their tune, be in control, she told herself. And she saw a growing competition between them to win her.

This was the hardest part! They were in such close contact day in and day out, sometimes alone, sometimes with others present, that if Malati did not see either of them even for a day, she felt restless and missed their company. She sensed that her real test to choose between them or even to really know what each meant to her was at hand and she was not sure she wanted to pass it!

Malati now played doubles games competently with Shyam against Chandra and Vivek in college competitions. Shyam trained her far more patiently than the coach, boosting her confidence and hence her game, even when her will was flagging.

'The interplay of logic and intuition in tennis that you Malati is getting a mastery over, distinguishes you now as a good player,' Shyam declared one day.

'But I am short and my legs and arms don't have the same reach as Chandra, you, and Vivek, let alone world champions like Kitty McKane,' said Malati.

'Yes, but you can make up that deficit with your strength, agility, speed, ability to return a well-placed volley, to assess and strategize, and to hit deadly shots. You should be in the tournament circuit by next year,' he asserted.

'Thank you, Shyam, for your commitment and your confidence in me that keeps me going,' Malati said.

'I marvel at your energy and stamina despite being on a goats' diet of grass and leaves that Hema Kaki serves you.'

'Don't make fun of her great vegetarian cuisine. She quietly gives us both two eggs every day. Baba sends money for us to eat chicken and mutton at the Parsi and Irani eateries. So, I have enough fuel to keep my engine roaring!'

'Your real fuel is your inner strength and will to succeed,' said Shyam admiringly.

Unlike Guru, Shyam was not a poet or storyteller and certainly not a dreamer—qualities that attracted Malati to Guru, but it was fun to spend time with him even when he constantly challenged her.

34

GURUDAKSHINA

Shyam often mocked and teased Malati. He called her Marathi Girl, Rani Lakshmi Bai; Marathi Gol Lal Mirchi—round red chilli; Ghati Kathi—the wand of the Deccan Ghats! In retaliation, she called him Ponga Pandit—a fake Brahmin priest; Pinocchio—long-nosed poser; nakli Angrez—counterfeit British; Kashmiri kofta—meatball.

One day, Malati was in top form. She hit a series of ace serves surprising her opponents. She got Chandra to make a forced error by attacking her backhand and Vivek by hitting the ball right into his feet. She also made her first attempts at short pacing. Shyam commended her. She was still casually dribbling around with the tennis ball when Shyam called out to Malati, 'Eh, Tennis Ball. You can join us here. You have done enough rolling around.'

Though Brahma the Creator made her short, Malati was by no means roly-poly.

'Is that the big-headed Tennis Racquet calling out? You better stop hitting on me first,' she retorted and opened herself up to teasing all around.

Chandra could not stop laughing. And Shyam was amused that Malati accepted that he was a racquet and she had to be tamed by him! Malati was furious and red-faced. She went running towards Shyam and nearly hit him with her racquet when Chandra intervened.

'Hey, you two. Will you behave yourselves on and off the court?' she admonished, quite enjoying the skirmish.

'Chandra, you tell your friend that I wield a mean racquet now and will out-smash him soon!' Malati retorted.

'But you and I are on the same side, remember? Partners in a doubles game? Besides, when I am training you, I allow you to win me over; oh, I mean allow you to win against me, most of the time,' Shyam played with words again.

'Then be prepared to lose fairly and squarely soon. I aspire to a 6-love win, maybe even a straight set win in the not too distant future,' Malati replied saucily.

'As long as there is some love in the game, I am OK with that! Even look forward to it,' Shyam said.

They all laughed as Malati conceded, 'OK, let's say there is much love gained and none lost on all sides in this game, dear tennis friends!'

After Malati had achieved enough proficiency in tennis, she suggested to Shyam one day that they stop the lessons.

'I don't know how I can thank you for your pains. What gurudakshina can I give?' she asked.

He smiled, put his hand on his forehead, and looked up, pretending to ask the heavens for guidance. He then glanced around to assure himself that they were alone and came across to where Malati was standing near the wall of the tennis shed, shielded from public view and pulled her gently to him, as if in jest. Before she could say anything, his arms were around her and her small, round frame was being squeezed against his tall, hard body. Shyam bent down and planted a firm kiss on her lips.

She could feel his soft, ample lips pressing against hers. His tongue sprinkled some saliva to cool the hot breath rising from the furnace of his body that was scorching her too. The raw scent of their perspiration rose in a mist and mingled in the air between them. His eyelids were half closed to draw in the pleasure, and half open to let passion dart out from his eyes to hers. Then he stepped back, took her face in the cup of his hands, and kissed her on the forehead and cheeks, pushing away her curls with the tip of his long nose. Malati then shuddered as if blistered by a flame and stared at him in stunned disbelief. It took her a few minutes to realize what had happened, to push him away fiercely, and run out of there in confusion.

She could hear Shyam calling out, 'Malati, Malati, stop! I have still to tell you what my gurudakshina is to be.'

Malati rushed towards the college to tell Kamala. She saw her coming towards the class with Ram and Guru. The tennis group quickly joined them. Malati imagined that Shyam gave her a look of someone who shared an unspeakable secret!

Malati was trying to calm her palpitating heart. She was more afraid of the disclosure of what happened rather than that it happened. She prayed hard to all her gods and goddesses that no one had witnessed their kissing for it is she who would be shamed!

In class, all the lectures passed in a daze for Malati. She could feel Shyam's eyes boring a hole in her back. Was he tracing the contours of her body that he had held with his gaze, her round cheeks, and luscious lips that he had felt and pressed against, her teasing curls that he had pushed out of the way? If it was his first kiss too, Malati imagined that he must be reliving the moments as she was.

She asked herself what she felt about Shyam's audacity. She must have liked it, otherwise she would have pushed him aside or resisted. Or even punched him. Instantly!

She was ashamed to admit to herself that she may have trembled with pleasure, not fear. And that she seemed to have let him linger over the kiss for some time and she may even have been guilty of throwing the dart back into his eyes. Was she surprised into submission or equally passionate? She could not say. It all happened so quickly was her excuse.

Then she wondered, was there something in her words, her gestures that invited this insolence, kindled the fire of his desire? The signals between young men and women of their ilk were not easy to decipher. There was no set code. Did her talk about gurudakshina trigger it?

Kamala, sitting next to Malati, sensed that she was tense. She clasped and unclasped her hands repeatedly, signifying the furious battle of thoughts raging in her mind. Kamala hoped Malati could hold back the munitions of her emotions long enough and not detonate them there and then, unmindful of embarrassment or consequences.

When the last class was over, they headed out quickly avoiding everyone. Once alone, Kamala asked Malati to spit it out! Malati told her in detail what had happened. Kamala looked grim at first, but then started smiling.

'I used to wonder which of them would dare to do it first—Guru or Shyam. Now we know that Shyam has more courage so he beat Guru to it. I marvelled at how you have managed to focus on the tennis instead of a romance with the obviously pleasing young man who is so attracted to you. This was bound to happen,' she said to Malati's surprise.

She relaxed a little. Then a wave of guilt washed over her, more because Kamala did not remonstrate with her.

'But, Kamala, what will Baba say if he comes to know?'

Kamala said that Baba did not need to know anything. Just as they did not need to know every bit of his struggle in Desaikheda. Whom he shot or when he was shot at. The girls were responsible for their own day-to-day actions and destinies now. They had to draw their own Lakshman Rekhas.

'OK, even so, have I not inadvertently crossed or allowed Shyam to cross some boundaries? I don't know how much of it was due to my own signals—conscious or unconscious—and how much of it was Shyam's moment of impulsive daredevilry,' Malati wondered aloud.

'Well, from what we have read in novels and poems—a first kiss is a once in a lifetime thrill. If Shyam's kiss ignited a pleasing sensation in you, then he must have picked up some inviting signals from you before. The antenna of men—and women—of our age and in this ambience of dissolving boundaries, are very sensitive and he must have responded to that!' said Kamala.

'Let's say I have been foolish enough and find myself in this mess. What next?' Malati asked.

'First, that nobody should have seen you. Second, you don't utter a word about this to anyone. I am the sole keeper of your secret,' Kamala said solemnly.

'But what if Shyam goes around broadcasting the incident as proof of his conquest over me?' Malati asked, worried.

'You either say he is a liar, or say that he aggressively tried but you escaped,' Kamala reasoned. 'If he is gallant, you won't need to lie. More importantly, is this just a momentary spurt of passion. Or something long term, Malati?'

'I don't know. He is just a good friend at present.'

'I suspect he thinks the same way too. But if you intend to be romanced by him, it has to be within bounds. Restraint and passion are contradictions, but restraint is also a test of the extent and depth of his passion and eventually, love, for you.'

Malati felt relieved of her burden of guilt and thanked Kamala for her advice.

'I take you so much for granted, our "we" has become so much a part of my "I". What would I do without you! And I have been so self-absorbed, that I have not asked you, Goddess Sita, about the Lord Ram in your life. I see he has replaced me in your morning walks from home to college, making a detour to accompany you?' Malati asked.

'Yes. Our friendship is growing like the waxing phases of the moon,' Kamala said.

'Well, it is at least a half moon by now,' Malati teased.

'For now, it is the spiritual awakening phase of the crescent moon!' Kamala insisted.

As for Malati, Shyam seemed to have awakened her body!

∽

'Big news! Pestonji is organizing my concert in the prestigious Empire Theatre. Part of the Edward Behr orchestra will accompany me as a novel experiment. Thank you, Malati, for making this miracle happen,' Hema Kaki squealed with delight and the girls danced around her clapping.

Mohan Kaka was all smiles and hoped that she will draw crowds despite being a relatively unknown singer. Malati assured him that since Mr Petit was supporting this, he would ensure its success. Hema Kaki was not a nonentity; she was the disciple of the legendary Ustad Salamat Ali Khan. That is what had been publicized.

Mohan Kaka turned in shock to Hema Kaki and asked angrily, 'You told them?'

'Yes. They wanted to know whom I had trained under and what gharana I belonged to. I did not give any other details,' Kaki said defensively.

'Do you realize what we are risking? Total exposure of your past. Do the girls know now?' Mohan Kaka asked, alarmed.

Before Hema Kaki was forced to lie, Malati intervened.

'Kaka, it makes no difference what her background is. She is your wife now. As a singer, what is essential is her musical training and lineage, which is the best. As for the rest, don't worry. The world of music is changing,' Malati assuaged his concerns.

'You are right. However, girls, you are not to tell anyone anything about Hema's past. Unless you want to ruin us and part from us,' Mohan Kaka pleaded.

'Of course not, Kaka. You are our family,' Malati assured him.

'You see, girls, your Kaki being recognized as a Muslim and daughter of a courtesan can affect my job, and my nationalistic activities besides the social stigma. That is why I made the cruel choice of not permitting her to sing, I set aside my concerns about this concert for Hema's sake. And, of course, the world must hear her voice,' Mohan Kaka declared.

∽

Shyam was waiting for Malati at the college gate. He took her aside and asked why she had not come for tennis that day.

'Are you avoiding me because of what happened?' he asked. Malati feigned ignorance.

'Something very special transpired between you and me. Lightning struck. I was the first to get the jolt when I kissed you. But I know you too were quivering.'

Malati was speechless. She had not planned this conversation.

'Look, Shyam. I may have given you the wrong impression by asking about gurudakshina,' she said defensively.

'I can read you very well by now, Marathi Girl. You know as well as I do that you and I are more than badminton and tennis partners, having spent hours together over two years. We cannot deny that we are charged like storm clouds. When we come together—opposites attracting—the fire within us suddenly comes to life and emits sparks, gathers enough heat to become an explosive bolt of lightning in an instant. That's what happened yesterday.'

'What you did was very sudden and presumptuous. I felt ambushed,' she said hesitantly.

'Miss Marathi Girl, romance is about the unexpected happening, the unseen waves of emotion propelling us to seize moments of closeness, to take it to new levels of intimacy and pleasure. I am sorry if you felt imposed upon, that too in a public place, without warning. However, something told me you were ready for it, even inviting me. If not, the incident never happened, I am sorry, and it will never happen again,' Shyam said solemnly.

Shyam was a gentleman after all, Malati thought and was greatly reassured.

'Well, I don't blame you, but I want us to forget it ever happened. I hope you did not go around boasting about it? In any case, if you did, I will deny it!' Malati warned him.

Shyam confessed that he had told his twin brother, as there were no secrets between them, but no one else.

'So, we are still friends, and partners?' he asked and Malati said yes. However, considering her shocked reaction, he deferred his right to ask for his gurudakshina in the future, at a time of his choosing. Malati clarified that she would pay it as long as it would be something she can give without compromising her honour, or something that would not be like Dronacharya in the Mahabharata asking for his best archery student Eklavya's thumb, so that he could never compete with his favourite student Arjuna.

35

A PLAY WITHIN THE PLAY

The next day, on their way to the college, Guru reminded Malati and Kamala about the auditions for *Satteche Gulam* beginning that evening. Dinkar, their classmate whose father was a patron of theatre and sponsor of the play providing logistics, food, and props, was going to join Guru in interviewing aspirants for roles in the play.

Malati showed off her familiarity with the play. She reassured Guru that she had read the play three times, memorized her lines well, and was ready to banter with her two suitors, Kairopant and Vaikunth. Of course, under Guru's direction.

Guru convened the auditions in the Rangayan auditorium owned by Dinkar's father. It was to be the venue for their rehearsals until the final performance at the college.

When Malati reached the auditorium with Kamala, Guru and Dinkar were set to test all the assembled candidates—and, to their surprise, there were many of them. Guru called Malati in first to test for the part of Nalini and asked her to act out any passage from the play. 'You must not disappoint Mama Warerkar, whom we have the honour of having with us to guide us with the casting this evening,' he announced.

Malati's heart pulsated so fast she could hear it go *dhad dhad dhad*. She pulled her padar tightly around her waist and tucked it in front. Was she hiding her nervousness or making an extravagant gesture of taking on the challenge? Guru wondered, looking at her with some trepidation himself.

What he did not know was that Malati had secretly gone, Demosthenes-like, near the ocean and shouted out excerpts from the dialogue, the roaring waves becoming her garrulous and demanding audience. Thereby she had learnt to face the fear, difficulty, and struggle to get started and to project her voice over other sounds in the universe.

She chose a dialogue, which expressed outrage at the ill-treatment of women by a lawyer character in the play—Martand. She strode on to the middle of the stage, stood erect, and recited her favourite dialogue, her voice reverberating the thunderous power of her friends, the ocean waves, in the auditorium.

'What do these men think about women? Are we only playthings or animals? Are all men trained to view women thus? How will they do anything beneficial for the country with this attitude? When they view the value, virtue, and goodness of their own daughters, mothers, and sisters in such a derogatory and distrustful manner, how can they be capable of saving humanity from its ills?'

Malati could not believe her eyes when Mama Warerkar, one of the tallest figures in modern Marathi literature, came up to her and smiled benignly.

'Malati, before I say whether you are fit for the part, I want to ask you to imagine that Nandini's atma has entered your body, how will it transform you?' he said. Malati's anxiety melted away before Mama Warerkar's kindly gaze. Her face shone with the eagerness of an amateur beginning her journey to be the thespian who would bring the play to life!

She took a minute to think. Then she said, 'Mama Warerkar, if I may call you that respectfully, sir. Do you not recognize me as your Nalini? I am educated. I am myself empowered and empathetic to others who are less so and urge them to change. I am idealistic and easily swayed by the actions and words of patriots. I am strong willed and once convinced, will commit to anything and anyone who is working for the motherland. Yes, at times I may be gullible, like any young woman is, to flattery or misrepresentation! I may misjudge people. But I also have a strong sense of rectitude and if I have erred, I make amends quickly, abandoning my ego. If there is any part of being Nalini I have left out, please tell me.'

Malati held her breath. Guru was beaming with satisfaction. His choice of Malati as Nalini had been validated.

'Yes, there is. I have conceived Nalini as an extraordinary woman, ahead of her times, but in some ways still unable to escape the weft and warp of tradition she is trapped in. That tension, and the one between her feminine weaknesses and assumed masculine strength, is what you have to reflect. Your emotions must sizzle, your passion must burn through the stage curtains to scorch the audience,' Mama Warerkar said.

She vowed to follow his directions.

'And remember, Guru has a triple role—as a medium to interpret my play for young college audiences, as director along with Dinkar, and also as the main actor playing opposite you in the role of Vaikunth—a pivotal character in the play and the carrier of my political and social messages. So, your somewhat tumultuous relationship with him—that of initial irritation and misunderstanding, turning to love and respect and leading to marriage, is crucial to the success of the drama. So, you both must bond well on stage and at critical points, the audience must hear the thunderbolt striking,' he emphasized.

'I understand, sir. We are good friends already. So, it helps,' Malati said shyly. Guru beamed.

'I think she is the one,' said Warerkar to Malati's relief and delight.

She impulsively touched his feet, thanked, and assured him that she will make Nalini so much a part of herself that no one will recognize her as Malati.

Mama Warerkar approved Kamala's choice for singing the theme songs. Some thirty other members of the cast and crew of the play were selected. After Mama Warerkar left, Guru addressed them, giving instructions on rehearsal schedules and explaining the import of the play.

'Know that this is not just any play we are staging. It's our offering to Mother India's freedom, to awaken Western educated Indian youth in our college and beyond, to contribute to it in whichever way they can—through their ideas, writings, and proselytizing activities. Without in anyway endangering our studies—the completion of which is an important offering in itself! We will spawn action groups to support the Gandhiji-led freedom movement.'

There was a chorus of support as they all shouted 'Bharat Mata ki Jai!'

∽

When Malati and Kamala returned home exhausted, Kamala warned Malati with a serious face, 'Guru positioned you very cleverly so you could get Nalini's part and he will be your Guru as director. Now, don't you go offering gurudakshina to him!'

What could Malati say? She was amused with the coincidence that Nalini, like her, had to choose between two suitors. She reckoned that her closeness to Guru during the rehearsals would help bring clarity.

Malati was more inspired by Vaikunth than Nalini, for she like him, wanted to blaze a trail as a lawyer and use her legal training and advocacy to serve the country. She was not deterred by Vaikunth and Kairopant's face-off demonstrating that most Indian nationalist leaders were lawyers but also that many like Tilak refused their sanad or like Mahatma Gandhi gave up law practice.

Guru's portrayal of Vaikunth Rao, the down to earth, altruistic lawyer, true patriot, and social worker helping peasants secure justice and using his pro bono advocacy to help those who were being exploited was brilliant. His sardonic witticisms, spoken sometimes in English, added zest and sophistication to the otherwise serious Marathi drama.

Dinkar played Kairopant, the wily gold digger and deceitful lawyer in bombastic style. Kairopant's put-on patriotism was to impress, woo, and marry Nalini, heiress to the rich Anna Saheb estate. Once he learnt that she was no longer the heiress, he tried to marry Anna Saheb's widowed daughter-in-law and real heiress, Rewa, whom he had reviled earlier.

Rewa was among the quintessential *Satteche Gulam* women characters.

'I have no authority or control over anyone, but everyone has power over me. I am a slave to other people's power—sattechi gulam,' she lamented in the titular line from the play.

Malati protested to Guru about Rewa's character, and urged him to change the script.

'I agree that she is the stereotype of a self-sacrificing Indian woman but she is Warerkar's creation. Moreover, not every character can be a Nalini living in the twilight zone between tradition and modernity. I believe making a sacrifice is an ennobling act—whether made by women or men. Who are we to deny that merit to Rewa?' argued Guru.

Being part of Warerkar's play was a lesson in the vocabulary of power relations between women and men. Kshama, Nalini's friend, called her 'Mahatma'—a masculine noun that could not be feminized. 'Even grammar has surrendered and failed women,' Nalini declared.

Malati was unhappy with Warerkar's showing an educated Nalini as still dependent on the affirmation of a man for life fulfilment and revolted against scenes where she as Nalini had to grovel at Kairopant's feet in supplication.

'I touch your feet. I plead with you. Don't leave me.'

She felt humiliated by Kairopant's kick in response and his saying that the 'kick is the only language you will understand'.

That Vaikunth had to come to her rescue did not redeem the situation for her. She too asked like Vaikunth: 'How can a strong, sensible woman like you become a weak goddess?'

Guru was exasperated. 'If I knew that I would have to deal with a suffragist every day on the sets, I would have advised against taking you on as Nalini. These are not cardboard characters cut to particular specifications. They are meant to resemble real people. And why do you think it's only women who need a man for affirmation? Men need women in their lives too,' he said.

'Well, too late for regrets. I am your Nalini for good or for bad. Like the madhumalati creeper needs a tree or a wall for support, to survive, climb, and flower, women are portrayed as clinging to a man. The man is shown to be a self-standing tree or wall, not needing any props,' Malati argued.

'Malati, I would rather focus on love and the interdependence between men and women including in a marriage. Sigmund Freud says that at the height of being in love, the boundary between the ego and the object threatens to melt away. Against all the evidence of his senses, a man—or a woman—who is in love, declares that "You and I are one", and is prepared to behave as if it were a fact,' Guru argued.

'Applied to Nalini, she thinks she is in love with Kairopant, her illusion of an ideal man, and surrenders her ego. She is devastated when he rejects her. On the other hand, Vaikunth, a man, swallows his ego and pride, bears Nalini's insults, and rushes to propose marriage to her when she is disillusioned with Kairopant, because he believes in their love,' Guru explained patiently.

'I accept that you are my Guru, and bow to your swamitva of love and logic over me, Vaikunth. I am your sattechi gulam—enslaved by your power of love,' Malati declared lightly and bowed before him.

'No, no. You must not do that, Nalini. I am your sattecha gulam,' said Guru, solemnly raising her up by her shoulders.

Dinkar, who was always around with his camera, clicked photos for posterity.

These were precious moments between them, leaving both

wondering whether they held a deeper meaning for their future beyond mere play-acting! Malati realized that love grows not only when one lets go of vanity, but when each panders to the other's vanity. On the sets of *Satteche Gulam*, Malati and Guru complimented each other. Sometimes Dinkar had to remind them that other actors also existed, and that they were not alone in the play or in the universe.

In the climax of the play, when Vaikunth and Nalini decided to get married, Guru said every evening for twenty-seven days to Malati, 'Just as I loved you, I was confident you would love me. The shadow of the malefic planet Rahu—that is Kairopant—did momentarily cover the moonlight of your love for me. But I knew that he could not cast his shadow forever on our love.' They also repeated daily their promises to keep alive the fire of their passion with their lover's quarrels. They sometimes forgot that it was a fleeting illusion that they created just for the play.

Warerkar highlighted how the exercise of power and enslavement of Indians at the national level by the British, cascaded down to individuals, families, and communities in the Raj. Linked to that was a subtle exploration of what is patriotism, serving the motherland, and working towards gaining swarajya.

The hypocrisy of some of the Westernized Indian elite, pretending to go swadeshi and supporting satyagraha, while seeking self-projection and material benefits from their engagement with British India, was another theme that resonated with them all.

Vaikunth's soul had captured Guru and provided some answers. He challenged Kairopant and set out what true patriotism was: 'To you, Kairopant, the motherland is an abstract idea visible only on a map. My Mother India is concrete, tangible, stretching from the highest peaks of the Himalaya to the southern tip of India, where the seas seek to swallow up Sri Lanka. It is encapsulated in the service to her poor, dispossessed, and oppressed children,' he declared.

A major change Guru made in the play with Mama Warerkar's permission was to insert a dream sequence as a climax where Vaikunth imagines Gandhiji's charkha becoming Lord Vishnu's Sudershan Chakra or divine discus. The charkha fiercely spins on Vishnu's index finger and destroys the Fortresses of the Enslavers, freeing the masses of people held in thrall—a subtle way of saluting the satyagraha movement's power to drive out the enslaving British from India.

Guru was afraid that the more imperialistic among the British professors might object to references to Gandhiji or the satyagraha movement. They were relieved when Professor Wodehouse and the Cultural Committee members cleared the staging of the play after viewing its dress rehearsal.

Dinkar contacted all the professors he thought would be interested and all Marathi knowing students, inviting them to attend. It was heartening that on the appointed day, they had more than a full house of 300 rasikas. Mama Warerkar was the guest of honour. The curtain rose. The show began and they artfully acted out scene after scene, to an appreciative audience. The closing scene between Guru and Malati, followed by the Sudershan Chakra dream sequence, drew the maximum applause. The beaming cast and crew took a bow to a standing ovation.

Mama Warerkar came up and gave a short, unscripted, but powerful speech. He praised the actors especially Guru, Dinkar, Kamala, and Malati. He was careful not to score any anti-British points directly. The only message he gave was potent enough:

> Remember to find your own true and right path to serving your country. And to help the poorest, the most exploited, and persecuted. Whatever you do, whichever profession you are in, find ways to pay your debt to our Motherland, Bharat Mata, and lead her towards liberation from the shackles of her political enslavement—from sattechi gulami.

36

ENSLAVED BY POWER

They thrilled to the percussion of a different type of clapping—the right hand raised in a clenched fist and then hitting against the left shoulder—*thap thap - thap thap thap*. Its vibrations rose upwards and sideways, sailing above the crowds and out into the halls and corridors of the college. Suddenly, someone from the audience shouted, 'Vande Mataram' and 'Bharat Mata ki Jai'. Spontaneously, everyone joined in the boom and swell of the chant even as it ricocheted around the minds and hearts of young Indians gathered there. The actors must have joined too, for Warerkar smiled at them with approval. The students mobbed him. His purpose of firing up their nationalist spirit beyond the the words of the play, was achieved.

Chandra, Vivek, and Shyam came backstage to greet and congratulate them. They all said they loved the play and particularly complimented Guru and Malati on their splendid acting.

'You two were so immersed in it that we could not tell whether it was acting or you were actually wooing each other. Guru, you must have loved repeating some special lines to Malati every evening of the rehearsal,' Chandra joked.

Ram praised Kamala's singing. 'You were amazing. I am sure Mama Warerkar must have been pleased by the innovative way the music and the theme song were seamlessly woven into the whole play. You are our nightingale.'

Ram's praise made Kamala very happy, coming as it did from a rasika who mattered the most to her. And one who was usually not so expressive.

'I admire your bravery, Guru, for mounting a history-making anti-British event in a British citadel,' said Shyam, striking a discordant note.

'Well, we had got clearance for it and the patriotic purpose was achieved,' Guru affirmed. Shyam turned to Malati and reminded her she now needed to focus on tennis or lose the opportunity to play singles this year. She assured him she would give her all to practise tennis until she meets her goal. Guru looked away.

The play had bestowed the riches of confidence and joy as orator and actor on Malati. But it also created an emptiness and sense of loss—the indescribable excitement of performing on stage, the affectionate chitchat, the little tiffs and tantrums in the *Satteche Gulam* family on the sets, and the make-believe intimacy with Guru—she missed them all.

The play would have become a pleasant memory and a personal and collective achievement to cherish, but for the shock when Guru and Dinkar were suddenly summoned to the principal's office the following Monday. The *Satteche Gulam* family, which had swelled to include some from the audience, waited for their heroes when they came out of his office.

The principal told Guru and Dinkar that he had received anonymous complaints that the play went off script, and included some anti-British dialogue, that Mama Warerkar's speech and patriotic sloganeering and the clenched fist and chest clapping went against the spirit of the agreement. Guru explained that the Cultural Committee had cleared the script and the play including at the dress rehearsal stage. It was about rousing a sense of Indianness and patriotism but the words 'British rule' were not mentioned even once. The chant and the clapping were not pre-planned and came up spontaneously. Also, since Mama Warerkar, the great Marathi playwright had given his play free of cost, they could not refuse him the honour of a brief speech which again did not mention the British.

'You can check with the Marathi knowing students who attended the play and with Professor Sukhtankar, the authority on Marathi language and literature,' Dinkar suggested, thereby deftly diverting the arrow coming from their unknown enemies, traitors all!

The principal demanded a list of the attendees for questioning. They denied having such a list and suggested contacting all Marathi students.

The principal let them off with a warning that if he found that they had broken the pact they would face suspension or even rustication!

'What will happen now?' Malati asked.

'Don't worry,' Dinkar said with supreme confidence. 'Our Marathi boys and girls will not betray us or incriminate themselves on either of those points, take it from me.'

Guru advised Dinkar against openly approaching the Marathi-speaking students. That would make Dinkar and Guru look guilty.

He believed that the best thing was to pray and do nothing. The principal very quietly instituted an inquiry, for the management did not want to publicize the 'embarrassing incident'. Fortunately, they put Professor Sukhtankar on the inquiry panel. He later told Guru that it was heartening to see that every Marathi student who was interviewed denied any treasonous material in the play. Some, who had qualms of conscience, apparently just denied having watched the play.

As for the sloganeering and clapping, no one could identify who had started them. The inquiry panel could not hold the whole audience present there responsible, nor could they find any evidence against Guru and Dinkar. They were both let off with a warning that any infraction in the future could cost them dearly.

Malati agonized about who the anonymous informer could have been. Guru insisted that they not be bothered about that and rejoice that they had served the purpose of awakening their college mates and converting them into potential recruits for the freedom movement. 'We ourselves are transformed. I, for one, cannot be the same again,' Guru exclaimed.

'How will we operate the freedom cells now? We will be under watch?' Kamala said.

'Each cell has its leader, and they will decide. I know the questioning may force some to postpone activism but most won't be deterred. Many like me will simultaneously devote themselves to their studies and to becoming lawyers who will practise in their system and change it from within,' declared Guru.

'I am the one who will follow Vaikunth's path to become a lawyer of the dispossessed and freedom fighters. On the other hand, remember what you, as Vaikunth, said about not needing to be a lawyer in order to be a patriot? You are going against your beliefs.' Malati teased him.

'I don't believe everything that I said as Vaikunth. You can guess which of Vaikunth's pronouncements I absolutely do believe in,' he replied, teasing Malati back.

'Hey you, Nalini and Vaikunth. I am Kairopant and I am materialistic and believe in opportunistic patriotism. I made my contribution. I will not allow the ghost of genuine patriotism and satyagraha to ride on my head. Henceforth, I am going to finish my studies and make money, and patronize Marathi theatre like my father,' Dinkar said half seriously.

After this sweet-sour moment of patriotic triumph and uncertainty about where the scrutiny of the British establishment would lead, they went to the 'freedom beach' near the college to celebrate. Guru held Kamala's hand and asked her to join him in singing his favourite patriotic poem penned by Yashwant, the sensational young Marathi poet they admired. Malati, Ram, and Dinkar joined in. A crazy quintet of wandering patriotic minstrels, all of them singing at the top of their voices in Veer rasa—their right hand raised, heads held high in a heroic pose, like the bards of the Maratha king, Shivaji!

Vadu de karagrihachya bhinti chi unchi kiti
Manmana nahi kshiti
Bhinti chya unchit rahe kaya atma konduni
Mukta to ratrandini
Bhakti la jo pur aala, wadto to antari
Payari ne payari.

Let the walls of the prison grow higher and higher
My strong heart will never be shaken or tire
My patriotic soul can't ever be kept in thrall
It is free to roam in the day and at nightfall
My devotion to my motherland rises within me
Step by step, like flood waters, gushing to be free.

Just when they thought that the brush with the British authorities in college was behind them, it came up to confront them again. Malati and Kamala returned from college one evening to find Mohan Kaka and Hema Kaki considerably agitated. The police had come to inquire about the girls for acting in an anti-British play and in the process, had cross-examined them thoroughly about the girl's political affiliations.

'This is what I was afraid of. How many times have I told you to be careful? Once you are in their sight, it's difficult to evade their continued scrutiny. I fobbed them off by telling them that you are simple daughters of a farmer, scholarship holders, loyal to the British, and with no interest in politics. I have saved you this time but you won't get a second chance with the British,' Mohan Kaka warned them.

'And, yes, tell your friend and my favourite boy, Guru, to be extra careful now. His career could be ruined if there is the slightest shadow of anti-British activism over him,' Hema Kaki piped in, quite firmly.

The girls promised that they would stay away from any anti-British activities and would counsel Guru likewise. They were more worried about Mohan Kaka coming under British lens.

'I told them my loyalty to the British empire was self-evident, since I work in a British company in a fairly high position. They also asked about Hema's singing patriotic, anti-British songs. She vehemently denied doing that and offered to sing abhangs to the Marathi policeman. Arrechya. That was a narrow shave,' he explained.

'Mohan Kaka, we are sorry. I hope this will not in any way affect your nationalistic activities,' Kamala said.

'Which nationalistic activities? I am a loyal British citizen and employee,' Kaka said surreptitiously glancing at Hema Kaki whom he seemed to have kept in the dark about his double life.

∽

Malati had resumed her tennis with Chandra, Vivek, and Shyam and managed to play singles games in college, but not in inter-college tournaments. She told herself she could not be the master of all things she learnt. A good actress, a successful debater, and a high scorer in academics she had become. So, doing moderately well in sports was reward enough.

Shyam, of course, did not think so, and was disappointed with her. He said he had invested in training her but she had slacked off due to her involvement in Guru's play. And giving priority to studies in the last semester meant that his efforts and Malati's talent went to waste.

They had no intimate moments since the time he had impulsively kissed her. Malati did think there was some attraction still between them, but she avoided fanning the fire. Chandra kept asking her whether she was avoiding Shyam, having heard about their famous kiss from Vivek.

Malati was irritated. 'You have the other twin. Are you not satisfied with that? We are friends. What more do you want us to do?' she said.

'The lady doth protest too much, methinks. It's OK for Malati to like two men at the same time. You don't have to make up your mind just yet about which one to marry! So don't avoid becoming close to Shyam just because you are also drawn towards Guru. Explore and enjoy both,' Chandra said, teasing and testing her. When Malati said she would not encourage Shyam to go where she was not yet ready to go, Chandra accused her of being so fixated on the destination that she failed to enjoy the thrill of the journey—to seize the joys of stolen moments from humdrum duties, to taste the forbidden fruits of a man's longing for her, to risk the heart bursts from dangerous liaisons.

'This is a new side of you, Chandra! You cannot preach to me unless you not only believe in all that you say, but also practise it. Tell me truthfully. How intimate are you with Vivek and anyone else at the same time. Have you slept with him?'

'Vivek and I are having a love affair with all that it involves,' Chandra said evasively. 'It's true, there is none else in my life at this point. Except you!' she laughed.

Malati was suitably outraged and accused Chandra of breaking the code of chastity before marriage that young virgin women like them were bound by. Chandra questioned the very basis of the code. Who had imposed that code? Men! From Manu, the Hindu lawgiver, down to their fathers! Who were complicit in the women breaking it? Men. They broke the code more than the women ever dared to. In Kalidasa's *Shakuntalam*, was it not Dushyant who lured an innocent young girl into breaking it? It was acceptable then and glorified with a gandharva vivaha. Over the years, men, out of jealousy, forbade women to make love, unless it was with their husbands after marriage. That too, only to endlessly bear children.

Remembering Malak and Baba's injunctions, Malati questioned her logic and granted that there could be exceptions for people like Chandra because they came from rich, educated, and elite families.

'Why? We can't have different standards. We both went to the ashram school and now we are both in Elphinstone College. You can no longer claim to be at a different, lower level of social evolution than me,' Chandra challenged Malati's reasoning.

'We are differently placed, also because of the sanskaras, the values, we have been brought up with. What passes as divine injunction is but an interpretation by people, mostly men, I agree. But for me, it is about keeping a pact I made with my father, who believed in us. It is in return for not throwing us motherless girls into the pit of marriage at the tender age of eleven and instead sending us to the ashram for making us—mere pieces of coal—into diamonds. And then not stopping there. Enabling us to go to one of the best colleges in India to study further. All this he did, overcoming the fear and risk of his daughters being "defiled", "raped", "dishonoured", or worse—tempted into illicit relations with men before marriage. The only assurance was our promise, our will power and our ability to defend ourselves, no matter what the assault or to resist the lure of young men like Shyam and Guru to surrender our bodies to them,' Malati said earnestly and with conviction.

Chandra assumed a condescending tone. 'OK, I understand. My parents are more liberal and they let me decide.'

'That's good of them and maybe it's the right way for you. Kamala's and my way is, and has to be, different,' Malati replied and abruptly changed the conversation. 'Do you intend to marry Vivek?'

'Yes, I do, but only after his career is on track, and I decide what I want to do. Which may be another two to three years. So, you see why we cannot wait that long for our physical union? Both our families are broad-minded but Vivek's mother wants us to get married soonest. There! Now I am pushing you towards Shyam because I want you to be my sister-in-law. That way we can continue our friendship, my darling Chhabi,' she said, and lifting Malati's hands, kissed them.

Malati was touched by her affection, but didn't want to encourage her line of thinking.

37

THE PROPOSALS

'I would only take my love life forward with someone—Shyam or Guru—if I wanted to marry him. It would not be fair on them or me. It might be a problem for Shyam's parents to accept me, a Maratha, and a farmer's daughter. Not someone from sophisticated Bombay society. And that question will arise only if Shyam is interested in marrying me, beyond doing some Radha–Krishna love play, as we used to call it, remember?' Malati pointed out.

'As I said, they are liberal and if Shyam is keen to marry you, they will accept you with open arms. But, should you and Guru think of marrying, there is no way his orthodox, Saraswat Brahmin father will agree to an inter-caste marriage. Don't you delude yourself about that.'

It set Malati thinking. Chandra retreated somewhat and clarified that she was not forcing her to consider Shyam, if she was not ready or willing. Malati held her hand and confessed that though she liked Shyam and would always be friends with him, she liked Guru more and had a deeper connection. However, she needed time to think and prayed that Goddess Parvati would show her the way.

'You had better be careful, because Goddess Parvati had made the wrong choice marrying Shiva, the ascetic with matted hair, ash on his forehead, a leopard skin sash over his bare chest and a snake around his neck, so choose your goddesses and men wisely,' Chandra said, laughing.

'Hey, don't blaspheme our gods and goddesses. Just because you are inclined towards Christianity,' Malati retorted with a smile, remembering the spat and the temporary falling out they had had over it in the ashram.

Chandra then launched into a tirade against Guru, describing him as a soft-hearted fool, too idealistic, and maudlin. His family life was complicated by the machinations of his beautiful but evil stepmother and uncaring father. He was always short of money and wore khadi clothes and wrote for magazines to earn some pocket money. He could not safely steer Malati through the jungle of the real world. He may have been exciting for the stage, but not for real life.

Malati rose to Guru's defence. She claimed that what Chandra listed as his weakness, Malati found attractive. He was rich in ideas and dreams for the country—that's why he wrote articles and wore khadi to spread the message of Mahatma Gandhi. His father was a successful advocate and once Guru started earning as a lawyer himself, he would be comfortable. Malati was drawn to him regardless: to his intellect, his romantic bent, and generous heart.

'I suspect you are also drawn by sympathy and worse, pity—never a good foundation for marriage. Shyam is your man, believe me—full of fun and manly vigour. He will keep your body and mind happy. And guess what? I will come as bonus,' she said, embracing and kissing Malati on her cheeks.

'Hey, I promise I shall consider. For now, I must go,' Malati said, extricating herself from Chandra's grip. But ironically, she had set Malati thinking about Guru more than about Shyam.

That evening, Kamala stayed back to study in the library with Ram. So, Guru and Malati walked back home together. They swung by their favourite spot on Chowpatty Beach. Like lovers who have no place else to meet, they had of late been making the crowded seaside promenade their 'hideout'. Guru always said that the crowds were mere blind dots and dabs on the pointillistic painting of the beach. It was only the sharp-rayed sun just before mellowing, whose stare they could not escape.

They always sat at a particular spot on a stone bench overlooking miles of a rippling shoreline. But it was occupied that day. Unlike Guru, who loved to sit on the 'thrones of sand' as he called the little mounds he shaped up high before lowering his tall, slim, dhoti-clad body down on it, Malati did not like to smudge her saris—the few that she had—with beige coloured wet sand. But that day she had no option. Both knew the mounds would give way the moment they sat on them, much like the weight of their separate realities, flattening the swell of their reigning dreams.

They watched the waves frantically rushing up to them, caressing their feet, and playfully receding from them. Moving away, Guru picked up fistfuls of dry sand, kneading them to feel the meaning of each grain in his life, and letting them glide through his long fingers back to where they belonged in the past. He then smoothed the wet sand around them in three concentric semicircles.

The sky was painted a brilliant orange as the sun set itself up on the sea's watery stage, mesmerized by its own reflection, before slowly immersing itself, like a devout pilgrim. Fluffy balls of clouds, white turning to blue and grey, vied to create a constantly shifting kaleidoscope of imagined shapes and sounds, captivating the people below, telling them untold stories.

Inspired by it, Guru held Malati's hands and kissed them passionately. She did not resist. He slowly let go and looked at her, flashing his dimpled smile. She smiled back shyly. Then he picked up a sharp-edged shell and started writing poetry on wet sand. He recited the first stanza from Balkavi's poem 'Prem Lekh' in a soft voice to accompany his writing, just as a tabla player must accompany and impart rhythm to song.

> Meghanche kari bhurjpatra dharuni, astanchali pratyahi
> Swargiche navlekha kumkumrase, ti sandhyadevi lihi

> Holding the birch bark of clouds in her hand
> The glorious sunset as a perennial witness grand
> Her pen dipped in the red sap of my love infinite
> The Evening Goddess writes a new missive exquisite.

Malati abandoned all restraint, and picked up a shell herself and humming the verse, she wrote over it. He held her wrist, as if teaching a child to write. Then he recited and made her trace another stanza.

> Lajja mugdha pari sheer kamal teh thevooni majhya uri
> Shwasanchya kavani lihi priyatama, hi prem lekhavali

> With enchanting shyness, her cheeks suffused
> My beloved rests her lotus head on my chest bemused.
> She creates our love epistle' mystique
> In the poetic language of our breaths unique.

Guru put his arms around Malati, pulled her towards him, and she rested her head against his bosom. She listened to the *dhak dhak dhak* of his racing heartbeat. They sat there silently, daring neither to speak nor to break the delicate glass of the sacred moment.

Then he recited the last stanza, looking down at Malati, his large expressive eyes trying to arrest hers in the lasso of his gaze. They strained to see each other's expressions in the last of the sunlight before it turned dark blue—the colour of Lord Krishna's body.

> Saare te mag lekh tucch gamati
> Chittachiya Lochani
> Teecha akshay lekh ekach ubha
> Mee magna parayani
> All those other lyrical outpourings magnificent
> In my heart's eyes seem so trivial and insignificant.
> For I am the sole, rapt and discerning reader vernal
> In the universe, of this, my beloved's love letter eternal.

Guru wrote the last verse, then kissed the frisky curls assembled on Malati's forehead by the wind.

'Here you are, you young lovers! We have been looking for you everywhere,' Kamala's voice broke the trance and Guru and Malati got up, embarrassed, to face her and Ram. They hoped the fading light had been their accomplice in hiding their guilty looks. All they could do was smile.

'Hey Guru, what are your intentions towards my sister? You can't hold her close to you like that—that too in public view. Of course, I don't mean you can do this in secret either,' Kamala admonished Guru. Then turning to Malati, she said, 'And you, young lady, I thought you remember our promise to Baba, never to dishonour ourselves or him.'

'Kamala, you of all people must know what I feel about Malati,' Guru interjected. 'I told you before coming here.'

'Yes. Question is where do we take them? And have you told her? I mean beyond the play acting and poetry?' Kamala asked, somewhat sarcastically.

Guru knelt again and made a declaration to Malati with Kamala and Ram as witnesses.

'My dearest Malati, I have reached the summit of my love for you. I can confidently say you are the dearest to me—above anyone else! It's not only the magic of the Evening Goddess or of the play acting or the poetry we share. I love every part of you—your expressive face, your sculpted body, your brilliant mind, affectionate nature, and your strength of character. I loved you from the first day that you complained about me to Professor Seal. You were right, I was following you. I noticed your gait, straight out of a Kalidasa play, and your combination of modesty and boldness. So, I am happy to have been following you in every other way since. Some days ago, when our Sanskrit professor read to us Dushyant's soliloquy in admiration of Shakuntala, I could not help looking at you and wonder like him: did the supreme creator first draw you in a masterpiece, and then touch life into his art? No, considering your extraordinary perfection and your maker's true omnipotence, I imagine you to be a unique creation in femininity's treasure house.'

For a moment, Malati forgot her earthly ordinariness! She felt now the heart burst that Chandra had referred to—a thrill incomparable to anything she had ever felt before. That he had proposed to her with Kamala, her lifelong companion goddess as witness, confirmed to her that it was not maya. Even if it was an illusion, she would not have it shattered.

'My dearest Malati, tell me that you feel the same about me, want to spend your whole life with me, want to marry me?' Guru asked.

'Yes, yes. I do love you, but how is marriage between us possible, Guru? You are a Brahmin. I am a Kshatriya Maratha. You are caught in a difficult family situation with your father and Mai. We both are poor. We still have studies ahead of us and want to become lawyers. Why the hurry?' She was surprised to hear herself parroting Chandra's concerns about their future together even though she wanted to luxuriate in the unfolding miracle.

'You, of all the people, should not have these doubts. If we believe in each other and are ready to make sacrifices, we will succeed. I am an eternal optimist, though I may appear sometimes to wallow in the happiness of melancholia,' Guru said. 'So, Malati! You can't but say yes to me. Ask your heart. Not your head.'

'I say yes from my heart, but my head must still weigh in for the next few years it is going to take for us to be married,' Malati replied. 'And I have my conditions, which include first and foremost, that we don't disclose this to anyone and behave as before—as good, close friends.'

'I agree to this condition and all others in anticipation of their being set,' Guru said, smiling.

'You might regret it,' she warned him with a smile too.

Then turning to Kamala and Ram, Malati asked. 'OK now Ram, have you proposed to Kamala? If not, then with the sea and us two lovers as witnesses, pledge your love, and loyalty to each other. Ram, you probably will face similar opposition from your Konkastha Brahmin family. So, you and Guru take courage from each other as you battle forth,' Malati usurped the role of a family elder blessing their betrothal.

'I have already proposed to Kamala and she has given me her consent—invoking all the gods of philosophy from Adi Shankaracharya to Aristotle to Kant and Nietzsche. That's my equivalent of Guru's poetic courting of you Malati,' Ram said, glancing at the semicircles of poetry written on the sand by Guru.

'You take inspiration from Adi Shankaracharya, who in his *Charpat Panjarika Stotra*, criticized marriage and wives?' Malati pointed out.

'That is far from true. In Shankara's *Prasnottara Ratna Malika*, he quotes Yudhishthira describing a wife as someone who is truly a friend, philosopher, and guide,' Ram replied.

'Don't forget that Shankaracharya admitted to women's intellectual prowess when Ubhaya Bharati, the wife of Mandan Mishra, ably took him on after he had defeated her husband in an iconic philosophical debate.' Kamala stated conclusively.

'Malati, our Ram has found his Gargi in Kamala. Let us all rejoice,' Guru said solemnly.

They held hands, raised them high, seeking blessings from the heavens. These came in as unexpected and auspicious thunder, lightning, and rain. The two men dropped their rain drenched fiancés home. No saying anything to anyone, they warned each other.

༄

Malati's foursome did well in the semi-finals of the college singles and doubles tennis tournaments. Chandra played singles against Malati in the finals. She won the first set and became complacent. In the second set, Malati recovered ground and in the third, she decisively defeated Chandra, the reigning champion. Chandra was visibly upset. Malati seemed to have gained renewed confidence to achieve anything.

'I am so happy and proud of you. Remember, I had said I will ask for my gurudakshina at the right time—I meant—a time of your victory. You have come up from behind to become the women's singles champion of the college,' Shyam said.

Malati's heart sank. What if he asked for what was not hers any more to give?

'Go ahead and ask,' she said courageously.

'Simple. I want you to come and meet my parents. I have spoken so much about you to them as my tennis protégé and as this little Marathi girl from exotic lands who has a fierce desire to prove herself to the world,' he said, smiling.

Malati relaxed and smiled and felt a warm surge of gratitude to him for all that he had done for her.

'Oh that? With pleasure,' she replied.

She told him that she was going to join the LLB course immediately after BA. He was surprised but said, 'All the more reason to show you off to my parents.'

38

FINAL LAP TO THE FINISH LINE

Kamala, Ram, Guru, and Malati passed their BA degrees with distinction. Malati's tennis family did well too. Guru and Malati decided to go to Bombay University Law College. Kamala and Ram were to do their MA in philosophy from Wilson College. Chandra wanted to teach. The Kaul twins wished to appear for the ICS examinations and set a record for the first Indian twin brothers to crash through a recently opened British bastion.

Chandra hosted a dinner to mark their reaching a lower Himalayan peak with aspirations to conquer Mount Everest as she said in her note. As they looked back and discussed their future, Malati became uncomfortable when she saw her two suitors clash.

Guru accused Shyam of reinforcing the British empire by joining the ICS—becoming direct, elitist instruments of oppression. Shyam argued that would be so for any profession—that it applied to Guru and Malati practising in British courts too. And that Indian administrators needed to be in place if India was not to fall off the cliff when the British leave.

'There is something to be said for modern methods of administration, finance, and governance which the British have pioneered. The Montagu–Chelmsford Reforms of 1919 have opened the doors to what they call the Indianization of the Imperial Civil Service. It is a historic opportunity for us Indians to storm the citadels of British rule and work from within to take over and prepare the ground for British departure,' Vivek joined the argument.

Malati tried to calm the waters but Shyam continued to provoke.

'I bet Guru would jump at the opportunity of joining the ICS if he could! See Malati, it could have been a matter of sour grapes for you too. They don't take women, do they?'

'Neither is true,' Malati asserted.

'OK folks! This is meant to be a celebration dinner for us—friends forever. We will look back on these three years as our halcyon days—as the best and most carefree periods in our lives. So, let's not allow our differences of opinion to cast a shadow on its celebration,' Chandra, the gracious hostess, intervened, much to Malati's relief.

Malati agreed that the three years might seem calm by comparison to the turbulence that could lie ahead. Guru looked pensive the whole evening—a little aloof, even troubled. Chandra tried to lighten the mood by asking everyone to relate his or her most embarrassing and most exhilarating moments in college.

'For me, the most exciting moment was when I dazzled the British professors with my memory and mathematical prowess—just when they least expected it from this provincial Marathi girl. I enjoyed their discomfiture and grudging admiration. The most embarrassing incident was when on the very first day of college, I wrongly accused Guru in Professor Seal's class of following us,' Malati flagged off the storytelling. Everyone laughed.

'Well, the same incident was both the most embarrassing and potentially the most fruitful one for me. After that, I could follow her every day and know that she could not complain!' said Guru smiling.

'Hey, that's not fair,' Malati protested.

'It was my first taste of the joys and perils of studying with young women in the same class, and most of all, with a cracker like Malati,' said Guru. 'The high point of excitement for me in college was directing and acting in *Satteche Gulam*, and cresting its dangerous political waves. The lustre on the gold was getting to spend so much time with my "play family",' Guru added, making no mention of the nationalistic activities that the 'play family' had generated.

'Interesting! My most exciting moment and my most embarrassing ones were also with Malati. But I am not at liberty to say more!' Shyam declared and looked conspiratorially at Malati.

On an impulse, Malati dared him to disclose what they were and instantly regretted it.

'Well, the most embarrassing thing was that I tried to embrace and kiss Malati and she ran away before I could. My most exciting experience was when Malati, whom I have been coaching, became the singles champion of the college. There, I have said it,' Shyam said, smiling and looking at Malati mischievously.

Everybody was silent. Guru looked crestfallen. Chandra came to Malati's rescue.

'Come, come, Shyam, telling a lie and a truth tied together in a bundle does not make a lie a truth. You would never dare do that,' she said and laughed.

'Well, this was supposed to be a fun game, so I thought I should try. You have caught me out there, Chandra,' said Shyam, laughing away the real lie disingenuously.

Malati blushed and was quiet for a change. She had embarked on a new voyage with Guru and their boat seemed to be rocking in the eddies that Shyam inadvertently stirred up.

'The fun moment for me was when Professor Holden scolded me for engaging in a "Hindu–Muslim scuffle" with our Muslim classmate Yusuf Meherally, only to be told by him that we are close family friends. The expression on his face was priceless,' said Vivek, breaking the tense silence. 'The most mortifying moment for me was when I kept commending Guru's play and its aftermath for being so forthrightly and cleverly anti-colonial and anti-British, without realizing that some British Professors overheard me and started the witch hunt against you all.'

Malati gaped at Vivek in disbelief. 'If you knew you had inadvertently betrayed us, could you not have warned us? Or did you tattle to build your ICS credentials? Since we have come out OK so far, I forgive you. I don't know about Guru, who bore the brunt.'

'We are not traitors to our motherland, nor disloyal to our friends,' said Shyam, vehemently.

'What's done is done. Fortunately, we all survived the inquisition including that by the police who came to my home and were handled adroitly by my father,' said the large-hearted Guru in a spirit of forgiveness.

'For me, discovering Kamala—a kindred philosophical soul—has been the high point of my three years in college. The embarrassment was to be mocked as a lakdi pehelwan and poor performer in sports, much against the Socratic emphasis on physical training as a complement to mind building,' Ram confessed.

'Well, you can't be a philosopher and jump around like us monkeys. Besides, that makes two of you. Now Kamala, your turn to return the compliment,' Malati quipped.

'The high point for me has been how Ram and Guru have respected us, cheered us on in our quest for perfection without feeling that their manhood is challenged by our achievements. Vivek, you seem as enlightened. Shyam worked selflessly to coach Malati to be a tennis champion—something she could neither afford nor buy with money. Chandra, our childhood friend, thanks for your friendship, for showing us the exalted life of Bombay, giving us motor car rides, inviting us to your home where we met inspiring people,' said Kamala sincerely.

'Stop! Stop! I have not yet become so old and eminent either, to be paid such fulsome tributes! OK, for me it was embarrassing, Chhabi, to be beaten by you. Thank God it was you, my darling not any other bitch! Socializing with the British and Anglo-Indians and still having our core group of patriotic friends was the best part of being an Elphinstonian for me,' Chandra explained. Then looking towards Vivek, she said, 'You all know he is the one for me!' Everyone clapped for the couples—declared or not.

The Maratha girls were unabashed in their enjoyment of Chandra's mutton and fish fare. The two Brahmins, Guru and Ram, looked on with fascination and a bit of disgust, as the ladies inelegantly chewed through the bones. Ram picked at his food, disconcerted by the carnivores around him.

'Hey Ram! Has Kamala the tigress not trained you to forage for something more than grass?' teased Chandra.

'Oh no! It is Kamala who is going to join me the goat, in grazing on grassy meadows,' declared Ram.

Malati announced that no one could get her to give up meat, as it was her soul food.

'Oh no Malati! The flesh and gore you so love will protest against the soul you invoke,' Guru, who shunned meat but ate fish with relish, joked.

∽

The next day Guru and Malati met for a heart to heart about their future before the girls left for Vaishali.

'Malati, now that we have pledged our undying love to each other, we must commit to erasing everyone else from our arc of affection. I belong only to you and you to me. Shyam admitting to forcefully kissing you upset me. Hope he has not attempted anything like that again?' Guru said, agitated.

Malati assured him that he had not and that he was just a tennis friend. Guru respected that, but wondered whether they should now take Shyam into confidence that they were now committed to each other so Shyam does not cross the line again.

'No. I can't. Unless I tell my father and Akka first and you tell your father. And I dare not till I start earning. Neither can you,' Malati stated firmly.

'We must have a code to fend off the barrage of marriage proposals we will receive from our communities,' Guru said.

'I agree. On my part, I will break off from tennis and Shyam to concentrate on law studies. Kamala and I will convince Baba to let us continue studying,' Malati said.

'Our love will have to be hidden like that of Dushyant and Shakuntala then, till the right time comes,' said Guru.

'But unlike them, don't think I will have physical union with you before we formally get married. That's a pact I have made with my Baba and on that I will not relent,' Malati said, a little embarrassed to have to spell it out.

'I accept. I would have expected nothing less from someone with your sanskaras. I will never cross the Lakshman Rekha until you cross it yourself. During the enactment of *Satteche Gulam* do you think I was not tempted or tortured later in my solitude by thoughts of possessing you? I have enough willpower and most importantly, love for you, to wait. But I have my own, conditions too,' he said.

'As long as it does not negate my conditions, I accept,' Malati smiled back indulgently.

'I must have your permission to hold the lotus of your hands and kiss their pink cushioned petals whenever we are alone. And perhaps the next stage will be to kiss your cheeks and forehead and then your lips. You won't deny me that, will you?' Guru asked.

'OK. Let's go step by step. My hands being kissed it is for now,' Malati conceded and elicited a triumphant, dimpled smile.

'I don't want to dampen your ardour. Neither you nor I have the luxury of meeting alone,' she added.

'Let me savour the thought and the hope that it will impel you to go to the next stage,' Guru said. 'Surely this is not one-sided, is it?' he asked.

'It is not. But also know that it is not within my power to go to the next stage, however much I may desire it.'

On their way back home, as they walked past a dark patch of the beach, Guru took both her hands in his. He asked Malati to close her eyes and gently furled the tips of his fingers like feathers over her palms and asked, 'Can you feel the vibrations pass from me to you?'

'Yes, I can,' she said, her senses straining to receive them.

He traced patterns on her palm intently, as a cartographer would a geoscape, up the mounds, and down the hollows and along the crisscrossing lines of the rivers of fate. She felt his vibrations and opened her eyes.

'Our palmist-astrologer says that I have the auspicious spirals of Lord Vishnu, signifying divine consciousness and good luck. You must have the corresponding ones of Maha Lakshmi,' Guru said.

'Well, there must be some force that made me choose you over Shyam,' Malati said, trying to make light of the ritual, although her excitement was mounting too.

He then kissed her hands softly and then deeply. Malati had to admit to herself that she thrilled to the touch of his lips on her palm and the deliberate yet spontaneous way he performed the ceremony of loving her thus. Was it natural or was she weak to melt in the fire of carnal temptation? She prayed that her defenses would not fall easily when they went further in their explorations.

'You are a sly fox!' she said. 'Your hands linger over me as if you are caressing my body, your lips simulating a kiss on my lips!'

'I am no fool, I humbly admit. So sensitive are my hands that awakening to their touch you can hear your nerve endings crackle to life, see the colours of pleasure explode as blood gushes underneath your skin and the perfume of arousal hits your nostrils.' Malati did not contradict him but withdrew her hands from his grasp once they emerged into light.

They returned to Mohan Kaka's home and sadly and reluctantly took leave of each other. Ram and Kamala had just returned from their lovers' tryst at the library too, preferring bookshelves to hide behind and exchange glances over. They cavorted with each other as only two philosopher-lovers do—with Kant's critiques of Pure and Practical Reason contesting with any attempts to create illusions of intimacy.

Malati often wondered what Kamala found attractive about Ram. Unlike Guru or even Shyam, Malati did not see a speck of romance in him. She teased Kamala, 'How can you fall for a hermit like Ram?'

'I do often feel like a celestial temptress—a Menaka come to seduce Sage Vishwamitra into the ways of love,' Kamala said, rather disingenuously.

'Stop the comparison there. Because in the legend, he goes back to being an ascetic and she reverts to being the eternally beautiful, celestial dancer. She leaves behind their daughter Shakuntala to be reared by yet another sage!' Malati retorted.

'Don't get carried away. Thankfully, we are living in the reality of the twentieth century, not in mythical times. So, he can be in a hermitage only of the mind,' Kamala laughed.

༄

Baba congratulated Malati and Kamala on their achievements. Before he could suggest that they now look to getting married soon, Malati and Kamala made a strong plea for them to continue their celibate scholar journey and be pioneers—as one the first women lawyers in Bombay Presidency and as a philosophy postgraduate who could then teach in a prestigious college.

'Well, you are fortunate that I do not readily have any suitable Maratha boys to marry you off to. Even if I had, I would be tempted by the prospect of my two daughters breaking new ground,' he said smiling. The girls were delighted to get Baba's blessing for their next sprint to the finish line!

BECOMING ARTEMIS

Baba told them that Govind was doing well, going to school and learning farming too. The Saraswati Vidya Mandir school now had more than 300 girl students. A big stride indeed. The dacoit problem was somewhat under control, thanks to Malak's action, and it had generally been peaceful. However, Baba did not want them to go there. He would bring Govind to Vaishali to meet them.

To their pleasant surprise, Malak welcomed them at the entrance to his wada, with Veena and her brothers in attendance. Surekha did a special aarti and put a sandalwood paste dot on their foreheads and a black soot mark near their ears.

Malak saw that the girls were overwhelmed and explained its significance, pointing out that they were celebrating the two women graduates' extraordinary achievements and removing the evil eye. They were like warriors returning home, unscathed and victorious after battle. These rituals were meant to create an unseen shield around them.

Malati and Kamala's chests certainly puffed up with swabhiman—a sense of the self. Malati never understood why apart from those who were enemies, near and dear ones too were said to cast an evil eye. Is it that even they could be jealous of you, or they gloat too much before God about you and thus bring down his wrath to teach you and them a lesson to be modest?

That evening they were reassured when Malak endorsed Baba's decision to let them continue their studies.

Sarala came across to meet them the next day with her toddler son Divyabh.

'Is Abhimanyu happy with you? Are you both truly together now that he has proven his virility and you have given him a beautiful son?' Malati asked her boldly.

'That is what I expected,' she said, shifting uncomfortably. 'But he has grown more distant and does not even seem to care for Divyabh. Krishna Rao supports me against Ramabai's machinations, dotes on his grandson, and makes up for Abhimanyu's neglect. He says it's as if I had given him another Abhimanyu!' Then Sarala, swung like a pendulum from despair to optimism.

'You know what? Under Krishna Rao's training I have become a fine rider and will soon be shooting down moving targets—a flying bird or a galloping deer as a mighty huntress,' she said proudly.

'And all your lovers from the past—are you finished hunting them?' Malati could not desist from teasing her.

She laughed wryly and said, 'The hunt is on!'

Sarala created a make-believe miasma of ill will and then, with equal dexterity, spread her wings and flew away or swiftly galloped out, much like the birds and the deer she was learning to hunt. And she still chased the game of her passion despite having the trophies of Abhimanyu and Krishna Rao on her wall.

Sarala's redeeming quality of dedication to her mother shone through in all she did for her and against those she thought had wronged her. Fortunately, as Surekha had assured, since her son's birth, Sarala was too preoccupied to engage in mischief. Maa Saheb, was very happy with the little Krishna who was in her life now and who loved his grandmother.

Shifting her focus on to them, Sarala asked why they were not planning to get married soon. 'I know Malak tried but none here are as noble as Malak to stoop down to marry a common farmer's daughters. Moreover, you could not live within the maryada—the bounds of our palace families,' she declared.

The girls just looked at her in silence. She realized she had misspoken and rushed to apologize, 'I am sorry, it's the royal men who don't deserve you both. Not men enough. Look at me, caught in this unhappy union. You are better off with enlightened men you must have already picked. So, tell me who you have chosen,' she said to retrieve the goodwill and dig for information.

'We have not yet decided. You will be the first to know when we do,' Malati said breezily. Kamala and Malati were stung by Sarala's 'stooping down' remark and uncharacteristically boasted about their achievements and ambitious plans. They claimed that marriage was secondary for now. Moreover, they would not have to depend on Malak's charity because they would be getting scholarships.

Sarala smiled and said, 'I am very impressed with my dear friends winning so many laurels. I too have tried to do something extraordinary, within the bounds of where I am imprisoned.'

'We admire you, Sarala, for that, and some day would like to see your riding and hunting skills in full play. Amazingly, instead of Rani Lakshmi Bai's sword, you will wield the shotgun,' Kamala, having made her point, was generous.

Sarala was pleased, though she thought that they should call her Artemis—the Greek goddess of the hunt—rather than Rani Lakshmi Bai. She had no desire to be a freedom fighter, or worse a martyr. Malati smiled at the memory of all the Greek goddesses Sarala had identified herself with over the years and agreed that Artemis was the most apt epithet for her. She was untameable too, like the goddess of wild nature that Artemis was. But she was certainly not Artemis, the goddess of chastity!

Sarala promised to arrange a hunting party before they returned to Bombay.

∾

After Sarala left, Malati and Kamala spent time with Surekha, who looked happy enough. Veena was a delight. Her princess looks and carriage added to her prodigy rider sheen. Surekha called her the 'gossip princess', relaying palace stories to her adoring father.

'Veena is going to be someone extraordinary,' Malati commented to Surekha and bit her tongue as she remembered Maa Saheb's prediction.

'I only want her to be happy,' Surekha said, pensively.

Veena bossed over her two brothers, Vishnu and Vishal, who adoringly followed her, the female Krishna, like calves hypnotized by the music of her invisible flute!

'Who would think this is a family that used to favour boys. If Malak was king, she would inherit his kingdom. His friends remind him of his patrilineal tradition,' said Surekha, laughing.

'And Malak married you so he could fulfil his duty to have a male heir,' Malati reminded her. Malati now understood why Sarala, even after her marriage, competed with Veena for Malak's affection.

Their time in Vaishali flew past and they had to leave for Bombay soon, but before that, Govind came to Vaishali to spend some time with them. Govind was now eleven. He looked hardy from the farm life and was a good-natured boy. Surekha's sons instantly took to their maternal uncle.

More excitement awaited them when, as Sarala had promised, Malak showed them the silk scroll they received with Krishna Rao's family coat of arms on it. It had two lions standing on their hind legs facing each other and Goddess Durga in the middle. Inscribed in ornate red and gold writing, the scroll invited them to join Sarala's hunting party.

'Normally, women don't do hunting. And here Krishna Rao is hosting it in Sarala's name to mark her hunting debut. I am proud that she will ride her well-bred horse, Anmol, to the forest and will join Krishna Rao, Abhimanyu, and me in the hunt,' Malak declared, his normally cold, grey eyes almost moist with emotion.

Maa Saheb was invited, but Malak felt she was too frail for the long ride. Sarala was disappointed and came across to get Maa Saheb's blessings.

She rode Anmol—priceless, as the name suggested—a handsome, moving sculpture of a horse in glistening brown, its muscular body taut and powerful, its large hooded eyes, rivalling Sarala's in the range and sharpness of their gaze.

She was dressed in the royal riders' dress—Jodhpur pants, long quilted blouse covering her narrow waist and shapely hips. To give it the Artemis touch, she wore a short cape. Special riding shoes, crafted by the royal shoemaker, completed the gear. Her long hair was tied up in a tight ponytail, that swung artfully from side to side as she, astride and erect on the horse, sauntered in slowly through the wada gate.

They all admired the majesty of the horse and its elegant, fully in command rider. 'Sarala, victory be to you,' they said. Sarala preened, glowing with pride.

'Thank you, dear family and friends, for joining us on this very special day. Enjoy your first hunting party, dear Malati and Kamala, and welcome Govind,' she said as they climbed into the carriage that Krishna Rao had arranged for the accompanying party.

Malati and Kamala felt so out of place in their cumbersome nine-yard saris like the zenana ladies—mere spectators in this hunting jalsa of their star performer friend, Sarala.

The forests of Shivpuri soon appeared before them. Quite unlike the beguiling lush and evergreen Van Devi of Ratnagiri. There, animals and birds hid themselves so insidiously in the armpits of the dense tropical trees and between the ponderous breasts of the Sahyadri hills, that the hunter often became the hunted. Snakes or foxes, hyenas or vultures even leopards made a feast of any human who dared to enter her dark recesses.

Shivpuri's Van Devata, was by contrast, casually spreadeagled with trees and shrubs sprouting like tufts of hair on his chest and arms, creating enough enclosures and canopies for the wildlife to hide, but ample open, well-lit spaces for the hunters too to seek them out. The not so tall, bent legs of forested hills, cupped grassy fields. The Van Devata wore swirling robes in shades of green—from the palest of pale to the deepest of deep, speckled artfully in bursts of yellow, orange, red, and purple flowers.

The rich array of trees in the Shivpuri forests amazed them. The thorny, thin leafed khair, the aromatic resin producing salai, large leafed tendu that turned into bidis for smoking, the flame of the forest, palash, tall kardai trees with light yellow wraps and the woody dhawda. They wrangled with the hunters bent on cutting through their thickets to squiggle pathways and clearings, prepare stakeouts or penetrate the abodes of their animal friends.

The hunting party finally reached the shikar ghar—hunting lodge—at a good pace and awaited the star rider-hunters to arrive. They were upon the biggest of Shivpuri's famous lakes with many species of birds, including migratory ones, flying around in a sweet cacophony.

'Ramabai has not joined us,' Malati observed.

'She would have come if it was Abhimanyu's hunting party,' Surekha said. 'It's for the best. Let Sarala cherish her moment of glory without any one with ill will around.'

The baits and traps for the birds were laid. Tempting morsels of food, including insects, were strewn on the ground. The shooters hid behind shrubs and piles of straw as they took aim.

'Sarala, you get to go first, as the best must!' Krishna Rao, her proud but nervous father-in-law and teacher, called out.

The spectators watched with bated breath, as Sarala took perfect aim, targeted with finesse different birds—each with a unique flight path—and shot down a good pile of them—mostly quail, red junglefowl, painted francolin, peafowl, and ducks. Her impeccable performance drew a big applause. Abhimanyu, clapped enthusiastically too and tapped her on her shoulder as did Malak and Krishna Rao saying 'shabash! shabash'. Sarala bowed and acknowledged the applause.

'Hail to you, Sarala. You are truly Artemis the goddess of the hunt,' Malati shouted excitedly.

Sarala looked at the girls triumphantly—happy she had proven her worth in something rare for a woman in Vaishali, and beyond. The feathered trophies were scooped up into canvas bags to be readied for Maharaj's culinary ministrations!

An advance team of spotters who had gone to identify locations where the graceful chinkara gazelles, boars, and tigers that hunters would chase on horseback and kill, returned just in time to guide the hunters to their next preys.

The 'spectators' came back home and awaited the return of the hunters in the evening. At dusk, they heard the clatter of galloping horse hooves and sudden uproar at the gates of the wada. Malati and Kamala rushed out eagerly to see what game and trophies the hunters had brought back. It was only when Malak and Krishna Rao leapt down from their saddles, and the rider behind them came into view, that they saw to their horror, Abhimanyu holding up a wounded, blood splattered Sarala.

The retainers came running and helped take an unconscious Sarala down from the horse and put her into the carriage that was standing nearby. She seemed to have been shot, not mauled by a wild animal.

Both Malak and Krishna Rao looked distraught, and Abhimanyu hung his head. Malati and Kamala were speechless with shock.

Surekha rushed out and held Malak's hand and asked, 'Aho! What happened to our dear Sarala?'

Malak did not reply.

She took one look at the blood splattered unconscious Sarala and demanded, 'Who is going with her to the hospital? We have to save her now!'

Without waiting for a response, she got into the carriage with Sarala and shouted to the driver to go as fast as possible to the royal hospital. She showed a woman's presence of mind, while the men were immobilized by the tragedy itself. Not for the first time.

Baba asked Malak, 'What happened, Jamai Raja? How did she get shot?'

'It is I who was foolish enough to teach that beautiful, precious girl riding and hunting. This accident would not have taken place if I had not encouraged her on this path,' Krishna Rao said, sobbing on Malak's shoulders. Malak was trying to look brave.

'No, Baba Saheb. It's not your fault. It is my bullet that hit her instead of the gazelle that I was focused on. I did not realize that Sarala had moved ahead on her horse towards the gazelle to get to the prey first! I am guilty and I am ready for any punishment from both of you,' said Abhimanyu, his shoulders heaving in a sob.

Ramabai arrived at the wada, caterwauling, her batwing arms flapping. She beat her chest and cling-clanged the armour plates of her gold necklaces. 'We don't want to lose her. She is the mother of our dearest grandchild. I am so sorry it happened this way. Oh God! What have you done?' she cried and looked angrily heavenwards and sympathetically at Abhimanyu.

Baba urged a shell-shocked Malak to rush to the hospital along with Malati. Krishna Rao told Abhimanyu to go home and change out of his bloodstained clothes and join them at the hospital soonest. Baba and Kamala stayed back with Veena and the boys. When they arrived at the hospital, before returning to the wada to take care of Maa Saheb, Surekha told them that the English surgeon was trying to take out the bullet, which had lodged in Sarala's back. After a very long hour, the doctor came to talk to them. He told them he had removed the bullet and though she had lost too much blood, he saw some chance of her pulling through.

Malati pleaded with Malak to let her stay till Sarala regained consciousness. He relented. Malati had never prayed as she did that night. As she sat there, wakeful and alert through the night, watching Sarala fight for every breath, she realized how everyone tends to take every living moment as a given. Sarala certainly did. Restless about her present, reckless about her future! Malati prayed to God to give Sarala a chance to cherish being alive and forgive her past contempt for life—her own and that of others.

40

THE ROAD TO PURNA SWARAJYA

It was nearly dawn, when Sarala regained consciousness and asked to see Malak. He was waiting outside. He came in and tenderly held her hands, looking into her eyes and said, 'Thank the lord you are safe now.'

'Baba Saheb!' she said in a weak, barely audible voice. 'I am not safe. Did you not see Abhimanyu tried to kill me? He is jealous of me. He and his mother. They resent my closeness to Krishna Rao, who loves me as you do—maybe values me even more than you ever did.'

'I surely do,' said Krishna Rao who entered the room just then. 'I know both Abhimanyu and Ramabai resent my fondness for you. The responsibilities, the freedom I grant you to do unconventional things. But Abhimanyu is not violent and did not deliberately shoot you. I did not teach you well enough. One never goes ahead of a hunting team member and unwittingly in the line of fire, as you did in your eagerness to be the one to shoot that gazelle. When you are in a hunting party, you must keep "half an eye" on your surroundings!'

Malati wondered if Krishna Rao was trying to blame Sarala? A patriarch, protecting his son and true vanshaj—his heir—after all?

'I am sorry then, Rao Saheb. I was at fault. I am the bad student. I not only failed the test, but I am paying the price!' Sarala said ruefully.

'No, no, Sarala. You have done what very few women dare to do! And done it brilliantly. We were witness to what an expert rider you are and the mastery with which you shot those birds like Artemis. And you will recover soon from this mishap,' Malati said reassuringly.

Sarala smiled wanly. 'But I cannot be called Artemis because I did not get the deer! At least I learnt to shoot birds well, did I not, Rao Saheb? I am a good markswoman, am I not?' she sought affirmation from her teacher.

'Yes, I am very proud of you. You were indeed matchless at the bird shoot, and it was you who did get the deer! A markswoman, better, perhaps, than Abhimanyu,' Krishna Rao belatedly assured her.

'Is that why he took aim at me?' Sarala countered, sharp even in her fragile state.

'No, dear. He would not go that far and you know it,' Krishna Rao again defended his son.

Sarala turned to Malati and said, 'You are a good friend, Malati, and forgive me if I have been less than fair with you both or your Akka, who has been nothing but good to me. But you should know that I dared to do all these extraordinary things to impress, if not outshine, you both!'

Malati gently pressed her hands in forgiveness on behalf of them all.

'Vilas Rao, you can punish me for my lapses. I love her more than you can imagine,' Krishna Rao now pleaded guilty on his son's behalf.

'What punishment? I don't know for what bad karma in my past life God has punished this child—not only now, but since her childhood! Let's just pray she recovers and is back to being her spirited self,' Malak said.

They both shook hands as sambandhis—fathers-in-law of Sarala and Abhimanyu—in commiseration.

Sarala smiled wanly at the two men and said, 'Baba Saheb, please don't tell Maa Saheb about this. I don't know what she will do to herself if she knows that she did not foresee this. When I went to take her blessings, she did ask me not to go hunting, but I told her it was important to prove my exceptional abilities to you all. Maybe she should have stopped me,' Sarala said, wistfully.

'I will take care of your Maa Saheb, like you did, until you are back with her. Don't worry, Baal,' said Malak, reassuringly.

'I am happy then. I can sleep in peace now. Baba Saheb do pray that I get well soon. I still have so many milestones to achieve, and yes, earn my place on that portrait gallery of your distinguished family members, Rao Saheb,' Sarala said.

'Of course, dear! You have already earned that special place and you will be the first woman in our family to have her portrait go up there. We will summon the portrait painter the moment you recover,' Krishna Rao promised her.

There was a smile of satisfaction on Sarala's otherwise pallid face.

The doctor advised Sarala to rest. Krishna Rao stayed back and sent Malak and Malati home. They drove home in silence. Their carriage had barely reached the wada gates, when Krishna Rao's messenger came galloping behind them and asked them to return. They rushed back to the hospital. When they got there, the doctor, Krishna Rao and Abhimanyu, who had joined his father, looked grave. He informed that Sarala had succumbed to her injuries and just breathed her last.

'It can't be. You must be mistaken. She seemed all right when we left,' Malak said, unable to accept what he was being told. 'Krishna Rao, what happened? We left her in your care,' he turned to a very distressed Krishna Rao.

'I can't understand. I was sitting here and watching over her. I just went out when Abhimanyu came to the hospital and I brought him in here to meet Sarala but she was gone already. I called in the doctor then,' Krishna Rao explained.

Malati was stunned. How could she so suddenly stop breathing? Abhimanyu's delayed appearance made her uneasy too. But she said nothing. Her heart was too full of grief for their friend who would be Artemis. However much young women like Sarala wanted to be goddesses, their exceptional courage, confidence, and stamina were never enough. Instead, their seemingly small weaknesses—Sarala's impulsiveness and vengeful nature for example—were enough to deny these aspiring goddesses their divinity. The mighty sun swallowing up Muktabai's ants.

∽

After Sarala's cremation, the two families decided that while Krishna Rao's family would have custody of Divyabh he would spend time with his maternal grandparents. Maa Saheb was devastated and clung even more to Divyabh, the only living symbol of her beloved daughter. Malak also tried to spend more time with Maa Saheb and Divyabh at Chhota Ghar—away from Surekha and her children—just as Sarala would have wanted.

Malati and Kamala dared not visit Maa Saheb after the calamity, unsure whether they could face her 'divine grief' and her bitterness that they were alive. They travelled back to Bombay in a sombre mood, but with a new value and zest for life, grateful to God for what they had and still excited about what they aspired to be. However, Sarala's death had tamed their expectations for themselves. They did look forward to the future, but with much humility.

Troubled Malati and Kamala accused all the men of closing ranks against Sarala. For they noted how nobody moved to punish the self-confessed killer, Abhimanyu.

Baba explained away the seeming inaction of Malak. He cautioned against judging people and their decisions only from the narrow peephole of the event itself but urged them also to try to look inside the whole room of the minds and circumstances of the so-called perpetrators and victims. Moreover, they could not allow suspicion to masquerade as proof of Abhimanyu's guilt.

Malak—a practised hunter himself had witnessed what happened. It may not have been easy for Malak to forgive Abhimanyu, whether it was a wilful act or an accident. Malak knew however that if he made it an issue, it would be disastrous for both families—the scandal, criminal inquiry, enmity, and the trauma of Sarala's death made worse all around. If Abhimanyu were to go to jail, Divyabh would lose his father. Baba had no doubt that Abhimanyu would somehow pay with a guilty conscience. He asked the girls to assess crime and punishment, actions and consequences, without emotion and weigh them carefully.

'You must remember that it must not end up harming the cause of those whose death is sought to be avenged. For Malak it was a question of salvaging what he could, of Sarala's dignity and legacy,' he stressed.

∽

Once back in Bombay, the girls got busy worshipping at their new temples of learning—Malati at the Government Law College and Kamala at Wilson College. They had literally to go their separate ways in opposite directions to college now. Guru and Malati went to Law College together, while Kamala and Ram headed off to the much nearer Wilson College.

Guru and Malati were in healthy competition and vied to get top marks and commendations from their mostly British professors. Malati was the sole woman in the class, so she felt both privileged and under pressure to prove her worth here, even more than in Elphinstone College. They told each other that they were going to tie for the gold medal, awarded to the best law student at the end of the second year. Guru secretly hoped he would beat Malati, a formidable rival and a woman, to it, while Malati aimed to beat the other men's all-time records

The two had been attending Mahatma Gandhi's public meetings

and providing covert support to satyagrahis from time to time, working through the *Satteche Gulam* discussion and action groups and secretly preparing pamphlets and articles. In their law classes they were deliberately understated on opposing British rule and advocating freedom to avoid raising suspicion. However, the nationalist upsurge against the Simon Commission in 1928 changed all that.

They now sought to participate more openly in the national movement, casting aside their earlier caution and joined their fiery nationalist classmate from both Elphinstone College and the Law College—Yusuf Meherally. Yusuf had defied his pro-British parents and founded the Bombay Youth League to get young Indians to agitate vigorously for India's independence.

Guru and Malati studied a range of law courses that helped them understand how British legal systems were adapted to put an impress of rule of law on an inherently unfair and illegitimate colonial system of governance in India. They also debated the changes towards greater self-rule and reforms that the British government had been proposing, in response to the growing demands from various sections of the Indian National movement for dominion status if not Purna Swarajya or complete independence within or outside the Commonwealth.

As a follow-up to the disappointing Montagu–Chelmsford Reforms of 1919, Indian national movement leaders of all hues strongly opposed the Simon Commission appointed by the British government in 1927. There was outrage over the absence of any Indian representation in a body that would decide the fate of Indians. All major political formations—including the Congress and the Hindu Mahasabha gave a call to boycott it when its members arrived in India in February 1928.

Malati and Guru skipped classes and joined the hartal and demonstrations against the Simon Commission. They did not however cross the Lakshman Rekha of courting arrest or quitting college for good as was being increasingly urged by Congress leaders. They participated in a mammoth Congress rally on Chowpatty Beach in Girgaum which sent an unequivocal message of widespread Indian opposition and resistance to the Simon Commission.

Simultaneously, Yusuf, who had become close friends with Guru, proposed an amphibious expedition whereby some boys would go on boats and accost the members of the Simon Commission delegation at sea itself. But it seemed that the police got wind of their plan and prevented it. Without telling Malati, Guru then joined Yusuf and his followers, dressed up as coolies, to get access to the Bombay Port where they greeted the members of the Simon Commission with black flags and shouts of 'Simon Go Back'. Malati was angry with Guru that they had not included her in this first foray, but understood that she could not disguise herself as a coolie.

Instead, she chose to actively mobilize and join the larger, 700-strong youth procession against the Simon Commission led by Yusuf from the gate of Alexandra Port of the Bombay docks. As they shouted slogans of 'Simon Go Back' and 'India Is for Indians' and marched forward, a large contingent of lathi-wielding policemen appeared before them and warned them to stop and disperse immediately. The protestors refused and doggedly pressed forward. Suddenly, before they knew what was happening, lathis began to rain down on them—the thick batons that looked defensive and harmless when held by policemen casually standing around, but were deadly when they hit unarmed Indian protestors' heads, shoulders, chests, backs, and arms.

As the front rows of protesters collapsed, the blows fell on those walking behind them. Successive waves of blows and falling protestors created a chaotic, untidy moving battlefield, in which one side was armed with only flags and voices that, despite the cries of ah, ooh, hey Ram, ayeega, Deva re, ya Allah of fallen heroes in pain and shock, still reverberated with assertive shouts of 'Simon Go Back'.

In no time, the police had beaten down enough rows of protestors to the ground. They proceeded to walk over the bodies of fallen heroes to reach and subdue those still standing. Soon the rest were forced to disperse helter-skelter. Malati was hit lightly by a lathi on her arm because she managed to duck the blow in an adroit move. However, Guru, who was next to Yusuf at the frontline, tried to jostle and argue with the police. 'This should teach you a lesson', a policeman said, as he hit Guru hard with the baton on his head. Guru fell on his back, bleeding profusely

Malati rushed to extricate him from the stampede that followed, and with another classmate's help pulled him out and dragged him to a nearby shop. She hired a covered Victoria and took him to Mohan Kaka's house, not a hospital, in case the police found him there and arrested him. Mohan Kaka, who Malati rightly expected to be experienced in handling such situations, took him to his freedom fighter doctor friend, who treated and bandaged him. It took a few days for Guru to be declared out of danger.

'Why were you risking death by being so close to the frontline and trying to grapple with the police. You are not strong or nimble enough to fend off the policemen's lathis,' Malati scolded Guru, trying to hide both her concern and admiration

'Well, my limbs may not be trained to evade blows and fight back, but I have a head with a brain that can wrestle with the toughest! See that is why they hit it, but it is intact. A lesser man would have succumbed to the injuries,' Guru joked.

'Guru and Malati, you both are now battle tested and should therefore join me in revolutionary activities. They are much more impactful than these one off, stop–go protests. After all, you have seen how the British have no compunctions in using violence to subdue peaceful freedom seeking Indians. Why should you?"

Mohan Kaka challenged them.

However, they both insisted that they were reinforced in their determination to follow Mahatma Gandhi's non-violent path. They felt gratified that they had at last seen action and dared to face blows in the ongoing war of independence and somehow had dealt a blow to British rule themselves—albeit through soul force and passive resistance.

Appa was not to be told about Guru's injury and his participation in the protests, so Guru stayed with Dinkar for a few days until he could face his father with a plausible story of an accident. Guru finally returned home with a long, still healing scar across the right side of his head and forehead. If Anna guessed what had happened, he did not make any comment or betray emotion.

Guru did not go to college too until his bandage was removed, lest his professors associate him with the protests and institute suspension proceedings. But it was clear that the British government was on the back foot and had to carry out an inquiry against Sergeant Carter who was in charge for ordering an unprovoked and brutal lathi-charge on a peaceful procession of youth, causing injuries to many. Yusuf, Guru, Malati, and others who had joined the protesters were allowed to return to college with a mild warning. All nationalists, including Mahatma Gandhi who had picked up their slogan too, applauded their courage.

41
READING THE LINES OF THE PALM

Guru and Malati were aware that they were now on the radar of the British authorities and had to be very careful and give up their activities for a while. Their return to college also spoke of the liberalism of some of their British professors, like Professor Addington who shared the vision of many of their countrymen that India would one day govern itself. They recognized that British rule over India was politically unjustifiable and economically unsustainable.

The dilemma was, how and in what manner and pace, power should be transferred to Indians and to which governing structures at different levels for such a large, impoverished, politically divided, socially hierarchical, and religiously riven country. Despite the confidence of Western educated Indian nationalists, there was also the often expressed doubt about whether Indians were ready to govern themselves—leading to Lord Irwin's cruel joke that Indians would perhaps be ready for independence in 600 years!

What pained Guru and Malati was that the Indian side was unable to present a united Indian counter proposal to the Simon Commission with the Congress's 'Nehru Report' being dubbed a 'Hindu Report' by Jinnah, who had broken away from the Congress, and presented his own '14 Points' on Muslim demands from the British! All it did was to get Mahatma Gandhi to raise the tempo of his Non-cooperation Movement. The cycle of inadequate reform, defiant protests, and brutal repression that followed, made discussions on these in their law classes sensitive.

Many revolutionary movements and underground factions stepped up their advocacy on armed attacks and rebellion against British rule too. The fire, sparked by leaders like Veer Savarkar and the triumvirate of Bal, Pal, and Lal, and more recently the martyrdom of Lala Lajpat Rai in police lathi-charge during Simon Commission related protests in Lahore, was burning bright.

Guru and Malati were therefore delighted when one day, Professor Addington called his students in groups and asked them to imagine a road map of constitutional, legal, and administrative reforms that would unequivocally lead up to India's independence. He emphasized its importance against the background of the Simon Commission still working on its report and he hoped the ideas of young Indian law students would set the compass right. It was also to be a major dissertation by which he would judge them for their end of year results. Malati was among the students assigned to work on the scenario of a telescoped in time, fifteen-year reform and transfer of power towards independence, while Guru was in the slow track reform group where they had the luxury of thirty plus years to spin out freedom.

Guru and Malati believed that at the least, it demonstrated British open-mindedness and tolerance of debate, and at best, it was meant to get genuine inputs to policymaking from young Indians and training future administrators, leaders, judges, and lawyers shaping the transition to Indian independence.

Whatever the motivation, they regarded it as an opportunity to prove their value and contribute in their small way to India's freedom. They vowed to give their best. Malati felt lucky to get the accelerated self-rule template but the challenge was to make for a smooth transition. Guru was determined to make his plan as front loaded as possible to satisfy the nationalist aspirations, while keeping the fiction of British suzerainty.

They thus got to work on their separate assignments. Malati and Guru sought to interview leaders of the freedom movement to get inputs. Chandra managed to secure a meeting for Malati with Mahatma Gandhi at Mr Petit's guest house. Reading his speeches and articles, she noted how he included women in his conceptual framework for everything, from cleanliness to khadi, to the concept of slavery and freedom and considered their emancipation and participation in his movement essential to India's independence.

She was surprised at how diminutive he looked, clad in a white loincloth, a symbol of solidarity with those rendered poor and wretched by British imperialism. He was seated on a white sheet but to Malati it appeared to be a flying carpet, held aloft by the levitation of that sage, lifting India to freedom with him. Chandra and Malati approached him, touched his feet, and introduced themselves.

'I am always ready to meet freedom-loving young women at any time and to be infected by their fresh ideas and enthusiasm. Come close, unless you fear being infected by my disease of nationalism,' he said, looking at them with his discerning eyes through round rimmed glasses and displaying his famed sense of humour.

They sat down cross-legged in front of him. Malati's heart pumped like a goldsmith's bellow. She summoned up courage and said, 'Bapuji, I feel privileged to meet you in person. Why would I, a woman who is already possessed by your spirit of nationalism herself, be afraid of further contamination? I have been participating in your satyagraha activities. I was part of Yusuf Meherally led Simon Commission protest, which was lathi-charged. Dare I say that it's courage, not fear, that you ignite in us—courage to be the wheels of the chariot of Indian independence equally with men! I wish to ask you a few questions about the freedom movement. I have been assigned a project at the Bombay University Law College and I want to excel in that project not only because I am the only woman in my class, but because I hope to humbly contribute to your cause.'

'I like that you are trying to be a pioneer in what has been a man's field. Go on,' he said, smiling.

'You have said that national independence is as necessary in the international context as individual independence is within a nation and that the legal maxim—sic utere tuo ut alienum non laedas—is equally moral. You have stressed that there is not one law for the atom and another for the universe. You see Indian independence as an inherent right for India to exercise, day before yesterday. Given the complex realities of India and our British rulers' calculations, what do you see as the shortest possible path to India's independence from Britain in the next fifteen years? How would you say we should proceed to that goal in terms of constitutional, administrative, and legal reform? That's my assignment,' Malati said.

He listened to her patiently and became thoughtful for a moment.

'Dear beti, please remember that the intention has to be pure, then everything else becomes possible and these so-called reforms become revolutionary. Our rulers don't yet have the will, so they sometimes find fault with us and divide us, and at other times, try to buy time through so-called progressive or incremental reforms. You fix the goal based on the pure intention of India's independence on the part of the British rulers and of all Indians themselves. Then you work backwards, and you will get the answers as to what constitution, which laws, and which policies you need to put in place to reach there soonest,' he said, giving her the essence of his wisdom on the issue.

'May I also ask another question that troubles me as I seek to be among pioneering Indian women lawyers. You are a lawyer but you gave up your practice for nationalist leadership. The Congress is urging youth to boycott colleges and dedicate themselves full-time to the nationalist movement. How can I best serve this cause of freedom without disrupting my hard won right to higher education now and after I get my law degree?' Malati asked.

'Finish your law studies if your heart tells you, and yes, it is your right and duty. Then later, as a lawyer, be an example to other women and men lawyers in serving the people of this country towards a free India. Freedom from British rule, freedom also from internal colonialisms of caste and the subjugation of women we suffer. Think of what you will put into the constitution and the laws to advance these essential causes too,' he said.

An attendant came in just then to remind him that he had to leave for the public meeting he was to address in Santa Cruz.

As Malati left the presence of Mahatma Gandhi, she felt she had seen in him the miracle-making Muktabai's scorpion. He with his eight stick legs moving swiftly all over the land of Bharat and beyond. The two magnetic pincers of his thought, grasping the unformed minds of masses of the Indian people. His ten eyes seeing the past, present, and future. His narrow, segmented tail, held up in a magnificent curve over his tiny body and stinging all with the tincture of protest and defiance, so it courses through the veins of every Indian. He was slowly, but surely, burrowing down to the netherworld of the British Raj. Soon the British shesh snake king, would bow his head unfurled, before this scorpion of a Mahatma.

∽

Curiously, although Guru could have independently met Mahatma Gandhi, he chose instead to interview the controversial lawyer turned freedom fighter, Jinnah, using the contact of Appa's Muslim colleague. Guru began by asking him why he did not join in presenting a United India constitutional package to the British in response to the all-white Simon Commission on which Jinnah had said, 'A constitutional war has been declared on Great Britain.' Jinnah was haughtily spirited, and gave him a clear perspective on the slow track to freedom. He attributed it to difficulties in resolving the Muslim question and the British using it to justify their reluctance to part with power in haste. Guru and Malati decided not to share notes from their interviews for fear of 'contaminating' each other's proposals as opponents.

They submitted their dissertations to Professor Addington.

Malati was under greater pressure, because if the shorter road to independence team had not made a convincing case, the cause itself would suffer. When Professor Addington summoned them to give his judgment on which side had carried the day, Malati was hoping for victory—not for her sake but India's sake. She was not afraid to be presumptuous about an Indian Government Law College student's ability to sway British imperial opinion and policy. She believed in what Gandhiji had affirmed, that every blow took a chip off the edifice of British colonialism, every good idea was important, no matter when it took wing and flew.

Professor Addington began with a caveat about being a mere teacher in a Bombay Law college, not a member of an Imperial Reform Commission or a viceroy. So, what he picked up and sent for the viceroy's consideration was likely to be of limited value and impact. But who knew? If selected in their entirety or in parts by the powers that be, they would have contributed to making history.

Malati's delight at her paper being his choice for the most daring but credible scenario was short-lived. He chose to send to the viceroy's office, Guru and another student's longer-term scenario for transfer of power. Guru was happy, but, both he and Malati went to see Professor Addington and argued for him to personally recommend the speedier independence scenario.

'Remember, Guru and Malati, we are not writing fiction. Nor are laws made at my whim and command. Don't think colonial structures built over a century and half are liable to be dismantled in fifteen years. Also, we are making recommendations to dyed-in-the-wool imperialists by definition, not freethinking academics like me, nor young freedom seeking Indians like you,' he explained, but relenting added.

'I am going to send your paper, Malati, just in case some liberal like me in Lord Irwin's office has the breadth of vision to pick up ideas from it and make a case.' They left his office amazed at his generosity of spirit as a British citizen working in the Raj and daring to dream with Indians about its early end.

They rejoiced when both Guru and Malati passed with the highest marks in class. Guru got more than Malati in some subjects, much to her disappointment. But he was miffed that she got higher marks than him in some other papers, especially in the Constitutional Law paper. They tied for the first place overall!

'Learn to be bested by your future wife, Guru, even in areas you think are your strengths,' Malati teased him.

'Could you not have gone a notch lower in this subject for my sake?' he asked.

'Are you joking? I will make sacrifices and concessions when faced with choices between your well-being and utter misery. Not on small matters of male ego,' Malati said laughing.

Despite all the turmoil at home, involvement with nationalist activities and academic pressures, Guru found the time to write articles for the *Times of India, Illustrated Weekly of India*, and other newspapers. His poems and plays were published in Marathi journals like *Ratnakar* and *Yashwant*. He wrote under an assumed name, Pushpak, after the mythical flying chariot of Hindu epics, to denote his intellectual and literary flights of fancy.

Monographs on modern Indian literature and on culture won him the Sir George Legrand Jacob Prize of Bombay University. Malati was vindicated in her appellation for him of Michelangelo. He could be as perspicacious and acute in his understanding of law and statutes, as precise in his drafting, as he could be imaginative as a poet and writer. His way of being a complete man, Integram Hominis, Guru told Malati.

Guru was most of the time happy when he was with Malati in college, but seemed to lapse into interludes of intense reflection and sadness. One day, he appeared so upset, that Malati demanded to know what the matter was.

'I don't want to burden you with my woes, nor blight your happy spirit,' he replied.

When Malati insisted, he indeed bared his grievances against his stepmother freely. Mai wanted to come closer to Guru, which he was resisting as tactfully as he could. Simultaneously she was filling his father's ears with complaints about him and his brother. Malati could not see the problem. She advised Guru to simply befriend Mai to defang her. He explained again that if he warmed up to her, she could portray him as having an affair with her, and thus estrange him forever from Anna. She suggested he find out any secrets she kept from Appa that she could be vulnerable on. Guru demurred.

'It's in keeping with the Bhagavad Gita's teachings—a just war for a righteous cause. Fighting injustice. Did Lord Krishna not resort to yuktis—and ruses to neutralize the Kauravas in the epic Mahabharata war?' Malati justified her advice based on what Guru humorously called 'other-worldly wisdom'.

'Surely you don't think I am at war with my Mai?' he asked.

'You tell me. I can't speak for you. In any field of life, be it family or community, college or workplace, there is a dharma bhoomi, the field of duty, and a karma bhoomi, the field of action. But you have to be prepared for these to become a rana bhoomi or a battlefield from time to time. And you have to use all the strategies necessary and be ready to join battle. At least that is what the Maratha in me thinks! The Brahmin in you may be squeamish about engaging in war by other means,' Malati counselled.

42
THE TRYST

Guru was finally convinced and agreed to monitor Mai's meetings with people inside the house and track her movements outside the house with Dinkar's help. He informed Malati that he had found nothing beyond her going to the community Swami's temple.

'In the Ahilya Ashram, I learnt that nothing is what seems to be. Danavi shaktis—evil forces—like your Mai, could be creating a smokescreen of piety behind which they may hide a million sins. One who is so religious can't be cruel to her stepchildren. Witness my angelic Akka,' Malati tried to strengthen his resolve.

'I agree. In fact, my uncle Jagdish performs puja twice a day. But a meaner and more unethical person is difficult to find, even if you go looking for him with a lantern! His only redeeming feature is that he manages to be a thorn in Mai's side,' said Guru, laughing at last.

'OK. Just execute your plan now. Meanwhile, pretend that you are on her side, without, of course, flirting with her. You have no permission for that,' Malati said, half seriously.

Later she had pangs of guilt. What if her advice only struck a match on the tinder pile of Mai's machinations against Guru? If she was playing Krishna to Guru's Arjuna in this Mahabharata, was there also someone advising Mai, or like Sarala, was Mai her own charioteer?

Malati had almost forgotten about Guru's problems with Mai, when Guru burst into Mohan Kaka's house one day, demanding urgently to speak to her. He told her that Dinkar's detective had stumbled upon the truth. He had observed that Mai entered the temple, joined the congregation, but after barely half an hour, left by a side door. She then rushed into what appeared to be someone's house in a side lane and emerged from it alone after an hour or so, returned to the temple and left by the main entrance. Anyone watching her would have thought she had been in the temple all along.

'Guru, Mai is up to something she does not want Appa to know! Ask Dinkar to get the detective to take photos as evidence,' Malati suggested.

A week later, Dinkar had the photos. The person who opened the door to Mai was a young man, as Malati had suspected. Dinkar showed the photos to Guru and he was identified as Surya, a cousin of Mai. They had wanted to get married in Udupi, but because he was from a poor family, Mai's father had forced her instead to marry a well-established householder, Appa. Later, Mai had persuaded Anna to help Surya come to Bombay for studies. They speculated that either he was being helped by Mai by way of money or that they were having a torrid love affair. Either way, it put Guru in a difficult situation with Appa, more than with her.

'If she is having a love affair with Surya, you have to find a way of scaring her off from continuing for your father's sake. But then, you will have a snarling tigress on your hands who has been denied her prey,' Malati pointed out. Then, trying to help a nonplussed Guru, she suggested that he find a third person to do the exposé.

'Malati, that is indeed a brilliant idea! Jagdish Kaka is visiting us in a few days. I will quietly sow the seeds of doubt, set it up for him to "discover" the liaison, and he will indeed pursue it with "religious zeal"!' exclaimed Guru, his spirits lifting momentarily, and then again drooping at the thought of his having to resort to Kautilyan ways.

Weeks passed. Guru did not raise the matter and Malati presumed the worst. Then, one day he agitatedly told Malati that the 'discovery' had happened through Jagdish Kaka who had followed her all the way to Surya's house, literally broken into it, and caught her 'in flagrante delicto'. Appa had confronted Mai. She had made no attempt to deny her 'sin of passion', but had fallen at Appa's feet, promising never ever to stray again and to cut off all contact with and support for Surya.

'Oh good! Happy ending, then,' Malati said with satisfaction.

'Yes, for Anna, not me and my brother. We have stepped on the cobra without killing it. We have to now brace ourselves to face a Mai who been cornered and provoked and will strike repeatedly at will,' Guru said ruefully.

'Why do you presume that? She should be on her best behaviour, now,' Malati assured, though inwardly worried.

Guru explained that Mai's surrender was not sincere. She resented Jagdish Kaka and suspected Guru had something to do with it. So, while pretending to be submissive with Anna, Guru feared that Mai may hit back at them. Besides, Appa seemed more embarrassed that she was caught in an act of infidelity, rather than by the act itself. It was almost as if he was not bothered about her gratifying her lust with a young man, as long as no one, including he himself, came to know. Moreover, Guru did not see him abandoning her, since he had a young daughter by her, and feared that she may diminiate Appa even more.

'What if she turns her attention to me now that Surya has been banished from her queendom?' Guru agonized further.

'No. She must be cured of her "sinful passions" as she called it,' Malati tried to pacify him.

He looked so despondent and vulnerable that Malati grasped his hands in reassurance. Though they were in a public place, outside Mohan Kaka's house, Malati did not resist when he started to take her hands, palms upwards and pressed his lips and planted a few quick, furtive kisses on them.

'My destiny is written in these beautiful, soft palms of yours, do you know, Malati?' he said.

'You mean alongside mine?' Malati smiled

'Yes,' he affirmed.

'Now show me your palms,' Malati demanded.

She raised his palms to her face, guided his fingertips to her lips. For the first time ever, she kissed him back. His face was rapturous with pleasure. His large expressive eyes seemed moved to tears and his lips trembled with desire. Malati, shivering from the memory of Sarala's aspiration to be an oracle and holding the palm of his left hand next to her right one, pronounced, 'Guru, you have greatness written in those lines and no Mai or even Appa can stop you from achieving it. See the lines on my palm mirroring your head, heart, and lifelines. They complement you and support you. They promise you that I will be there to pick you up when you stumble or fall, to give you resolve when you hesitate from seizing greatness, and give you pleasure and lift your spirits when you put yourself down. Most importantly, the lines on my palms take you to your highest destination. As long as I am by your side, don't be afraid of anything.'

Guru pulled Malati towards a flamboyant gulmohar tree nearby. Its masses of flame red flowers surrounded by delicate fern like leaves, formed a perfect, domed pavilion for the lovers. Guru stood still, faced her and said, 'Malati I want to recite to you the "Song Divine" I

composed especially for you entitled "Madhu Malati—Majhich Devi".'
Before Malati could say anything, he knelt down on both his knees
and recited.

> Madhu Malati, you are the goddess
> Installed in my temple's sanctum sanctorum
> To the exhilarating heartbeats of celestial drums
> My fevered chanting and joyous, limpid songs.
> You accept me as your devotee
> And I pledge my whole life to you
> My dreams—dreamt and undreamt
> For you to see and turn into miracles
> The nightmares, those ghoulish pretenders
> To chase away with your trident and discus
> Your love fills my cup of yearning
> To be great—for your sake, not for mine.
> I aspire to reach distant horizons
> And swing back to my cove where calm, inner rivers
> Of happiness, flow, meander and rest.
> I will in turn shield you from non-believers in your divinity
> We will be iconoclasts in other ways too
> Show them we can be and do anything
> The world will turn around us and be at your feet.
> Seeking your benediction.
> For night and day my votive incense burns
> Wrapping you in spiralling wafts
> Of grey smoke, protecting as it churns
> Its distilled holy ash I smear like Shiva's Vibhuti
> In surrender of my supreme Self
> The sweet, ambrosial scent of Homa the ritual fire
> Ignites our sacred desire.
> None dare thwart our love's purpose
> Nandadeep, the ever-glowing lamp of love
> Its sword of pure luminosity
> Cutting through seams of darkness
> Its little ruby tongue of flame,
> Scorching all ill will, all blame.
> I pick red roses for your worship

And bear the prick, pain, and wounds
Of the thorns of sorrows, the hail of arrows.
The kalash pot brimming with amrit
I raise trembling to your parted petal lips,
The heavenly nectar of immortality we together sip
Passing from me to you, you to me, until infinity.
Forgive me, if I seem still so awkward,
I am but a priest newly initiated,
I know not the mystique of these rites
But I promise to rise up to be the best
Sacrifice everything at your altar
Never failing even your most implausible hopes
My Pancha Praan—the five vital life forces
Drawn from cosmic springs
I consecrate to you my Devi,
Let the spirit divine
Merge my soul with yours
And our bodies entwine
O Madhu Malati, let the beguiling veil of Maya
Once and for all be pierced and fall
Between the Manifest and the Truth
Between the Striving and the Attainment
Between the Worshipper and the Worshipped,
Between Me and You!

Malati was thrilled to the core at such unbelievable adulation. He, who was a vidvaan—a brilliant scholar, a Brahmin no less and a lawyer to be, was in love with her—a mere rural Maratha belle. And that too in a worshipful, priest to goddess way! However, she could not hold back from expressing her self-doubt.

'I am honoured to be installed in your temple but I don't measure up. I am a mere mortal and whatever divinity I thought I had, was shaken out when I saw Sarala die in its quest.'

Guru shook his head reproachfully at Malati, his face drained of all poetic ecstasy. 'Malati! You have to accept your divinity to be my goddess, not question it,' Guru exclaimed.

'OK, my devotee. I will keep your faith. I will also ensure that you do not bear sorrows and arrows alone, that I do indeed ward them off and bring only good fortune to us, tathastu.'

She stood on tiptoe to reach his bent head, making the gesture of a goddess blessing him. She realized just how puny she was physically, just when Guru was putting her on a high pedestal.

Guru was pleased that he had moved the 'stone idol of his goddess' to tears at last. 'Please don't cry even if they are the tears of joy,' he said.

'Guru, you are my true love, I see. Your poem is your vow to always love and cherish me. Will you write it down in a bhurjapatra leaf and present it to me?' Malati asked.

'With pleasure,' said Guru. They embraced each other in silence, transported into their own world, impervious to the sights and sounds of mundane existence around them—the rhythmic *tat tat tuk* of the horse carriages ferrying people around to their destinations, *dhap dhap dhanpak* of bullock carts carrying the loads of the world, the *trin trin trin* of bicycles circling around them with curiosity, *ghya ghya, nahitar ata mi jatoye*—calls of street hawkers discounting their wares before they wound up, *caw-caw, chir-chir, tityu-tityu*—the harmony singing of birds flying in v-formations to their nests before they roost at night, the intermittent chatter and amused glances of passers-by heading to their homes.

'Hey, you young people! Don't do your prem pradarshan on the road. Such public display of affection could cost you!' Mohan Kaka called out.

The lovers were shaken out of their trance and a rush of shyness overcame an usually brash Malati. Guru, too, was embarrassed, more for her than for himself.

'Guru is going through a difficult time at home. I was trying to calm him,' Malati blurted out.

'You seem to be crying too, Malati, which is so rare for you. You don't have to explain, dear. I understand but be careful not to display such affection in public. One never knows who is watching. It's OK by me if you both intend to get married. If not, I have an obligation to report to your father, Malati. I would say the same to Kamala and Ram,' he warned kindly.

'But, Kaka, we beseech you not to tell either of our family members as yet. There will be opposition from both our fathers. We do intend to get married only after we start earning and hopefully, by then, their opposition would have melted away in the fire of our love,' Guru took Mohan Kaka into confidence.

'Mohan Kaka, whatever you may have seen today, Kamala or I have not given up our vow of celibacy,' Malati assured him.

'Young lady, you are talking to a hero in matters of sacrificing for love. Guru, ask me what I have gone through to marry Hema, daughter of a Muslim father and courtesan mother, who were never married,' Kaka said sardonically. 'You cannot even imagine how my Brahmin family berated me, threatened to even kill me. For I was besmirching the name of the family forever. To Hema's mother's credit, she was convinced that I will make her daughter happy. I have a hard task to live up to her expectations,' said Kaka, smiling.

'Turban raised to you, Kaka, for crossing the highest mountains of prejudice—religious and moral—for the one you love. An inspiration for me and Ram who will face fierce resistance from our families. I am determined to marry Malati, no matter what. And you are a witness to that resolve,' declared Guru.

'Unfortunately, even Baba may not favour Kamala and me marrying Brahmin boys,' Malati made a case for not telling Baba.

∽

During vacations Kamala and Malati spent time between social work at the Sewa Sadan and catching up with their old Elphinstonian friends. It was during one such group trysts that Guru did not turn up and Dinkar came all breathlessly upset and called Malati aside and informed her that Guru's stepmother, had finally taken revenge on Guru. She had wormed her way into Jagdish Kaka's good books, pretending to turn over a new leaf, plied him with his favourite dishes and in his weak moments extracted a confession out of him about exposing her.

When Malati asserted that Guru could truthfully deny any direct role, Dinkar informed that Mai never confronted Guru. Ironically, she put Jagdish Kaka on the task of following Guru after college and he then informed Appa about Guru and Malati having an affair. Malati was taken aback. Mai was a wily snake goddess after all.

Malati stoutly defended herself to an invisible Appa by claiming that she and Guru did not have illicit relations in the same way as Mai and Surya. They had been classmates for four years. It was natural and Appa could not object to that. These defences collapsed when Dinkar informed her that Jagdish Kaka had tailed her and Guru to their beach trysts and most recently outside Mohan Kaka's house and even reported their conversations and pledges to each other, clinching the matter before Appa. Moreover, Guru, always truthful like King Harish Chandra, did not deny the accusations, although he could have, since they had no photographic evidence.

Malati's heart raced with trepidation about what this would mean for her and Guru.

43

EXCHANGE OF SACRIFICES

A very agitated Guru arrived soon enough. Kamala, Ram, and Chandra, also joined them.

'You heard what happened, Malati? Remember, I had an instinct that sooner or later this calamity would fall upon us and our love will be tested. You thought I was being overly anxious when I in my "Song Divine", warned of sorrows and arrows,' said Guru.

Guru then described how his father, like a true lawyer, put him in the dock and asked him three questions. His fate was to be decided by the answers he gave. A brilliant lawyer that Appa was, he went on to demolish Guru, playing on his respect for his father, his adherence to the truth, and his commitment to Malati.

He began the trial by recalling that Guru as the eldest son, had certain responsibilities towards the family and in carrying forward the family name. Then Appa confronted him with Jagdish Kaka's testimony about his 'illicit affair' with Malati including his 'Song Divine' recitation before a deified Madhu Malati. The first question was, 'Do you, Guru, deny your liaison with Malati, a Maratha girl, who has no standing in the Saraswat Brahmin community? If yes, then are you willing to resile from it?'

Guru told him that he and Malati had been close friends for four years and may have shown some affection to each other in public, but had never crossed the Lakshman Rekha. Guru asserted that he would not resile from his relationship with her and that Malati's standing was higher than that of any Saraswat girl of her ilk, because of her brilliance, educational achievements, and strength of character, besides her beauty.

Guru's pride in Malati and love for her glinted through his narration.

The second question Appa asked was whether Guru was willing to break with Malati completely until they both decided on marriage. Guru told him there was no need to do that because marriage was not being discussed. But then, Guru was not prepared for the third question Appa asked—that he should therefore commit to marry the best Saraswat girl in view, Lata, whom he had grown up with. Since her father was a lawyer too, practising in the high court, Guru could join his chamber once he began practice. She was fair and beautiful, a good cook, and homemaker. She would forgive Guru his dalliance with Malati and be a wonderful companion for Mai. Guru responded that he would not marry anyone until he got his law degree, started earning, and became independent.

'Oh good. That settles it then,' Chandra butted in sarcastically.

She gave Malati a 'I told you there will be trouble' look.

'No, no. Far from it,' said Guru. 'When I refused to even get engaged to Lata, he forced me to admit that I am committed to marrying Malati after we finish our law studies.'

Malati was relieved that Guru resisted his father's pressures and declared his commitment to marry her. This satisfaction was blown away when Guru told them the climax of the story.

'When I stood up for you, Malati, Appa was upset like I have never seen him before. His eyes blazed with anger, his face turned red. He asked me in stern voice to be prepared for his verdict. He announced that he would no longer support me in my further studies and that I should start working immediately to support myself. Because of the promise he made to my dying mother, whose darling I was, my punishment was restricted to this. He said he would allow me to stay under his roof and provide for my board and lodging, but nothing more.'

Guru stopped and there was total silence and consternation all around.

'Unbelievable! How could a father do this to his son!' Chandra exclaimed.

Malati was too stunned to speak.

'So, what was your response, Guru?' Kamala asked.

'Well, what else could it be than to say, well if that is your verdict Appa—then so be it? I will marry Malati, whatever happens,' Guru recounted emphatically.

He explained that Anna probably thought that he could blackmail Guru, but he was stumped by his son's response. Appa asked whether he was willing to sacrifice his law studies and his family for Malati. He wondered what Malati was willing to do in return. Guru affirmed that Malati too was committed to him and would be willing to do anything to support him in every way. Appa stiffened, ordered Guru to abide by his verdict, and wished him well. Guru's narration reflected the first flush of the heroism of his decision to defy his father for Malati.

Malati wanted to know what was Mai's reaction to this 'trial'.

'Mai pretended to support me and came in to mediate. Jagdish Kaka also seemed repentant and pleaded with Appa to forgive my youthful infatuation for Malati. But Anna could not be moved, and nor was I budging—like father, like son,' Guru said with an ironic smile.

Malati was silent and pensive. She blamed herself for letting things get to this stage. Had she let matters rest when Guru had complained about Mai, she cobra-like, may not have struck. As Guru had anticipated, she was provoked, bid her time, hid her malefic intentions, and then bit Guru when and where it devastated him the most.

Now what was Malati to do to get Guru out of this morass? His father probably guessed that Malati had no money to bail him out. She barely survived on the scholarship money replenished only marginally by Baba. Guru was sacrificing his dream of a legal career for her without a second thought. She had to do something for him too to reward that act of renunciation with a sacrifice of her own! But how?

'Malati, don't be sad and dispirited. I will do part-time work, apply for a scholarship, and keep studying law,' Guru said.

'That's not possible—the law course is very intense. You can't get away with part-time work, nor get a scholarship midway, and it's for needy students. Your father is not poor,' Dinkar pointed out.

Suddenly, Malati had an epiphany. She closed her eyes and summoned her heroine, Annie Besant in her mind. Malati strained to hear her, to read her lips. At first, all she could hear and feel was the clamour of the sea waves, curdling into a storm in her mind.

'Malati, come to teach at the Banaras Hindu University—a nationalist institution I have co-founded,' Annie said finally, her outstretched arms beckoning her.

'She is calling me,' Malati said opening her eyes.

'Who Malati? Who is calling you? Are you OK?' asked Guru concerned at Malati's behaviour and declaration.

'I am responding to Annie's invitation to teach at the BHU,' she declared, her eyes shining brightly.

'What? You have to finish your law degree first. You are not giving up your dream to be a lawyer,' Kamala said agitatedly. Everybody joined in to dismiss the idea.

But Malati turned to Chandra and said, 'Please help me to get a lecturership at BHU. I am equally well served if I become a teacher like you,' Malati explained.

'I am deeply moved by your offer, but I will not allow your dream to be crushed to fulfil mine,' Guru said outraged.

'I am only postponing the realization of one dream and fulfilling another—of serving the country by imparting education to young women—creating many more Malatis! And since when do we talk about separate dreams? Your dream of becoming a lawyer is part of my dream too,' Malati replied.

'But why go to BHU?' Chandra asked and Malati explained how it was a special mission for her.

Guru sat next to Malati on the sand and rested his head against her shoulder.

'Don't go anywhere, Malati. I won't be able to live here without you,' he said, despondently.

Malati shook him lightheartedly and said, 'Raise your spirits, Pujari; if you are my true devotee and worshipper, you will be strong and give me courage to follow through with my plan—our plan. We will keep meeting, not on the streets of Bombay, but may be in my home in Benares on the banks of the Ganga, away from prying eyes and jealous hearts.'

Guru's eyes lit up at the prospect and he raised his head and smiled at her.

'I will allow you to quit law and go to Benares only on the condition that once we marry, you will come back and finish your law course. Then, I will earn and support you,' Guru said.

'I promise to do that,' said Malati. 'I will send you money from Benares for your fees, clothes, and books. So, you don't have to beg your father for mercy or money.'

She was filled with cold anger now.

'Thank you, my goddess. I will never be able to make it up to you for your supreme sacrifice even in seven rebirths. What can I do for you in return?' asked Guru.

'I want you to hold your head high when you are with your family and in the world and make them realize their folly in not believing in you,' Malati replied.

'You both are behaving like sentimental romantics with no practical idea of the world,' Kamala argued. 'Mai has succeeded in driving a permanent wedge between Appa and Guru, and maybe, between Guru and you, Malati, whilst you are declaring a chimerical victory in anticipation.'

'Victory will be ours. You will see,' Malati declared firmly.

She was trying to stay optimistic and cover up the inner dread of the unknown that was rising within her.

'And what will Baba say? You are taking such big decisions on your own, on the spur of the moment,' Kamala demanded, upset and unconvinced.

'Baba, I know, will bless my going to Benares as a college teacher. He wanted us to start working even earlier, remember?' Malati responded.

∽

Later that night Kamala tried to dissuade Malati again. She had always supported her even in her sometimes impulsive decisions. But never had they been of this magnitude or likely to cause as much disruption, and perhaps even harm, to Malati and her career. This was against men's and women's equal rights they believed in, Kamala argued, and asked whether Guru would have done the same.

Malati affirmed that Guru had defied his father and expressed readiness to give up his law education for her. So, there was full reciprocity and equality of sacrifice here. Kamala was unconvinced and pointed out that Malati would be the one to sacrifice first and Guru's was a notional sacrifice. What if he were to make up with his father and agree to marry Lata, or that Appa were to relent and let him continue his law studies? In both cases Malati could have continued her studies in Bombay and been among the first women lawyers of India.

'Kamala, I trust Guru. Yes, my heart reigns at the moment and I do this as his lover and soulmate. But my mind tells me that it's good for me too. When I met Annie Besant, and later Mahatma Gandhi, their spirit touched me. I cannot ever do even a fraction of what these great people have done and achieved, but I want to live up to some of their ideals,' Malati said with determination.

Kamala sighed in resignation.

'Please don't abandon me to bear the burden of my decision alone. Support me, bless me, please, Kamala,' Malati pleaded and embraced her like a frightened child clinging to her mother for comfort. Kamala assured her.

They agreed that their two heroes, Annie Besant and Ahilyabai Holkar, blessed Malati's 'Benares Project'. Ahilyabai enriched the sacredness of the eternal city, through rebuilding the holy Kashi Vishwanath Temple.

Kamala suggested that Malati bring out the serendipity of this to Baba to convince him.

'I agree. It is my decision, but I must show Baba the respect of seeking his final blessing, which he has never denied us. But yes, he will be concerned that I go without you, my inseparable sister and my pathrakhin!'

Kamala did not say anything but hugged Malati hard, sudden tears in her eyes. Malati gathered herself quickly and fell asleep thinking of all the preparations she had to make.

∽

Malati contacted Annie Besant through Chandra's parents. To Malati's delight, she was in Benares to inaugurate the Banaras Hindu University College for women—the Mahila Maha Vidyalaya or MMV, just when Malati was ready to join it! After a lot of correspondence and glowing recommendations from her Elphinstone College and the Law College professors, Malati finally got an offer letter for the post of a lecturer to teach history, maths, and political science. She would be living on campus in faculty accommodation, much to everyone's relief.

Baba rushed to Bombay as soon as he got her letter, predictably very worried; but they had satisfactory answers to all his queries.

One unexpected question caught her off guard. 'Are you running away from someone or something? I know my Malati well. She is not the kind to quit and give up her ambition midway, especially when she is doing so well. Tell me the truth,' he demanded, looking at her searchingly.

'Baba, I am inspired by Annie Besant to carry forward your torch,' Malati said sincerely.

'But what about marriage, Kamala, Malati?' Baba asked.

'Baba, don't worry. We will find our life partners when the time is ripe. You used to say that to Ayee, remember?' Malati reminded him.

'I am not happy, but I am proud! Malati go forward. Kamala, you go with her to settle her in,' said Baba

Guru and Malati finally spent some time together after her Benares arrangements were finalized and Baba had left.

Guru was meanwhile going through extremes of emotion. Sad because of their impending parting. He was also the happiest person in the world that Malati thought him worthy of her love and sacrifice. While she had snatched away the martyrdom from him, he enjoyed a sense of vindication and savoured a strange position of power with his family. He felt liberated from them and invincible, because he had Malati as his anchor and shield.

Guru invited Malati to visit his 'home'—his room with a separate entrance before she left for Benares.

'Oh, all right. Finally, our own indoor sacred space? All these years we have been carrying an invisible canopy around us under Bombay's blue and grey skies,' Malati joked.

'Yes indeed. Come in the afternoon and I will order in some tiffin snacks from Dinkar and we will sit and talk till dawn, if our spirit moves us. Don't say no to me. I promise I will behave,' Guru pleaded.

Malati was unsure. She wondered if he had checked with his father.

Guru asserted that he was twenty-one and his father had made it clear since their showdown that he was on his own. So that freed Guru from the burden of asking him what he should do or not do and Appa had forfeited all authority to tell him whether, when, and where he met Malati.

'So come without hesitation. It's your home now that you are my patron, not just my lover,' Guru said nonchalantly.

Malati assured him that she will come but asked him not to let his guard down. Mai and Appa could still find other ways to harass Guru and his younger brother, Ganesh. Moreover, Malati did not want them to think she was a woman of loose character. It was in his interest that they maintained decorum and Malati not spend the night there. Guru reluctantly agreed.

44

THE BIRCH BARK OFFERING

Malati wore the best khadi silk sari she had with a fashionable Magyar sleeve blouse and gold and pearl earrings. She applied kohl, a red bindi, and put on green glass bangles to cover her bare wrists. She tied her hair in a loose bun. She resisted Hema Kaki's attempt to put a jasmine gajra on it to avoid looking like a seductress.

'You look so beautiful. Since you already know how to act in plays, consider films your next career—after Benares,' Hema Kaki said, smiling.

'Oh, come on, Kaki. Don't give her new ideas. She is in such an adventurous mood these days, she may jump at any crazy prospect,' Kamala teased Malati.

'That's true. But not so much as to stray completely from my original purpose. Just because I dress up a little for my first and last meeting in Guru's home, does not mean I am anything other than a prim and proper college-teacher-to-be. Not a wanton actress. I want to dazzle Guru, that's all. Sometimes I must indulge my feminine side, instead of trying to be like a man all the time,' Malati said.

What she did not say was that she wanted to impress Mai and Anna, just in case she encountered them. She figured that they would be very curious to see this woman that Guru wanted to give up everything for. They would have to concede that she was beautiful and radiated the strength and grace that Guru found so irresistible.

Guru picked Malati up from Mohan Kaka's home.

'You look lovely. So appropriate for the surprises which I have in store for you when we reach home,' Guru exclaimed.

As always, they walked to their destination. He took her through Laburnum Road, which she had never travelled through before, with its pendulous bunches of glorious amaltas blossoms turning the vista a bright, golden yellow. It was as if the gods had prepared a sun-specked, fragrant arbour, unrolled a soft floral carpet, and showered a rain of petals on the couple in blessing. Their hands swung and touched from time to time and a sweet-sad sensation passed from one to the other about a never before meeting and ever after parting.

They soon reached his neat two-storey house. This was the first time since Malati met Guru that she was going to see where he grew up and where his spirit resided. They walked up the winding stairs at the back of the house to his room. Quite symbolic of his relegation in importance in the household, and her entry into it by the back door.

Malati looked around as she climbed the stairs and caught a glimpse of a woman, who she guessed was Mai, looking out from one of the windows. She was fair with delicate features and curly hair. Malati smiled at her. She looked embarrassed but tentatively smiled back.

'Here, we are,' Guru said, unlocking the door and they entered his room. 'Welcome to my humble abode, dearest Malati.'

He shut the door, but did not lock it from inside. This was the first time they found themselves alone in a room. Malati stood hesitantly at the door.

'Please, don't be shy. That is not like you. Make yourself comfortable. This is the indoor temple for you, my goddess.'

He made Malati sit on the solitary chair at the study table. His sparsely furnished room had two shelves crammed full of books and a mirrored cupboard for his clothes. A vidvaan scholar's room all right, she observed. He wore his classic dhoti and white shirt and looked even more handsome framed by his four-poster bed. He offered her snacks and sherbet. Uncharacteristically, Malati was not hungry or thirsty. A sudden awkwardness, wandered in like an unwelcome cloud, its soft, shadowy folds, caressing them. Then Guru flashed his dimpled smile and said, 'Imagine, how this intimate sacred space silences us! We are better off under God's great, blue, open sky!'

Malati laughed and the cloud wafted away as easily as it had arrived.

'No, no it is wonderful to be here. Just the two of us. You do have a nice room. And it's very clean and neat,' Malati said.

'Well, I am very particular and it's in your honour too!' he said.

'I think I caught a glimpse of Mai as we were walking up and we exchanged smiles. Has she spoken to you since the showdown with Appa?' Malati asked.

'Yes. Just yesterday, she came here and said she was sorry about what happened with Appa. I did not accuse her of incitement, but my silence said it all. Then she said how lucky I was to love someone so intensely that I was ready to give up everything for her. And then she asked about you, because I had told Appa that you were going to interrupt your law studies and take up a job to support me,' Guru said.

'Really, why did you?' Malati asked.

'It's important that they all know that I am off the shelf forever for any marriage arranged by them. Apart from curiosity, Mai also seemed to want to unburden her own guilt. After wishing me well, she criticized Appa saying that he was as unfeeling and uncaring a father as he was an indifferent husband,' Guru said.

'She may be setting a trap,' Malati warned.

'I may sometimes be too trusting, but I am not a fool. I stoutly defended my father and told her that my love and respect for my father was undiminished,' Guru replied.

Then Guru's 'ceremony of surprises' commenced.

He opened a brown envelope and pulled out three photographs. The first was of the two of them as Vaikunth Rao and Nalini in the *Satteche Gulam* play, holding hands and looking at each other intently. The other two photos were separate portraits of her and Guru from the play.

'This is indeed a wonderful surprise. You got these out of Dinkar three years later, hah!'

'That is where it all started in real earnest, did it not?' Guru asked.

'I thought you said it started much earlier!' Malati recalled.

'Love is an eternal mystery—when it takes seed, when the sapling sprouts, when it becomes a plant and when it grows to assume the form of a sturdy, unshakeable tree,' Guru philosophized.

'So where are we now?' she asked.

'Well, our love right now is like a leafy plant and will require constant nurturing. So, don't forget me, and water our plant of love from afar with letters. I will write every day. Please find the spring of love within you and write to me regularly, too,' Guru pleaded.

'I promise, but don't expect me to write every day or too frequently. Remember, I will be alone, putting my roots down in a new place, working for the first time, and running a house too,' Malati said, suddenly nervous at the thought of all these coming together.

'All right, you are allowed some leeway in the beginning. After that you should write as if you are responding to the prayers of your one and only priest and devotee, every day my goddess,' Guru pleaded and Malati agreed.

The next surprise was a package wrapped in beige khadi cloth, tied together with sacred red and saffron thread. He knelt and presented the package to her and asked her to open it. She eagerly pulled it open to reveal a birch bark manuscript written in Guru's fluid, cursive handwriting. It was the Madhu Malati poem! She was delirious with joy and her wonder-filled eyes said so.

'Oh, you give me a most precious gift, just as I am about to leave for Benares—away from my devotee! It's a talisman I shall always cherish and should your love ever wane, I shall also wave this before your eyes and make you sing your "Song Divine" all over again,' Malati exclaimed.

The casket of surprises had not been emptied yet. Guru took out a faded red velvet box and opened it to reveal an exquisite, filigree work gold necklace and earrings set.

Guru presented the set as a memento of his mother—something she gave him at her deathbed for his future wife as a blessing. Anna had allowed him to keep it. He wanted Malati to accept it from a poor man who could not offer anything else in gratitude. It would also remind her of Guru and of their future together and mean so much to him.

Malati politely refused to take it since it was meant for his bride. They were not yet married and would not be for some years. She asked him to keep it for when they become husband and wife. She did not want Mai or Anna to accuse Guru of pawning the jewellery to her!

She could not however refuse Guru's request to have herself photographed by him, wearing his mother's gold threaded sari and jewellery. Guru's clumsy attempt at putting on the necklace and earrings on Malati, opened up her bun.

Guru sighed. 'Uff. Your tresses cascading down your shoulders and back in naughty black waves are like those of the Yamuna River, darkened in contemplation of Sri Krishna! My goddess looks ever more alluring,' he said.

He then scooped them up and gently kissed the nape of her neck, shoulders, and earlobes. He looked at her with longing and veneration.

'Are you not going to photograph me?' Malati reminded him.

'Yes, yes. I want to first adjust the lens of my eyes to your beauty,' he replied laughing.

He took shots like a professional photographer and said he would keep the photos with him for his happiness and equilibrium.

They drank the sherbet, reminisced about the past, and shared their fears and plans for the future. Time flew and soon Malati had to go. Guru instantly became sentimental. He put his head on her lap like a child, cried, and kissed her all over—cheeks, forehead, neck, hands, and even her lips, saying, 'I don't want to let you go.'

Malati didn't resist but said, 'Guru, you are making it more difficult for me than it already is.'

Malati got up to leave and as they both climbed down the stairs, they could see Appa, Mai, and Ganesh peering at them through a window. On an impulse, Malati waved at them. They withdrew from the window to Guru's amusement. Guru dropped Malati at Kaka's house and left without a word, unable to bear another farewell.

'I am bereft. But who am I to stop you from your high destiny! I am proud that my lioness has courageously struck out on her own perilous jungle path, meandering far from her cave. May you repel all dangers and maul any enemies to bits and emerge victorious,' a heartbroken Hema Kaki, bard-like, exhorted Malati. Kamala said that Malati was more a fearless warrior queen out to win the Battle of Benares!

ო

Malati and Kamala got off the train at the Benares Junction station with some trepidation. Kamala tried to hide her nervousness for Malati by stressing that this would be easier than becoming Elphinstonians. Malati smiled, not wanting to reveal her fear that this time, Muktabai's ant might fail to soar.

Both the station and the city were a contrast to Bombay. Its heartbeat was very Indian. Harsh Singh from the registrar's office came to receive them. Memories of Indore came flashing back as their horse carriage went past the tableau of old palaces, havelis, temples, bazaars, and forts.

They finally arrived at the gates of Banaras Hindu University—a city within a city. The calm of its lush green avenues and parks filled with trees, the majesty of its pillared buildings in old Hindu architectural style, and rows of peaceful classrooms with large open windows seemed to belie the tumult and the everyday battles that she as its freshest frontline warrior teacher was going to have fight on all fronts.

Malati completed her joining formalities at the registrar's office. She insisted on being given a two-bedroom apartment like the male teachers. She hired a capable looking middle-aged household help, Shantabai, to work and live with her, so she could feel more secure. She set up house from the advance on her first salary, which, at one hundred rupees a month was quite substantial. She was exhilarated but also daunted that she had become an independent householder.

After Kamala's return to Bombay, Malati felt the weight or the lightness—she did not know which—of being alone, without family and friends. She immersed herself in teaching, preparing her lessons meticulously. She made efforts to make new friends and engage in her favourite sports, participate in the drama society, and sightseeing.

Although this was a women's college, and it was an all women faculty, she did have to come in contact with men professors of BHU though, for academic consultations and syllabus setting. With her Bombay University first-class degree and Law College experience, the principal recognized her outstanding credentials and gave her advanced classes and freedom to weigh in on the curriculum. This naturally roused the jealousy of other faculty members.

Malati found that it was not easy for a young single woman to reach out to colleagues. The men were either haughty or too forward and women faculty members had their own complexes towards this 'bold import from Bombay'. Professor Gupta, a bespectacled, plump man with a permanently sardonic smile, lived next door to her with his wife. He tried to be too friendly with her. When she repelled his advances, he started picking fights with her. She reckoned that these were the usual tensions of power in a newly established institution, where even the great Madan Mohan Malaviya, the founder vice chancellor, often faced criticism, if not insurrection.

Malati did not let anything get her down. She instinctively took to playing the role of a female guru. She shaped the curriculum and set her own distinctive pattern of teaching in a new college trying to find its Indian soul, but also absorbing and propagating all that was modern and progressive from the Western world, even if some of it was transmitted through a colonial prism! Soon her popularity with her students began to rile other old-fashioned faculty members, even outside the MMV-like Professor Gupta.

She fended off complaints from colleagues that she was 'spoiling her students', 'subverting their minds with new-fangled ideas'. Malati did not care. She basked under the respect, even adulation, she seemed to evoke, when teaching a whole generation of fresh-faced young women like her, who came out of schools they were lucky to go to in the first place, and were probably the first ones in their generation to attend college. They hailed from different parts of India, some on scholarship and some paid for by enlightened parents moved by Pandit Malaviya's and Annie Besant's appeal.

The women students seemed as fired by the freedom movement as their men counterparts—if not more. Most were followers of Mahatma Gandhi's satyagraha path, but there were a few who lionized the revolutionaries of Benares—or the Gundas as they were affectionately called. Malati, while encouraging debate, and patriotic activism, tried to steer their boat to safer shores of Gandhian non-violence, but she knew that some of her students were carried away to banks that were more dangerous and became Gundis!

As a teacher, Malati had to be circumspect and look out for what the Mahatma in his speech at the 1916 inauguration of the BHU had referred to as 'India in her impatience', producing 'an army of anarchists', 'the bomb throwers', and 'assassins' fighting the British authorities. Benares had a large number of these. And BHU, the largest congregation of awakened youth in the city, was apparently infested with them. Malati had a hard time deciphering which of the faculty members sympathized with revolutionaries, which of them were afraid of being marked as collaborators, and which ones actively kept a vigil on students and fellow teachers and reported on them.

Malati put up the photos of Guru in her bedroom. Shantabai noticed the 'the deluge of letters' with the pressed flowers that came for Malati almost daily. Malati told her that she was engaged to Guru and among colleagues, parried questions about her marital status.

Malati sent Guru a princely sum of fifty rupees by money order as the new academic year began at the Bombay Law College. For her, this offering of the 'fruit of her sacrifice' and Guru's act of receiving it with gratitude, swallowing his manly pride, created a unique bond between them—one that was not without its pulls and stretches for both—especially as they lived apart.

45

LOVE, LETTERS, LIFE APART

Malati felt that she could never be alone when her long-distance lover, Guru, constantly embraced and pushed away, praised and berated, cajoled and mocked her through his letters. They were prolific and poetic, beguiling and eloquent, an endless source of inspiration and validation to Malati. His fountain pen traced lyrical word patterns, his fluid handwriting breathed life and voice, feeling and fragrance, colour and movement into mere inanimate sheets of paper.

So alive were Guru's letters that they threatened to incarnate into Malati's alter ego. Teasing her mind with riddles about the universe. Dipping into her soul in contemplation. Whispering confidences into her ears. Serenading her unabashedly. Touching her body with the feather of his words. Giving advice when she was in a quandary. Affirming her actions when she took 'adventurous decisions'. Sharing her disappointment at setbacks, yet not allowing her to rue her mistakes.

Wherever she was and roamed, Malati was beginning to silently talk to Guru come alive in his letters—her second self—and sometimes even her lips moved. Soon Malati realized that she had to detach herself from Guru's letters if she wanted to retain the integrity of her own self and not appear insane in public.

So, she bought a tin trunk to collect Guru's letters, lined it with a saffron cloth and began performing a ritual of unfolding and folding, reading and rereading Guru's letters till they got frayed at the edges and blotchy from occasional tear drops. Every night, she laid the letters to rest in the trunk's 'cloth bed', shutting away her second self with them—until the next time.

Paradoxically, the letters aided Malati and Guru's discovery of each other—the good with the bad—more intimately than they would have if they were living together. About how quick he was to feel hurt by a complaint or a reproach from Malati or allege her lack of interest and warmth. Sometimes his letters were love-filled harbingers of joy, sometimes they made her feel morose and guilty, quite against her nature. No wonder the poets declare that letters speak to both the agony and the ecstasy of lovers!

> Do write to me, Malati. I do not mind what you write—there are things and things to write of. Besides, there is that sweetest thing—the fountainhead of all my fondest thoughts and highest emotions—yourself. Your own doings, Malati, would be of the greatest interest to me, be they ever so trifling. I have done nothing here since you left, but think of you and thirst for your letters as a Nectar of Life Immortal.

Guru urged Malati in one of his earliest letters!

Malati did not always live up to his expectations. But then which goddess ever lived up to the expectations of her devotee, she argued. They had their lovers' quarrels through letters and about the letters. And about waiting!

> I do my usual pilgrimage to the letterbox and feel crestfallen when your letters do not arrive. I see this as a punishment for my coldness and formality perhaps, for I deserve no better than death—cold silence.
>
> It is such a horrid torture to wait for a letter that never arrives or which sluggishly arrives the next morning, if at all. A troubled day, a sleepless night, an anxious heart and an ailing body—that is all my gain, dear Malati. How can you be so superbly careless, Malati, when I am so punctiliously careful?

Once, Malati had a rough day in college with an altercation with a woman colleague. In that frame of mind, when she received a complaining letter from Guru she shot off what Guru called a 'very crushing' reply, signing herself off as 'yours sincerely' instead of 'yours affectionately'.

> It has oppressed and depressed me. I have given myself away to you. You may do whatever you want with the gift—you can get angry with 'it', be sincere to 'it' or be indifferent.

Malati apologized to him. He was pacified too, quickly.

> My consolation is that you love me so intensely that you feel that you have absolute right over me. And when reason reigns

> over me and not sentiment or impulse, you cannot hurt me. Hot words are but bubbles that rise up to the surface of this sea of love, short-lived and baseless, and as such, I treat them, at least for now. Please try not to misunderstand me again. To whom can I look up for being understood than to you, my own, my dearest Malati.

Malati scolded him for not concentrating on his studies now that she was not there to compete against and impress, and urged him to seize his ambition by its reins. He wrote back a playful reply.

> I have already made some unsuccessful attempts at serious reading of law and that ill success I attribute to that sweet, loving girl, whose naughty eyes are now running over these lines. No sooner would I begin reading seriously, then would an elfish creature float into my room, humming melodious ditties in my ear,
> The fringed curtains of thine eyes advance
> And say what thou sees yonder.
> And command me. And on my obeying, would be enacted a thousand all too familiar scenes, memories or dreams in which that sweet elfish creature aforesaid, would take the prominent part along with me.

When he reached out to her in his loneliness, it stirred her profoundly.

> I found that spring is beautiful, even in Bombay. Down Hughes Road for example, beautiful red and yellow flowers are blooming bountifully on trees and are being showered continuously on a hard, unanesthetic humanity. But the 'Rift in the lute which sometimes makes the music mute' is that I am alone here—so far away from the person I love.

Malati was consumed with the struggles of making a mark at the college and her correspondence with Guru that she had barely been in contact with her tennis friends. Malati was therefore delighted when one day Chandra, to whom she owed so much, Vivek, and Shyam—came to Benares to visit her.

The visitors were impressed by the way Malati had settled into her own not so little world and had adjusted to living and working as a single woman in a completely new city. They met, talked, and laughed like old times, as they explored Benares together.

They first went to the famed Benares ghats on the Bhagirathi River. Each stepped embankment had a distinct identity and was fringed by majestic, storeyed temples, alongside humbler shrines, casually clustered among ancient banyan trees, the overlapping whorls of bamboo-matted umbrellas in deep conversation with each other and with those that gathered beneath them.

Rising up from the waters, the ghats seemed to fan out into a tangled network of narrow gullies running pell-mell in no given pattern, making it a veritable maze where visitors were lured into losing their way by design. It was where the local Banarasis with a flair for playacting—priests and devotees, shopkeepers and residents, rushed about, rubbing shoulders and elbows with each other, argued fiendishly, played the hide and seek of romance, shouted across crossings to exchange gossip, and whispered confidences at street corners.

The theatres of their lives were their inns and homes, shops and hand carts, music academies, and Vedic schools, the food and paan stalls, fortune-telling booths, naach ghars, and brothels and, of course, the temple yards and bhajan mandalis.

Pilgrims and visitors jostled with locals to pass through these clogged arteries. Eager buyers thronged the bazaars of Benares, attracted by their gorgeous silk weaves and by the lovingly moulded, lifelike images of gods and goddesses in clay, brass, wood, and marble for countless believers and doubters alike.

As they threaded their way through the winding lanes strewn with dirt, slush, and dung piles, dodging collision with 'sacred' cows and monkeys, bulls, and stray dogs, they were overwhelmed by the stench of decaying rubbish and urine. Malati was reminded of Mahatma Gandhi's famous speech here in 1916 where he had 'self-castigated' Indians and Hindus for letting their holiest of holy city become so filthy. She told herself that she would encourage her students to come here and do a clean-up 'shram daan'!

They tried to exit the gullies in time for evening worship. A veritable stampede ensued. Shyam and Malati got separated from Chandra and Vivek. Malati had so far avoided being alone with Shyam but now, there was no escape.

Shyam said loudly into a startled Malati's ear, 'You and I seem to have lost our way!' He held her hands protectively and then reminded her that she had not paid her gurudakshina.

'When you never followed up, I presumed you were joking,' she defended herself.

'No, Malati, you were afraid you will be drawn into my charmed circle and away from Guru! You did not trust yourself around me. You slunk out of tennis, avoided meeting me. I did so much to make you something of a pioneer in sports. But you threw it all away, including your dream of becoming a lawyer—all for that good-for-nothing Guru. What man worth his name would allow the woman he loves to do that?' said Shyam.

Malati was furious.

'Guru also sacrificed for me. We love each other and intend to marry the moment he gets his law degree next year,' Malati said curtly.

'How would you define our relationship? Tell me you don't feel a thrill in meeting me, or enjoy my manly company more than that of that effeminate and melancholic poet?' Shyam demanded.

Malati's eyes spit fire now. Her words came out like the seven tongues of Agni deva.

'Please don't conjure up a relationship of love, when there was nothing more than a special, sports-ignited friendship between us. I never misled you and I even told Chandra that Guru is the one for me. And for the future ICS Shyam, I must mean nothing more than a passing flirtation.'

'I can give up my ICS dream for you,' Shyam offered.

Before Malati could answer, Chandra and Vivek joined them and they fell into an uncomfortable silence.

'Where did you lovers of yore get lost?' asked Chandra, taking the liberty of an old friend.

'Oh, I was reminding Malati of it. I was also demanding gurudakshina from her,' Shyam retorted.

'OK, the next time I am in Bombay I will pay it,' Malati forced herself to respond.

'I want to show you that unlike Guru's family, my parents are enlightened and that's what you will miss, if even now, you don't change your mind and come back from Guru to me. Ask Chandra,' Shyam said openly.

Malati let it pass.

They moved to the famous Dashashwamedh Ghat where the evening aarti of the Ganga had commenced. They marvelled at the multi-tiered brass lamps held aloft by rows of red and saffron clad priests against the starry skies, their concentric light patterns mirrored as bright moving flecks on the water and mingling with the reflection of the heavens themselves. Amidst the meditative chants, the orchestra of clamging temple bells, tinkling cymbals, the *thumpadumpa* of drumbeats, the hallowed, vibrating boom of the conch shell being blown to invoke the blessings of the gods above, Shyam whispered into Malati's ear, 'If you believe in God, then here is a message for you and me. To find ourselves together once again.'

Malati did not reply. Her mind was tracing its own concentric circles of momentary doubt—about her choice of Guru—as fleeting as the flames that extinguish when the oil is sucked into the last drop by the wicks before they turn to ashes themselves. She knew that Guru's family might never accept her even if she did a yogic headstand to please them. But so what? Guru had made his choice just as she had made hers, she told herself.

They returned to Malati's home and sat down to dinner. Before Shyam left, he demanded that she pay gurudakshina by honestly replying to the letter he would write to her on return. Malati could not refuse.

Malati soon received a letter from Shyam demanding that she give a point-by-point rebuttal to his arguments on why she should choose him and not Guru. So, she penned a very tactful letter praising Shyam, his many qualities of head and heart, his fun-loving nature and what he had meant to her as a coach, partner, and friend. But every time she tried to say why she rejected him for Guru, she got stuck. Comparisons, she knew, were odious, but even more so between two able suitors. So, she put the half-finished letter in her study table drawer to be completed later and sent off to Shyam in full and final payment of his gurudakshina.

ട

At the start of the summer holidays, Kamala, Ram, and Guru came to Benares. Guru brought along his camera, Malati's birthday gift to him, 'to capture and imprison' her, his goddess, against the backdrop of the Ganga and the holy sites of Benares. So, early one morning, they went to take a ritual bath in the river around Assi Ghat. There was much merriment as he tried to get the rest to pose as true pilgrims spontaneously taking a dip, joining their hands in veneration to the sun god and river goddess Bhagirathi.

Posing and spontaneity were a contradiction in terms, they pointed out, but Guru did not agree. Ram took off his shirt, entered the water just wearing his long loincloth, and offered his prayers, his Brahmanical sacred thread slung across his narrow chest.

Malati teased Ram about his ultra-orthodox kin hiding their 'impure' European ancestry.

'All I know is that I am jivan mukta, a seeker of self-realization—the oneness of the self and the universal spirit that is Brahman. And that's what I pray for—even here, dipping in the Ganga,' he said, crushing Malati's attempted joke, much to Kamala's amusement.

Kamala took a dip fully clothed. Guru's camera detected a dainty water nymph, her sari fanning out on the water like diaphanous wings, her long hair floating up around her—a suspended black halo.

Then Guru went into a frenzy photographing his goddess Malati who was self-conscious about entering the water and being silhouetted by it, especially with her full figure.

Later, Guru described what he saw and felt in a letter to Malati enclosing the prints of the photos.

> Malati, that evanescent image of you, taking a dip in the holy Ganga in Benares, and rising from it, is forever etched in my consciousness—beyond photographs. Your sweet, round face and dewy complexion glowed. Your doe eyes glanced shyly at me—returning my gaze.
>
> Then you half closed your eyes and joined your hands in pretended prayer. Your wet black curls played hide and seek in the morning breeze—now with your face, now with your swan neck and now with your marble smooth, outstretched arms. With your hair swirling in the waters, you evoked the image of a beautiful water lily, blooming out of a dark pool to face the orange ball of the ascendant sun. Do you blame me for not being able to separate my dreams about you from reality, dear Malati?

Malati blushed reading the second part of the letter.

> The river had painted you with a sensuous, liquid brush. So, when you emerged out of it and walked towards my camera, shaking off water droplets, it subtly unveiled your form to me—more than if you were standing naked before me. Your wet blouse and sari clung to your body in tiny, delicate folds. They embraced—to my great envy—your perfectly round and taut breasts. As you walked deliberately under the weight of your damp sari, your curvaceous cheeks swung gently from side to side, showing off your narrow waist and exposing the firm calves of your legs. Will you promise me, Malati, never again to look so seductive until you and I are married? For you are testing your Guru's self-restraint and power of penance beyond limits. You can't be the heavenly nymph, Menaka, who tempts the sage Vishwamitra into a bodily union with her and also be the one to prohibit it.

46

A FLICK OF THE PUPPETEER'S HAND

Ram and Malati forced a protesting Guru to take off his shirt and pushed him into the water. Ram became the photographer.

'You look like a priest straight out of Kashi Vishwanath Temple, minus the belly. You should give up law and come here to become a priest since you are vidvaan enough,' Malati laughed.

'I will, but only if you are going to be installed here forever as Goddess Saraswati,' he teased Malati.

They explored Benares and its environs together. Guru looked so happy. Malati saw no sign of the tortured soul his letters reflected. Being with her seemed to have that 'ebullience effect' on him as he confessed. The foursome coming together again, buoyed him up too. Even when Guru and Malati were alone in a room, they strayed dangerously close to the line of lost control but they never did cross the Lakshman Rekha.

The vacations soon got over and it was time to return to Bombay. Guru lapsed into sadness as he left with Kamala and Ram. Malati told him that the next year would pass as quickly as this one, and that she would meet him soon on the other side of it, never to be parted. As they bid goodbye at the train station, Malati realized that she would miss him even more than he professed in his letters to miss her.

Guru's letters used to overwhelm Malati and make her feel guilty about not replying immediately. But this time, it was nearly three weeks and he had not written a single letter, even to say he had reached safely. So, she sent three expansive and unusually affectionate letters in a row before she heard back. She eagerly opened Guru's letter.

Dearest darling Malati,

Now you understand how I feel when you don't write to me! I have discovered that the way to get you to write to me real letters, not those merely marking attendance, is to starve you of letters from my side! My silence for three weeks and you send me three letters—full of the kindness and love I have been craving. Guess what? I have not written to you all these weeks because I am extremely disturbed and in mental pain. I have in my possession, Shyam's letter to you and your unfinished letter in reply. You can imagine my sense of shock and betrayal on reading them.

He then went on to explain that when he was in Benares, while he was working on his thesis, he kept his manuscript in Malati's study table drawer. As he was leaving, he seemed to have inadvertently picked up Malati's unfinished letter.

'If not intended for my eyes and meant to give notice to me, I wish to God, I had not seen them. I would not have suffered the torture that I have,' he moaned.

Malati was aghast. She wrote back instantly to apologize for the disquiet she had caused. She accepted that she should not have left an unfinished letter carelessly in her drawer. but it also showed that she had nothing to hide. She reproached him for taking so long to express his anguish. She truthfully explained that this was meant to be a letter rejecting Shyam and assured Guru that she only loved him and no other man.

But Guru was not satisfied. He argued that her unposted letter did not give him the impression that Malati had no feelings for Shyam. He questioned whether she had sent another, more ardent letter instead and discarded this one because it was not loving enough.

> Can you ever be mine wholly and spiritually? Were you fancy free before you committed to me—had you the control of your heart last year and had it not gone to someone else? Have you never been another's, even mentally or principally mentally—never? Prove it to me, Malati, and you will save a wretched soul from the tortures of hell. If you care for me enough, please tell me immediately, or you will be too late.

He pleaded earnestly.

> Just because I cannot be like Princess Mirabai, crazed by her love for Lord Krishna, singing devotional songs in your praise, thinking of you every moment or seeing your image in everyone and everything, does not mean I love you less. About that have no doubt.

Malati explained and vowed to finish the gurudakshina letter to Shyam for Guru to post it to him, so she did not mislead either of them.

He replied with a sense of relief and vindication, happiness at conquering doubt—about himself and about Malati, both of which were the same to him. Love was, in his view, self-surrender in its highest stages. Man was naturally egoistic but his egoism evaporated, be it for a few moments, before this potent love and he delighted in self-surrender, merging in his love.

'Today I discovered that you are capable of such surrender. Remember, I have surrendered my all to you and my future is in your hands,' he said, his concerns allayed.

Malati replied to Shyam's letter, very tactfully expressing her gratitude for all that he had done for her and gave reasons why Guru was her choice without saying why Shyam was not. Guru trusted her to send it directly to Shyam. Shyam's debt was paid. Thankfully, Malati did not hear from him any more as he went on his ICS path.

Guru's mood was more cheerful. He now turned his complaints about her into playful, titillating questions and repartee—as in a Marathi lavani song and dance. In an effort to be more jovial like Shyam, Malati guessed.

'When I said please keep your cheeks soft and supple for me, you asked me defiantly what do I have to do with your cheeks? Have you become mad? As if you don't know,' wrote Guru.

When Malati asserted that her cheeks belonged to her and her alone, he retorted, 'You don't write letters to me and trouble me. So you have to make sure that the hand giving the pat has less "trouble" and greater pleasure!'

When Malati warned that she could retaliate too, he replied that he would gladly bear up with her revenge, knowing it's coming from the 'honeycomb of his Sweet Malati'.

Malati pursued her teaching career with passion but she was equally ambitious for Guru. She asked him to derive his happiness from success in academics, and set him the target of standing first in Bombay University in law. Guru did not disappoint her. He excelled in his final year exams and won the Bombay University Inveracity Gold Medal in Law and other prizes.

This was a moment when Malati and Guru felt confident that with the filaments of ability, effort, and ambition perfectly knotted into a rope and anchored firmly to the rocky mountainside, they would quickly climb to a higher, more coveted destination. But then fate—the great sutradhar puppeteer, by a flick of his finger, misdirected the forces around them in family, society, and nation, affecting their individual destinies, delaying the desired milestones being reached, or thwarting their purpose altogether.

She and Guru had planned that once he became a lawyer he would get a job, they would marry, he would take his turn to support her, whilst she finished her law studies. Having qualified as a lawyer with distinction, they thought, doors would open for Guru immediately to a good job. Or that he would get to practice as a junior with one of the other big lawyers in Bombay at the highest courts in British India.

With the Great Depression affecting British-ruled India as well, the demand for freshly minted lawyers in Bombay was low. Guru applied for all kinds of government positions, including as a sub-judge or deputy collector, but those too were limited and rarely open to newcomers.

Guru even dared to think for a while that he could start his own practice, but realized he could not afford the luxury of being a briefless lawyer, given that he had no 'tied up bundle of inherited money'. So, he had to willy-nilly fall back on working with his father as an unpaid legal assistant, clerk, and understudy all rolled into one.

There were opportunities that came up from outside Bombay, in Sholapur, Dharwad, or Poona. However, Appa ruled them out on the pretext of it being the wrong place or wrong job at the wrong time, for launching the 'promising legal career', Guru truly 'deserved'.

Guru wrote to Malati in frustration.

> I do agree with Appa about my potential, but not about having to wait. I am in despair! I know my abilities are far ahead of even the seasoned advocates I meet. But I argue in vain with Appa. The way he is directing my career, I shall be practically a shiftless man, entirely dependent on him. Like Rossetti, I seem to be living in 'alternate fits of industry and indolence' without a regular job. It crossed my mind—a very undutiful thought it was—that he is refusing me a chance to gain economic independence on purpose, so that I cannot marry you for a number of years, till at last, as he once hoped, I may give up the idea of marrying against his wishes.

When Malati commiserated with him, he exclaimed. 'Malati, I am so disturbed by it all that I cannot even get down to enjoying the most rollicking of Shaw's plays! Escaping these surroundings shall be the rebirth of me!'

Guru had expected that as his first-born son who has done him proud in academics, Appa would commend and build his morale. Guru yearned for his validation, but it never came. Instead of congratulating him and telling Guru he was happy and proud of his achievements, Appa lapsed into a sullen silence and indifference. When Guru took his precious prize books to the high court to show them to him, he barely glanced at them while another lawyer admiringly asked questions.

Malati tried to explain away Anna's reactions as the false modesty of his generation that ordained that parents never praise their own children. It could invite the evil eye. Guru disagreed and wished that was true. Appa would then at least have been more appreciative when they were alone. But no. When Guru asked for money to buy Stroud's *Legal Maxims*, Appa looked derisively at his prize books and questioned why he opted for those useless books, thus trivializing his achievements and choices. Moreover, Guru's prize books were 'rotting in the university office' because he did not have the money for printing the university coat of arms on the covers. While Malati could not change his father's attitude, her money orders enabled him to get the prestigious university coat of arms for his prize books.

'Thank you, Malati. I have received all my prize books from the university. Well's *The Outline of History* is a beautiful book with many illustrations. I fell in love with it, which, however, need not make you jealous.... When are you going to inspect this, my wealth?' Guru wrote in gratitude and celebration.

Malati had to keep boosting his morale and countering his growing cynicism about a profession he had just about embarked on. He confessed that he was no longer in love with his profession, he had seen through that it was neither an intellectual profession nor any use to society. In the famous Sati Bribery Case the offenders were released and went back to their positions of power. That made him think of dharma-adharma, niti-aniti, samaj—society and state institutions involved.

Guru continued to contribute to the freedom movement as these activities provided a purpose in life, which he had been intently thinking of in relation to what he saw on the streets and the country. He had surreptitiously joined Mahatma Gandhi's Civil Disobedience Movement of 1930, participating in some of the marches, boycotts, and picketing. He was lucky he had not been arrested so far. Malati applauded him for doing his bit for Bharat Mata.

Guru felt that to live a simple, honest, and pure life, to be as useful to the country and the world as possible was the highest and most beautiful goal that a man could have. Name, honour, power, and wealth were but dusty dreams, and nevertheless, he seemed to be striving for them. However, he vowed always to keep the ideals in mind.

Apart from the frustration about not being gainfully employed, Guru recognized that his idealism and goodness were also the source of his unhappiness. While a wicked man had no compunctions about anything, a good man's conscience was especially alive and felt strongly about his own least unimportant faults and was always unhappy.

Malati agreed and told him that she too experienced the same dilemmas in her work and life in Benares—even with a regular job! But he replied with a letter pointing out the reversal of role and fortune that had now placed him on a lower pedestal than hers.

> Two years ago—after filling the law degree forms, I said to you that you will become an important person by virtue of your law degree. Then, when I come to see you, you will say, 'You look so poor, who let you come inside and sit down? You have ruined my carpet'. At that time, you said so nobly 'Galicha wait hou naye manhun majhya prana che tyavar awaran ghalin. (I will put a shawl of my being over the carpet to welcome you.)' You remember that? Now you will not say this, I think.

'Well,' Malati wrote in all modesty, 'you are the one who became the lawyer and it's you who is going to be rich. And I, a poor teacher, will come to you and you will question who I am! Will you lay down the shawl of your being for me?'

'It is already under your feet,' he wrote back.

Malati agreed with Guru that their separation must end. They had waited six long years and both felt ready to take the plunge, bear the consequences. Ram and Kamala joined them as co-conspirators in planning a secret double marriage! They had both secured teaching jobs in Bombay and Ram was, therefore, in a better position to defy his parents.

47

TO DELAY IS TO DENY

They finally decided on their date of marriage. It was to be Purnima—the full moon day of May when Lord Buddha was born. Malati promised to give Guru 'whatever he wanted' on their wedding day.

> I am delighted by your decision to give me whatever I want this Purnima. But take care, I'm very greedy. And what I ask will not be only for that day, but its repercussions will last for our lifetime. You must give me a present, which you have never given and will never give to anyone else, and I will give you a similar present myself. You will receive it in the very act of giving. On that day, two beings shall be united into one.

Malati surprised him with her reply.

> Dearest Guru, I know that we feel frustrated by the delayed gratification of our mutual desires. Please enjoy the intensity of our longings too and the thought that when we are eventually fulfilled in each other, we will forever cherish it. Remember Proverb 13:12 from the Bible, 'Hope deferred makes the heart seek. But when the desire comes, it is a tree of life.'

Instead of abating, Guru's passionate longing to be with Malati only increased after their decision to get married soon. His letter writing was now about memories of their being together and dreams about their future union. He wrote about how he had kept her curls and glass bangles in his black deal wood box. As in Barclay's book, *The Rosary*, he regarded these as being among the beads of his rosary—things that belonged to Malati and were held sacred in his possession.

Malati once joked with him that since his father wanted him to remain a bachelor, maybe she should become his maid.

> There are two concepts of a maid. In Shakespeare's *The Tempest*, Miranda says to Ferdinand 'I am your wife if you will marry me. If not, I will die your maid. To be your fellow. You may deny me,

but I will be your servant, whether you will or not.' I will not go by your choice. I will combine the two. Meaning, you will be mine no matter, but you will also have to accept bondage. Is it acceptable to you? Pressing my feet, ministering to me when I fall ill? Paha bai! It's not an easy pledge to make.

Malati mocked him for espousing patriarchal ideas of women's servitude to men rather than that of worshipper to a goddess he had claimed to be earlier. Guru contradicted her, reminding her of his 'Song Divine' which he stood by, and took a pledge to be Malati's slave for life. He recalled that he had proved his credentials in Benares when he pressed her tired feet. Malati could not quarrel with that.

Guru began to share his nocturnal fantasies about Malati in his letters. Malati could not remain unaffected. It was one of the letters that did not go into the letters trunk.

> The single outcome of sitting and writing this letter at night is that the feeling that we are together remains with me the full night through. In my sleep, when I turn, I expect to fall on the shoulder of my cuckoo! Your arms are tightly encircled around my neck, and I'm gently kissing your face and hair, and all over a hundred times. Your breasts rise and fall. They make me feel guilty that I'm neglecting them—so I pleasurably remove the cause for that jealousy. Then you start laughing.

Then stirring in memories, he wrote.

> Remember, in Benares when I was with you in your bedroom, you gently pressed my temples and ran your fingers through my hair? One night, so I dreamed, you kissed the palms of my hands, a thing that you rarely do. I asked you, 'Is this in reward for their service at your breasts?' You punished my lips for uttering 'impertinent' words.

Guru accused Malati of not reciprocating his ardour. He complained that even in his smallest actions, the expressions of his eyes and choice of words, he showed his immense love for Malati and felt very strongly that her love should be visible in equal measure. He however suspected sometimes that Malati was just tolerating these expressions of love by him and that she chose to suppress her love deep in her heart or not to express at all. Malati did not want to tell him how she had deliberately cultivated detachment from him and his letters, to avoid spawning a second self. She merely admitted to being less demonstrative by nature and professed her profound love for Guru.

Another time he worried about his future infidelity. He told Malati that his friend Banerjee had inspected his palm and predicted that he will be rich and that Guru's heartline had many tributaries indicating plurality of affaires de coeur. He confessed to being upset as he speculated upon the 'the Hyde in him' and set about reproaching himself.

He dreamt about wrapping a rich wedding sari around her but joked about his own humble clothes. He recalled the khadi material they had bought for his pajamas. He had got it stitched and alas the pajamas turned out to be big enough—24 inches at the foot. 'I wore one today and felt I was walking in huge sacks! I hope it improves with familiarity!'

Guru also sent Malati news about the 'marital conquests' of their friends with much delight.

> Gaitonde has returned from Hubli a 'quadruped'. Guess what? Dinkar is going to present Gaitonde's wife with a copy of Douglas Jerrold's *Mrs Caudle's Curtain Lectures*, so that she may sharpen her wits and her temper with its aid.

Malati wrote back in jest that she had now read the book and Guru would have to brace himself to have a Mrs Caudle acolyte for a wife! Like her, Malati was not a woman to 'wear chains without shaking them' and would take 'whole and sole possession' of Guru's ears to 'convey the wisdom that will continually flow from her lips' every night and unlike wine, it shall 'not be sugared'. Like her, Malati will trust the sweetness of Guru's disposition, to make it agree with him. For example, Malati threatened to enforce a prohibition on Guru's tea drinking once they get married, as it was not good for his nerves and turned him into an insomniac and a compulsive late night letter writer!

Guru however counselled against it and in turn gave a sermon on how to avoid the pitfalls of being a shrew. A shrew he said was none other than the devoted wife, who unfortunately lacked wisdom.

She loved her husband but she disliked some of his ways and was bent on correcting them at all costs. She meant well, but she was impatient and therefore adopted the wrong means to dictate to her husband—a big baby. It resulted in unhappiness, disharmony, and exhibition of temper.

Malati needed to learn to deceive Guru into obedience by playing upon his moods and feelings and by adopting a sweet tolerant attitude, reasonableness, and imagination and a great deal of romance. He was amenable to covert not overt disciplining. There was great credit and much pleasure in seeming to obey while in fact Malati would command.

Malati hastened to agree and looked forward to command by subterfuge for a fulfilled marriage. He was pleased and replied that community of life and interest, mutual sympathy and help, and something as deep as to be inexpressible—constituted the aim of marriage. He hoped that their life would be one long honeymoon of the type Malati had described.

Malati had kept herself gainfully busy with her participation in the newly established All India Women's Conference. She addressed meetings and advocacy groups to advance women's and girls' education and secure the outlawing of harmful social customs. Her advocacy on the Child Marriage Bill came straight from her heart, as did the need to legislate to give women the right to divorce, inherit, and to vote. She mobilized citizens to meet the local administration officials as well as legislative assembly members. She campaigned around Benares at the community level too, as Baba had done in Ratnagiri and Desaikheda. While it was even tougher to convert the orthodox Banarasis to reform, BHU fortunately was a lighthouse!

She continued her advocacy on Gandhiji's khadi movement, and learnt to spin yarn on the charkha wheel and quite enjoyed the peace that came from the meditative act of spinning! And seeing the delicate tendrils of yarn being born from cotton balls was sheer joy and sweet reward for patience. She took her students on Clean Benares expeditions at the risk of denting her popularity!

∽

One summer evening, just as she finished penning a letter to Guru after dinner, there was insistent, knocking on the door. Shantabai opened the door and they were shocked to see two young men and her star student Ruchika, rush in and close the door behind them. They said that they were BHU students accused of being revolutionaries and were being chased by the police. They wanted Malati to give them shelter until the police left the campus and they could safely escape into the gullies of Benares.

Malati had to think on the spot. She could hear some commotion outside and realized that the police were going from apartment to apartment in search of these three students. So, she asked them to hide in her bathroom behind a large brass water pitcher as best as they could, so that any cursory glance by the police did not reveal their presence.

Shantabai was surprisingly calm. They decided together how they would deal with the police. When the inevitable knock came, they opened the door and looked askance at the three police officers—all Indians—who had come with the BHU security guard.

'What's the matter? Why are you disturbing me—a single woman teacher—at this time of night?' Malati asked with feigned indignation.

'We are sorry, madam. We are looking for three students who are accused of plotting armed action against the British officials and who may be a threat to peace and security in the university campus,' one of the policemen said.

'You are looking for them in my house? Would I allow anyone like them to enter my home without raising an alarm?' Malati demanded sternly. They looked sheepish. She allowed them to have a cursory look around and not finding anyone, they left. Malati locked the door and heaved a sigh of relief. Shantabai drew the curtains. Malati cross-examined the three revolutionaries. They admitted to having plotted to attack British officials and premises and were therefore on the run. They were inspired by the defiant guerilla actions of the Gundas against the British occupation of Benares and by the Anushilan Samiti, impatient to drive the British away.

'I admire your bravery but I feel, and I know for sure, that a whole generation of young revolutionaries like you would have sacrificed themselves only to provoke more repression and delay the granting of independence to India. You will have to drop out of college, as you are now branded as terrorists and even a lenient BHU administration won't be able to help you. Our vice chancellor has clearly taken a stand against any faculty or student involvement in even the Non-cooperation Movement protests, and, of course, disapproves of revolutionary activities by any student,' Malati warned them rather half-heartedly. After all, she was no one to counsel them since she had herself crossed boundaries to serve the national movement.

The three listened to her politely and then explained their position with vehemence.

'Didi, we knew that when we chose this path. But, we as Banarasis have revolutionary patriotism pounded into our being. We are now too deeply involved to retrace our steps. Thank you for saving us this time. Who knows when we will be caught and be martyred,' Sunil said with bravado. They boasted that they knew the Kakori case revolutionaries, including the mysterious bangle seller and Pravesh Babu and her own connections to Vaishali and Bombay HRA revolutionary movements through Malak and Mohan Kaka! They therefore urged her to join their movement, as educated women leaders were rare. When she denied any such revolutionary connection and refused to join them, they turned around and mocked her.

'Why would you—a woman who has a comfortable teaching job and possibly a rich, lawyer husband waiting in the wings—have the courage to embrace a life of danger and sacrifice for the country?' Sunil said.

Ruchika too vehemently berated her for her doublespeak as a teacher extolling the virtues of nationalism, but lacking courage when it came to action.

Malati was touched to the quick. Her face hardened, she got up from her chair, looked each of them in the eye and said furiously, 'How dare you cast aspersions on the courage and patriotism of any pioneering Indian woman, let alone your teacher. I have done my bit of joining non-violent protests and borne lathis. Even now, I am serving the nationalist cause and Mother India in my own way and it does not have to be your way. You do your best to unshackle her. And don't come to the campus, because the police are hunting for you here. Do your recruitment, advocacy, and organizing activities outside, where you may be safer and more effective.'

Ruchika rushed to apologize on the trio's behalf and touched her feet. Malati softened and found herself compelled to give some money to help them in their life on the run. They left without further argument once the coast was clear.

The next day, Malati inquired at the registrar's office about the triumvirate. She was told that though bonafide students, they had disappeared into the revolutionary maze of Benares and had been quietly struck off the university rolls. The British government was involved in the university, so while Indian nationalist spirit was to be encouraged, the university administration could not brook violence against the British state.

Malati noticed soon after that the surveillance on the faculty and on her had increased. Her colleagues too seemed somewhat hostile and wary of her.

Meanwhile Guru followed political developments keenly in Bombay besides joining civil disobedience activities. Every time Gandhiji came there, especially to Laburnum Road and Gam Devi, 'places of pilgrimage' both, Guru attended his public meetings. He wrote to Malati in detail about the Gandhi–Irwin Pact of March 1931 and expressed his happiness that the Poona Declaration, agreed in the main with the terms of peace, which Mahatma Gandhi gave to Mr Slocomb, representative of the Labour Party in England.

That meant that the Congress could just accept the terms and attend the Second Round Table Conference, so there would be an end to the high mental tension in which they had lived for a year, also due to the 'kindness' of the economic depression through which they were passing. Guru was convinced that they were truly moving towards getting the British to work around the constitutional reform plan that he and Malati had worked out for Professor Addington—what the Mahatma called the 'substance of independence, not the shadow'. As it turned out, the British went on to give communal and vested interests the preeminent voice at the conference. It failed and the Civil Disobedience Movement was now re-launched. Hopes belied!

48

A POND EAGER TO MEET THE OCEAN

As the date for their marriage drew near, Guru was given to inordinate dreaming. He told Malati, quoting the great Kalidasa, that a thought was more vivid than an act to a lover. However, he also became desperate. He felt that his father and Mai seemed to push him to the edge of a cliff and that Malati was the only one who could save him from a precipitous fall. He urged her not to tarry!

Malati realized that any postponement of their marriage could break his spirit. So, she, Guru, Kamala, and Ram rushed to legally register their marriages in Bombay and then proceeded to Nainital by train. Whilst their grooms-to-be said that they were at heaven's door, Kamala and Malati feared that their betrayal of Baba's trust would land them in hell! They relived their many conversations with Baba in trains between life-changing destinations and wondered why they did not trust him to agree to go with them to this all-important one!

Kamala rationalized that if it was just Baba, they could have convinced him and used Surekhatai and Malak's good offices. But since it involved convincing both the grooms' and brides' families, they had no other option.

Malati agreed and added that much as they may owe their lovers who waited for them for years and defied their own parents, she and Kamala would not have gone ahead with their marriages if Baba had objected strongly.

'Then this will remain one of the many "what ifs" of our lives. We will just have to bear Baba's ire when we confront him with the truth, after the wedding,' Kamala declared.

They sent a very respectfully worded letter to Baba explaining whom they were marrying and the reasons why they could not tell him beforehand.

Ram and Guru too wrote letters postmarked Bombay to their fathers informing them of their marriages. None of the letters mentioned how, when, and where they were getting married.

They arrived at the idyllic Himalayan town of Nainital built around the bowl of a shimmering, jewelled lake, marvellously oval shaped like a goddess's eye. It was surrounded by seven sentinel hills, covered in the green, grey, and brown shawls woven from exotic trees like the ash, cedar, and walnut. The trees rose majestically around the deep blue lake, which chameleon-like, changed colours with the varying light of the day and night.

The pure, cool mountain air was a refreshing change from Bombay's oppressive heat and the two couples felt transported to a much desired and awaited Shangrila. Ram's friend Gokul, had made arrangements for their stay and for the Arya Samaj wedding ceremonies to be held the next day.

The brides-to-be wrapped themselves in handwoven, green, nine-yard saris, as Guru and Ram had wanted. Malati asked Guru not to insist on her wearing his mother's jewellery, for Kamala then would have nothing comparable to wear.

Instead, they adorned themselves with 'flower ornaments'—fuchsia earrings, pink rose garlands, jasmine hair decoration, and marigold waistbands! Their grooms gave them black bead mangalsutras with two small concave gold cups as pendants. They put kajal on their eyes, geranium petal paste to paint their lips red, and perfectly etched a bold red dot between their brows with a small round silver mould filled with kumkum powder.

Malati had brought ivory coloured Benares silk shirts with gold trimmed silk dhotis, orange stoles, and Marathi pheta turbans for Guru and Ram.

Malati thought that she and Kamala looked the part of latter-day Shakuntalas living in a hermitage and King Dushyants from another land in Kalidasa's play that resonated with all four of them. Their alliances were as unlikely. True, *Shakuntalam* had a sad interlude. But it did have a happy ending!

They went through a simple, moving ceremony conducted by a young Arya Samaj priest in the small pavilion of a garden near Talli Taal. Guru got Gokul to take photos during the wedding ceremony as evidence of the marriages solemnized.

The chants, the symbols, and the messages in the shlokas, the quick saptpadis around the fire, the garlanding of each other—simple gestures they made with the intermediation of the priest, miraculously seemed to seal years of friendship and desire into a lifelong pact of togetherness, blessed by the gods residing in their high Himalayan abodes!

Kamala and Malati considered themselves fortunate that they knew their life partners intimately, unlike their own parents or Surekha and even Sarala, whom God introduced to their husbands after the marriage ceremony! Though it was a small, private event and only Gokul and his wife were witnesses, its sanctity in binding the couples together in an indissoluble union was equal in their minds to that of the most elaborate ceremony, the pomp and pageantry of a royal wedding celebration with elephants, horses, palanquins, and music bands!

After the wedding, they returned to the guest house, a strange shyness enveloping all four of them. So, this was it! The moment they had all agonized over so much had come and gone! As expected, Guru was the most affected by it all. He was almost in tears, holding Malati's hands possessively.

They returned to their rooms in the evening after a walk by the lakeside and a long, tranquil boat ride. They were overwhelmed by the sense of having achieved the impossible, but also with the anxiety about facing their respective families when they returned. Guru and Malati had another period of separation staring at them, unless Guru got a good job and Malati could then move back to Bombay.

For the first time ever, Guru and Malati were free to be alone in a bedroom together without feeling guilty or conscious of boundaries.

They embraced and wiped each other's tears of happiness and laughed. Guru presented Malati with a notebook in which he had neatly transcribed his favourite Marathi poems. He promised to read a poem from it to her every evening for the rest of their lives together—along with his own poetry, which he said Malati would continue to inspire as his muse.

For their nuptial night, Guru chose a poem not one of love fulfilled, but of love eternally expectant! 'Sangam Utsuk Doh', the great Madhav Julian poem.

> Ekatra gunfun jivit dhave
> Preeti che nartan nachlo mage
> Ekata ubha mi ethe
> Bhovati shodi Priyete

> Pulsating with life intertwined, we together flowed
> The gift of the dance of love once bestowed

A solitary Pond, muddied and parched now I stand
Searching for my beloved in this wasteland
Eager to join my long-lost soulmate in vain
Surrounded by sand, yearning for rain.
So, I can swell with water and course through it fast
To be one with my True Love—the Ocean vast!
Wracked with pangs of desire unfulfilled, wait laborious
Dazzled with visions of a union, sweet and glorious.
Peacocks dancing on earth in splendour
King frogs singing on streams yonder.
In that moment, overcome with love and with grace
Will you run unswerving into my tight embrace
Gods in heaven will festoon welcome arches along
While we like crazed minstrels sing an auspicious song
Amazed and rendered unconscious by love newborn
The saffron colour of passion we must don
Throwing ourselves down from the edge
To surrender our life force we earnestly pledge
Then we will finally attain our union with the Ocean supreme
But alas, ending the cursed season of Vaisakh remains but a dream.

'But why should it be recited on the night of our "Union accomplished, Sweet and Glorious"?' Malati asked.

'To enhance the poignancy of our attaining the unattainable! Don't you see? It might well not have happened. The rains may not have come. And we would still be like the pond and the ocean, separated by a wasteland. Malati, let's just celebrate every good thing that happens by recalling how parched we were and have been all these years,' Guru said, collecting Malati into his arms.

Guru eagerly pulled at Malati's sari and removed all nine yards of it as she twirled dizzily to free herself of the restraining cloth. He clumsily tore open the buttons of her blouse instead of freeing them meticulously one by one from their eyelets. Then there was the last knot of her bodice he gave up on opening, because, in his impatience he had tightened rather than loosened it. She laughed indulgently and managed to untie the knot while he fretted.

'Forgive me, if I seem still so awkward. Am but a priest, newly initiated, come forward,' he whispered the lines from his 'Madhu Malati' song and smiled sheepishly.

His desired wedding present was within his grasp, but Malati liked that he did not rush to claim it. Instead, he did his usual 'palmistry ritual', proceeded to kiss her face and lips and then fondled her breasts with his long, probing fingers, and hungry mouth as she throbbed to his touch.

Malati was shy and excited. He lifted her and laid her down tenderly as he would a flower on a pillow. Then he undressed and came atop of her. Malati obeyed meekly, for a change. She had no excuse, nor needed one to allow him to take over her body as he already had her heart and soul. Then they gave themselves to each other, tearing through all the self-erected boundaries to unleash the pent-up passion of years.

They spent the next week enjoying the solitude, the enchanting scenery of Nainital, and each other's minds and bodies. Guru was like an eager boy delighting in the new sport of love with an animated playmate in Malati. Although he had known her for seven years, there was a freshness in this new unfettered relationship. They were both novices in the act of lovemaking, so, they found themselves spanning each other's rainbows of desire with their sometimes frustrating, sometimes joyful, colours and fragrances of surprise.

All four of them found that at this time, when they reminisced about the past, the distinction between the good and the bad that happened to them on the way to this destination seemed to get blurred. They cherished good, for the pleasure it gave them and would always give them. The struggles reinforced their sense of heroism in having lived through and overcome them. They could accumulate niggling regrets and store them away in the recesses of their minds—like Malati's not becoming a lawyer yet—but what was the point, they reasoned.

Equally, they tried not to dwell on the future with its demons of uncertainty and conflict, waiting to waylay them on their return. They suspected that these were already at work in Bombay! Unlike Guru, Ram was less worried because he had a job and his parents did not live in Bombay.

As soon as they reached Bombay, they went to meet Mohan Kaka and Hema Kaki and took their blessings. Their guardians told them they had to tell a very agitated Baba that they did not know where the foursome had gone to get married. He had extracted Guru's father's address from Mohan Kaka. He was now camping with Arjun in Bombay at the state guest house.

Malati and Guru decided to visit Appa straightaway. They knocked and entered through the front door this time. Mai opened the door, smiled, and ushered them into the large living room without saying a word. Appa was sitting on a high backed carved wooden chair behind a table. It almost looked like a judge's bench to Malati. They respectfully stood before him, 'in the dock', guilty as charged! He looked at them impassively, his face turning red like an Irishman, the only giveaway of the anger boiling up within him.

Guru and Malati touched his feet and sought his blessings. To their surprise and relief, he got up to tap their heads with the tips of his outstretched hands in reluctant benediction. He asked them to sit down. Mai, who had been watching from a corner of the room, now came and sat next to Malati and surprised her by clasping her hands to show acceptance.

'So you have had your way. I can only hope things work out well for you both, Guru and Malati, for you are on your own now. I confess I am doubly disappointed in you, Guru. You have embarrassed me in the Saraswat community, not only by marrying into another caste, but also by doing so secretly without the goodwill of our community. While you gave me notice two years ago, I thought I could coerce you to change your decision through the pain of withdrawing my support for your legal education. I was wrong. You stayed the course and were honourable to Malati, who too showed herself worthy by sacrificing her legal career. So, I guess I will have to accept what you have done, but we will have to work out a way which does not make the whole family a pariah in our community,' Appa delivered his interim judgment.

Although Guru had told Malati to be silent and submissive through their meeting, Malati could not restrain herself. All those letters of Guru complaining about his father coursed through her mind to compel her to speak out.

'Respected Appa, thank you very much for your recognition of our union and the extent to which we have gone to realize it. However, I am aghast that false and antiquated notions of caste should shackle an enlightened vidvaan like you. Even within the realms of caste dharma, I am a Maratha Kshatriya, the ruler and warrior caste, almost at a par if not above the Brahmin one. In any case, is it not that a higher caste man can marry a lower caste woman and she and her children get elevated?' Malati questioned the very premise of his caste-based objection to Guru marrying her.

Guru was encouraged to speak up.

'Appa, besides the caste issue being moot, she is an educated Vidushi and a college teacher—a guru, which is the calling of the Brahmins, is it not?'

Appa looked taken aback at this joint attack from them. He changed tack.

'You see, I may be enlightened, but the society we live in is not. For now, Guru can stay in my house while he tries to get a job. You, Malati, will presumably return to Benares to resume your job there.'

They were relieved, as it gave them the time they needed and they thanked Appa.

49
A LONG-DISTANCE MARRIAGE

'Don't be so quick to thank me. I am not done yet. I am appalled that you, Malati, did not deign to tell your father about your intentions at all. He is the real injured party here. Do you know, he came visiting here when he was informed by a letter, after the fact, about your secret marriage? He brandished, what I presume, was a loaded gun to shoot you, Guru. Since you were not there, he was ready to take me down instead!' Appa said.

'Oh no! I am so sorry and mortified! I seek forgiveness on Baba's behalf. He is a hot-blooded Maratha, but he wields the gun only to protect his people from the dacoits in Guna. He would never harm you or Guru,' Malati said rather defensively.

Appa showed them a side of him Guru had never mentioned, nor perhaps discovered before.

'Well, we had a tragicomic moment. He burst into the house saying to me, "where is Guru, why has he kidnapped my daughter, and where has he taken her?" I allowed him to look around the house and when he was done, I said in all sincerity, see that makes two of us. I too have been duped and I am looking for him and Malati. Let us go find them, and I have no objection if you shoot them both. Madhav Rao realized that both families had been kept in the dark, cooled down, and apologized. Guru, you had better be warned—any misbehaviour with Malati and he will come gunning for you—literally! That is what happens when you marry someone from the warrior caste, is it not, Malati? Instead of protecting the Brahmins, your father was all ready to kill them—including the newly anointed one, his daughter,' Appa said.

'It will never happen again!' Malati said foolishly, only to have Appa come back with another repartee.

'Better not, or you will either become a widow or a culprit yourself or both!' he said, the hint of a dimpled smile like that of his son, making an appearance on his handsome face. 'Now redouble your efforts to find a job,' he said to Guru. 'How long can you depend on your wife's earning or on me?'

'Well, respectfully Appa, it's not Guru's fault. If you set him free, he will get a legal job tomorrow. He has earned his keep by working for you and the rest he earns through writing work. He has always conducted himself with self-respect and dignity,' Malati said assertively.

Appa looked uneasy—not used to women, that too, young women, speaking up. Mai announced she was going to bring some tea and sweets to celebrate the occasion. The awkwardness melted.

∽

Then Malati and Guru, along with Kamala and Ram, went to meet Baba at the state guest house. Alerted by Mohan Kaka, Baba was pacing up and down the hallway waiting for them. He stopped and looked at them with blazing eyes when they entered the room. They touched his feet, but he moved away angrily.

'No, no, not so quickly will you get my blessing. I need some answers first, you renegade daughters! I trusted you all these years with my honour and boldly supported you so you could be more than the fifth caste of women your mother referred to. Is this how you pay me back? By not trusting me, nor keeping my trust?' Baba said. His big black eyes sent out streaks of lightning to shock them out of self-satisfaction. The words coming through his dark plump lips and greying moustache, made them momentarily recede into guilty speechlessness. His thundering voice stirred up a tempest to almost make them roil in regret.

Guru spoke to return the favour Malati had done him with Appa.

'Baba, both Ram and I are privileged to have as our wives, women of such ability and high moral character and that's your legacy. They have always been conscious of living up to your expectations and keeping faith. Unfortunately, they happened to fall in love and be loved by Ram and me, both I am sure, suitable grooms in your eyes, except for our caste. That meant that since our families would never approve, we had to present them with our marriage as a done deed that they could not unravel. So, it had to be kept secret from you too.'

Baba softened, but turning to Kamala and Malati said sternly, 'What prevented you from at least telling me that you were interested in these young men? Every time I asked, you evaded the question. I would not have objected. After educating you so well, I did not expect you to be yoked to less educated Maratha men like me! Sure, I wish Guru and Ram were blue-blooded Maratha men. But they will do as they are!' Baba said and proceeded to embrace all of them by turns to their great joy.

'Thank you, Baba, for your grace. Guru's family has agreed to accept the marriage and you have blessed us. Now my parents remain to be convinced. I am in no hurry,' Ram said.

'I want you all to visit Vaishali and pay your respects to my eldest son-in-law, who is also Malati and Kamala's benefactor. I dare not invite you to Desaikheda to be warmly welcomed by the Chambal dacoits,' Baba said, smiling.

Kamala's and Malati's happiness was complete at last. Malati was bold enough to ask Baba about his feisty call on Appa. Baba apologized for acting impulsively as a protective Maratha father. Ram and Guru got on well with Baba. His wisdom and sense of humour did charm the city-bred, English-educated boys.

∽

Baba left for Desaikheda and Malati for Benares the next evening and Guru was very sad again. Malati assured him that their separation should be over soon because the stars at last seemed to be getting favourably aligned!

Malati's announcement about her marriage to Guru and her returning to Benares alone, led to gossip about her having had a gandharva marriage. Malati let the legend about her being a free-spirited Shakuntala build.

She went to notify her marriage to the college and insisted on retaining her maiden surname. The shocked clerk quoted the rule about married women assuming their husbands' surname as the only proof of change of status. She pointed out that her name was Malati Desai and that the marriage certificate she had given him was evidence on record.

When he threatened to refer the matter to the authorities, she was furious and complained to Guru about patriarchal systems being perpetuated in a new university with a supposedly modern outlook. She wondered why she was expected to merge her identity into her husband's and thereby obliterate it. After all, she was the one working in BHU in her own right.

To her surprise, Guru was offended. He reminded her that Malati was the one who wanted to get married to him. He sensed that because he was jobless and she was the breadwinner, Malati was somehow ashamed to assume his surname.

Malati was outraged and reminded him that it was he, who had pleaded with her to marry him and the onus was on him to also surrender the ego of a traditional husband and to keep their pact strong and free of self-doubt. To this, she got an anguished reply from Guru.

> You may be right, Malati, that I obtained your consent unfairly—which fact has resulted in such awful trouble for myself, as I am now undergoing. Have I not placed you on the highest pedestal of my heart and worshipped you every minute of my life? And in return, you have trampled upon the heart that I gave you for a throne, have torn it to pieces, and consigned it to the gutters.

Malati rushed to explain and apologize. He cooled down and entreated her to retain her maiden surname. She in turn assured him that she would happily and proudly bear his surname and asked where his love for her had gone.

He replied that his love for her was not so ephemeral. His love for the Malati of his heart remained strong as ever: it only suffered a momentary severance from the Malati of reality from time to time.

Months passed and neither was Malati able to go to Bombay nor could Guru come to visit her. The BHU community began to speculate on his whereabouts. Professor Gupta and a few of her other men colleagues, seemed to think they had a licence to romance her without the hint of a scandal because she was 'married but single', as her husband was not around. Guru had still not found a good job. So long distance husband–wife love talks and quarrels by letter continued.

Money matters were a delicate subject between them as Malati was still the primary earner and sent Guru money. When she apologized once to him for delay in sending him money, he asked her not to think that he was a hopeless spendthrift and always asking her for money. He believed that Malati was more eager to give him help than he was to receive it. In fact, Malati had to remonstrate with him because he differentiated between her money and his.

When Malati asked him to work hard so their separation can end soon, he blamed his inability to do so on her.

> My incessant desire to be with you races through my veins and inflames my whole body. I yearn to feel the gentle pressure of your limbs against mine. I yearn to rest my head on your lap and feel the soft touch of your hand on my heated temples, to bury my lips in the softness of your bosom. These and a thousand such sensuous images and desires haunt me, waking or asleep. I once read of 'the desire of the moth for the star'. Mine is not a hopeless one, for I know I shall attain my star within a few months. But I am exasperated with the period intervening. The letters we write; are they not symbols of our separation? Are not words but weak and meaningless things? Can they ever hope to express the intensity of our love, of our desire? They are, at best an imperfect substitute....

Malati was surprised that he, the original 'Letter Man', was disenchanted by the medium, just when it had most value. She tried to make him believe in its power to bridge distances and got herself to write regular, longer, passionate letters, but they did not quell his storm. They discovered that the problems of living apart were greater when they were married.

He explained that if they were living together and he had said something that hurt Malati, he could have immediately rectified his mistake. And if she found it unsuitable to forgive him, she would have put her arms around his neck to imprison him and sentence him. But living apart was another matter. As he explained.

> When I get angry with you, I'm more upset and unhappy than you. Why bother? You're not going to give me the alms of pandering to my anger. Kashala cut cut kara? Majhya ragala thodi tu bheekh ghalnaar aahes? I'm writing down for you a sweet poem of Coleridge which beautifully expresses my feelings. 'If I had but two little wings and were a little feathery bird, to you I'd fly my dear, but thoughts like these are idle things, and I stay here!'

When Malati told him to come to Benares quickly as she felt frustrated, his answer surprised and pleased her. He reasoned that Malati's irritability had sprung up because their marriage had been postponed by so many years, and even after they got married, they had to be apart and were thus denied sexual pleasure. Guru declared that he was among those men who believed that women had sexual desires too, which men as their partners, needed to cater to. He promised to come armed with insights about sacred sexuality and fulfilment and how best to practise it. They could then truly live up to the essence of Vatsayana's *Kama Sutra*, and cherish their sambhog, as an emotional and spiritual, as much as a physical union and pleasure.

Guru fervently hoped that he would get a job that purposefully engaged his mind. He poignantly envisioned a time when he would be an enormously busy man, the one working the whole day in a job he loved and coming back to Malati, tired and weary, yet joyful and happy that the long-sought hour of union with her had come. And he knew that Malati would not allow him to keep awake as late as he now stayed, but that hour they certainly would have!

On his mother's death anniversary, he related how his angelic mother's memories haunted him still. He remembered vividly how she had called him when she was on her deathbed in the gathering dusk of the evening, when the lamps were still unlit. There, holding his hands in hers, she had told him in a sweet plaintive voice that she would suffer less in leaving this world if he assured her that he would be brave and look after himself and his brother. He had bent his head and cried, instead of giving an assurance—a regret he would carry all his life. Since then, the poet Yashwant's ode to a mother lost, always stabbed him like a knife.

> Ayee Manhooni Konhi, Ayees Haak Mari
> Ti haak yeyi kaani, Maja hoye dukh kari
>
> Hark! is that someone calling out to his beloved mother
> When his cry reaches my ears, to intense sorrow I am moved
> The name Ayee sounds like a cruel taunt
> Now whom can I call 'oh mother' and show off
> The Lord of the Three Worlds though anyone may rise to be
> Without his mother, he is but a woebegone beggar like me

Malati responded with empathy. She urged him to celebrate her legacy of love. She asked Guru to not just look for her in the painful crevices of his memory, but in the pleasurable living essences of those around him, here and now, who could mean the same to him in kindness and beauty of spirit.

Guru indeed saw his Ayee's reflection in Malati, though they both could not be more different. His Ayee was a meek lamb; Malati was a lioness. She was easy to hurt and cry, Malati was made of sterner mettle. But both women were equal in the largeness of their heart. While Malati would one day be an Ayee to Guru's children, god-willing, he looked to her to fill the void of his Ayee's affection, for both him and his brother. Malati recognized from her own loss that nothing could indeed fill the void left by his Ayee, but she vowed to try her best to be everything Guru wanted her to be for him!

50
THE BENARES CONSPIRACY

One day, when Malati returned home in the evening, she found a pamphlet of the Benares South Revolutionary Group on her study table. It exhorted all Banarasis to join the movement and take up arms against the British state. There were no names or addresses given, just the numbers 8,80,808, which she presumed was a code, along with a drawing of the Benares ghats. Shantabai was startled when Malati showed her the pamphlet.

'Shantabai, did the triumvirate come back despite my telling them not to? We could be booked for sedition if we are found to be in possession of this,' Malati asked sternly.

Shantabai looked flustered. 'No, no. No one came back. I don't know how it ended up on your desk,' she said.

'Ideally, we should burn it. But, first let's decipher what it says. Either there is an urgent call to action hidden in this or it could be a trap from the British to smoke out all those involved. Can you decipher it?'

'Well in Benares we all look for Hindu symbols connected to numbers, places, deities, and time. So, there must be some related pattern,' Shantabai suggested.

The next evening, when Malati returned from her classes and tennis practice, she found Shantabai missing and the door unlocked. Unusually so. Against her better sense, she asked her neighbour Professor Gupta whether he had seen Shantabai. He laughed and said cryptically, 'Don't worry about Shantabai. She is quite the woman about town like you.'

She went into her bedroom, took out the pamphlet to open the secrets locked in it, and get a clue to Shantabai's disappearance.

She began with number 80 or assi in Hindi and linked it to something being organized at Assi Ghat—the largest of them. The number 8 coincided with it being 8 March so something could be happening that very day. Assi Ghat also had aartis at night, so could the time of the event be 8 p.m.? Would it not be ideal to organize a clandestine activity at night, drowned out by the sound and frenzy of evening prayers?

But then where specifically, on the big Assi Ghat was the activity scheduled? 808—and connections between numbers and deities could hold the key to the temples where the event was planned.

She quickly tried to locate the temples closest to the Assi Ghat. She knew that in Hinduism, the deity most associated with the number 8 was Goddess Lakshmi. So, one of the temples could be hers. The second temple could be that of Lord Vishnu reclining on the Adi Ananta Shesha serpent—numerically visualized as one-infinity-zero.

The last 8 of 808 she guessed might be linked to Lord Ganesha, the elephant-headed god of all good beginnings. She guessed that the one temple with all three deities could be the newly-built Lakshmi Narayan Temple, which overlooked the Assi Ghat. It seemed too obvious a venue but Malati was excited that she had, perhaps, cracked the code. But what next?

It was already 7 p.m., and Shantabai had not returned. Had she been abducted and was she in danger? Was the pamphlet a trap for Malati? Malati was too restless to stew in her doubts at home and decided to go to the Assi Ghat and find out what was happening, if anything.

She took along her favourite short, stout stick for protection along with the pamphlet. As she walked, she began to feel afraid, not of the dark alleyways nor the leering looks of passers-by. She feared that she was being reckless in entering revolutionary territory, where violence was justified as a necessary evil—something Guru would not have allowed. Their patriotism did not extend that far. The very thought of the peril raised the level of her excitement. A strong gust of wind tussled with her sari wrap. She pulled it back tightly around her shoulders and marched on.

Malati reached the riverside embankments now so overflowing with people that the stone floors could scarcely be seen through the dense thickets of sweltering, noisy bodies. How would she, a novice in the 'patriotic games of Banarasis' find Shantabai? Or break the hard diamond of deception of the revolutionaries with nothing but the solitary mallet of her guess work?

As she neared the Lakshmi Narayan Temple, she felt as if someone had pushed her from behind. She bumped into one of the wilful bulls of Shiva that roamed free there and it butted her. She managed to escape with minor bruises by reflexively holding up her lathi against the animal's horns and pushing back.

Though shaken, she persisted and went into the packed temple and prayed for divination. As if the deities answered her call, a young man dressed in the saffron robes of a sadhu with a Swami Vivekanand type turban, came to the side of the sanctum sanctorum—and drew a figure of 8 in the air. She noticed that some devotees quietly went to the temple backyard, ostensibly to offer prayers and receive special benediction. When the young sadhu spotted Malati, he looked alarmed and rushed towards the backyard himself. It was Sunil! The leader of the triumvirate who had sought shelter in Malati's house. She too went into the backyard, discreetly flashing her copy of the pamphlet sideways as she saw others doing. She was allowed in, but as soon as she entered, Sunil took her aside on the pretext of giving her prasad, snatched the pamphlet from her, and urged her to leave.

'This here is our contact meeting,' he said urgently. 'You should not have come. You must have been followed. Now you have put both yourself and us in danger,' Sunil hissed.

'I will go once you tell me where Shantabai is,' Malati insisted.

Before he could reply, they heard some shouting and disturbance at the nearby Ganesh temple. Malati rushed out to see what had happened. The police were raiding the place and they had picked up a few suspected revolutionaries. She could hardly believe her eyes when she saw Shantabai being handcuffed and taken away by the police. She also spotted Rahul, the other revolutionary. But it was when she saw her star student, Ruchika, in custody that Malati grew seriously concerned. She went running to the police and showed her university identity paper and vouched for Shantabai first. The policeman looked at her quizzically.

'Madam, she is the head of the women's cell of the Benares South Revolutionary group. We caught her red-handed preaching sedition and planning violence against British officials,' he said.

'You are mistaken. She has been my housekeeper. She may have just come for aarti,' she cried, looking at Shantabai and expecting her to protest too.

But Shantabai did not say a word. Her eyes were downcast and there was a shadow of shame, in an otherwise proud moment of making the supreme sacrifice for her country as a revolutionary. Malati wondered if Shantabai felt a tinge of regret at betraying her mistress's trust, or for even luring her into incriminating herself. But then, if Shantabai had told Malati what her mission was, she could not have served her country as she wanted. My patriotism, right or wrong, Malati supposed!

'And this young boy, Rahul, is Shantabai's son and a leading light in the revolutionary movement and Ruchika too is Shantabai's niece and an accomplice! I am surprised that you have no idea about their real identities,' the policeman continued, mockingly.

'What are you going to do with them?' Malati demanded.

'It's up to the British authorities, and depends on what crimes they have actually committed,' the policeman replied.

'As Shantabai's employer, please keep me posted,' Malati requested.

The policeman took down her address and other details and signalled that he may call her to give evidence.

Malati could feel a combustion of emotions. Sorrow about Shantabai's fate, the humiliation of a vidushi being outsmarted by the cunning of an eighth-class pass woman revolutionary, helplessness in rescuing the three self-willed martyrs, and most of all, niggling self-doubt about whether her own patriotism went deep enough into the bowels of violence. She went down the steps of the ghat, dipped her hands and feet in the waters of the Bhagirathi, and splashed her face to smother the fire and damp down her feelings of disquiet.

She looked up towards the many boats passing by, their lanterns hanging from poles, and noticed the better ones among them, ferrying British officers in full regalia. She was alarmed when she spotted Sunil, now in the disguise of a boatman with two other boys in a ramshackle boat, almost tailing the British ones. When they saw her, they broke into the Banarasi folk Kajri song, '*Barasan lagi badariya, jhoom, jhoom ke*', even though it was not monsoon season. What was Sunil up to? She remembered that just last year, a revolutionary, Mahindra Nath Banerjee had been convicted for assassinating the Benares DSP. Were the triumvirate targeting these British officials as a follow-up?

When the boats went by peacefully, she sighed and wiped her face with her sari padar, walked up the steps, bent to pick up her stick but her feet slipped on the steps. She was about to fall when Professor Gupta, suddenly came up from behind her and hauled her up.

'How are you here? Have you been following me?' she asked and freed herself from his hold.

'Madam Desai, I had told you, you need friends like me and as your colleague, neighbour, and admirer, I have to save you from yourself. Otherwise, you know what they say about Benares? Save yourself against widows, bulls, stairs, and sanyasis and you may worship gainfully at Kashi. See how your revolutionary widow and sanyasi priest befooled you, you hit against the bull, and slipped on the stairs distracted by something you should not have seen, huh! You are up against not only the omniscient British but also the crafty and fearless legatees of Bhangar Bhikshuk and Dattaram Nagar for whom life is as temporal as the pasing of the monsoon season and they are ready to kill and be killed. Only I could be the means to your salvation,' Professor Gupta said.

Not caring to respond, Malati almost ran out of there until she reached her home. She realized that no dips in the Bhagirathi could purify her, nor bestow her with the guile and strength required for attaining the salvation that was reserved for the ascetic-warrior freedom fighters in Kashi.

Malati was now under the scrutiny of the university and local government authorities—as the employer of a 'designated revolutionary' and being present near the scene when she was arrested. She was foolish enough to have gone and identified herself to the police trying to vouch for Shantabai's innocence.

Sure enough, the next day the principal of the Mahila Maha Vidyalaya summoned Malati and gave her a talking to. Malati told her everything truthfully, except the part about her giving asylum to the triumvirate.

The principal listened impassively and said, 'I understand, dear, that a young, single woman can get carried away with patriotic fervour. The college is imbued with Indian nationalism, but can't be party to violent means to achieve it. You will be relieved to know that for the sake of the reputation of the college, we will protect you from any further police involvement and questioning.'

'Thank you, madam. I am indeed grateful to the college for shielding me, but also sad, because I would have liked to help Shantabai and her son and niece—BHU students both—with her case. They might be defenceless. Now my hands are tied,' Malati said, feeling genuinely concerned.

The principal sternly asked Malati to completely detach herself from the case, even if Shantabai approached her. There were ways in which the BHU helped its people. Malati could not be the instrument. Then she went on to praise Malati as an exceptional teacher. She was brilliant, thorough, and most of all, so respected and loved by the students that they identifed with her completely. Malati was a friend to them, and she had taught them to value sports and drama, too, besides academics. Malati had given young women students a voice and they saw her as a shining role model to follow.

'Thank you, madam. I am gratified,' Malati said, truly pleased. She worried though that praise from superiors rarely came to elevate. It came either before something that was due being denied, or to prepare the one being praised, to take a fall.

'It is, therefore, all the more distressing that this unfortunate incident has happened,' the principal continued and paused. Malati instinctively braced herself. 'Some of your colleagues say that the fact that your housekeeper was all along a revolutionary and that Ruchika your star student, also took to arms, indicates that either you are easily fooled or you are one of them. I have to regrettably ask you to consider moving on—not immediately, or it will look suspicious, but in the next few months. We will, of course, give you glowing references and certificates as you truly deserve.'

Malati was shocked and angry, but responded with dignity.

'Thank you, madam, for your appreciation. I myself wanted to give you notice, since I have to move back to Bombay to be with my husband,' she said and left immediately, not wanting to show any emotion.

So, the great puppeteer played tricks with Malati yet again. Just when she was getting comfortable and Guru had started thinking of moving there to teach at the Law College, Malati was handed this honourable 'Quit Benares' order from the BHU she had come to love. She asked the puppeteer if he had something nobler and higher in mind for her and Guru, because their struggles had been far too protracted and their triumphs too short-lived.

Malati decided not to share her trials and tribulations in Benares with Guru, though he sensed her newfound impatience and urgency for him to get a job so she could join him.

I am hopeful that soon our streams will merge and flow together.
We will enhance each other's good qualities, not fall into a rut

of coming and going, and we will spend our lives with deathless consciousness and with the fire of love always burning.

As though the puppeteer decided to hear her plea, Guru was soon selected for the Bombay Judicial Service and his first posting was to be as a sub-judge and magistrate first class in Kopargaon. It fitted Appa's scheme of things—to banish Guru from Bombay so that their inter-caste marriage did not 'tear the eye like a piece of rock' in the Saraswat community for him.

With all her respect for Hinduism, it was this caste fetish Malati could not accept or condone. She agreed with Veer Savarkar's concept of Hindutva where the divisive and debilitating caste system was to be smashed once and for all. His call for one country, one God, one caste, one mind—brothers all of us without difference, without doubt—truly moved Malati even though he left out the call to 'sisters all of us'!

Malati added that idea in her sermon to herself. Mahatma Gandhi too had been rightly trying to peel off the encrustations of caste from Indian consciousness and yet it seemed as difficult as peeling off the skin itself.

As soon as Malati got the news, she hastened to tell Guru that she would leave her post in BHU immediately. She now had the supreme satisfaction of giving notice to the BHU.

Malati's students organized a heart-warming farewell dinner for her. Their evocative speeches celebrating her as a guru, as shakti incarnate, as a brave freedom fighter, and extolling her human qualities, filled her with pride and renewed confidence that she had just been drained off.

One of her favourite Marathi students recited a poem by N. V. Tilak, 'Poorey jaanto meech majhe bal', which held a potent message she vowed to carry with her always.

> Bola have te mala kai tyache
> Poorey jaanto meech majhe bal
>
> Jauntily holding an elephant calf in one hand
> In the other, with a mewling lion cub, I stand
> The majestic tiger, half dead with fear
> From his cave cautiously does peer

These mountains are mere rocks to deceive
The waves of the ocean are like trembling leaves.
Recognizing myself, my name I proudly bear
I am truly self-realized and self aware
Of a mirror I have no need
Or a path free of stone and weed
Am I not complete and auspicious?
Of God's creatures felicitous
I have no more regard for your opinion
I well know my own strength and dominion.

51

FAREWELL, MY DOMAIN

Some colleagues, who had envied Malati, stung her with the comment, 'This was inevitable. How long could a woman continue to work after marriage?' It hurt Malati because it was true, wasn't it? She had to shelve her law studies for now, if not for good. Moreover, she had a responsibility to Guru, to run his household, and to play mother soon enough to their children.

Just before she left Benares, Malati had a brainwave. She decided to meet the vice chancellor, Mahamana Malaviya. She was delighted when she was summoned to the VC's office to meet the great man. She was nervous too. After all, he was a living legend, a seventy-year-old patriarch, and she a slip of a girl, deigning to give her own views on matters on which he was a master and had overriding jurisdiction.

He was credited with translating 'holy madness into the accomplished fact of the great monument that was the Banaras Hindu University against all odds, and of nurturing it into a world class institution in a short time'. Besides that, he had the distinction of being the Congress Party president for four terms and the founder member of the Hindu Mahasabha. Moreover, he had been the lawyer/advocate for revolutionary freedom fighters. He had defended the Chauri Chaura violence accused and also pleaded for clemency for the martyred Bhagat Singh.

When Malati entered his office, she was struck by its aesthetic design and the beautiful paintings and idols of Hindu gods and goddesses on display. The great man sat behind a large wooden desk, dressed in a white dhoti, kurta, khadi stole, and his famous white muslin turban. His distinctive handle bar moustache only partially covered the warm smile with which he greeted her. It lit up the room for her.

'Come, Malati. The principal told me all about you. I was as curious to meet you, as I know you were keen to meet me. So, tell me, daughter, what is your message for me?' Malati was pleasantly surprised and humbled.

She began her presentation.

'I bow my head before you, O great guru! Thank you for giving me the honour of meeting you. None can imagine the respect, even veneration, I have for you.'

'You are a champion of women's education, widow remarriage, and you have campaigned against child marriage—all of the causes I am personally very committed to. You so adroitly straddle the leadership of the Congress and the Hindu Mahasabha, both of which I follow keenly and believe in, though some think they are at cross purposes with each other. You are one of the greatest Indian educationists and a collaborator of my other idol, Annie Besant, who brought me here!'

'Thank you for your quite accurate description of what I aspire for every day, but the results, as the Gita says, are not always in my hands,' the Mahamana said.

'I have a few humble suggestions and questions for your consideration and guidance based on my experience here at BHU,' Malati continued.

'Go on,' he smiled.

'I was upset that you were thwarted in your attempts to get women to join humanities courses and to teach Sanskrit in the regular BHU. So, you opened the MMV. But we need both—women's only colleges, but also women studying with men in all the disciplines. It makes the world of a difference. I have seen that in Elphinstone College. So, I plead with you to not give up on that effort.'

He looked a little startled.

'I have observed how a university like BHU with its avowed aim of being the crucible of the Indian nationalist spirit and soul, is challenged to deal with revolutionary nationalist movements swirling within and around it. The BHU administration is cautious. I understand that as a university in the British Raj, you don't want to give them an excuse to take it over. But we could find ways to help our BHU family members who get involved in revolutionary activities but have not actually engaged in violence, In the case of Shantabai, Rahul, and Ruchika some legal defence should kindly be provided,' Malati pleaded.

The Mahamana gave a thoughtful nod.

'Guruji, I sacrificed my law studies and came here to teach and to support my husband. Now when I rejoin him, how do you think I can serve my country better—by resuming my law studies and defending freedom fighters as a lawyer or continuing as a teacher?' she finally asked.

The Mahamana replied to her questions diligently.

'Left to myself, I would open up all the disciplines in BHU to women, too. But we have to make haste slowly, lest we fail too early, too irreversibly. MMV is the first step. By and by, we will have other cobblestones laid on the path to equality in women's education.'

'On the delicate matter of our supporting revolutionaries, I will reflect upon your request. About which is more important, imparting education or becoming a lawyer to defend satyagrahis, I have said it to Gandhiji himself, education first!' he said emphatically.

'If children don't study, how can they prepare to run the country,' she, quoted him. He smiled approvingly.

'But you know what? I see you best as a fiery and powerful woman advocate defending our freedom fighters in court. So, I would say nothing like it if you rejoin and complete law studies and become a lawyer. The British, as they get nervous about the power of the freedom movement to dislodge them, are going to use sedition and treason laws more and more against Indian freedom fighters. Either way, you will live up to the faith of those like me and Annie, who lay so much store by women's education as a means to achieve independence,' he said firmly, and got up to signal that the meeting was over.

∽

Malati was leaving for the station the next day when a messenger handed her a letter from the VC in a sealed envelope.

> Dear Malati,
>
> I am happy to have met you. Your suggestions were profound and taken to heart. I assure you that I will act on helping the people you referred to. May you carry the learnings from this institution on the path of greatness you seek for yourself and our Bharat Mata.
>
> My best wishes for your future endeavours!

Malati left Benares with her head held high.

When all who had come to see her off at the station had left and she was settling down on her seat in the train compartment, Sunil suddenly appeared and said with folded, hands, 'Thank you, madam. Our movement will always remember what you did to help us. We are finally getting someone to defend Shanta Ma, Rahul, and Ruchika—all because of you! And I am free to continue my revolutionary mission.'

Malati looked around and said almost in a whisper, 'I am glad. God bless you all who work and sacrifice to free Mother India. But remember, violence will not work, find other ways....' Her words lost on him as he jumped out of the moving train with practised ease and dissolved into the multitudes in a fast-disappearing Benares station of Malati's life.

Malati sat back in the train headed to join Guru in Vaishali to seek Malak and Surekha's blessings. A new chapter in her playbook was about to be written, and she would have to play a role for which she was ill-equipped. But she was determined to prove, especially to Guru's family that she is as good a homemaker as she had been a scholar, tennis player, or teacher.

Malati and Guru reached Vaishali at almost the same time. Guru embraced her and then, looked her over anxiously—as if checking whether any piece of her was missing. They rode silently in Malak's new motor car to the wada, possessively holding hands and taking in the scenes of Vaishali, he as a newcomer acquainting himself with his in-law's universe, and she as one looking for changes in Vaishali over the years! Not much had changed and the Karuna River flowed on as calmly as before, no matter the whirlpools of the swarajya struggle the denizens of Vaishali were being sucked into.

At the wada, Surekha welcomed them warmly. They both touched her feet. 'Thank you for receiving me into your home as Malati's husband,' said Guru, respectfully.

'You are welcome, our jamai raja. I like your pandit and pujari, Malati,' Surekha said, alluding to Malati's letter confiding that Guru had called her his goddess and himself her priest worshipper. A ruffled Malati walked forward to hurry past both Surekha and Guru, stumbled, but Guru held her up.

He joined Surekha in teasing Malati and recited B. R. Tambe's ode to bashful new brides ever so tunefully.

> Nava vadhu priya me bavarte, lajte pude sarte phirte
> Look the new blushing bride is bewildered and stumbles.
> Bashfully she walks forward, meanders and tumbles.

Surekha laughed out loud.

'You two are already ganging up against me!' Malati said feigning anger, but a smile lighting up her eyes and tugging at her lips.

Before they could respond, Veena, who was standing close by, ran to Malati and said, 'Maushi, we will both gang up against them.'

'You should join me. I will take you to Bombay and show you plays and films. If not, I will tease you with a poem too,' said Guru, smiling at her.

Veena, now a beautiful teenager, looked suspiciously at Guru and said, 'I am on my maushi's side. I am not afraid of your poem. Bring it on.'

'All right. Here it goes,' and Guru began to sing the poem, 'Phool Rani' by the great poet, Maaydev, suitably adapted to apply to Veena.

Hirwe hirwe gaar galiche,
Harit trunachya makhmali che,
Tya sunder makhmali varti,
Khelat hoti tee phulrani.

On the cool, cool carpets verdant
Of soft green grass abundant
Beautiful, luxurious, velveteen
Joyfully frolicks our Flower Queen,
Surrounded by the sweet, blue atmosphere
She roams carefree, innocent and unaware
Swinging and singing on her mother's lap
She is not yet caught in cosmic love's trap

Veena demanded to hear the full poem.

'I will sing to unravel the mystery of life as you grow up in age and wisdom, and let each new stanza "way lay" you!' Guru wove his poetic tapestry right in front of her eyes!

'All right,' said Veena and thus began that very special journey of affection and 'play way' between her, Malati, and Guru.

Like Veena, Guru amused her two brothers, Vishnu and Vaibhav, with songs and storytelling about boys.

'Now, I want to know which one of you likes to go to school and which one finds excuses to skip school?' Guru asked.

'We both like school, but also like to skip it and stay at home sometimes!' replied Vishnu.

'OK. This poem is dedicated to the malingerer most inclined to skip school,' Guru said and sang.

Ayee shale madhe kasa jau,
Majhi shala kiti tari door,
Mulay geli palun bhur bhur!

Oh mother, how can I go to school this morning,
My friends have already gone there running
Let me stay home awhile and talk
My school is way too far for me to walk

'And the schoolboy goes on to make all kinds of excuses, it's too hot, or the stones will prick his bare feet. What are your excuses?' Guru asked the boys.

'That I have fever and my head aches.'

'That other boys tease me. Call me cat eyes.'

The two boys rattled away their excuses.

Guru then sang the last stanza.

OK, I will go somehow to school in a dash, however far,
But first will you give me my favourite sweet from the jar?

'What's your sweet inducement?' Guru asked them.

'I want a horse like Veena's.'

'A violin.'

'A toy car....'

'A gun to go for shikar.'

'Stop! Stop!' cried Guru. 'Don't you two want the actual sweet the boy in the poem asked for?'

'We get that without asking—thrust upon us by the dais,' they both said in unison.

'Oh, OK. Now what did you learn from this poem?' Guru asked.

They fell silent. Veena replied for them. 'That there is no real reason to avoid going to school—your reasons are made-up ones. Secondly, what you get without asking, you don't value and covet any more.'

'That's right!' said Guru, and he and Malati blessed the precocious Veena.

When Malak returned from the court that evening, Guru had a formal audience with him in his durbar room. He was a bit nervous because of Malak's reputation of a stern and officious demeanour. He wore a new pant-suit Malati had ordered for him to look like a prospective sub-judge and first-class magistrate! She wanted to show off his noble mien to Malak at first sight.

'So does the Nalini in you want to project the materialistic Kairopant in me, rather than the idealistic khadi-wearing Vaikunth Rao? I am sure your Malak is shrewd enough to see through and recognize the true me! At least he will be flattered that we made an effort to seek his approval,' Guru smiled.

'Malak will like all of you and has no option but to approve my choice,' Malati replied confidently.

Malak welcomed them warmly. They sat on chairs flanking Malak's throne, much like courtiers do. He casually appraised Guru from head to toe. Looking pleased, he said, 'Congratulations to you, Malati and Guru, on your marriage. I understand you have courted each other for six years—and you, Malati, and Kamala kept denying any "entanglement". Then you secretly got married. You hoodwinked us throughout, did you not, eh?' Malak asked Malati with mock annoyance.

Malati explained the reasons why they had to keep it secret.

'I understand. Anyway, you have our blessings. But given that this is not a usual marriage between two consenting families, but essentially between the two of you, the responsibility for its success lies with you. Malati has made sacrifices for you, Guru. If you at any stage forget that, and give her any unhappiness, we Kshatriyas know how to avenge any wrong done,' Malak warned.

Before Malati could come to Guru's rescue, he said. 'Malak, that threat is an unfair way to bless our marriage! It does not do justice to the love and generosity you have showered on Malati and Kamala all these years. They both are discerning, educated women, who would not have chosen us and then tested us for six years if they were not satisfied that we are committed to them and we will make them happy. Anyway, I don't speak for Ram, but I give you an undertaking to love and cherish Malati always,' Guru said sincerely.

'And protect her from all harm too!' added Malak.

'I wield no gun, nor brandish a sword. But I will protect her in every way with my Brahmanical mantras!' said Guru.

Malak smiled at Guru's riposte to his Kshatriya jibe.

52

GURU'S RIVER OF ACHIEVEMENT

Malak ceremonially presented Guru with a suit of clothes, a turban, and a ten tola gold coin as a token of respect and kinship. Surekha gave Malati a silk sari and four gold bangles, telling her to always wear them as a married woman, not be bare-wristed.

The talk turned to politics and Malak seemed unusually reticent. Later, when they were alone, Surekha told Malati the reason. Malak had been under severe strain because of the constant carping of the British Resident against him after the Kakori incident. He had accused Malak of aiding and abetting the HRA in Vaishali and sympathizing with the Congress and urged the Maharaja to remove him from his ministerial position, if not book him for treason. Malak had stoutly denied the 'absurd allegations' and dared the British Resident to come forward with proof. The people of Vaishali were with Malak and did not betray him. So far, the Maharaja had held firm but the relaunch of the Civil Disobedience Movement by Mahatma Gandhi last year, which had its reverberations in Vaishali, had destabilized the Maharaja too. He now worried about the Congress-fomented insurrection.

'So, for now, the rulers of Vaishali prefer the British as the lesser of the two evils—better their overlordship than dethronement by the mobs, huh!' remarked Malati.

Surekha smiled wryly.

Guru and Malati returned to Bombay after their 'pilgrimage' to Vaishali. They stayed in Appa's house to pack Guru's meagre belongings and treasure of books and to prepare to set up their home in Kopergaon. Malati gave up the effort to make friends with Mai when she saw that her meanness was replaced by a new jealousy about Guru and Malati starting a 'romantic journey' away from her intrigues. Instead, Malati learnt Saraswat cooking from Guru's aunt and got under the skin of the mores of the family she was married into.

In Kopergaon, Guru and Malati were warmly received with garlands by a small group of officials and staff from the District Magistrate's office. They soon settled into their three-bedroom home with a large but wild garden, overlooking the Godavari River—one of the greatest and longest rivers after the Ganga.

'We should thank our ancestor King Bhagirath for doing the penance, so we could all be blessed with the life-giving waters of the Ganga and her riverine sisters. The Godavari is Kopergaon's lifeline, apart from imparting a unique beauty to it. Kopergaon is now my Benares and the Godavari my Bhagirathi,' Guru said.

Malati looked askance.

'In Benares, you were the head of the household and supporting me. Now this is my turn. You need not work at all and can enjoy the comforts of home. Also, you have to take care of me and our children in the future,' he reminded Malati. Malati agreed—for now.

Guru was already fired up about his job. He was among the first Indians to be a first-class magistrate and sub-judge, thanks to the progressive Indianization of the civil services. He combined both executive and judicial functions. The district magistrate, Paul Johnson, and the district judge, Thomas Wright, who were Guru's bosses, sat in Ahmednagar. Soon after he took charge, Guru had to travel almost eighty miles to meet them. He came back elated by his meeting with his bosses.

'You know, Malati, you and I have always viewed the British in India as invaders, colonial masters, and as arrogant, overbearing and uncaring rulers and administrators, out to rob India of its riches and Indians of their dignity. Judge Wright today showed me that there are exceptions,' Guru said.

Malati was a bit sceptical and wondered whether the judge was not being double-faced like the British are known to be.

'Well, not this one. He was very pleased to have me, an Indian, as his sub-judge. After we discussed my duties and issues that come up at the subdivision and district level, he said he was very impressed that in a short period I had picked up the key pulse points of my job. When I asked him for his general guidance and advice to me, he said, whenever and whatever decision you take as an administrator and judge, use the test of how it will help or hinder the interests of the common Indian. Be it the farmer toiling in his fields under the blazing sun or the labourer carrying heavy loads or even the small producer and trader providing goods and services to the community,' Guru said, becoming emotional.

'That's wonderful,' Malati exclaimed.

'Wait. He said two other things that sound straight out of our own lawgiver Manu's books: "Whilst interpreting and applying laws, remember they exist for the welfare of the people and must not harm them. Secondly, uphold equality before the law and make no distinction based on caste, creed, or status or even race in your work".'

Malati was happy that Guru had found an inspiring mentor and his purpose in work.

'Mr Johnson by contrast is a typical British colonial officer. Condescending and full of imperial purpose, alas! Warning me that I watch out for the contagion of any anti-British activities in Kopergaon. And make sure revenue realization is effective,' Guru grimaced.

They soon found out that Kopergaon had other more urgent problems for Guru to address. It was the monsoon season and overnight they witnessed the fury of the raging Godavari going out of bounds, a watery giantess churning forth with her powerful arms and feet and gulping down trees and temples, homes, and embankments. She trampled on the fields, inundating crops, gushed into homes, pummelling them. She snatched livelihoods and left people displaced, homeless, and hungry.

Guru immediately evacuated those living directly on the banks and arranged to provide relief. Meanwhile, Malati set off on her own to investigate the cause and reported to Guru that every monsoon the sluice gates of a reservoir at the Nasik border were opened automatically and excess water was released downstream, flooding Kopergaon. At her suggestion, Guru worked out a solution with his counterpart in Niphad Subdivision, which would solve the problem of flooding for both.

They agreed to release excess water from the reservoir in spaced intervals and direct into irrigation channels for fields. He also secured approval for building a large reservoir in Kopergaon. In the three years they spent there, this became Guru's signature monument, dedicated to the welfare of the people of Kopergaon and he gave Malati abundant credit.

Malati and Guru received much love from Kopergaon. It was where Guru and Malati had their first child.

Malati gave birth to a baby girl—Kashi—in a small taluka hospital in Kopergaon where an English-trained doctor attended on her.

Although people around them were lukewarm in their good wishes because their first child was not a boy, Guru celebrated her as a reincarnation of his mother.

Kashi was a healthy baby with fine features, a round face, large eyes, and curly hair like Malati's and an arched smile like Guru's. As she grew and flourished, Guru transferred his adoration and poetic attention from Malati to her. The moment he returned from court and office, he picked her up, played with her tiny fingers wrapped around his, tickled her small pink feet to the marvel of her giggles, and kissed her plump cheeks softly as she gurgled intently up at him. He held her delicately against his heart resonating to the *lub-dub-lub* of her heartbeat, assured by the rhythm of his!

Malati was getting used to the novelty of motherhood, but taking time to accept that she had to share Guru with Kashi and Kashi with him. Guru reassured her saying, 'Vedi ga vedi! How can you be crazy to think that my love for you can diminish. It has only grown and deepened, with Kashi as the new, potent, and indestructible bond between us—a living symbol of our union?'

Malati slowly got to embrace him and her motherhood sincerely; enjoying Kashi with the same intensity with which Guru, her teacher in love, had been doing all along.

Soon it was time to leave a peaceful, yet fulfilling Kopergaon, for Bombay. Guru's good work had been noticed and he was called back on promotion to serve in the Legal Department of the Government of Bombay, in charge of the conduct of civil litigation.

Malati was happy to be back in Bombay after being in a kind of exile for nearly five years. It was great to be reunited with Kamala and Ram, who too, had just had a daughter, to reconnect with Chandra and Vivek, who had got married and had a son. And so good to be able to catch up with Hema Kaki and Mohan Kaka, who were delighted to have them and Kashi to indulge with their affection. Kaka had left Britannia and worked for a swadeshi company and Kaki's musical career was flourishing.

Most of all, it was good to be the wife of an emerging star in the Bombay government like Guru. Setting up a separate and well-appointed home put them in an unassailable position in the Saraswat community that Appa could no longer be embarrassed by. He could only be proud! In keeping with her promise, Guru's brother Ganesh, who was now in college, occasionally came and stayed with them.

Appa too was lured to their home by Malati's culinary excellence and by her offering him his favourite fish delicacies in authentic Karvari style, which Mai had shunned. He often came across straight from the High Court, even when Guru was not around, and felt honoured to be indulged by Malati. He had to concede that she was a true Goddess Annapurna, transcending caste and community! As Guru said jokingly, Malati had conquered Appa through his taste buds and stomach!

Appa also took to Kashi instantly, the first grandchild in his family. He taught her Konkani, her father tongue, and Kashi soon became fluent enough to teach Malati. Anna was proud of her 'Brahmanical intelligence', though Malati insisted that she had inherited her 'tactical Kshatriya brain' too!

From Vaishali came the good news that Veena was getting married to a Maratha boy from a noble family. They were unable to attend the wedding due to work. Kamala managed to go and came back very pleased.

Just ten days after her marriage, Guru and Malati's doorbell rang one evening. To Malati's utter shock, it was Veena looking dishevelled and distraught, carrying a small trunk. Her uncombed hair was knotted into an untidy bun. Her eyes had turned red with crying, her unwashed pink skin had become ashen and drawn. Her usually buoyant mien carried sword wounds of a battle she seemed to have ferociously fought and lost.

'Veena! What happened? Are you OK?' Malati exclaimed, opening the door wide.

Veena fell into her arms and sobbed uncontrollably.

'Please help me, Maushi, Kaka. I have run away. I have to hide from my husband, my in-laws, and from Baba Saheb and his cruel inquisition. He forced me to marry Sandeep Rao because he comes from one of the richest and most influential families in the Central Province,' she cried.

Malati led her to the sofa and sat her down.

'Veena, you are not a docile calf to be leashed and sent away with any man as a bride. Malak has always respected your free will, educated you, and allowed you to wear pants and breeches and tame and ride horses! Surely, if you did not like the match, why didn't you resist,' she asked her incredulously.

'I don't know under what light and star I saw Sandeep! To please Baba Saheb, I said yes. But when I met him in our nuptial chamber, I was repulsed and could not bear to spend the rest of my life with him. I ran away from his house that very night, and came back home ten miles on my horse that I had taken along!'

'Arrey deva! What have you done? No wonder Malak was upset with you. He has no face to show in the Maratha community, let alone in the Maharaja's darbar,' Malati exclaimed, horrified.

'When I refused to go back to my husband, Baba Saheb was furious and asked me to leave the house, and swore never to see my face again. He was very angry with Ayee because she tried to plead on my behalf. It was Ayee who told me to come to you, knowing that you would not turn me away,' Veena explained.

Before Malati could say a word, Guru assured her of their support in every way possible.

'Thank you, Kaka, for giving shelter to your phulrani—and becoming the vanmali—the cosmic gardener!' she said, reminding him of the phulrani poem he used to sing to her.

'If Malak finds me, he will have me killed on the spot,' Veena warned.

'Don't exaggerate, Veena. How could a father who loves you so much do that?' Guru asked.

'After the crime I have committed in Baba Saheb's eyes, he feels entitled to eliminate me—the symbol of his shame. I am worried about what he must be doing to Ayee,' Veena said, her eyes filling with tears.

'Why would he blame Akka for your willfulness? He is the one who gave you freedom!' Malati tried to reason.

'Oh, he had already started tormenting her day in and day out. He told her that she should either persuade me to go back to Sandeep to redeem Malak's honour or do away with me. And you know how your Akka is. Just quietly soaks in the insults,' Veena said.

Later, when they were alone, Malati applauded Guru for his generous offer to Veena to live with them. However, both worried about how explosive this matter could become and about Surekha's well-being.

They sent Veena away to Kamala in Poona and conveyed to Surekha that Veena was safe in Kamala's watchful custody, had taken up a teaching job there and was happy. Surekha sent them a poignant letter through Baba.

Dearest Kamala and Malati,

Since our own Ayee left us, I have tried to fill her void for you two and you have in turn called me your little Ayee and given me love and respect. Today I am asking you to please take care of my child, Veena, be her guardian and save her not only from her father's wrath till he comes to terms with her 'devastating act of defiance', but also from her own impulsive, egoistical madness!

I now realize how much Veena is like Sarala. Both girls wanting to be wilful like men in shaping their own destinies. Sarala paid a price with her life for this delusion. I don't want Veena to suffer a similar fate.

I am counting on you. I know you feel a certain loyalty to Malak, but in this matter, I need you to disobey, even deceive him, for a while, until Veena is forgiven and safe with him.

Please thank Guru and Ram for me for putting up with this Veena tornado in their lives.

Ocean full of love to you all and your babies,

Your Little Ayee/Akka.

Guru conjectured that Malak wanted to show his extreme displeasure to Veena and at the same time demonstrate his outrage at her actions to her in-laws, a way of apologizing to them and redeeming his and their honour. However, knowing how much he doted on her, he must have wanted her to be safe with them. Arjun must know and report to him.

53
THE TRIAL

Not all the domestic bliss that Malati was basking under, quelled the storm of restlessness that was rising within her. She yearned for a purpose of her own in life. One morning she told Guru that she had had an epiphany again—that she must now keep her promise to him to resume her law studies and fulfil her 'dream interrupted' to become a woman lawyer.

That Malati had had two miscarriages and the thought that perhaps they were not destined to have another child, strangely strengthened her determination. To her delight Guru agreed immediately and Malati joined her old Law College, pledging not to leave midway, come what may!

Going back to her studies after an interregnum of five long years was daunting. Malati worried about having lost her academic spark and the stamina to study long hours. Did she still have that fierce competitive spirit, that resolve to prove her worth and excellence? Would she be able to manage it all while being the ideal, ever-nurturing wife and mother? she agonized.

'Banish these doubts. That's not my Malati!' Guru said, holding her hands. 'You are destined to mark another milestone—of a woman who came back after a gap to reclaim her purpose! "Poore Jaanto Meech Maajhe Bal!" Remember the Tilak poem. You well know your own dominion. Go forth courageously. Don't worry about anything else!'

That boosted her confidence. She rediscovered her old academic flair and rigour. She lived up to Guru's expectation and earned her law degree with distinction.

Malati joined the Chamber of Guru's classmate and friend, Upendra Salve, and supported his practice at the High Court. She chose him and he chose her because he was something of a Vaikunth Rao in his idealism. He dedicated a portion of his law practice to pro bono work to support poor litigants and freedom fighters who were caught in the British net of prosecution for sedition.

Sometimes Malati's work sat awkwardly with Guru's government litigator role but never once did he stop Malati from representing even those labelled enemies of the state by the British Raj he served. His bosses warned him a few times that Malati's work was in conflict with his, but he successfully argued that they were both upholding the rule of law.

Hema Kaki was a regular visitor at Malati and Guru's place, taking care of Kashi when they were both busy. However, they rarely met Mohan Kaka. He was often travelling outside Bombay—they had no idea where—ostensibly on business. There followed a long spell when they did not see him at all. Then one evening, Hema Kaki came over very agitated. On Malati's questioning, she finally admitted that Mohan Kaka had been arrested along with two of his friends for anti-British activities and had been in jail for over three months. He had told her not to inform Malati and Guru, as he wanted to die in prison a martyr!

Malati and Guru were shocked.

'There have been mass arrests of Congress leaders, but why the swoop on Mohan Kaka? Was he active in revolutionary movements?' Guru asked.

Hema Kaki said that only Mohan Kaka knew and she was completely out of the loop. Whenever she had asked, he said that his choice of freedom streams was eclectic like her repertoire of music! She requested Malati to go meet him and persuade him to be defended by her. 'I do not want him to be martyred like this in jail,' she sobbed.

Malati went to meet Mohan Kaka in the Arthur Road Jail in Bombay. When she saw him with his friends Bhim Rao and Shiva Prakash weighed down by heavy chains, she knew that she must defend them. The stink of torture—the unwashed sweat, layers of dirt on the skin and patches of dried blood on their clothes, the suppurating wounds of the flesh and the soul, the suppressed screams of pain on their brave faces, hit her senses. She was dismayed to see her Mohan Kaka in his prisoner incarnation, looking almost cadaverous, his light green eyes sunk in their sockets, his fair skin sallow and crinkling into folds, his head, back and shoulders bent forwards, but not in submission! For his spirit still seemed to be ascendant, held aloft and unfurled on a pole of patriotism, she was happy to note.

'How are you, Mohan Kaka? Have they been ill-treating you?' she asked with concern.

'Vadu de karagrihachya bhinti chi unchi kiti, manmana nahi kshiti!' He evoked the patriotic daredevilry of Yashwant's poem, 'Turungachya Darat' that Guru had also sung after the *Satteche Gulam* imbroglio.

'Let them do their worst, they cannot imprison my soul,' Mohan Kaka's still stentorian voice, reverberated against the real prison walls and he smiled, wanly, revealing two broken teeth.

'This is not a place I, as your former guardian, would have liked you to visit. I had told Hema not to trouble you, but obviously she could not restrain herself. Always defiant!' he said, smiling with affection.

'Mohan Kaka, you do not deserve to be martyred—not yet. You have many more hills—nay mountains—of patriotic action to climb before you lay down your life for your beloved Bharat Mata. I offer to fight your case, unless you think that I, a woman lawyer, can't succeed in freeing you. You once said that women can't do much in the freedom movement!' Malati provoked Mohan Kaka.

'No. No. I gave up that idea long ago. Truth be told, Hema has been my right hand in my revolutionary activities, part of my cover story, my courier and adviser even as she was cooking at home or singing on stage. She never faltered and even fooled you girls. That apart, I have been watching you, my dear niece, defend other freedom fighters very ably. But this case is a very tough one to win and I don't want you to sully your brilliant record with a defeat. Nor do I want Hema's role to be divulged, since they have seized some "incriminating letters",' Mohan Kaka explained.

'Kaka if you trust my abilities, you will not deny me the opportunity to prove myself—the harder the case, the more my glory—even if I fail. But I will not. I am sure of that,' Malati said firmly.

'Right then if you have come down into the Kurushetra of desh bhakti, you will have to wield the guns and swords of your legal acumen, and also get your feet and hands dirty, if need be, in the marshes. Are you ready to deploy saam, daam, danda, and bhed?' he asked.

Malati smiled and whispered that she had come there with that very resolve, but she first wanted to know the truth and nothing but the truth. She would use that truth to gather and shake the Mayavi magical dice of law, and play to win always like Shakuni Mama of the Mahabharata.

She asked Mohan Kaka what the charges were and whether they were guilty as charged. He told her that all three of them had been charged under the most draconian provisions of the Indian Penal Code, she would have to get the papers from the police, and then they could plan a strategy for defence.

'My own inclination was to admit these charges and become a martyr, but you have convinced me that my Motherland is still in chains and I must continue my service to free her. So, we must fight out of this prison and you will build our escape chutes. And remember, you get all three of us out or none at all,' he said.

Malati learned that Mohan Kaka had been the Bombay leader of a revolutionary cell with connections to the HRA and Anushilan Samiti. The cell had been quiescent for a while, but frustrated by the ineffectiveness of the 'do or die' Quit India Movement and the British suppression that followed, it had become active again and prepared to hit out against British government targets to force them to quit India. None of the three had broken down so far under interrogation. Since the police were still hunting for his more pliable associates, she needed to start work on their case quickly. This was the first time she would be defending someone who was close to her. She told herself that it should only add coal to her blazing furnace of determination and ingenuity.

Malati went to the police station and demanded to see Mohan Kaka and his associates' files as their attorney. A burly Marathi inspector in charge, greeted her.

'Malati?' he said, incredulously. 'Remember me?'

She looked at him closely. It was Bhika from Ratnagiri!

'We still have a dangal left to fight,' he said laughing. After all these years! Malati was delighted. They talked about each other's families and their journeys thus far. Then Malati turned to the court case.

'We shall have a dangal in court, Bhika Bhau. And I will win this time with the help of Lord Hanuman whom you introduced me to, remember?' she said, smiling.

'How can a mere woman lawyer win?' he teased her.

This time, instead of getting angry, she sought to win him over.

'See, your sister Malati is putting everything on the line for justice for our fellow Indians and I expect no less from you, my brother and classmate. Moreover, Mohan Kaka is like a dear uncle, so the political is personal here,' Malati said earnestly.

Bhika handed over the case files and said, 'Sister, you can try, but you will not win this one—take it from me. And not because I don't want you to. As for helping you, I serve the British sarkar and I have to do my duty!'

Malati went through the case files and realized why Bhika had predicted her failure. She was aghast that Mohan Kaka and his associates had been charged under Section 121A: conspiracy to wage war against the government; Section 122: collecting arms to wage war; Section 123: concealing the design to wage war against the government. Section 124A: bringing or attempting to bring into hatred or contempt or to excite disaffection towards the British government.

Besides this, the police seemed to have marshalled a formidable body of evidence. It included letters written by Mohan Kaka to Hema Kaki and to other known and unknown friends seen as collaborators, some propaganda material and pamphlets and 'discoveries of weapons, ammunitions and explosives in sites they used to visit and congregate in'.

When she confronted Mohan Kaka with it, she realized that she would have to use all her legal guile, agility, and much else besides. She told him about the serendipity of meeting up with Bhika after all these years as the inspector-in-charge. Mohan Kaka, to whom she had long ago described the Big Fight in school, smiled and said Bhika will be Bhika! Hema Kaki who had accompanied Malati to the prison this time to meet Mohan Kaka, looked thoughtful, but uncharacteristically said nothing.

Malati discussed her moral dilemma with Guru. He reminded her of the conversation between Lord Krishna and the patriarch Bhishma Pitamah lying on his deathbed of nails. The patriarch asked Lord Krishna in torment why he had resorted to deception to get victory over the Kauravas. Lord Krishna had famously replied that each age had its own circumstances and its own Evil and to end that Evil, everything—even a lie—was justified in every way.

With over a hundred thousand political prisoners in crowded jails, getting a quick trial in the right courts and with impartial judges was a challenge, but with Upendra's connections, she managed to get dates in a court which had an Indian Judge, not a 'contaminated one', so she expected a fairer trial.

When the trial began before Judge Shafiq Ali, the British prosecutor Malcolm O'Brien presented a strong case with all the evidence laid out in a cool, precise manner.

Malati sought to demolish the prosecution's case with a combination of law, politics, and righteous indignation.

'Milord, in the prevailing fraught political environment, is it not astonishing that the prosecution began with the fallacious assumption that every Indian patriot is engaged in conspiracies to wage war against the British government and every assertion of patriotic view, however expressed, every aspiration for the ideal of freedom for India is seen as sedition, treason, waging war? Surely, at a time when His Majesty's government in India is itself engaged with Indian parties to seek a path to Indian independence and when thousands of Indian soldiers are fighting for the British in World War II theatres, this kind of persecution and witch hunt is not justified for a government which claims to uphold the rule of law.'

Based on this logic, she questioned each piece of propagandist literature and epistolary evidence and cross-examined the police who claimed that they were coded signals for some terrorist activities.

'These letters that the first accused has written to his wife are private correspondence. As Hema Agashe or Hirabai is a well-known singer and Mohan Agashe is a connoisseur of natya sangeet, the letters have nothing but poems and songs. Yes, some of the songs are patriotic, but since when is that sedition or waging war? To read into them some code language is absurd.'

She then took up each of the so-called 'incriminating letters' supposedly between Mohan Kaka and his collaborators. She cast doubts on the signatures and at least two of the most incriminating ones she showed were forgeries because of the language used and discrepancies in the handwriting, while some others she proved were not material to the matter.

O'Brien then pounded her on the discoveries of weapons and explosives and looking at her with a sardonic smile said, 'Now will the esteemed lawyer for the defence claim that her clients had nothing to do with them?'

'Yes, Mr Prosecutor, I categorically affirm that Mohan Agashe and his two co-accused had nothing to do with them. The weapons were not found in their own residences, the accused were not in the venues when the weapons were seized, those so-called hideouts did not belong to them. Indeed, the weapons seemed to be planted and then a connection made post facto to implicate them. The burden of proof was on the prosecution—to show that Mohan Aghashe and his friends habitually met in these places, collected and concealed these weapons and plotted to wage war against the British government. Most importantly, no link had been shown to any incident of attack or violence that had taken place against the British government or public assets. Milord, the, prosecution has failed to establish any conspiracy to wage a war or to overawe the British government,' Malati affirmed masterfully.

In her cross-examination of Inspector Bhika and his two constables, she rammed home this point as they admitted that at no time had they seen or caught the three accused in these venues carrying or possessing weapons.

'Milord, I am sure that the honourable court will uphold the rights and freedoms of every Indian and the rule of law. It must not add to the injustice of the torture these innocents have been subjected to and endured. I challenge the prosecution to prove their alleged crimes beyond reasonable doubt.'

The Judge seemed impressed by her arguments. O'Brien was clearly upset at how she had turned the tables and demolished his case. When the court met after two days, she was shocked to be confronted by so-called new evidence brought forth by the Prosecution. They produced a fourth accused who had turned approver and confessed to not only being part of the revolutionary group led by Mohan Kaka, but also to witnessing them collecting weapons and preparing to attack British government targets. That was a blow!

54

VENUS GLOWS AGAINST THE SETTING SUN

The new development threatened to demolish the whole case so painstakingly built up by Malati. After conferring with Mohan Kaka, she decided to take the offensive.

She put Inspector Bhika in the dock again. 'From where did you materialize this so called fourth collaborator, Munna Lal? From thin air, I suppose! After I exposed the bankruptcy of the evidence you had presented, did the prosecution pressure you? You needed a fourth so-called collaborator because you were unable to unlawfully extract, a confession under torture from the three original accused! In violation of their fundamental rights and the common law principle, I may add, of no one being forced to be a witness against himself.'

The prosecutor strongly objected and the Judge upheld the objection.

'I insist that we were looking for other possible collaborators and we found Munna Lal. He readily confessed to the police and provided credible proof of his being a member of the group and witness to the alleged crimes of Mohan Agashe and his associates,' Inspector Bhika said without blinking an eyelid and looking straight back at Malati, as if in combat.

Malati then demanded to question Munna Lal. When Munna Lal took the stand, he first looked confident and quite gung-ho at the sight of a woman lawyer. But as Malati began to bombard him with piercing questions, he became increasingly nervous. He seemed to be unnerved also by the stern gaze of the prosecutor. His hands shook violently, as he held on to the rails of the witness box for dear life, beads of perspiration trickled down from his bald head and big wet patches of perspiration appeared on his shirt. He glanced repeatedly at Inspector Bhika.

'So, Munna Lalji, you have confessed that you know Mohan Agashe well and have collaborated with the three accused. So let me test you on how well you know them and their activities.'

She asked him a barrage of questions about Mohan Kaka, Munna Lal faltered so badly under her questioning that at one point he broke down and admitted to the court that the police had forced him to pose as a collaborator turned approver. Inspector Bhika was taken aback and pleaded not guilty to fabricating evidence and forcing Munna Lal to 'becoming a fourth collaborator'.

Malati was relieved and delighted when the Judge acquitted Mohan Kaka and his two collaborators for lack of evidence and chided the police for overreach. Upendra, her boss who had attended some of the sessions and listened to her closing arguments, complimented her. She had earned her place as one of the first female lawyers to win such a difficult case. She had achieved this by the sheer exercise of her fearless advocacy and the 'soaring forensic eloquence' of some of the great Indian advocates in political trials in British India that she was heir to. Local Marathi newspapers made her out to be a 'legal hero' and 'star' on the patriotic horizon and even the Bombay English newspapers noted her unexpected success, pointing to how it had set several precedents that favoured freedom fighters. Malati sent these newspaper cuttings to a very proud Baba and to the Mahamana in Benares.

Malati went to felicitate Mohan Kaka and Hema Kaki at their house. They welcomed her warmly and asked her to join the 'gang'. Shiva Prakash and Bhim Rao were beaming and savouring the sweets Hema Kaki had prepared. Malati was startled when Bhim Rao said, 'Hematai, you should have invited Munna Lal too, for he deserves to share in the celebration of our freedom.' Hema Kaki gave him a warning look and pretended she had not heard anything.

Malati smiled, embraced Hema Kaki, and said, 'You have turned out to be a closet freedom warrior and the best of them.'

Soon thereafter, Mohan Kaka disappeared. Malati and Guru suspected he had joined the INA and taken to arms to fight alongside Netaji Bose, somewhere in Burma. Hema Kaki was left a freedom fighter's grass widow for two long years. When the world war ended, many INA fighters were martyred. When Mohan Kaka did not return, Hema Kaki pretended to be in the dark, too, though they guessed she was assured of his being alive for she had not yet broken her glass bangles. Then one day, she came to Malati and Guru, all flushed and excited.

She informed them that she was going to cross the Seven Seas at last! Mohan Kaka had arranged for her to join him. She was to sail for Malaya that day. She would have liked Malati to accompany her on this adventure, as she had on her singing one! And later on, Mohan Kaka's freedom trial. But she knew this was a voyage she had to undertake alone.

When Malati asked her whether they were going to settle down in Malaya, Hema Kaki denied it.

They would return eventually to an independent India—and Mohan Kaka knew that time was near. Meanwhile, he wanted her to help with some mission. She could not imagine how a woman like her could be of any help to him. But, then a woman like Malati had saved him. Therefore, she too could.

Malati was intrigued. She only realized what the mission was when a year later they returned to Bombay, a young boy and girl in tow. They were the children of one of the captains in the INA, who had been martyred along with his wife. They had adopted the children. Hema Kaki, long troubled about being childless, said proudly that she had won a 'ready-made' family!

Guru and Malati introduced Kashi to their romantic journey in Bombay. They showed her where Guru first saw Malati in Gamdevi, the Elphinstone College auditorium where they acted in *Satteche Gulam*, the spot on the beach where Guru proposed to her! Once when they were on a typical fishermen's boat on the sea, he sang the 'Kolyache Geet' by poet Kanekar and asked Kashi to sing and clap along. Malati felt a twinge of jealousy as this was their song.

Aala khushit saminder,
Tyala nahi dhir
Hodila deyi na tharu
Ga sajni, hodi la baghto dharu
The sea is ebullient, dancing with glee
He will not let his darling boat go free
Keen to hold her tight in the waves of his arms
Besotted he is with the delicate boat's charms
Look Sajani! The sea's waters—a deep emerald green
The white foam churning and rising up to preen
Reflecting the toss and turmoil in my heart
The fury of my passion for you from the start
The sun rises, spectacular in the eastern sky

> *On the sea its ruddy reflection does lie*
> *Some of that glow is on my beloved's cheeks*
> *It's the sign and the signal that my mind seeks*

As he sang, Guru looked at Malati adoringly to wash away all stains of 'the otherness' from her consciousness.

Kashi embraced them both and said, 'I want you both to love each other and me like this always.'

Nobody was prepared in Bombay for Chakravat—the storm with inward spiralling winds, such that had not been seen by anyone in their lifetime and what it brought in its train. On that ill-fated afternoon, menacing storm clouds gathered in the sky, imprisoning the sun behind their furious, growling and heaving shutters; wailing winds came gushing in from the sea and went whirling through the streets like crazed dancers of destruction. Trees, beaten by the rain, swayed wildly, weaker ones were uprooted and fell to the ground. An epic churning propelled giant sea waves that strode in arrogantly, some as high as the buildings they battered on the seashore.

Arjun managed to come through the tempest to bring them news more devastating than Chakravat—Surekha had passed away! Veena, who had returned to Bombay and had started an exciting new career in Marathi theatre, and Guru and Malati now battled the storm within, even as it raged on outside.

Surekha had been a brave mediator between an apoplectic Malak and self-willed Veena with little success. She had therefore aided in Veena's escape and arranged for her to get asylum with her sisters, hoping that Malak's anger would soon subside and his deep affection for Veena would propel him to accept her back, eventually. That did not happen. Veena's in-laws justifiably felt affronted by her running away on her nuptial night, thus casting aspersions on Sandeep's manhood and virility.

They were relentless in demanding that Malak send Veena back to her husband's house, so he can remove that blot. It was humiliating for Malak to admit that, she had run away from his jurisdiction too. He the Kshatriya patriarch had no control on his own daughter or that, he had been complicit in her vile escapade! Malak faced deep embarrassment in Maharaja's court too.

The tragic loss of Sarala, and then, his beloved second daughter's fall from his own grace, as much as the world's, had become unbearable for Malak. Since he could not express his shame and anger in public, he turned on Surekha like never before, forgetting as she once told him, that he had promised never to hurt her in word or action. From morning until night, he berated her. He blamed her for Veena's original sin and subsequent infraction of running away. Surekha emphathized with Malak and let him vent his frustrations on her, accepting all the venomous epithets showered on her, as if they were the inevitable thorns that came with flower offerings.

In Surekha's life, Malak had been the sun—his rays protected her from mishap, warmed her with his affection, and lit her up with his trust. Malak, too, had drawn strength from her and joy from the children she had gifted him. But that sun had been eclipsed, if not exploded, leaving behind a toxic debris.

There came a time when she started becoming sick in the absence of that sunlight. Also, it was as if, all of Malak's thorns of blame, were perforating her being, without any balm of solace. She started getting headaches, high fever, and vertigo and the doctors could not say why. She began locking herself away from Malak, hiding from him. He would nevertheless seek her out to release his own pain.

One day she was looking through the medicines that Baba had given her to see if anything could cure her malaise. She came across sealed powder pouches of medicines against snakebites. Baba had meticulously indicated the dosage and warned that it was a form of poison for 'only poison could be an antidote to poison!' That echoed in her mind and she thought aloud.

'This is the only way to eliminate the poison of blame that courses through my body, mind, and heart. Let me take this antidote and end it all. If there is no flute, no one will be able to play a pitiful tune on it.'

She fearlessly swallowed three pouches of the snake venom antidote in the creeping darkness of one fateful evening near the well of the Bada Ghar. Immediately after that, she started to climb the stairs of the well so she could jump into it. For had Malak had not asked her to drown herself in the shallow waters of ignominy? Of shame? However, the poison acted so fast, that she collapsed into a heap and died on the stairs itself. Badi Dai found her inanimate body soon thereafter, when she came to draw water and informed Malak.

'Arrey Deva! She was still young. Whole life ahead of her!' Malati cried, on hearing the news.

'It's all my fault. My actions brought her the sorrow that took her life away,' Veena sobbed wretchedly.

Maa Saheb's prediction, or had it been her curse, had come true, Malati thought, but did not have the heart to tell Veena about it. Not only to spare her the guilt, but also because, as Baba had told them, the chains of cause and effect and credit and blame in life and death are complex and inscrutable.

Malati's heart went out to Surekha's young sons, to Malak, but most of all to Baba. Losing Ayee, and then his firstborn like this! It could not have been more tragic. So, Malati went as the sole mourner for Surekha from Bombay to Vaishali and joined a heartbroken Baba.

'I have been asking myself since then how my strong and cheerful Surekha could have surrendered so suddenly to the death force of Yamraj,' he moaned.

For the first time ever, Surekha was not at the door of the wada to greet them when Baba and Malati reached there.

'What happened to my darling daughter? Why did you allow her to die?' Baba asked Malak, breaking down.

Malak told him the whole story.

Baba was completely devastated by the revelations. Malak unexpectedly touched Baba's feet and started sobbing. Baba embraced him.

'It is my fault. It was I who drove her to this. Please forgive me,' he confessed.

This was the second time Malati witnessed a son-in-law confessing to having caused the death of his wife to his father-in-law.

'Only one of pure heart could have confessed the way you have done. She also did it for Veena, I suspect. Now, it's not a question of my forgiving you, but your forgiving Veena. My Surekha would have wanted that,' said Baba quietly.

'Malak, our heartfelt condolences! It is as if we have lost our mother all over again. We will miss her terribly. We, too, have a confession to make. We have been sheltering Veena for the last one year and she is well. She seeks your forgiveness, but also the permission to pursue her life in Bombay,' Malati said.

Malak melted.

He gracefully agreed to forgive her, and to send her money if she needed it. He sought a promise from Malati and Kamala that they would not allow her to go astray. He reckoned that Veena's in-laws would no longer hound Malak since her mother had sacrificed her own life for Veena's freedom. He urged them to find a good husband for her, like they did for themselves.

Malati returned to Bombay and told Veena about Malak's conditions of forgiveness. She asserted that she could not be married or be a touch-me-not flower of virtue, as it conflicted with her new flourishing star avatar in theatre and films.

As soon as Veena's success earned her riches, she bought her own flat and moved out of Malati's. As if to mock Malak, she started living with the most talented playwright and filmmaker of the time, Master Valmiki, a married man. He had given her all the big breaks, claimed to love her, and promised to leave his wife to marry her. When Malati questioned her about her behaviour, she asserted her independence, asked Malati to live up to her modern and educated maushi role, and try to convince Malak that she was Valmiki's second wife like Surekha had been his!

In the next few years, Master Valmiki and Veena scored success after success. She was among the top Marathi and Hindi film stars who commanded a high price. Malati kept Malak, torn between pride and embarrassment, posted about her ascent.

Malati's friends and acquaintances requested her to organize parties where they could meet and talk to the Silver Screen Goddess—Tara, the star. At one such party, Master Valmiki turned up too and he and Guru got on very well. But throughout the evening he glared at Veena whenever she spoke to any male admirer. After Malati served dinner, he came up to Veena and said in a loud, commanding voice, 'We have to leave now. Enough with your admirers!'

There was an awkward silence.

'I will quickly have dinner which Maushi has herself made. Don't worry, I will come for your film's shooting tomorrow morning,' Veena said graciously, but firmly.

Valmiki fumed at her defiance. Guru persuaded him to eat his dinner.

'Thank you for a wonderful meal, Malati and Guru, for your stimulating company,' he said warmly as they took their leave. 'Malati,

I hear you have acted in plays in college. You are beautiful and photogenic. I could give you roles in my films. Think about it and let me know.'

'Oh, I leave acting to my most beautiful and talented niece Veena who has found success as an actress and stardom too—a rarity!' Malati said admiringly. Veena embraced her.

'All is not well in the Veena–Valmiki universe. I sense that there are both ego and money issues and something else I could not put my finger on,' said Guru to Malati later that night.

'I agree. Valmiki had made her a star. But the creation had now become bigger than the creator!' Malati mused.

One of Veena's ardent fans described her as Shukrachi Chandni—the effulgent glow of Venus to Valmiki's Suryasth—setting sun. When Veena's Venus and Valmiki's sun were in rising conjunction, they both radiated light and illuminated each other with their incandescent magic! But as their trajectories of fading out diverged, the waning into darkness of Valmiki's sun on the cinematic horizon, threatened to engulf the brilliance of Veena's Venus.

'Their relationship is enmeshed in this play of light and dark!' Guru said.

THE REJECTION

Malati and Guru did not hear from Veena for months after that, so one day Malati went across unannounced after court to check up on her.

A maid opened the door. Veena was unwell and resting. Malati went into the bedroom and found Veena lying on her large ornate bed with sheets pulled over her. The curtains were drawn, the room was dark and the unmissable camphor smell of Zandu balm mixed with stale alcohol floated in the air. Malati switched on the light revealing Veena's drawn face. She squinted up, at Malati, then rose with a start and exclaimed, 'Maushi, why have you come unannounced?'

'As your Little Mother, I can come to check up on you anytime, Veena. Your parents asked me to watch over you. To use Akka's exact words: to save you from yourself,' Malati said.

Malati then noticed blue bruises all over Veena's face and hands.

'Oh my God! Which brute has done this to you?' Malati demanded, angry and concerned.

She touched her tenderly. Veena recoiled at first and then started crying. Between sobs she said, 'Maushi, I wanted to be strong and deal with these terrible demons myself. I did not want to trouble or alarm you or Malak.'

'You do us great injustice when you don't tell us about your ordeals,' Malati said gently.

Veena then confided that for the last one year, since Valmiki's career has started waning and hers had been rising, they had been having fights. He wanted to control her, whom she met, what roles she accepted, what money she got, and how she spent it. He was jealous of all the men she worked with and resented the adulation of her admirers. Under the influence of alcohol, all these devils of insecurity came jumping out of him and Veena become the reason for his failures and target for venting his frustrations. Even when she helped to secure contracts for films for him, he accused him of playing the goddess giving alms and rendering him a beggar!

'Oh, the distorted sense of pride and humiliation men have!' Malati exclaimed.

'Yes, Maushi. These days nothing I can do is right, and he just lashes out at me—with his powerful tongue and fists. I don't know which is more hurtful, his damning words hurled at my psyche or his blows on my face and body meant to disfigure and incapacitate me!' complained Veena.

'All the love and tenderness, the joy of creative success that brought us together is no more. What remains is bitterness, his narcissism turned into self-hatred and projected onto me.'

Veena fell silent, almost as ashamed of herself for having confessed to Malati as for the predicament she found herself in.

'You are a strong woman, Veena. Surely, you can walk out of the relationship that is tearing you to shreds. You are not married to him. He is a much older man, not even handsome. He does not deserve you,' Malati advised.

'Oh, Maushi, he always reminds me of how he made me Tara, the star from the putty of nothingness that I was in his hands,' Veena said.

'Oh, consider that debt paid. He controls your money and has been using it to finance his own pet projects. You are now an established actress. You don't need him for anything and certainly you must not brook his mistreatment of you. We will fully support you,' Malati assured her.

Just then, Valmiki walked in. 'Oh, so you called your aunt to complain about me,' he remarked. 'Malati, Veena is becoming crazy because I told her I can't leave my wife and marry her just yet. She hit out at me,' and he showed Malati scratches and bruises of his own to prove it.

'He is lying. I, a true Maratha, have to defend myself against his attacks. Besides, I have better things to do than to marry you, Valmiki. In fact, I want you to leave my house this instant,' Veena told him off fiercely.

Malati was proud of her, but only for a moment, because as Valmiki immediately looked contrite and begged her forgiveness, even touching her feet, she relented.

'As Veena's Little Ayee, I warn you that Veena will no longer put up with your brutishness and Guru and I will expose you as only two lawyers can and you will not know where to hide your face in the film world or in Bombay,' Malati warned him.

Valmiki looked obviously affronted, but controlled himself and said, 'You will have no occasion to use that threat, dear Malati.'

Malati left the two, not sure if Veena and Valmiki could ever knit up the obviously torn tapestry of their life together. She hoped and prayed for new beginnings for Veena. Unfortunately, as Veena starred in one Hindi blockbuster movie after another, Valmiki's sense of insecurity grew. Malati's involvement in the Valmiki–Veena affair and attachment to Veena started taking a toll on her mental stability and emotional well-being. Guru wanted her to stay away from it all to avoid being caught up in a scandal, if not worse—a tragedy. He warned her that this rocky relationship could play out in the public eye, given that Veena and Valmiki were celebrities in the drama and film loving city of Bombay and the country.

How could she be detached, Malati asked. Akka had placed Veena in her care and Veena was clearly in mortal danger. She had sought asylum three times, completely distraught after being grievously assaulted by Valmiki. Every time Malati saw her niece battered, a tooth broken, an arm sprained, hair pulled, back injured, lip cut, she died a thousand deaths thinking of how pained her Akka would have been.

Every time he hit her, he would tell her, 'Now let's see how you rise after this punishment.'

Punishment for what, Malati asked? For being successful? For paying his bills and getting him contracts? Or for bearing his temper tantrums? That was some way of serving up gratitude as punishment, Malati fumed.

They felt helpless because every time Veena relented and went back to him despite Malati and Guru's advice that she throw him out and quit living in this loveless hell of jealousy and conflict.

Veena was afraid that he would tarnish her name in the theatre and film fraternity and in the media, where he was a master of all he surveyed and owned a leading newspaper. Declare her insane. Throw acid to disfigure her beautiful face. Malati tried to give courage and tell her that he would not dare to do all those things for his own sake and that the longer she stayed with him the more likely he was to resort to the things she feared most. But Veena always went back to her ordeal as usual.

One day, Valmiki invited Malati and Kashi to his studio where Veena was shooting for what he said would be the most lavish film that he was directing based on the iconic courtesan of ancient India, Amrapaali.

Malati presumed that the invitation was from Veena too, and happily went with Kashi to Bombay Talkies, the legendary studio where many Hindi films were shot. When they reached there, Veena was not around. Valmiki was sitting in his director's chair, resplendent in a cape. He welcomed Malati and greeted Kashi charmingly, praising her beauty and star quality. Kashi was now thirteen years old and had indeed turned out to be a beauty.

The way he talked to them, Malati could see why Veena was taken in by his enticing web of words and courteous manner. It was hard to imagine how he transformed into a devil incarnate at night. Malati asked for Veena and Valmiki blamed her delayed arrival on her makeup man. In the meantime, he offered to take their photos and screen test for possible roles. Malati refused. But Kashi persuaded Malati to relent—quite against her instincts—for the fun of it.

The make-up man worked on both of them and they wore studio clothes and jewellery and found themselves transformed into Amrapaali era princesses. They were photographed against the backdrop of magnificent palace sets and then short recordings were made of them speaking a few lines from the script of the film. Malati and Kashi gave impressive screen tests and felt elated. When after more than two hours, Veena did not come, Valmiki declared pack up and they came away.

An excited Kashi told Guru all about the screen test that evening. Guru scolded Malati for fraternizing with Valmiki in Veena's absence. He smelt intrigue and forbade her from responding to him in future. When they didn't hear anything from Valmiki for a while, they dismissed the whole episode as a joke that Valmiki had played on them. But Malati felt rather uneasy when there was silence from Veena for almost a month.

Then came the news from a friend, who was also close to Valmiki, that Veena was in hospital, recovering from injuries to her back and arms sustained from an 'accidental fall'. Malati rushed to see her. Veena was lying on the hospital bed. Malati patted her head with affection and sympathy. But she pushed Malati's hand and sharply turned her face away.

'What have you allowed to be done to yourself? Why didn't you call me? I would have rushed to your rescue. I told you to get out of this relationship. It is draining you of your very dignity and swamitva—your ownership and control over your mind and body. My darling, I will not allow this any more. I will ask Malak to come and take you away till you see light and resume your film career on a new footing!' Malati said with anguish.

'Why have you come, Malati? I will not dignify you by calling you Maushi. You claim to be my Little Ayee, but I have now seen your real avatar. I have heard all about your visit to the studio and seen your photos and screen tests. All you want is for you and your daughter to be film stars and your advice to leave Valmiki is selfishly motivated. You want to replace me in Valmiki's life so he can launch your film careers as he did mine,' she retorted bitterly.

'This is a preposterous accusation! My advice to you is purely motivated by my concern for your well-being. I have no desire to join the film industry ever, especially after seeing what darkness hides behind the glitter and glamour of it all. I have a fulfilling career. As for replacing you in Valmiki's life, I am repelled by that venal man, quite apart from being happily married to the love of my life, Guru—something I know you have always envied. Kashi will not go anywhere near films either,' Malati said vehemently.

Veena then went on to ask why Malati had asked Valmiki not to tell her about the screen tests. During one of Veena's quarrels with him, when she threatened to go to her Maushi and Guru, he had apparently alleged that since Malati had been wooing him for film roles, she would no longer side with Veena against him or give her shelter. Angered by her Maushi's grand betrayal, Veena never came to their house and broke off all her ties with them.

Malati was flabbergasted.

'Veena dear, Valmiki spun a story only a diabolical fiction writer like him could imagine, to isolate you by framing me as a self-seeking relative, out to take advantage of Valmiki, thereby cutting the umbilical cord—yes that's what you have with me!' Malati asserted.

'If there was one, it is truly and finally cut, and cannot be rejoined. And if he is trying to isolate me, he is mistaken to think that you are my only support. I have left him and I am moving into the flat of one of my co-stars and friend for a while. I will fight to get back my flat and other assets, which Valmiki has deviously transferred to himself,' she asserted.

She offered to help Veena get her property and assets back, to fight for her in the courts.

'I don't believe anyone now—neither him nor you. Keep away from me forever! I don't ever want your inauspicious shadow fall on me and my life,' she said, brutally crushing Malati's spirit of a loving, duty-bound Little Ayee, and turned her face away.

Malati trembled with sadness and outrage.

A handsome gentleman in an English suit walked into her room. He was John D' Silva, the well-known Anglo-Indian actor. Like Valmiki, he too was much older than her, but looked more congenial. They greeted each other warmly with an embrace and a kiss, indicating to Malati that Veena had begun another liaison.

Veena did not bother to introduce Malati to John. They gathered her things and walked out of the hospital. As an utterly dejected Malati came out, she saw Valmiki accosting Veena.

'You can't leave me and go with this imposter. Besides, you risk losing your flat. I will destroy you and let everyone know how crazy you are. No director will touch you!' Valmiki ranted loudly in public view.

'Don't you ever dare to smear my reputation. I will expose you to the world, and tell them that behind the exterior of an intellectual and creative genius, you are a swindler and a vicious demon who seeks to assert his manhood by raising his hand against women,' Veena replied spiritedly.

Valmiki tried to get close to her, but John stopped him.

'Valmiki, let her go. I have a battery of lawyer friends I will let loose on you for trying to murder Veena, and they will put you behind bars for life,' he threatened, and Valmiki retreated.

'At least promise me you will finish my remaining two projects,' Valmiki pleaded.

Veena did not respond. He stood there watching silently as John's red Buick receded from view. In the midst of Malati's misery, this one scene calmed her heart. Valmiki spotted her standing at the hospital entrance and walked up to her. Malati tried to look away.

'We both lost her, didn't we?' he said sardonically.

'No, you lost her. Nobody can take my sister's daughter away from me. Not even she herself,' Malati replied and walked away.

Malati went home dejected. Guru, who had returned from a long day in office, took one look at her and asked, 'Are you feeling well, dearest Malati?'

'Oh, Guru, today I went to hell's gate and came back humiliated as never before,' Malati said and burst into tears. She told him all that had transpired at the hospital and exclaimed, 'I have borne the death of my mother when I was a mere child and then of dearest Akka more recently, with relative equanimity—comforted by my powerlessness before Yamraj. But the death of a cherished relationship with my beloved, living niece is a loss I will never recoup. A grand failure in human bonding I will never live down!' Malati said shivering at the memory of the cold currents of Veena's rejection.

Guru gave Malati perspective. Veena did not want to take refuge with her Maushi. She wanted the sympathy and company of a male film star. She was the one being dishonest and self-seeking. Whatever Malati had promised her Akka, there was a limit to which she could keep it on her own. In Akka's book, Malati had done her best. Veena, a twenty-six-year-old, must find her own destiny, make her own mistakes. It should not be allowed to stir the poison of regret into the nectar of Malati's life with Guru and Kashi.

'I know you are a truly honourable person and Veena and her capricious narcissism can't take that away from you,' Guru tried to restore Malati's equanimity.

56

AMONG THE CLOUD MESSENGERS

For the next few months, Guru and Kashi complained that Malati was not herself, that she was erratic, temperamental, and insomniac. She could not concentrate on her court cases and Upendra had to politely nudge her on to deliver her briefs. She told a perplexed Guru that, after many years she felt like the existentialist philosopher Kierkegaard, wondering 'What if everything in the world were a misunderstanding, what if laughter were really tears?'

Good news finally arrived in the form of a promotion for Guru, requiring him to move out of Bombay. This should have made Malati unhappy since she would have to give up her law practice. But she seemed to strangely rejoice at leaving Bombay. She told Malak everything about Veena and relinquished her responsibility. As expected, Malak was upset about Veena's 'unstoppable wantonness' but felt helpless as he had lost all authority over her.

Guru, Kashi, and Malati moved to Shimla, the summer capital of the British Raj, in the autumn of 1946. They had heard that it was called Chhota Vilayat or Little England for it was the creation of Raj officials, lovingly built over the years as a paradise and playground to escape from the oppressive heat of their other centres of power, Calcutta and Delhi.

They arrived at this charming hill station in a train which wound huffing and puffing up the hills for a hundred miles, through a hundred tunnels from the plains below. From the design and architecture of the city and its public buildings, homes, bazaars, and gardens, its storeyed layout, its segregation of the British elite from the rest, and the sheer number of them concentrated in it, it surely evoked a British Raj aura like no other place—not even Bombay.

They were lucky to come there at a time when the brown-skinned Indian babus, traders, coolies, and rickshaw pullers living in the lower parts of Shimla were surfacing up into the upper echelons of the city, as the scent of the Gora sahebs' imminent departure waltzed around everywhere in the cool Shimla breeze!

'Shimla seems to have been "Made in England" and pitchforked out from there and planted onto the Himalayan foothills. If they had their way, the British would take Shimla back with them when they leave India, just as if it were the Indian Kohinoor diamond wrested from the ten-year-old Sikh king,' Kashi remarked sarcastically.

Kashi, like young men and women of her generation, had mixed feelings towards the British—she was fiercely patriotic, hated their occupation, and wanted them to leave India soonest, but also loved and lived their art, literature, music, and films.

'Well, the British have occupied these Himalayan foothills for long, but Indians are retaking it from them,' Malati said, admiring the majestic views.

Shimla had an allure that was integral to it. No one could take that away. Their eyes detected a new self-assurance. In the stunning visions of the red sphere of the sun, rising from behind the steep-sided Himalayan mountain ranges, permeating everything with a golden light—of hope realized of India's multitudes. Then the same sun, slinking away into the twilight, to expose the soaring, jagged knives of the Hatu and other 'freedom peaks'—Kinnaur Kailash and Dev Tibba, plunging vengefully into the hitherto impenetrable imperial skies. The sloping pine and deodar forests, standing up to become the canopied sentinels of the sovereignty of all life beneath and around them. The padmakh trees, with their cascading domes brushed with delicate light pink flowers, now exuding their true fragrance, to exhilarate the body and spirit of Indians coming together at last to reclaim their earth.

The houses in the city that the British built, according to their whims and fancies, with the filigreed frontages strung from the roofs, were now being emptied of their white, privileged residents. The three-dimensional, multi-level tapestry of these wood, brick, and metal edifices on the ledges and pathways cut into rocky hillsides, seemed welcoming of new Indian residents. It was the right of the brown Mohans and Miras now, to play the game of peeping—not only into the lives of neighbours on either side of them, but on the terraces, gardens and houses below, while surrendering themselves to scrutiny by their higher level-and high flying-neighbours too.

For Malati, Guru, and Kashi, the winters in Shimla had a special enchantment. As it started getting colder, the Magician of the Hills cast His spell and assembled Kalidas's Meghdoots in the sky. They were delighted with their misty cousins suddenly descending and rising, accosting affably, shuffling along as companions, holding conversations of silence, and enveloping them into momentary anonymity.

The trio also revelled in the novelty of the first snowfall in winter. Its white furry blanket wrapped itself ever so softly on everything in sight—from the conical trees lining the streets, the slanted roofs of the Christ Church, the Gothic Gaiety Theatre, the curlicues of the tall black wrought iron lamp posts to the serpentine paths and meandering steps. Kashi and Malati ran around crunching the snow on the ground beneath and uninhibitedly bid it to cover them with its pearly shawl.

Not everything about Shimla and the change it brought for them was pleasant or easy to get used to though. The winters were very cold. They all had to get boots and English style woollen clothes to adapt to the 'up and down' terrain and inclement weather. The smoke from damp wood in fireplaces in their bungalow, choked them and they longed to be rid of it and for the first green shoots of spring to break out from the bare branches of trees, and the birds to chirp and sing again.

Shimla's Vice Regal Lodge and other government buildings set themselves up as the stage for crucial agreements for India's independence. The Shimla Conference and the Wavell Plan for Indian Self Government in 1945, before they arrived, had failed. But in May 1947, the Lord Mountbatten-Nehru talks on the Partition plan and the rather arbitrary and hastily convened Radcliffe Commission boundary demarcation meetings for India's partition took place in Shimla's Vice Regal Lodge—a hub for final decisions on the fate of India.

As Deputy Secretary in the Legislative Department of the Government of India, Guru had to draft key laws and regulations preparatory to India's independence and its aftermath. He sat in the closed circuit of Indian officialdom in Shimla to whom the power was to be transferred on the ground and who had some say on the terms of British disengagement. He and his colleagues were often frustrated by the top-down approach followed in decision making and their sound political and legal advice on matters of India's vital interest being often ignored or overturned in trilateral political negotiations and games of deception between the British Viceroy, Jinnah, and Nehru.

When Pandit Nehru declared the independence of India on the

midnight of 15 August 1947, India was rapturous with joy. It was also convulsed by the tragedy of one of the biggest and most violent and bloody migrations in history, brought about by the partition of India into two countries and the creation of Pakistan.

As Hindus and Sikhs from West Punjab and East Bengal flooded into India, surviving bloodshed and massacres, a massive relief and rehabilitation effort had to be mounted. Moved by this colossal humanitarian emergency, Guru went beyond his remit of duty and worked like a fiend to draw up both a law and a scheme for refugee evacuee property management for ensuring the resettlement and compensation of incoming refugees.

With great persistence and difficulty, he persuaded the first chief minister of Eastern Punjab, Gopichand Bhargava, to adopt and implement them. As the CM himself acknowledged, Guru had, at one stroke, saved the government hundreds of crores in resources and facilitated the convenient resettlement of millions of refugees coming across from Pakistan. Guru's model was adopted by other affected states too.

There was the other side of Shimla, which Rudyard Kipling had highlighted that both excited and scared Malati—the 'frivolity, gossip and intrigue' side. And she did not just mean of the political, official kind which thrived in those days of the transfer of power and of changing loyalties from the British Raj to Indian swarajya. It was also of the social kind. Whilst the outgoing British elites tried to cling on to fast receding authority and glory, the incoming Indian elites made heady assumptions of self-worth and preened themselves on being the new masters of all they surveyed in Hindustan.

The social broth was truly bubbling. They were thrown into this cauldron as soon as they arrived; and it singed Guru and Malati's marriage.

Guru had been deservedly catapulted into playing a role way above his age and official designation. That was intoxicating. The ability to make a difference in the lives of so many people by a stroke of his pen and through the power of his ideas, did give him a new sense of self-importance. It put him in a different league from Malati, who felt reduced to a non-entity.

Their beautiful and brilliant Kashi was in a convent boarding school, Tara Hall. Guru had taken to drinking whisky occasionally, to cope with the cold weather of Shimla, in the intellectually and 'spiritually' stimulating company of a Sikh judge, Harbhajan Singh, who lived there without his family—a curiosity in itself.

The Judge was a tall, fair, sharp featured, and attractive man, erudite, yet jolly, and a witty conversationalist. He had a gallant way of touching his turban when greeting a lady. So, Malati couldn't fault Guru for seeking out his company. Their love of poetry and of the law bound them together and Malati felt left out. The poet in Guru was lost to her and the law in her she had left behind in Bombay.

Guru was not the same under the influence of whisky and when Malati raised her concerns with him, they ended up quarrelling. It also went into other realms of real and imagined discord. Malati felt her attraction had waned for him and they rarely made love. He came back from his drinking and 'strategy sessions' with his Judge friend quite late at night, and Malati was usually asleep by then.

Malati struggled to make sense of the change. Guru was suddenly no longer proud of her; not showing her off to friends and colleagues as the love of his life, the intellectual lawyer companion and soulmate, as he used to in Bombay. He insisted on her switching to a six-yard sari and wear high-heeled shoes. He wanted her to look taller and less provincial in cosmopolitan Shimla and so she could meld easily into high society.

Malati reread Guru's Benares love letters and wondered whether the professions of his undying love was merely transient passion, born of distance, of the allure of the unattained, and the fear of losing her? Was the sheen of being a woman extraordinaire fading? Then she had only herself to blame. She had made no effort, despite Guru's encouragement, to practise at the courts in Shimla.

Guru accused Malati of being insecure and delusional when she said he was drifting away. At the very least, their marriage seemed to be in trouble. His astrologer friend's prediction that he would have many affairs of the heart seemed to be coming true—twenty years later.

Dorothy Atkinson, an Englishwoman and the widow of a judge, who had died a year ago, befriended Guru and Malati, courtesy Judge Singh. She looked younger than her forty plus years. She was pretty to Indian eyes, though Malati found her nose a bit too sharp and her lips too thin. Her white skin was beginning to wrinkle under the clever make-up. She was tall and thin with golden hair.

Dorothy introduced Malati to the pleasures of Shimla and to the cream of English and Indian society, which was being churned anew. Malati was grateful as she found it easier to fit in. Moreover, she got to play tennis with her.

Malati was impressed by her stories of how she had organized soirées when her husband was a judge, which the viceroy, Lord Wavell, and his wife, Lady Wavell—'Dear Eugenie' as Dorothy called her affectionately—were delighted to attend. She even claimed she curated the grand wedding of their daughter in New Delhi, a claim that seemed to someone even as credulous as Malati to be too far-fetched. She did dazzle her though, when Dorothy produced a photo of herself and her late husband at the famous wedding!

Among Dorothy's other awe-inspiring claims was that in this sunset hour of the British empire in India, her salon brought together the who's who of the English and Indian ruling elite and literati that earned her the sobriquet of Shimla's Madame de Pompadour!

Of course, with her husband gone, her salons were not the same nor was she on first name basis with 'Dear Edwina' the current viceroy, Lord Mountbatten's, elegant, aristocratic, and somewhat aloof wife! Instead, it was rumoured that Edwina was involved in high politics herself!

'Well, this Madame Pompadour has no Louis the XV Bien Amie, to back her. Who knows, Shimla may no longer be the summer capital of independent India. And mark my words, the halo of the white skin will disappear without the power behind it. I am sure those very elite Indians whom she and other British people dominated, are hot under their kurta collars and itching to soon treat them as outcasts! Then she will go crawling back to a drab life in England, where too, she will be an outsider!' precocious Kashi opined.

Within a year after India's independence, Kashi was proved right. As their compatriots left in large numbers, British residents realized that Shimla was no longer the dreamland it had been. Indians no longer fawned over them. Instead, many made it a point to show who owned the country and Shimla! They gatecrashed into British only clubs, restaurants, and theatres, and dared to dance at the dancing halls at Scandal Point. Malati noticed that Dorothy was restive and not her usual vibrant self either.

Gossip about the unlikely friendship between a senior Punjabi

Sikh judge and a young rising Maharashtrian legal officer began to circulate in the hilly whispering gallery of Shimla. Malati therefore decided to drop in on the duo unannounced. They were not alone! Dorothy, wearing a long flowery dress, was ensconced comfortably close to Guru, on one of the love seat sofas, both with glasses of whisky in their hands. Judge Singh welcomed Malati very warmly, but Dorothy and Guru looked ambushed. Malati was unnerved and felt betrayed, but put on a veneer of graciousness.

57

MARTYRDOM

'Hope I am not breaking into a happy ménage à trois in the new salon of Madame Pompadour,' Malati said mockingly.

'Come, Malati! This is a "spiritual", intellectual, and empathy-sharing ménage. You are welcome to join us and make it a ménage à quatre!' said Judge Singh good-humouredly.

He gestured to Malati to sit beside him on his sofa and gallantly kissed her right hand.

'Oh Malati, I don't have my salon any more, but with these two gentlemen, I feel that all the politics and poetry in these extraordinary times is being brewed together here in a delightful and heady concoction. Judge Singh is the inheritor of my Harold's legacy—legal and social. You, an educated Indian lady must partake of the concoction too,' Dorothy said patronizingly.

'Well, had I known Dorothy is here too I would have gatecrashed earlier,' Malati said, her displeasure spilling.

'Dear Malati, remember you had refused. Dorothy has just recently joined us as she is missing her English friends, most of whom have chosen to leave India. She is among the last few hold-outs among the "Shimla Swans" as they call themselves,' Guru explained.

'We try to give her a reason to stay on!' the Judge added.

'Of course! What would Shimla be without her,' Malati chimed in trying to be genial.

They all had a light Western dinner brought in a picnic wicker basket—soup, salad, and shepherd's pie from Dorothy's kitchen which to Malati's surprise Guru praised and enjoyed. The evening passed pleasantly and Malati was somewhat relaxed, though she kept a hawk's eye on Guru and Dorothy.

'Your Guru is quite a poet. I don't know how he can combine this with brilliant legal draftsmanship,' said Dorothy.

Malati looked at Guru accusingly, and said, 'I am glad you have rekindled the poetry in Guru. Because to me, he has confessed to the sentiments expressed in his favourite poet Wordsworth's 'Ode to Immortality'. How, when he and I were younger and in love, "everything, every common sight" seemed "apparelled in celestial light" and everything had the "glory and freshness of a dream"! But now, the things which he has seen, he can see no more. And we both ask ourselves, "whither has fled the visionary gleam, where is it now, the glory and the dream"?'

Malati savoured the Judge and Dorothy's dazzled look and Guru's sheepish one. Her triumphal Elphinstone College moment of twenty-three years ago revisited!

'Guru, you surely can't be surprised by this. You wooed me with poetry through seven years of courtship and until we came to Shimla. It is, perhaps, my turn. And count me in to come and join you,' Malati said, looking at him with deceptively innocent eyes and offering to host the Salon at their home with exotic Karwar fare instead of the bland English one. 'And Madame Pompadour, you can still preside over the Salon, along with the Judge,' she added generously.

She seemed to have pushed her luck too far, for Malati had never seen Guru so angry with her.

'Now, now Malati, you are crossing the limit!' he admonished her. He apologized to the Judge and Dorothy and explained how since her break-up with Veena and Surekha's death she had not been herself.

Guru got up and asked Malati to leave with him.

'But I have just started to enjoy myself and they both know I meant no insult to either of them. I plead not guilty, Your Honour and Madame Pompadour,' she said smiling sardonically still.

Guru angrily grabbed Malati's hand and led her out. She followed meekly, leaving behind the puzzled duo.

That night, when they reached home, Malati and Guru had the biggest fight of their married life.

'How could you do this to the senior Judge who has been my friend, philosopher, and guide. Without him, I would have been lost in this jungle of British-Indian bureaucracy and elite circles. The way you reacted, confirms to me that you are not yet ready, if ever you will be, for this high voltage society game,' Guru said sharply.

'For nearly eighteen months, I have borne the loneliness of evenings spent alone at home and put myself to sleep without complaining about your fraternal evenings with the good Judge. Then comes Dorothy, and throws me off-balance. Am I not good enough to join your merry bunch? I can be as much fun or as melancholy as the mood of the group dictates, even without whisky!'

'Well, you are clearly not Dorothy's kind, who can uninhibitedly socialize with men,' Guru said and checked himself.

'Ah you forget, I began my career living alone, dealing with men and worked in a nearly all male court system. Unless, with Dorothy, either the Judge or you or both, truly have a ménage à trois! What were you doing sitting with her on the love seat, your bodies touching? Is that why you don't look at me with love and desire any more? You lust after Dorothy, the willing gori mem.'

Guru was outraged.

'You have truly lost your mind. I was comforting Dorothy because she was crying. If you persist with this paranoia, you will drive me to other women. You should seek some treatment!' Guru said, much to Malati's chagrin.

'I am perfectly sane, thank you. It's you who are intoxicated, not only with wine, but with power, and feel that I don't measure up. The burden of proof is on you,' Malati cried vehemently.

'No, you have to give me evidence that I have strayed. Presumed innocent unless proven guilty, remember?' Guru said, assuming a tender tone and his old caring look and embracing Malati.

'OK, then I will come with you to the Judge's hangout sometimes and keep a watch on your extracurricular activities,' Malati declared, smiling.

'Malati, all these years, you have taken me for granted as your worshipper and lover. Now is your turn to come down from your goddess pedestal and make me feel desired, omnipotent, and immortal! It's that time in my life, where I am on the brink of greatness. I need a devotee. Will you be mine?' Guru said disarmingly.

Malati was still agitated, but chose to reciprocate his gesture. That night they made peace with themselves and love to each other. Malati was transported back to their first sublime moments of intimacy.

But alas they soon reverted to going their separate ways. The Judge was good enough to invite Malati from time to time, but she maintained a dignified distance and went only when invited. Dorothy and she no longer met.

One night Guru came back home from the Judge's house very agitated. He told Malati that Judge Singh had been promoted and transferred to Delhi and would be leaving soon and worried about

Dorothy being left behind. He revealed that the Judge's wife lived in Delhi in a mental asylum. It pained him but she tended to get violent and needed constant monitoring. For him, Shimla had been a getaway from that sorrow and he and Dorothy were star-crossed lovers. Malati was relieved.

'Rumours have it that Dorothy's husband's death was not natural. Something about a dose of cyanide extracted from apple seeds!' Malati informed him.

'Don't believe such vicious rumours. When the Judge goes to Delhi, he cannot take her with him. Such open Indo-British moral turpitude will not be tolerated in a senior Judge by the new Indian government. The Judge has asked me to take care of her, till such time as they find a way out!' he added.

'She is a grown woman and perfectly self-reliant. At least until now, your liaison, if any, with her was under the cover of the Judge's friendship. Now if you support her, it will taint your godliness, harm your brilliantly launched career, and our marriage too,' Malati warned.

'Don't worry, we will be careful,' Guru assured her, without really allaying her concerns.

In his farewell speech at a dinner hosted by Guru, the Judge thanked Malati for sharing Guru with him in his time of need. Looking at Dorothy, he requested that Malati bear with the one he was leaving behind for a little time more.

He left Malati with no option but to be gracious. She smiled reassuringly and looked at Guru and Dorothy, who seemed despondent at his departure, but strangely excited at the same time—or was she imagining?

Just before the independence of India, Baba had persuaded Malak and Maharaja's government to painstakingly work out a 'Freedom Project' to deal with the dacoit problem in Desaikheda and Guna. He offered the dacoits freedom from living as outlaws and fugitives on the run, from a life of hardship and violence, and from their image of 'danav avatars' of evil in society. Baba had gone and met most gang leaders of dacoits at great risk to himself and passionately argued that they should legitimize themselves before the end of British rule so that they could join the new post-independence governments at the local and provincial levels through elections that were sure to be held. That way they could defeat the high caste oppressors and landlords they claimed to be fighting, get a chance to have their own legitimate sarkar, and become popularly accepted leaders over ground. He had got a majority of dacoit gangs to join in the Freedom Project.

Malak had convinced the Maharaja to agree to the dacoits surrendering their arms and taking an oath of allegiance to him in return for clemency, their being able to hold on to most of their ill-gotten assets and some rehabilitation assistance.

But this was against the advice of the Internal Security minister who thought it was a foolish idea because dacoits would be dacoits. He argued that since the Maharaja was going to sign the instrument of accession for Vaishali to become part of the Indian union, he saw no benefit in expending the Maharaja's dwindling resources on these 'vermins'. Moreover, where was the guarantee that buying some gangs will not start a gang war and attacks against villages that have joined the pact? And won't the villagers fear that the Maharaja's government had given the dacoits a free run to loot and pillage?

The British Resident endorsed this line as he was in no mood to leave a parting gift for the incoming popularly elected Indian government.

'These pretenders to your throne, these riff-raff aspirants to power from the Congress and others must know what it is to tame these vicious motley gangs and govern!' he said to the Maharaja. That Malak, whom he had accused of treason had recommended this project, also irked him.

The Maharaja, nevertheless, went ahead with Project Freedom and ordered the reluctant Interior Minister to convene a maha panchayat of Guna including all village councils in Desaikheda. The surrender by the dacoits and their gangs would be staged and launch of the project would be announced there. Baba, its architect was given pride of place in the ceremony held around a massive banyan tree—the same one where Baba had years ago convened a maha panchayat for the Saraswati Vidya Mandir. A Shiva idol was now installed beneath it. One by one all the designated dacoit leaders and their followers started assembling and putting down their rifles and swords in a trough in front of the idol. They took their oath to abjure violence. The assembled villagers of Guna could scarcely believe this miracle and rejoiced. 'Maharaj ki Jai Ho! Madhav Rao Desaiji ki Jai Ho!' rent the air. Whilst the ceremony was in progress, they heard the sound of horse hooves and saw a pack of riders coming towards them. Baba hoped that it was the recalcitrant Shambhu gang whom he had unsuccessfully tried to persuade, coming to surrender after all! Yes it was!

Baba called out to him to join the ceremony. 'Ya, ya Shambhu bhau. Tumhi pan mukta hua. You too become free.' Shambhu smiled at Baba and holding his rifle aloft he went straight towards the enclosure where other dacoit leaders were laying down arms. He did not dismount from his horse. He surveyed all the dacoits who had joined Project Freedom and hectored them.

'You fools! What you have done by surrendering your arms. You think these people will let you live free. Each of the villagers whose homes you have damaged or burnt, whose women you have violated, the landlords and moneylenders whose treasures you have looted, will take revenge. The police and the government will bless their vigilantism, if not themselves hunt you down and eliminate you. There is still time. Pick up your arms and run! And continue the fight,' he exhorted. Baba called out to him and said 'Shambhu bhau! Don't go against the call of Lord Shiva that all your brethren are heeding.'

Shambhu turned towards him, trained his gun at him and shouted 'We Shiva bhakts forbid you Madhav Rao to invoke Shiva's name. You have plotted our destruction and you will pay for it.' The Interior Minister signalled the posse of policemen guarding him to shoot at Shambhu.

Baba got up, came forward and shouted, 'No don't do that. They have all come with my assurance of safety.'

But it was too late. Police started firing at Shambhu's gang. They fired back and fled. Baba was struck down. No one was sure whose bullet hit him.

Khandoba met shocked and grieving Malati and Kamala at the station. For the first time they saw him beaten. Baba's death had sucked all courage out of the perennial warrior.

'I had warned your Baba not to undertake this enterprise but he was so determined to root out dacoity in every way that he put his life on the sword and before the bullet,' complained Khandoba. The girls held his hands in sympathy.

They got to know Govind closely for the first time as a grown, young man. He was the spitting image of Baba and possessed his spirit—tall, muscular, swarthy, with a handlebar moustache and full of valour. He expertly wielded both a gun and a plough, with pride. His wife was a local girl who had attended Baba's school and now taught there. She had learnt to shoot at dacoits who dared to come calling with ill intent.

Malati suggested to Govind that he move out of Guna and build a new life in Ratnagiri. They feared that since the beehive of dacoits had been smashed, the manic bees will come after Baba's heir to sting him.

'I would not dream of moving. I am heir to Baba's glorious legacy and I have to carry on the noble fight. Don't worry, sisters. I am quite capable of safeguarding his villages and his farming heritage, here in Guna—his sacred karma bhoomi. I am going to contest elections and be a leader in the New India project! It will transform our Desaikheda further,' he said firmly.

After the incident, Malak had resigned from Maharaja's cabinet as he held the jealous Interior Minister responsible for thwarting the Freedom India project and for Baba's death. He also announced that he would be playing the polo game of electoral politics with the Maharaja's blessing—an aristocrat navigating the ball of public approval from atop his agile horse, with a long mallet of experience.

There was a moving Pagri Dharan ceremony, transferring Baba's turban to Govind, as his son and inheritor of his role as leader and defender of his villages. It took place with thousands of villagers gathered under the banyan tree, where Baba was martyred. To the sound of traditional bugles and drums and the chant of protective mantras and with the Bhagavad Gita in his hand, Govind took an oath to carry forward Baba's mission for Desaikheda and Guna, to make it a peaceful and prosperous place.

There was another poignant moment in Kamala and Malati's lives as women and as daughters. When they went to immerse their father's ashes into the Chambal River with Govind on the thirteenth day. Govind insisted that they share in this ritual as Baba wanted, although under Hindu tradition, only the son performs it. They saw that even in his going away, Baba had empowered his daughters.

They scattered Baba's remains—the nebula of the grey-white ashes and fragments of bones that once were this warm, sentient and noble being—into the swirling waters of the Chambal. The ashes turned to a luminescent gold in the early morning light before dissolving into the Ananta, the Great Infinity.

58
THE SEPARATION

Malak came to Desaikheda just before they left and condoled with them, blaming himself for encouraging Baba on a course that he as a realist should have known to be treacherous. He assured them, that he will avenge Baba's death and follow through on his dream of a dacoit free Guna in a British free India.

Malati was shocked to hear from Malak that Veena had renounced everything in Bombay and returned to Vaishali to her father, after taking the vows of a sadhvi. Veena told Malak that she quit being a Kasturi deer, who, unaware of the musk of happiness in its nave, but crazed with its perfume, wandered in its quest only to be thwarted and lost. Now she had come home to her nave and will seek her happiness within.

This was just on the heels of a prestige Valmiki film fetching her a best actress award. Malati was consoled that Veena left filmdom while she was still the reigning queen and not under the crippling shadows of failure. But she was tragically too young, only thirty-two, too beautiful to behold and hold, to shrink into bodily nothingness, retreat into a transcendental shell; too outwardly expressed to dig tunnels of consciousness towards some invisible, inner spiritual centre. For too long, had she as Tara, been nourished on the elixir of fame and public adulation to starve herself of it, and padlock away her unbelievably majestic beauty in a temple of 'nobodyness'.

Malak seemed happy that Amrit Wada now had a sadhvi mistress. He did regret that Veena had not remarried and that her stardom, which he had secretly come to applaud, was all in the past. He gave Malati a letter from Veena. She opened and read it with trepidation.

Dear Malati Maushi,

You will forgive me for daring to put pen to paper and sending this message after the way we parted. I was too arrogant, blind, and impetuous to see you in your true light and to return your affection and grace.

You correctly saw through Valmiki's deception and how he vilified you to estrange me from you, so he could completely dominate me.

Most importantly Maushi, I acknowledge your love and your true motivation to help me, to be my Little Ayee and protect me from being burnt by the blistering flames of other's egos, amid my own loss of the shield of reason!

Will you forgive me in the name of your Akka and my dear mother? Someday, I must unburden myself and tell you all about my Pilgrim's Progress. I cannot claim to have arrived at the Celestial City, but maybe at the Wicket Gate, and on to the 'straight and narrow path'.

Please give my love to dear Kashi, and my respects to Guru Kaka. I thank you all for your forbearance.

Much love,
Your aspiring pilgrim,
Sadhvi Veena.

Malati felt vindicated and touched by Veena's poignant reference to John Bunyan's allegorical Christian work which Malati had introduced her to. Indeed, Malati had followed Veena, the Pilgrim's Progress from This World to That Which Is to Come, and from the City of Destruction to the Celestial City. Valmiki had played a dual role—as Mr Worldly Wiseman helping her progress and as Beelzebub, Satan's companion, hindering it. Malati had fancied herself as the Faithful/Hopeful trying to guide her to the Wicket Gate—until Veena had so rudely broken her ties with her.

Malati rushed to send her a loving and much too effusive a reply of forgiveness and reconciliation. It was more for her own sake, to recover a big chunk of her self-belief.

Malati asked Kashi on her return to Shimla whether the Judge's going away had freed Guru and Dorothy up to have a full-fledged liaison. Kashi assured her that they had been correct with each other and if they met, it was in company. Now that the cloud of Veena's rejection of her had lifted, Malati told herself that she must no longer imagine other rejections—especially by Guru.

But not for long. Dorothy's visits to their place became frequent. It seemed as if Guru was emotionally, though thankfully not physically, standing in for the Judge in indulging her. And Malati was in no position to protest, having given her word to the Judge.

It only made her more frustrated and irritable. Guru too felt judged and they began to have fights. Kashi tried not to take sides when she was around, but ended up counselling restraint to Malati more than to her father. He now gave Kashi the pride of place in social gatherings, taking her with him or treating her as his hostess with company at home. Malati was reduced to protesting and she was sorry about the effect all this was having on Kashi.

Malati's prayers for this ordeal to end were answered soon enough. Impressed with his outstanding work in Simla on crucial legislative agendas, Guru was called to serve in the capital of free India, New Delhi. He was to go on a promotion to join the Constituent Assembly Secretariat team supporting the Drafting Committee tasked to evolve a new Constitution of the Republic of India.

Malati was delighted. Guru would now be able to jettison his so-called responsibility towards Dorothy. The downside was that family accommodation was not immediately available in Delhi. So, he asked Kamala in Poona whether Malati and Kashi could stay with her for a while. Kamala readily agreed. Malati secretly hoped that some distance between them would make Guru's heart grow fonder. The night before they left, Dorothy interrupted their quiet family dinner. She presented a book of Shakespeare's sonnets to Malati and stayed on.

With delicious irony, Malati opened the page to 'Sonnet XXXIX' and read select passages.

> Oh, how thy worth with manners may I sing.
> Even for this, let us divided live
> And our dear love loses name of a single one
> That by this separation I may give
> That due to thee which thou deserves alone.

Guru took the book from Malati and recited another verse, looking at her but also directing his glances at Kashi and Dorothy.

> Oh absence! What a torment wouldn't thou prove
> Were it not thy sore leisure gave sweet leave
> To entertain the time with thoughts of love
> Which time and thoughts so sweetly doth deceive.

Dorothy, not to be left behind, had the last verse.

> And that thou teaches this to make one twain
> By praising her here who doth hence remain.

They all laughed at this poetic passing the parcel game—a rare flash of bonhomie amongst them.

That night, Guru gave Malati a glimpse once again of the man who she knew and loved and who had chased her, loved her, worshipped her for years. He was surely one in whom desire was ignited by the anticipated pangs of their coming separation! He invoked the sweetest and freshest of odes of the lovelorn Yaksha from Kalidasa's *Meghdootam*.

> Shaama Swangam Chakita Harini Prekshane drishtipaatam
> I see your supple limbs in the Priyangu creepers,
> Your innocent gaze in the eyes of a startled fawn
> The beauty of your face in the roundness of the pale moon,
> The beguiling ringlets of your hair in the plumages of
> peacocks,
> The playful movements of your eyebrows in the ripples of
> rivers:
> But, alas!
> O passionate one!
> Nowhere in the universe
> Does your likeness exist in its entirety.

'Remember, how I used to recite the poem actually for you, but pretend it was a poem for poem's sake,' said Guru softly.

'Yes, only later did you admit to me what I already knew—that it was for me and me alone,' Malati replied.

'Yes, and I would add that I see the whole world in you and you in everything,' Guru continued down the poetic memory lane.

'Yes. I would protest that I am not the one who has cheeks with the pallor of the moon, nor am I a chandi—the passionate one!'

'Yes, and I would change the lines to the glow of your cheeks in the moon but insist that you are indeed the passionate and bold one!' Guru recalled, his dimpled smile making a welcome reappearance from behind the storm clouds of their discord.

It was a precious moment indeed, one, which Malati wished, would never pass. Almost like their nuptial night!

The next morning, they went to the station and he put Malati's luggage into the train compartment. Guru explained he had to stay back to attend to one last piece of legislation before he left for Delhi so would not accompany them. When Kashi complained, he asked her to visit him in Delhi and study close by at St Bead's College in Shimla under Dorothy's guardianship. Malati did not argue in public and whispered to Kashi that she can decide herself where she wanted to go to college.

'Goodbye and take care of yourselves, Malati and Kashi. I love you both. I will keep sending money orders regularly, so you do not want for anything,' Guru said.

He quickly embraced Malati and Kashi.

As the train left the station, Kashi called out, 'Dada, don't forget us in Delhi.'

'How can I?' Guru shouted back and waved wistfully amidst the loud whooshing of the steam engine and the shrill whistle of the guard.

Malati looked at him out of the train window lovingly as he retreated into a blob and then a fleck in the distance. Suddenly Malati felt a stab in her heart. She told Kashi that she saw Dorothy at the station. She had hidden herself from their view but once the train was leaving, she came to claim Guru.

Kashi cast a pebble of doubt in the clear pool of Malati's perception by asking whether she was not hallucinating.

'Are you worried that Dada is going to abandon you, Ayee, and me too?' added Kashi anxiously.

'Kashi, don't ever say that. Your Dada loves you and me. He may have just lost his way, thanks to the Judge. That Dorothy is trying to colonize his mind and heart,' Malati said firmly and laughed a hollow laugh.

'You are not giving me any reassurance,' said Kashi with an edge to her voice.

Malati turned a brave face to her.

'Nobody abandons a self-respecting woman like me. I can always restart my law practice. And your Dada owes me everything he has and is today. I know he will come back to me. Besides, you are a magnet in your own right,' Malati said confidently.

Kashi smiled and said, 'Yes. Dada does adore me the most!'

She might have dispelled Kashi's misgivings, but was she able to conquer her own fears?

Kashi's question about whether Guru had ever told Malati that he missed having a son, unnerved her. She emphatically denied his ever saying that. This was despite his relatives' cluck-clucking and saying how they were sorry that he had no son and heir, no one to perform his last rites, and provide a passage to heaven! Malati recalled how Guru would laugh that off and say that any man's passage to heaven has to be paved with his own noble deeds, not by any funeral rites!

Malati assured Kashi that he had been very happy with his one in a million, brilliant daughter, who he believed would go places. But a new weed of apprehension had been planted in her mind. She dismissed Kashi's suggestion that she have a baby boy to mend everything with Guru. She was too old and if Guru and Malati could not repair their relations now, a baby boy would not help.

Kashi persisted with her doubts and wondered whether Malati was still mentally disturbed because of the Veena affair. Malati was able to say truthfully that she was at peace with Veena now. She did admit that she had never been as mentally disturbed as when they were in Shimla! Kashi then raised another spectre and asked whether her Dada was going to marry Dorothy and take her to Delhi.

'No! They have a platonic friendship. It's the Judge and Dorothy who are committed to each other. Your Dada is ensuring Dorothy keeps faith with the Judge. Moreover, he will never double cross the Judge, who has the first and only claim on Dorothy,' Malati explained, as much to herself as to Kashi. Suddenly she seemed freed from the claws of the beast of suspicion that had dug into her and been tormenting her.

They were warmly welcomed in Poona by Kamala, Ram, and their daughter Manya, who too, was an only child. Malati had deliberately not told Kamala anything about the twists and turns in her relationship with Guru. Only that they would stay for four months and Guru would pay for their upkeep. Kashi chose to join the Wadia College in Poona and Guru was satisfied it was the best college and that she would be overseen by Kamala.

59
THE RING OF RECOGNITION

For Guru, apart from the striking difference in weather, Delhi meant a change of his mindscape from Bombay and Shimla. Delhi's Seven Cities folded into one, yet each marked a distinct phase in the march of history over centuries. It overflowed with monuments in different hues of arrogance and decay. However, it was the spanking Lutyens Delhi which most manifested the nascent energy of the recent transfer of power. A turn over by a colonial master who ruled this unwieldy Indian empire for 190 years, into the hands of English-educated and home-grown nationalist leaders and bureaucrats such as him.

Its central boulevard linked the majestic Presidential Palace and the symmetrical government buildings of North Block and South Block with the arched India Gate. It was here, that the first post-independence government of India was seeking to pick up the pieces after the tragic partition of the country, to undo the damage wrought by colonial oppression and criminal neglect, and weld a disparate territorial entity with a 5,000-year-old civilization, into a modern nation state and democracy.

Guru's office was in Parliament House, built in red sandstone, its pillared, wraparound veranda, chasing a circle. Guru's field of action was the Constitution Hall, where the Constituent Assembly had been meeting, to deliberate on, tweak and approve or reject versions of draft articles of the Constitution that he prepared after intensive consultations within the Drafting Committee led by the great Dr Ambedkar. Guru worked directly under the Secretary of the Constituent Assembly, Dr S. N. Mukherjee.

He felt humbled, yet proud to have the opportunity to shape the first Constitution of India. The Drafting Committee, mirrored in a microcosm, the wider, spirited discourses in the Constituent Assembly on each article Guru's team had drafted and redrafted. He witnessed how a thoughtful leader like Dr Ambedkar was constantly torn between his ideals and what he could realistically push through—from preferring a presidential, not parliamentary form of government, his idea of the United States of India, to not wanting an exception to be made for the special status of the state of Jammu and Kashmir! Guru's team scrambled to draft a via media that had to satisfy him, the Drafting Committee and eventually the Constituent Assembly.

Guru worked day and night to meet tight deadlines. He told Malati that though he missed not having her as an intellectual sounding board and emotional sanctuary, he did not want her to suffer the vigil or lead a nomadic life. He lived in Western Court—an iconic building where the likes of Lala Lajpat Rai had lived, but in single room bachelor accommodation. He hoped to get family accommodation in the heart of Lutyens Delhi soon, so Malati and Kashi could join them.

Over five months passed and Guru did not ask Malati to join him in Delhi. Malati tried to disabuse Kamala and Ram of their concerns on Guru's intentions, but she soon started to have doubts herself. As Guru's letters became more infrequent, as he sounded evasive about her joining him, she had to tell Kamala and Ram about the turbulence her marriage had gone through in Shimla. They worried even more.

Soon thereafter, Kamala remarked that Malati was developing a belly!

'It is your Puneri cuisine that must make me balloon,' she joked, when actually she barely ate their vegetarian, bland fare.

'Malati, this is no joking matter. When did you last have your periods?' Kamala asked.

Malati confessed that she had missed her periods ever since she came to Poona and attributed it to her getting menopause as she was in her forties.

The sky seemed to fall down on Malati when Kamala insisted on taking her to the doctor and he declared that she was pregnant! After nearly sixteen years! She guessed she had become pregnant the night before she had left, when Guru and she had made love after a very long time.

They would have another symbol of their love to look forward to, maybe the son that Guru coveted, despite his professions to the contrary. If God so wished, it might be the end of one tumultuous phase of their life together and the mother of all beginnings!

Kashi wanted Malati to inform Guru immediately. Kamala felt that Malati should go and tell Guru in person. The dilemma was that, if they informed him about Malati going without citing a reason, he would ask her not to come. If Malati told him that she is coming because she is pregnant, he may not believe her and think she was pressuring him. Ram pushed them to go immediately. So, Kamala, Malati, and Kashi landed up in Delhi without giving Guru any notice.

They went straight from the railway station to the Western Court, passing the Red Fort and other Old Delhi monuments and towards the very green and leafy New Delhi. It did indeed, have the imperial swagger of a city that had witnessed the rise and fall of empires and been the crucible for melting down and recreating the idea of India, again and again. They identified themselves at the reception desk, and asked to see Guru. The receptionist told them that Guru was at work and usually came back very late.

It occurred to Malati that Judge Singh, too, may be living close by. So she got his address and they went to his house. Malati had no qualms about landing up there unannounced. After all, as he himself had admitted, the Judge owed Malati much. He had taken away her Guru from her, rendering him unrecognizable as her lover, her worshipper. She had to put up with the Judge's lover, Dorothy leaning on Guru as a crutch, while she and the Judge searched for their salvation.

So, Malati sallied forth, ready to be politely rebuffed. She was, therefore, pleasantly surprised that when they announced themselves at the gate, not only was the Judge at the door to warmly welcome them, but Dorothy was by his side. She looked splendid in a crisp, white cotton and lace dress as a tribute to Delhi's hot summer. By contrast, the visitors from Poona, the 'native' flowers in crumpled cotton saris, were wilting in the heat.

Malati muttered an introduction.

'How wonderful to see you all,' the Judge and Dorothy said, almost to a cue.

'Let me guess. Guru missed you at the station and you went to Western Court, where they must have told you that he is at work. So, you came to the only friend you know here—me. Please make yourselves comfortable while I send a message to his office. You know he is doing such vital and commendable work,' the Judge said.

Malati did not contradict him and simply thanked him. They were served refreshments and while they waited for Guru, Malati asked the inevitable questions.

'So, Dorothy! What a pleasant surprise to see you here, away from your beloved Shimla. But then sometimes you have to give up one beloved for another! I am happy you are reunited with the good Judge,' Malati remarked.

'Indeed, Malati, after you and Guru came away, it was difficult for Dorothy to live alone in Shimla. So, she decided to join me here,' the Judge explained.

Guru rushed into the living room from his office asking agitatedly, 'What happened, Malati? You came unannounced. Unless you sent me a letter and the postal system let us down.'

He thanked and hugged Kamala.

'I know our coming here is sudden. Guru, is there a place where we could talk alone?' Malati asked.

Guru looked worried. The Judge and Dorothy excused themselves and Kamala and Kashi joined them in another room.

'Guru, I am expecting our second child—after all these years! Your Cloud Messenger seems to have done it! I did not realize it until Kamala saw signs and we went to the doctor last week,' Malati told him, a little shyly.

She watched Guru's expressions carefully—his thoughtful frown betraying disbelief, his eyes widening in wonder, and his quivering lips stretching into happiness—a cavalcade of emotions chasing each other.

'Arrey deva re! Malati, this is the best news I have had in a long time! Having a child after sixteen years seems like your Muktabai's miracle!'

And he embraced her.

Then his face clouded over. He wondered where he would put Malati up. At his level, he might not get family accommodation soon. He therefore proposed to request Kamala to take Malati back until Guru worked something out.

'Guru, for some time now I have felt that you, my Dushyant, are rejecting me, your Shakuntala of Abhigyan Shakuntalam. I have been wondering whether I have inadvertently earned the curse—maybe, as Maa Saheb predicted long ago, and lost the "ring of recognition" you may have given me,' Malati said to him, baring her heart.

'Malati, you are hallucinating! We may have had differences and quarrels, but that as you remember from *Satteche Gulam*, is part of our vow to keep the fire of our marriage burning,' Guru said.

Malati continued her plaint! 'Guru, that rejection was evident in Shimla itself. Then your sending me away to Poona and not wanting us back here on the pretext of no family accommodation, confirmed it.'

'Malati, you are being unfair to me. If I have indeed sinned, it has been in spending too much time away from you at work and socially with the Judge, and because of him, with Dorothy. But I have always loved you. It's you who cannot see me as your Lord even though I see you as a Goddess always,' said Guru sincerely.

'Then this is no way to treat the goddess who is one, not because you called her so, or made her so, but because of who she is and what she did for you!' Malati said angrily.

Malati was warming up to this 'either here or across the bow' confrontation to settle matters forever.

'Malati, my goddess, you misunderstand me completely,' Guru protested.

'I have been willing to go to the ends of the earth with you, as long as you continue to worship me as you pledged that day outside Mohan Kaka's house. Because of that, I gave up my ambition to become a lawyer, went alone to work in Benares, so that your dream to be one comes true. Even when I reclaimed my dream of becoming a lawyer and had a thriving and fulfilling law practice, I went with you to Shimla chasing your dreams as your shadow, not your light!' Malati said, her pent-up grievances and sense of loss speaking up for her unshed tears and her innate pride then gushing forth to flood out Guru's field of complacency.

'Remember you gave me a birch bark manuscript of "Madhu Malati"—your "Song Divine" to me when I first visited you in Anna's home. It had got lost and I found it in Poona. That is my Ring of Recognition,' Malati said. She took out the bhurjapatra from her bag and handed it over to him.

By now, Guru had fully incarnated back into a worshipper. Malati the Goddess had held a live flame to his incense of remorse, of respect and gratitude, creating its own self-fuelling embers and long-lasting fragrance. And he himself lit the nanadadeep—the lamp of bliss and reconciliation.

'I am sorry if you ever got the feeling that you are less than my better half! I am a fallible devotee, like all devotees are, always expecting and asking for boons, but not keeping up their side of worshipping with ardour and single-minded devotion. This poem—a sign of our pure, unalloyed love, is indeed a Ring of Recognition, though it is not needed,' he said, overcome with emotion.

He embraced Malati and they walked together, hand in hand to the room where the rest were waiting for them. He announced the good news. The Judge and Dorothy congratulated them.

Guru however confessed that it came at an awkward time for him when he was expected to be a workhorse at the Constituent Assembly, slaving away day and night. Also, he still had no government accommodation where Malati could stay comfortably and it was urgent now because he had no ancestral home in Delhi. The Judge promptly offered that Malati could stay with him and Dorothy till such time as Guru was able to get government accommodation. He also promised to speak to the Law Ministry leadership to expedite Guru's house allotment. Guru and Malati embraced the Judge with gratitude.

60

SWALLOWING THE SUN

Kamala and Kashi returned to Poona and Malati stayed on at the Judge's place until something that she had been expecting to happen, took place. The Judge's mentally disturbed wife, Jasmeet, escaped her confinement and landed up at his residence one morning. Malati, who was in the living room reading a book, happened to open the door.

'Where is Harbhajan? Who are you? Are you the woman living with him? Are you carrying his child?' she bombarded Malati with questions in a loud voice. The Judge and Dorothy came running out.

'Oh, so you have one Indian and one English mistress, do you?' she turned to the Judge and asked viciously.

The Judge explained who Malati was and why she was there to Jasmeet patiently.

'And who is this Englishwoman? Don't tell me she is your colleague's wife, too,' she said sarcastically.

Malati was amazed at her clarity of thought—not the sign of someone who was supposedly mad.

'As a matter of fact, she is the widow of the late Judge Harold Atkinson and my former colleague. She lives in Shimla,' said the Judge.

'So that is why you took a posting in Shimla and put me away in an asylum? I will kill her and you, both,' she said and rushed towards Dorothy.

Two of the Judge's attendants ran to protect the Judge and Dorothy from her wrath. She tried to hit and scratch them, but was restrained by one of them whom she slapped fiercely. Freeing herself from his grasp she said, 'Don't touch me with your dirty hands, you dog.'

Malati stood frozen and helplessly watched everything that was taking place. Finally, she took out Guru and Kashi's photo to calm Jasmeet down, but Jasmeet turned on her and attacked her instead. The Judge rushed to hold Jasmeet. Thankfully, her nurses came in just in time, and she was taken back to the asylum. The Judge looked stricken, his face lost colour and he sat on his favourite sofa with his hands on his head bent.

The usually confident Dorothy seemed truly shaken, trembling almost.

'How will this work out, Harbhajan? We cannot continue like this. Is insanity not a reason for divorce?' Dorothy demanded.

'In Indian society, as you know by now, it's not about a legal divorce, it's about my humanity—that I abandoned her when she was in her lowest and most vulnerable state—the stigma of that is as much as of Jasmeet's mental illness. Jasmeet's parents are from a prominent Sikh family. Also, with the new government, this will be a scandal I will not survive,' the Judge said.

Dorothy looked crestfallen.

'I will find a solution, don't worry, Dorothy,' said the Judge and turning to Malati asked whether she was injured.

'No, no. I am stronger than that. I am truly sorry about all this!' Malati said.

That evening a very excited Guru visited them, unaware of what had transpired.

'Dearest Malati, the child whom God is gifting to us is very lucky for me. I have just been told that I am being promoted to the post of joint secretary and that means I will get a bungalow soon. Dear Harbhajanji, thank you for all your encouragement and mentoring. I will always cherish your friendship. I owe Malati much of my success too,' he said.

Everyone congratulated him. Then Malati told him what had happened with Jasmeet that day.

Guru immediately apologized. 'I am sorry, Harbhajanji, that I got carried away with my own news and didn't sense that something was wrong. I am distressed to hear about what happened today. I know you are torn between your conscience and your heart. I can't tell you how to make a compromise between the two in this case. Whatever you decide, Malati and I are there for both of you.'

'Sometimes these dilemmas resolve themselves and decisions of others guide you to your destiny. I have an intuition this is what is going to happen to me on this matter,' the Judge said philosophically. 'I am asking Dorothy to go to Shimla for a short while, till I work things out here.'

'What a quagmire we are in and getting further dragged into, Harbhajan! I feel I should release you from this misery,' she said.

'Don't you ever say that!' the Judge said.

'Dearest, I am so despondent at this moment. The vision of our life together fades away by the day,' Dorothy said and for the first time Malati noticed how she gathered her dress on either side with her hands and crushed it in frustration.

'Dear Dorothy, do not weaken my resolve. Give me courage to do the right thing by you and by the law,' said the Judge.

Malati recalled Tennyson's epic poem about King Arthur and the Holy Grail the Judge was fond of reciting in Shimla. It must seem to the Judge, who saw himself as being 'upon a Holy Quest' of love, that Dorothy was being 'too dark a prophet' in saying that 'he was lost in a quagmire, following wandering fires'. It was also true, that some like his wife Jasmeet would declare that his was but an unholy quest. Others would probably say that the Judge, with his love of the law, 'like a King must guard that which he rules, and may not wander'. What a cruel predicament!

Guru assumed charge as a Joint Secretary in the Ministry of Law. A government bungalow, in the prestigious Robert's Lane area, close to the prime minister's official residence, was allotted to him. They moved in as soon as they could, because they needed to settle in well before Malati's delivery. They bought their first car—a sky blue Hillman.

Meanwhile, Dorothy did leave for Shimla saying that she awaited the Judge's 'Final Judgement'. From there, she continued to cajole him to make a choice quickly, threatening that she would otherwise leave for England soon. The Judge tried hard, but was unsuccessful in working out an amicable divorce even with his in-law's good offices. Then one day, they heard the shocking news that the Judge had resigned from his post, citing personal reasons.

'Why did you have to cut short your brilliant career like this?' asked Guru, in anguish.

'You showed me the way, remember? I could not in good conscience continue as Judge and subject that office to slander. So, I resigned and did justice to the "love in my life". That way I get my freedom from bondage to Jasmeet, without worrying about what people will say. I also do not have to fear the opprobrium of the government about my personal life. I get to keep my pact of love with Dorothy to join her, a free man, in Shimla. At last to live happily ever after,' explained the Judge to Guru and Malati. They shook his hands in solidarity and wished him luck and bliss.

On reaching Shimla, he wrote to them.

Dearest Guru and Malati,

Arrived safely. Happily home with Dorothy. I have reached my supreme destination! Hope you both are not missing me too much! I forgot to wish you all the best for the birth of your child. You know, I think he is going to be someone exceptional. Promise me, you will name your baby Bharat, because he is going to be born around the time of the adoption of the First Constitution of Independent India—one which his father has wielded his mighty pen to write and when the Republic of India that is Bharat, will truly be born.

Guru and Malati replied saying that they would honour his wishes, asked him to be the godfather, and invited him for the naming ceremony.

That was not to be. Three months later they got the tragic news that the Judge had died in an accident, as he went trekking, falling off a cliff in Jakhoo Hills. On further inquiry, they learnt that Dorothy had left for England just a few weeks after his arrival in Shimla. He had been left alone in her house, which she had bequeathed to him. Apparently, the Madame Pompadour in Dorothy, could not bear not being able to convene the cream of Shimla society and hold court, now that most of her British friends had left and the Judge was no longer a Judge!

Guru was crushed by the thought that the Judge must have been heartbroken and bereft at losing both his loves—the law and Dorothy. He could not have survived without them and perhaps had taken his own life. They would never know. Their regret was that he was too proud to reach out to them.

It was the end of the ninth month, but the baby seemed to be in no hurry to enter this world. Malati got herself admitted into Delhi's Wellington Hospital, with a capable lady doctor Dr Pasricha, attending to her. After a thorough examination, she declared that Malati was actually in her tenth month of pregnancy and in danger. She ordered an immediate Caesarean section to be performed on

Malati. As they prepared for the surgery, Malati overheard Dr Pasricha asking Guru to choose between his wife and his baby since she could probably save only one.

He hesitated for just a minute and said, 'Please, please save both. But if you have to make a choice, save my goddess Malati. She has a greater claim to life and immortality!'

Malati drew strength from that and woke up from the operation groggy, but with the will to live. Guru handed over their baby—their shendephal, the last fruit of their life together—all bundled up and alert with big black eyes, first surveying the world and then looking intently at both of them.

Malati said to Guru, 'Aho, we must call him Bharat, as we promised the Judge.'

Guru smiled and said, 'It will have to be Bharati! But look at her hands, the way she grasps with her little fingers. She will surely dare the lion cub to open his mouth so she can count his teeth, just as little Bharat, the legendary Dushyant and Shakuntala's son, marvellously did, and went on to found a dynasty that created the original Empire of India—Bharatvarsha!

'Ah, yes! A true Muktabai's ant, she too will be swallowing the sun.'

And Malati laughed.